P9-BIO-396

ALSO BY LORI BRYANT-WOOLRIDGE

Hitts & Mrs.

Read Between the Lies

Weapons
of Mass
Seduction

LORI BRYANT-WOOLRIDGE

HARLEM MOON
BROADWAY BOOKS
NEW YORK

PUBLISHED BY HARLEM MOON

Copyright © 2007 by Lori Bryant-Woolridge

All Rights Reserved

Published in the United States by Harlem Moon, an imprint of
The Doubleday Broadway Publishing Group, a division of Random
House, Inc., New York.
www.harlemmoon.com

HARLEM MOON, BROADWAY BOOKS, and the HARLEM MOON logo,
depicting a moon and a woman, are trademarks of Random House,
Inc. The figure in the Harlem Moon logo is inspired by a graphic
design by Aaron Douglas (1899–1979).

This book is a work of fiction. Names, characters, businesses,
organizations, places, events, and incidents either are the product
of the author's imagination or are used fictitiously. Any resemblance
to actual persons, living or dead, events, or locales is entirely
coincidental.

Book design by Diane Hobbing of Snap-Haus Graphics

LIBRARY OF CONGRESS CATALOGING-IN-PUBLICATION DATA
Bryant-Woolridge, Lori.
    Weapons of mass seduction / by Lori Bryant-Woolridge. —1st ed.
        p.   cm.
    1. African American women—Fiction.   2. Female friendship—
Fiction.   I. Title.

    PS3573.O6863W43 2007
    813' .54—dc22

                                                        2006034828

ISBN 978-0-7679-2665-2

PRINTED IN THE UNITED STATES OF AMERICA

10 9 8 7 6 5 4 3 2 1

FIRST EDITION

This book is dedicated to my two incredible children, Eva and Austin. Your wise, beautiful ways make me so very proud. And to my dear and courageous friend Heather Bond Bryant, whose grace under fire inspires me daily.

Age cannot wither her, nor custom stale
Her infinite variety: other women cloy
The appetites they feed: but she makes hungry
Where most she satisfies.

—William Shakespeare, from Antony and Cleopatra

A Note to the Girls

Even way back in the early 1600s, William Shakespeare, speaking of Cleopatra, got the joke: A confident, sensual woman is ageless and unforgettable. And then centuries later in the 1920s the godmother of seductive, feminine sensuality, Coco Chanel, brought us Chanel No. 5, the indispensable LBD (little black dress), and the mind-set that "for one to be irreplaceable, one must always be different."

But somewhere between Coco and Nicole Kidman, sensuality and seduction became a spectator sport. We "normal" women sat back and watched the famous beautiful people have all the fun, settling for living vicariously through the loves and lives of Hollywood celebrities and literary characters.

Well, I agree with Justin Timberlake, sweet man-child that he is: It's time to bring sexy back! And that "sexy" is YOU!

This book began as a reminder to myself, and now to you, that we cannot neglect for too long the vibrant, sexy enchantress within. We women get so bogged down underneath all of life's details that we forget the soft, sensual sides of ourselves. And by the time we can exhale, sit down, and remember, society is telling us that part of our life is over. It is my hope that *Weapons of Mass Seduction*, part flirt manual, part fiction, will help you find your way to (or back to) your elegant inner bombshell.

I would like to acknowledge some sexy women in their own right: My mom, Mable, and my mother-in-law, Judith Ann. My editor, Janet Hill. Marie Brown, a graceful warrior and a loving, supportive friend. The hottest moms on the planet—the ladies of Mothers Off

Duty; the coolest authors on earth and my Femme Fantastik tour mates—Nina Foxx and Carmen Green; and the best mentor in the world—Beverly Hemmings, a woman who makes aging gracefully look so damn good and sexy!

To my handsome focus group: Craig Woolridge, Joe Nunn, Douglas Neri, Madison Jackson, Ken Holley, and Ted Bell, thank you for being so candid about what makes a woman attractive.

Clarence Haynes and Christian Nwachukwu, thank you for your patient assistance.

And thanks to all the Boy Toys, Big Dogs, and Sweeties who inspire us and make being a seductive woman so much damn fun.

Enjoy this journey and, as always, Expect Good Things!

Lori

P.S. Check out www.inspireandaffirm.com for gifts for dreaming and believing and www.weapons-of-mass-seduction.blogspot.com for my musings and well-intentioned ideas on sensuality, flirting, and S-E-X.

Weapons

of Mass

Seduction

When

the

student

is

ready,

the

master

will

appear.

Chapter One

Where am I? Pia Jamison wondered, turning on the light and looking around the beautifully appointed yet unfamiliar room. A momentary burst of panic rushed her body, replaced her morning grogginess, and cleared the way for the facts. It was December 7, and she was in Annapolis, Maryland, at the Loews Hotel, a two-hour Acela train ride away from her chic New York apartment.

The panic was unusual. Waking up in lonely hotel rooms in strange cities had been a part of her life for years now. As a senior vice president at SunFire Productions, she was constantly on the road, traveling to the far corners of the globe, overseeing the making of million-dollar videos for some of the biggest names in the music business. From Mary J. to Madonna, from Seal to Sting, from Alicia to Beyoncé to Ciara, it was her job to make sure that the images and music of these artists were presented as attractively as possible. It was a tough job and success had cost her plenty—a family of her own, for starters—but after nearly fourteen years it was one she did well and still adored.

Interview . . . Theo Johnson, she reminded herself.

Pia glanced over at the clock and noted with a groan that it was only 7:47 A.M. She wasn't supposed to meet with Theo until noon. If her fretful mind would only cooperate with her body, she'd have at least another three hours of sleep. Pia wanted and needed to look as beautiful and as fresh as possible for this encounter. Her future was riding on it.

Calm down, she instructed herself. *If he turns it down there are others on the list. There is no such thing as only one man for the job.*

Nervous energy led her from the bed onto the floor to commence her daily yoga exercises. Standing straight, her arms in prayer position, Pia tried to calm herself by repeating a new mantra: "It's just an interview. It's just an interview." Arching back and then gracefully diving forward and placing her hands on the floor and her head on her knees, she stretched her body and tried to determine just who she was kidding.

She was hoping that Theo would at least hear her out and consider the position, while knowing full damn well that his interest and acceptance had everything to do with her ability to enticingly sell herself. This could be a problem. Pia Jamison could sell a skinny teenager with a mouth full of gold, as well as the inability to pronounce most words of the King's English, as a worldwide sex symbol, but sell herself? On this front, her confidence sagged.

Pia finished her sun salutation and moved to the full-length mirror to inspect herself. Even in her just-out-of-bed state, Pia still had it going on, she had to admit. Her mocha glazed skin was smooth and wrinkle-free—a sign she was aging well. The notable features of her face came together in a pleasing mosaic of interesting angles. The shapely pout of her mouth and slightly flared nostrils of her dignified nose balanced the stop-and-look beauty of her most striking feature—large, wide-set, golden brown feline eyes that appeared to hold the mysteries of the universe in their gaze. All this loveliness was framed by a head full of healthy black hair, cut fashionably short and fringed.

Her arms, legs, and butt were toned from years of practicing healthy eating and yoga. Gravity had been kind to her round and still firm breasts, and Pia's stomach, never stretched to its maximum by pregnancy, was still flat. Tight abs were a coveted prize by most women her age, but for Pia they were a daily reminder of the baby she'd always wanted but hadn't gotten around to having.

You can't have a baby until you start having sex, she told her image. *Girl, face it, you are a no-sex-havin' total used-to-be.*

It *used to be,* as any man familiar with her womanly wiles would testify, that Pia Clarice Jamison was built for sex. It used to be that Pia, closer to forty-one than most realized, had a dangerous combination of sexual expertise and unbridled lust. She had the wisdom of more than twenty years of erotic experience and up until a few years ago had the confidence and technique to work both mind and body to their best advantage. In the old days B.C. (before celibacy), Pia had never met a man who, if she had the will, could resist her way. It *used to be* that seducing a man into bed or the back of a limo was second nature to Pia, and her list of "whupped" suitors was discerning and distinguished.

But that was years ago. A damn lifetime ago.

Today, she was standing in a hotel room three states from home, hoping to snag Mr. Right. But now, having gone from supersexual to damn near asexual, Pia had no idea how to attract what she needed to get what she wanted.

ᗡᗡᗡ

Walking into the Captain's Table, a popular new restaurant on the Chesapeake Bay waterfront, Pia confirmed their reservation and took a seat at the far end of the bar to await Theo's arrival. She'd chosen the eatery, now tastefully decorated for the holidays, for its welcoming ambiance—ambiance she hoped would help sway Theo to her way of thinking.

"Excuse me, miss, the gentleman would like to buy you a drink," the bartender informed her, gesturing to his left.

Pia's eyes followed his nod and rested on the face of a pleasant-looking black man. She gave him a quick smile of acknowledgment before turning back to the bartender.

"Please tell him thanks, but no."

Before the message could be delivered, the man's casually dressed, average-size frame was by Pia's side, blocking her view of the front door.

"Okay, I had to come over and find out for myself," he began with a flirty twinkle in his eye that didn't match the matter-of-fact tone of his voice.

"The answer is, no, thank you," Pia replied, quickly dismissing his unasked query. Despite his warm smile and friendly demeanor, she'd seen his type before and wasn't interested in getting tangled up in his web of please-baby-please while waiting for Theo.

"But you haven't heard the question."

"Doesn't matter. My answer is still no, thank you. Now if you'll excuse me, I'm waiting for someone."

"I hope he's got a blowtorch to take the chill off," the man sniped, stepping back down to the bar to clear his tab.

Several minutes later, the bartender placed a glass full of ice in front of her. "From the gentleman," he revealed. Without looking over, Pia felt herself cringe at the man's final statement. She hadn't intended to come off so rude, but lately, when it came to flirtatious men, "cold" seemed the only temperature setting she knew.

"Pia Jamison. Girl, how you doing?" Theo asked, shaking her from her embarrassment. Forsaking all formalities, he drew her into an enthusiastic bear hug. They both could feel her body stiffen before she awkwardly eased away.

Relax. Don't screw this up.

"Theo. It's nice to see you. You look well."

"You too," he said as his eyes roamed her torso.

"Um, why don't we grab our table so we can talk," Pia suggested.

"Sure," he agreed, chalking up her distant demeanor to long-standing embarrassment. It'd been a long time since their series of three dates had ended in anything but a fairy tale. He'd definitely been into her, but the last time he went without sex he was fourteen and Theo had no interest in backsliding, not even for someone as fine and intelligent as Pia Jamison.

Theo followed Pia into the dining area, taking the opportunity to check out her curvy physique. For someone not giving it up, the woman certainly chose clothing that worked to her best benefit, like today's chocolate brown pencil skirt, leopard-print cardigan, and red high-heel pumps. Pia's ensemble managed to show off her dynamic assets but leave the discerning eye wanting more.

The hostess led them to a window table for two overlooking the Chesapeake Bay. Just as his mama had taught him, Theo held the chair as she settled into her seat, all the while enjoying the rose-scented fragrance of her perfume.

"So . . . Pia Jamison . . ." he tried again, singing her name like it was a lyric in a John Legend song.

"That would be me . . ." Pia responded, sounding totally inane even to herself. She was nervous and it was showing.

"May I take your order?" the waiter mercifully interrupted.

With her lunch request of tofu and vegetable stir-fry and his of crab cakes and fries, the waiter departed. Theo stared out at the water. The view provided a beautiful natural diversion, and a grateful Pia scurried to collect her thoughts. Already this was not going well. Pia was desperately out of practice when it came to making date-friendly small talk, and the silence between them was awkward and heavy. Definitely not a primo way to begin such a delicate negotiation.

"You're making quite a name for yourself in the sports world," Pia said, trying to find a safe topic to tackle while she attempted to get herself together.

"I'm flattered that you've been keeping up with my career," he said. Pia couldn't help noticing that charm still oozed out of the man's every pore. "And what about you? It's no secret that SunFire is the place to go if you're looking to pick up a MTV Moon Man."

"Well, it looks like work has been very good to both of us."

"I'll toast to that," Theo said, lifting his water glass, "and to that sexy body of yours," he said, once again returning to his flirtatious self.

"Hmm. So, are you dating anyone?" Pia asked, awkwardly dismissing his compliment while trying to sound nonchalant.

"Uh, not at the moment. I recently ended a relationship. Why do you ask?"

"Just curious. Any kids?"

"Not that I'm aware of? You're awfully direct, aren't you? So much so, I'd say what's fair is fair. So let me ask you: Are you still uh . . . going without?"

"Yes, and it's actually very liberating not to be beholden to your libido. I am in complete control of me." Even to Pia her response seemed stiff and rehearsed.

"Sounds very Oprah . . . and lonely," he commented. "So I'm guessing you don't have a man."

"Well, no. I mean, not at the moment." Damn, he was making this harder than she'd thought it would be.

"Okay, so, no man. No sex. You don't smoke. And all you eat is rabbit food. What do you do for fun? How do you live?"

"I live very nicely, thank you. I have a great apartment, though I don't get to see it too often because I'm always working, but at least I get to travel regularly."

"Sounds like you have a nice existence, but what do you do to *live?* To experience life? To feel alive?"

"Don't be silly. Of course I feel alive," Pia insisted, but when he laid it all out on the table like that she now wasn't so sure.

"Not the way you'd feel if you and I hooked up," Theo said in a very matter-of-fact tone. His eyes spoke a different language, full of lusty promises and resuscitative powers. "Come on, Pia. You know we'd be *amazing* together." He reached across the table and placed his hand on top of hers. He flashed that mind-blowing smile at her, and she could feel herself grow flustered as she quickly reclaimed her hand. "What do we say we end that nasty little drought of yours?"

"I don't want to have sex with you. I want to have a *baby*."

A big, fat, very pregnant silence fell over the table. Theo sat in stunned amazement, and Pia was furious at herself for being so tactless.

"Sorry. I didn't mean to just blurt it out like that."

"That's why you called me?"

"Well . . . yes. So what do you think?"

"I think you've been celibate a little too long. In the real world, if you wanna make a baby you usually have sex."

"I mean, of course we would have to have sex."

"*Have* to have sex? Damn, it *has* been a long time, hasn't it?"

"Look, Theo. I'm forty-one years old and have a history of female problems. I've always wanted to be a mother and thought I still had time, but according to my doctor, it's now or never, and I think you're the perfect candidate."

"Candidate? Hell, I don't know whether to be flattered or pissed. Why me?"

"Because I know you're smart and successful and you obviously take care of yourself, though of course I would like to check out your medical history."

"You really do cut to the chase, don't you? No finesse . . . no seduction . . . just hand over your vaccination records and let's go make a baby."

"You don't have to be involved. I'm not looking for a partner, just a father."

"Then why not go to some sperm bank and make a withdrawl. It's damn obvious you don't need or desire a man, just his seed."

His last remark sounded biting and cruel, and unfortunately she'd heard the crack about not needing a man too many times before. Pia brushed it off and continued her pursuit.

"I considered it, but then I thought that in the future the child might want to know who his or her father is, and I don't want it to be some bar code on a test tube. I at least owe my child a name."

"Well, so much for your 'you don't have to be involved' theory. What about adopting? Plenty of kids out there need a home."

"Just because I don't want marriage or a man doesn't mean I don't want to experience pregnancy. So are you interested?" Pia abruptly asked the question, frustrated by her poor showing.

"Sorry, but no. I am already too busy looking after these grown-ass babies I represent. I'm not ready to take care of a real kid."

"Look, I'm financially secure. I don't need anything from you other than a little help right at the beginning. I'm prepared to take it from there by myself. I'll even have a contract drawn up relieving you of any parental or financial responsibilities. You'd never have to see me or the baby again."

"You know, for a millisecond I might have been flattered that I was your chosen one, but right there you just screwed it up. I'm not a stud service. And I'm not the kind of man who would father a child and walk away. Damn, what happened to you? You've become one of those ain't-nothing-a-man-can-do-for-me types of chicks. Well, that's not the kind of woman I want and certainly not the kind of mother I'd want my kid to have."

"Theo, I know it sounds crazy, and I haven't done a very good job at presenting my case, but I'd really appreciate it if you'd give it some thought." Pia felt the heat of humiliation creep through her body, but she was too desperate to give up.

"You seem to really want this, and I really hope this works out for you, but I'm not the one. A word of friendly advice: With the next dude you approach, you might want to soften him up a bit first before you spring a request like that on him. Maybe go out on a date or two. Use some of that charm I know you still have locked up wasting away inside of you. Good luck. Nice seeing you." Theo unceremoniously stood up and dropped several twenty-dollar bills down on the table. And with a slight shake of his head and a befuddled smirk, he turned and left.

The scraping noise of metal chair on tile floor punctuated his departure. Pia watched him walk away and was disgusted with herself for botching this meeting so badly. Twice today she'd managed to turn a man off to the point that he'd left her sitting alone and feeling like a complete and utter failure.

Chapter Two

"*Chica*, you screwed up," Darlene "Dee" Perez said with all honesty and little fanfare as she propped her tiny size five-and-a-half feet on her boss's desk.

"I'm well aware of that. So this is why I pay you such a generous bonus every year? For you to tell me things I already know?" Pia asked, ignoring her secretary's physical and verbal informality. After six years of daily contact with this petite Latina, Pia often wondered just who was in charge.

"No, you pay me the generous bonus because not only am I one hell of a great assistant from nine to five but because I'm willing to sit here *after* hours talking about your pathetic love life."

"Hey, insubordination is a fireable offense," Pia threatened with mock bravado. But they both knew there was no bite behind her bark. Darlene was way more than Pia's employee. She was the heartbeat that kept things running smoothly while Pia was out on the road. Darlene managed to out-diva the divas and sweet-talk the suits, and all the while make her manager look good. Dee was also her closest confidante and the sister Pia wished she had. Twice she'd tried to promote the woman, but Darlene refused, choosing instead to enjoy the best of both her worlds—an exciting, glamorous, and manageable-stress-level job she enjoyed and a happy home life with a hunky husband she adored.

"Touchy, touchy. Now, like I said, you screwed up. The plan was to rekindle the interest, go on a few dates, get to know each other better, and then, *maybe, if* it felt right, *after* a few months, approach the baby subject. You weren't supposed to go in there with both ovaries loaded, shake his hand, and ask to borrow a cup of sperm. No wonder the man took off running."

"I know, and believe me, I felt like a real ass just spitting it out like that."

"Maybe it's time for Plan B," Dee suggested.

"I didn't know there was a Plan B."

"Plan B: Make sure you're fertile. Get drunk. Find a nice guy at a bar, take him home, do the deed, and make a baby. No fuss, no messy strings attached. You're a mommy and he's none the wiser."

"There are so many holes in that strategy, I don't even know where to begin," Pia replied.

"Just go with the top three. I'm still a newlywed. I need to get home early."

"You've been married three years, and Hector is in Iraq."

"Yes, and I should be home writing my brave husband who is fighting for freedom and your right to have a baby out of wedlock. Now, back to your reasons for not going with Plan B."

"First, I'm not going to just screw any stranger. I'm trying to get pregnant, so that right there kind of discounts safe sex, now doesn't it? I mean, I am dying to have a baby but there ain't no way I'm *dying* to have a baby."

"Pick a nice bar where nice guys go."

"Haven't you seen and heard the PSAs? You can't tell just by looking. It's just not safe."

"And reasons two and three?"

"Reason two: It's not fair to jerk a guy around like that. I think it's only right that the father is a willing participant. And it's the only fair thing for the baby, especially if he or she wants to know who the father is at some point."

"Okay, both are valid. And three?"

"Because maybe this whole plan is just crazy," Pia pronounced.

"It's not so crazy that an old chick like you would want to have a baby."

"I'm not that old."

"Look, *chica,* the facts are the facts. You're over forty and, according to Dr. Montrae, with all your fibroid issues the factory may be closed before it even opens. It doesn't seem crazy at all that you want to get into production before it's too late."

"*But . . . ?*" Pia asked, already knowing the topic of the next barrage of comments and advice that was to be thrown her way.

"But what does seem *muy loco* is this love/hate thing you've got going with men. And I still don't understand how a pretty girl like you doesn't like sex . . . not with boys *or* girls. Those are the two biggies you're going to need to get over if this baby-making is ever going to happen."

"How many times do I have to tell you that I don't hate men, I just hate the games they play? Men and I just don't seem to get along beyond the bedroom, and that's not enough for me.

"And I happen to love sex, but not at the price of my sanity. I don't plan to be celibate forever. Just until sex isn't a game but part of a real loving relationship."

"Or until you find yourself a baby daddy."

"Exactly."

"But you messed up with Theo, which means only Grand Nelson is left on the *papi* list."

"Which means?" Pia inquired, suspicion coloring her query.

"Means it's time to change up," Dee declared, looking inquisitively at her boss. "You're not ready yet. I think it's time to bring in some professional help. You're rusty, *chica,* and I hate to think what kind of shape that *chocha* of yours is in. You must pee dust."

"What are you brewing up in that sick little mind of yours, Darlene?"

"Nothing yet, but I'll think of something," Dee promised before returning to her own desk.

Pia plopped down on the office couch in a swirl of disgust. She hated to admit it, and would never do so out loud, but she was actually hoping Darlene would come up with something, because her flirt gene was severely atrophied and she was teetering on the verge of becoming some sort of a sexual nerd. And as the tick-tick-tick of her biological clock kept reminding her, time was running out.

Chapter Three

Wednesday—Welcome

*"Passion is what makes a woman sexy. The body may not
be perfect, the face may be more interesting than beautiful,
but if a woman has charm, then I want to know her."*
—Giuseppe, 56

*"Ultimately what makes a woman sexy is how comfortable
she is in her own skin, and how comfortable she makes you
feel in yours."*
—Danny, 45

Pia Jamison stood at the door of the
Pacific Ballroom of the Surya Hotel and Spa and tried to quickly recuperate from her forty-yard dash down the corridor. Taking fast,
shallow breaths, she peered into the dark room, illuminated only by
the video presentation. Damn, she hated being late. Particularly
when she had been booked as a panelist at a conference she had only
cursory knowledge about. Because her flight from New York to San
Francisco had been delayed, she now had to make the embarrassing

walk up to the head table with all eyes following her every move and figure out what to say that wouldn't make her look like an uninformed idiot.

Her eyes, now accustomed to the dark, rested on an empty chair on the outskirts of the room. Clutching her welcome tote and unread registration packet, Pia quickly crossed the room and slid into the seat, trying not to disturb the others who sat watching and listening intently to the presentation in progress.

What the hell does this have to do with music videos? Pia thought as she tuned in. Confusion clutched every part of her mind and body as she reached inside the black nylon tote and pulled out a lavender binder, opened it to the cover page, and lifted it into the meager light. WEAPONS OF MASS SEDUCTION: UNLEASHING THE SENSUAL YOU. *What the hell?* As confusion turned into tormented realization, Pia knew there was only one person responsible for putting her in this mortifying position.

When I get home I am going to kill you, Darlene Teresa Anna Maria Valencia Perez, for tricking me into attending this foolishness, Pia telephathically promised her secretary. *I don't care if my love life does suck. I have neither the time nor the inclination to travel three thousand miles from home to attend some stupid romance clinic.*

—

"Brains make a woman most appealing. If I say something about a current event or the news and it sails over her head, that conversation is over."

—Donnel, 37

—

As the montage of handsome international faces continued to parade across the screen, Pia felt herself cringe in the dark. Was she that off the mark from what these men were describing that Dee thought it necessary to subject her to this torturous humiliation? Was she that socially inept?

Apparently, considering you haven't had a second date in two years, her pesky inner voice chimed.

~

"What will win me over every time? Great tits and a slam-ming ass."

—*Jason, 26*

~

"Okay, there's always one Neanderthal in the bunch," a female voiceover added. "So, there we have them, the answers we seek to the question we've all been asking ourselves: 'What about a woman magnetizes a man?'"

The age-old query lingered in the air as the video presentation ended and the lights came up. Pia took a quick look around. The room was filled with women whose body types and personal styles were as diverse as their wardrobes. Apparently those wishing to amp up their seduction skills to a nuclear level were a vast and varied lot. Their ages spanned from early twenties to late sixties, their figures falling everywhere between Mary-Kate Olsen and Mo'Nique. Surprisingly, with the exception of a few Pamela Anderson and Mariah Carey wannabes, most appeared normal. Not the desperate losers Pia would have imagined signing up for this kind of seminar.

But looks can be deceiving, Pia reminded herself. Right now she certainly felt like a big loser and wondered if the rest of these women felt the same. This had to be the ultimate low. She'd always frowned on Learning Annex–type classes that taught tips on how to snag a man, with workshops with titles such as "How to Date Out of Your League," "How to Make the Right Man Fall in Love with You," "How to Find Your Soul Mate." There had to be something wrong if you had to pay someone to teach you what Mother Nature had already supplied you with at birth—mating instincts, pheromones, and such. Damn it, Dee knew this about Pia, and yet here she was, sitting in a workshop with the corniest title of all, "Weapons of Mass Seduction."

There was a hesitant silence in the room as the assembled women waited for the workshop leader, Joey Clements, to materialize. There was no effort made toward introductions. Pia exchanged a nervous, courtesy smile with the five other women at her table. Each sat silently engrossed in her own thoughts, sizing up the others while waiting for instruction.

Not an extroverted flirt in the crowd. Guess that's why they're all here, Pia surmised with an inner grimace, turning her attention to the binder and the biography of the instructor. A quick scan informed Pia that Joey Clements was billed as a world-renowned sensuality and flirting expert revered in Hollywood for transforming small-town *blah* celebrities into Tinseltown *ahh* sex symbols.

Time to blow this estrogen fest and plan Dee's murder, Pia decided, rising to leave. Just as her bottom left the seat, Goldie Hawn's not-as-well-preserved-but-still-with-head-turning-appeal look-alike waltzed into the room and gracefully positioned herself behind the orchid-bearing podium.

Her escape foiled, Pia turned a groan of despair inward as she sank back into her chair.

"Whoa. Is *that* Joey Clements?" whispered the young biracial-looking woman sitting to Pia's left.

Pia totally understood her confusion. She too expected to see a tall, buxom sex bomb. Instead, standing before them was a plump, frizzy-haired, fifty-something flower child. The woman was dressed in a canary yellow figure-concealing caftan with a long string of coral beads dangling between her bountiful breasts. It was clear to Pia that this wasn't the boho chic look now trendy with all the L.A. and New York fashionistas, but rather a lifestyle uniform.

"Hello, lovelies. I'm Joey. Welcome to the first *fabulous* day of your *sensual* life," Joey Clements said, pronouncing each word with a sultry and hypnotic Kathleen Turner–like growl.

As soon as Joey opened her mouth and her smoky and suggestive voice—with its just-climbed-out-of-bed rasp—caressed Pia's ears, Pia was immediately intrigued. The hippie had disappeared, replaced by a compelling sensual goddess. With the dramatic voice and movement reminiscent of a legendary silver screen diva, Joey exuded a riveting sensuality and a certain *je ne sais quoi*.

"I'm very well aware that you lovelies are here to 'unearth your inner bombshell,'" she continued, "but before we get started, I'd like to clear up some probable misconceptions about what this workshop is and what it isn't. In our four days together you will *not* receive three hundred and sixty-five tips on how to drive your partner wild in bed. You will *not* learn the ultimate techniques for giving fellatio or the secrets to talking dirty. And this is *not* four days of bad girl sex for good girl lovers, though that is an *intriguing* topic for the future!"

Four of the women at Pia's table joined the rest of the room in a giggle. A few disappointed "Awws" and "Oh no's" could be heard. Judging from her open mouth and wide-eyed frown, the young lady sitting next to Pia seemed particularly disappointed by Joey's seemingly bait-and-switch advertising. "Not to worry, lovelies," Joey continued. "Though you won't receive actual instructions on these topics, you'll learn enough this weekend to make all those things happen quite naturally." A wave of applause quickly spread around the room. Pia raised a curious eyebrow as she noticed the young girl's frown quickly turn into a delighted and relieved grin.

Once the clapping died down, Joey went on. "When you hear the word *sensuality,*" she said, pronouncing each syllable slowly, as if she were in the middle of an orgasm, "what is the very first thought that pops into your mind?"

"Sex!" the bottled blonde sitting at their table enthusiastically responded.

"Please, a show of hands, how many of you agree?" Joey asked.

By Pia's count, at least two thirds of the hands were airborne. She and the white woman with the big hairdo and the Chanel suit were the only two in their dinner group with both hands in their laps. Pia didn't know the other woman's rationale, but Joey's question was too thought-provoking for her to offer an immediate response. And truthfully, she wasn't quite ready for any group participation.

"Yes, most people do think that *sexual* and *sensual* are synonymous, and for sure, sensuality is a key ingredient in achieving a richer, more satisfying sexual experience. But, my lovelies, sensuality is *much* more encompassing than just a mere sexual perk. To be sensual means to be acutely aware of your surroundings. It's the joyous preoccupation with what you smell, touch, hear, taste, and see. With the right state of mind, you can make *anything* a sensual experience—eating, walking, dancing, gardening, laundry . . . you name it.

"How many of you have taken the towels out of the dryer and instead of plopping them down on the folding table, have brought them to your nose and smelled the fabric softener, or rubbed the warm terry across your cheek?" Joey asked, describing the action in a way that made doing wash actually sound interesting. "No? Why not? Because it is just laundry?

"Sensual people *savor* the world around them, not simply observe it. They *experience* each task rather than rush through it to get at some imagined end, and in so doing, live a more passionate and appreciative existence.

"So by living sensually, you begin to see the world in vivid color and delight in the goodness that envelops you daily. You're always in the moment and aren't hung up on the future or the past. And this, my lovelies, has a huge bearing on how you perceive life . . . and sex," she said ending her statement with a conspiratorial wrinkle of her nose.

While interested in her words, Pia found herself mesmerized by the strength of Joey's individualism, the power of her sexual energy, and the effectiveness of a coquettish aura that didn't match her appearance but still seemed completely natural.

"The Weapons of Mass Seduction workshop is designed to help reawaken this lost side of your womanliness—your sensual side—the side that easily gets pushed away as life becomes more demanding and age and other people's opinions take their toll on your feminine confidence."

A soft chorus of "Mmm-hmm's" drifted through the atmosphere. It was obvious that Joey had the audience's rapt attention.

"Over the next few days, you'll discover ways to awaken your soft, alluring feminine side and live life with greater pleasure and joy and less stress. From the living room to the bedroom and everywhere in between, we'll explore the sensual *you* and learn how to use your unique sensuality to create an extraordinary atmosphere in which to live, love, and, of course, make love. Because when you feel like a sensual woman you behave like one. And that confidence, my lovelies, is the true secret to driving your partner wild in bed."

With that comment the room erupted into a thunderous ovation accompanied by the hoots and hollers of a room full of women ready to explode. Though Joey's words had resonance for her, Pia remained seated, taking in the scene, still unconvinced that staying had been the right decision. After years of playing hide-and-seek with her sexual self through celibacy, was she really ready to step into the open?

"Now, before we enjoy our sumptuous opening night supper," Joey continued as the applause tapered off, "I'd like you to take the next few moments to get to know the other incredible women in your group. Please introduce yourselves and tell the others a little bit about you and why you're here. After that, I'd like you to divide yourselves into teams of three. Each team will work together for the duration of the workshop."

Attention turned from Joey in the front of the room to the individual dinner tables. The chatter of introductions buzzed throughout the room. Sitting with Pia was Julie Morgan, a single and, based on her outfit, hot-to-trot thirty-three-year-old native Californian who was now a parole officer in Seattle, Washington. Tracy Lun, a married, childless certified aerobics instructor from San Francisco in her late thirties, was followed by sixty-year-old Rhonda Gardner, a widowed elementary school principal in the San Jose school district with three grown children and four grandchildren. While Tracy was there to add to her marital bliss trick box, both Julie and Rhonda were looking for skills to help get them ahead in the dating game.

"To be honest," Julie revealed, brushing her bangs from her heavily lined blue eyes, "I'm interested in marrying up. So I'm here trying to get a leg up on the competition—specifically my boss's wife." Julie's wide, superwhite smile revealed her pleasure at stunning her tablemates. It was obvious the woman delighted in being provocative in more ways than one.

"Well, I guess it's my turn then," announced a loud Texas accent belonging to a large and curvy woman on Pia's right. "Hi, y'all. I'm Florence Chase, but my friends all call me Flo. I'm a housewife and mother from Dallas, and I have three boys, two in college, both on football scholarships, and my oldest is in the military. Right now he's at Fort Sam Houston trainin' to be a medic. I love scrapbookin', the Dallas Cowboys, and a good ol'-fashioned Texas barbecue. I guess that's about it."

"Why are you here?" Tracy asked.

"Well, honey, let's see—I'm fifty-three years old and been married half that time. And now after twenty years of havin' kids around, my house is empty and so is my 'amorous arsenal,' as Joey's ad put it. Figured I'm too damn old to catch me a new man, so I better figure out how to hang on to the old fart I got. Kind of beefing up my own homeland security, as it were," she said, cutting a teasing eye toward Julie. While Florence's comment triggered laughter from the rest of the group, the slight break in her voice said what Flo didn't—that this was more an exercise in relationship rescue than refreshment.

With that, all heads turned to the young girl sitting next to Pia.

"Hi, I'm Rebecca Vossel."

An awfully white name even for such a light-skinned sister, Pia thought, inspecting Rebecca, who was one mess of a woman-child. Her crinkled, honey-toned mane was brushed back into the standard can't-do-anything-with-this-damn-hair ponytail, leaving the girl's nut-colored face wide open for inspection. Hers was a genetic collage of biracial features—full lips and broad nose, high cheekbones and blazing green eyes—and the ultimate sign of mixed parentage—hair too curly to be straight and too straight to be curly. She wore no makeup, a denim dress that screamed "help" instead of "hip," and sensible "feet don't fail me now" sandals. Pia had seen the type before. Looking like she did, this girl knew what it was like to play second fiddle in an orchestra filled with Barbies.

"I'm twenty-two and from Iowa . . ."

Well, that explains the name and the dress, Pia thought.

"I just moved to Chicago to work as a receptionist at an advertising firm. I maxed out my credit card and borrowed the rest from my best friend, Cris, 'cause I really wanted to take this workshop, even though my parents would die if they knew I was here."

"I can't imagine a cute thing like you having a problem getting a date," Rhonda offered.

"The men in Chicago are way different from what I was used to in Cedar Falls. I haven't had one date since I moved . . . not that I dated much at home either."

"Anything else you'd like us to know?" Pia asked.

"Just that I hope Joey Clements is as good as they say, 'cause she doesn't look like someone who knows how to flirt. I mean, she has a really cool voice, but she looks like somebody's grandma."

"Hey, we grannies are sexy too," Rhonda said with bemused admonishment.

"But let's be honest. Isn't Rebecca sayin' what we've all been thinkin'?" Flo asked with a conspiratorial smile. The truth of her statement caused the rest of them to burst into laughter and nod.

"I don't know," Pia said, "there's something . . . kind of sexy about her."

"And you are?" Tracy asked, directing everyone's attention back to the final introduction.

"Hello, ladies. I'm Pia Jamison. I'm from New York; I'm an executive in the music video business."

"Whoa! You must know a lot of celebrities. Why are *you* taking this class?" Rebecca asked, in awe.

"Actually, I was tricked into attending. I *thought* I was speaking at a conference on the impact of sex in music videos on culture. Apparently my secretary felt it was in her job description to schedule an intervention."

"Why would she do that?" Flo asked.

Pia quickly threw to the back of her throat the real reason Darlene would hoodwink her like this. She had no intention of following Rebecca's lead and bearing her soul to these strangers. "I guess she thought I needed a little help and knew I wouldn't come to this . . ."—*bullshit*—"this kind of workshop on my own. All the long work hours and traveling haven't left me much time to date these past few years, and to tell the truth I'm a little rusty with my girl skills," she explained, settling on the half truth.

"At least all of yours are just rusty. I haven't got any skills at all," Rebecca interrupted.

"Well, we all need something. That's why we're here, isn't it?" Rhonda added.

"Lovelies, it's about suppertime. If you haven't selected your groups, please do so," Joey Clements interrupted.

"How should we do this?" Flo asked.

"Let's make it easy," Tracy suggested. "You three—one squad. Us three—another." The six women murmured and shrugged their consent and immediately turned their attention from the whole to the newly formed parts.

Pia quickly sized up her partners. Florence Chase seemed perfectly nice, in a loud, colorful Texas kind of way. She was sure her story was deeper than what she was telling, but then again, whose wasn't? And that Rebecca Vossel was a mess. Her personality cocktail of youth, enthusiasm, and desperation could prove to be an annoying combination for the team. Still, Pia fought the impulse to judge her.

"Woo-hoo!" Flo cheered, lifting her wineglass to everyone at the table. "To the future weapons of mass seduction."

❧

"Book me on the first flight back to New York tomorrow," Pia barked into the phone while navigating the hotel lobby on her way back to her room. "And then pack up your desk. You're fired. And I really mean it this time."

"*Chica*, you just got to California. You're supposed to be in class learning something," Dee said, ignoring her boss.

"Yeah, well, we just finished dinner and here's what I've learned: There's no way I'm doing this. I'm not going to subject myself to some stupid workshop with a bunch of desperate housewives and man-hungry singles. You punked me. The confirmation letter said this was a workshop called Weapons of Mass Seduction: The Impact of Video Vixens on Society, not some bombshell excavation . . . Oh my God, you actually created that letter yourself, didn't you?"

"Well, you wouldn't have gone otherwise. Come on. Make this your resolution. It's a new year, only two weeks old. Time for a new, flirty you."

"I don't do the resolution thing."

"You need professional help, *chica*. Stay and get it."

"I'm not crazy, Dee," Pia hissed into her cell phone. "I can't believe you tricked me into coming to this thing. Do you know anything about this workshop?"

"Yes, I'm looking at the ad right now," Darlene said, and began to read.

Need to restock your amorous arsenal?

**Is there someone you'd like to meet or a relationship
you'd like to renew?
In four days you can become a deliciously dangerous**

Weapon of Mass Seduction

**The WMS workshop will teach you the skills
necessary to create a loving, sensual relationship with
yourself and others.**

You'll learn everything you wanted to know about

- **sensuality vs. sexuality**
- **winning the flirting game**
- **making your life a more enjoyable,
  passionate and awe-inspiring experience**

"Sounds like fun," Dee concluded.

"Well, it's not. There are lectures, homework, and tests. And Joey Clements, well, she's a piece of work. She's supposed to be some sort of international flirt expert, but she looks more like an escapee from a commune. I mean, she is kind of sexy, but what is some hippie broad going to teach me about flirting with New York men? And"—Pia shook the workshop folder—"I can do this myself."

"I have just two words for you . . . Bill Dorante."

"So our date only lasted an hour. We just didn't hit it off."

"Okay, two more words: Theo Johnson."

"Woman, you need a bigger vocabulary," Pia said, cringing in residual embarrassment. Even though it had been more than six weeks since their crash-and-burn lunch together, she still felt mortified by the mention of his name.

"Well, we had to do something. Grand Nelson is the only man left on the *papi* list, and that makes him the golden sperm. If you blow that, then what?"

"I have no damn clue," Pia replied as she opened the door to her room.

"Exactly. And that's why you are out in California trying to learn to be a civilized girl again. Now you go do your homework and I'm going home to write my Hector. God willing, we'll both get laid soon."

Chapter Four

Thursday—Individual Sensuality

It was 7:50 A.M. and Pia sat alone in the WMS makeshift classroom, taking her first exam since graduating from Brown University too many years ago to count. The title, "The Sensual You Self-Test"; the questions, such as "How do you feel about public displays of affection?"; and their multiple-choice answers all had the ring of a cheesy women's magazine self-help quiz. Last night she'd refused to partake, but this morning, while waiting for her teammates, guilt had set in. She was already here, so what the hell. And, as Dee had drilled into her head, she might just learn a thing or two.

"Shopping, and not sure if it's real or faux fur? B . . . feel it," Pia declared, and marked her answer. "Free hour? A . . . get a massage. Sexy elevator music? Meeting? B . . . listen, lust, and then get back to work."

She continued down the list of queries and possible answers without incident until she got to question number eight: "What qualities are you most looking for in a lover?"

"A high sperm count," Pia joked aloud before her giggles quickly fell silent. Even when sex and relationships had been a steady part of her everyday life, she hadn't thought much about what she really *wanted* in a man. She usually just took the package as presented—accepting and valuing the noble qualities and ignoring the flaws for as long as she could before moving on or being pushed aside. Never had she sat and definitively decided what special qualities she was looking for in the man she wanted to love.

"Passion and adventure? Looks and humor? Stability and wealth? Why is there no 'all of the above'? Because that would be way too easy," she asked and answered for herself. Pia thought for several minutes before her choice came to her. She had to say that the qualities that would in fact aid in the pursuit of all the others were passion and adventure.

Testing complete, Pia quickly checked the answer key and equivalency table and added up her score. Consulting the "sensuality index," she was pleased to learn that based on her score of six B's and four A's, she was still a solidly sensual woman at least on paper.

Satisfied with her results, Pia sat back and watched as the steady flow of workshop participants began, and within ten minutes they'd all gravitated to their newly formed teams. Rebecca arrived and the two women waited several more minutes before a visibly upset Flo joined them.

"How'd you do?" Rebecca asked as she nodded toward Pia's self-test.

"Okay."

"Well, according to this, I'm Supersensual." Her smile was a combination of pride and disbelief.

"Go 'head, Jessica Simpson," Pia responded, keeping her surprise in check. Of all people, Rebecca was the last she'd have pegged as living a hedonistic lifestyle.

"Well, I didn't do so well," Flo volunteered in a flat voice. "It looks like I am about as sensual as a rock. My score makes me too sensible to be sensual. It's no wonder . . ." Her voice trailed off into a void of self-pity. Pia and Rebecca traded looks, not knowing whether the polite and proper thing would be to probe further or leave it alone.

"Remember what Joey said," Pia offered. "This test isn't to make you feel bad about yourself but to give you an indication of where you stand and what you need to work on."

"Yeah, well, too late. I feel horrible and apparently I need to work on everything," Flo said. Silence, heavy with the embarrassment that comes when strangers confess the intimate details of their personal lives, settled around them.

"I don't know how much to believe this test, 'cause my score definitely doesn't match my love life," Rebecca revealed, politely trying to take the focus away from Florence. "Guys just don't get me—at least not the ones I like. When I go out, it's like I'm invisible. They want hot girls who love to party. So what chance does someone like me have?" Rebecca asked, her eyes almost pleading with Pia.

"Well, you know what they say, 'Beauty is only skin deep.' " Pia's words sounded scripted and insincere even to her, but what else do you say to someone you've just met who insists on unpacking all their personal baggage at your feet?

"Wonder what that's all about," a woman seated behind them commented, gesturing to six easels draped with lavender silk.

"I think we're about to find out."

"Good morning, lovelies," Joey Clements's husky voice rang from the doorway. She floated to the front of the room, wearing another gossamer caftan, this time in purple. There was an alluring lightness that surrounded the woman. Despite what Rebecca might think, it was clear to Pia that Joey Clements possessed the much-coveted "it factor."

"I hope you each had a wonderful evening and are ready to begin in earnest the transformation into your sensual selves. Today we are going to delve into the realm of *individual sensuality*." There was an enticing lilt to her voice that was both seductive and commanding.

"Society erroneously teaches women that we should *feel* sensual only when we are *acting* sexual. But a true weapon of mass seduction revels in her feminine side and strives to feel good even when there is no one around. How? By surrounding herself with comforting textures, sounds, scents, tastes, and a visually pleasing persona and environment. This increases a woman's sense of beauty, pleasure, gratitude, and, most important, self-worth.

"Let's do a quick exercise. I'd like each team to put together a list of items to be included in a gift basket for a newborn. Please note the purpose for each item."

Pia felt her heart expand and contract ever so slightly. The last thing she'd expected in a flirt workshop was baby talk. It was disconcerting to participate in an exercise focused on preparing for the arrival of an infant when she was so far away from home trying to expand her chances of creating one.

"Good thing we have a mother of three on our team," Rebecca remarked.

"Yes, but it's been a long time. My babies are old enough to make babies of their own. But I guess the basics never change. Let's see: receivin' blankets, gowns, onesies, socks, and a few bibs are really about all the clothes they need when they first get here."

"And lotion, shampoo, powder. I love the way babies smell. Fresh and sweet," Rebecca added, furiously writing the list.

"Pia?"

"Ah, I don't know. You two seem to have it covered."

"You New York career girls, too busy workin' to think about havin' babies," Flo remarked. She noticed the subtle drop of Pia's eyes and slight twist of her lips before moving on. "Well, every baby I've ever known has needed diapers and wipes."

"What about those wipe warmers? Those things are cold on a little bottom. And a mobile over the crib. They're supposed to stimulate the baby," Rebecca offered.

"And a lambskin rug to lie on," Pia softly voiced. "And music. Soft, soothing tunes. Smooth jazz, classical, new age."

"That's good. I say we add a few books and we're done," Flo said, just as Joey brought the group's attention back to her.

"So why, do you ask, in a workshop about turning women into sensual weapons are we making lists more appropriate for a baby shower? To prove my point: that from birth to around age four or five, there is nothing surrounding our children that isn't intended to stimulate every one of their senses with tastes, scents, and textures that are varied and appealing. We intentionally buy things that feel good to the skin, smell pleasant, and sound soothing. And then, somewhere around the time kids discover self-pleasuring, we begin to associate sensuality with sexuality and things change drastically. Suddenly, sensuality is discouraged and becomes something we adults pull out of our trick bags when we want to spice up our sex lives.

"Honesty Moment: You walk into your seven-year-old daughter's room one morning and find the pajamas she went to bed in are on the floor and she is sleeping happily nude. 'Why?' you ask. 'Because the sheets feel good on my skin,' she says. Please, a show of hands: How many of you would be shocked and bothered and insist that she sleep with pajamas so she wouldn't catch cold or some other concocted reason?"

Slowly the hands of nearly three quarters of the room rose into the air. Apparently Joey's point had hit home. Why was sensuality considered an imperative in early childhood and then snatched away before puberty?

"Whoa, that is so my mother," Rebecca whispered to Pia, keeping her hands defiantly in her lap. "Once she and I went shopping for school clothes. I didn't put on a bra under my slip 'cause I liked the silky feeling, and she got so upset she slapped me. She said the boys would think I was a slut."

"Shhh," Flo gently admonished, putting her index finger to her lips and tilting her head toward the front of the room.

"So it is time to take back your sensuality and *revel* in it once again," Joey was saying. "A woman's sensuality truly takes root in her *individuality*. A woman comfortable with her uniqueness is a *confident* woman. And a confident woman is a *sexy* woman! So you must first find the things about you that are unique and interesting and make you feel good about being you.

"Yes?" Joey interrupted herself to acknowledge Rebecca's waving hand.

"What if there's just nothing that's interesting about you? What if you've spent your entire life trying not to be noticed and now nobody does?" Her comment raised the curious eyebrows of her teammates.

"Or maybe you've spent most of your life being somebody else's somebody," a voice called out.

"Yeah, like a mother," added another sympathetic participant.

"Or a wife or lover."

"Or a wife *and* a lover," Julie quipped, making the group around her snicker uncomfortably.

"Or all of the above plus about a hundred other job titles," Flo added.

"So the question is," Joey stepped in, "how do you wear all of those hats and find your authentic self beneath them?"

"Exactly. How do you find someone you never realized you'd lost?" Flo asked.

Or have kept hidden for so long? Pia wondered in her head.

Or never knew, thought Rebecca.

"Well, you dig deep and excavate. You dust off the precious relic, polish her up, and *voilà*: You discover what Dubya and others couldn't—a bona fide WMS.

"This morning we're going to talk about ways to bring out the incomparable you hiding behind all those titles, expectations, marketing campaigns, and celebrity endorsements. And we begin with identifying your personal charisma."

With all the flair of Vanna White, Joey walked to the easels and dramatically removed the fabric from each, revealing poster-size photographs of six very famous celebrities. Staring back at the audience with their perfect toothy grins were Sharon Stone, Whoopi Goldberg, Angelina Jolie, Reese Witherspoon, Oprah Winfrey, and Halle Berry.

"*Charisma*. Every woman has her own distinctive brand of 'star quality.' You don't have to be famous to own and use it to your best advantage. Charisma is not *what* you are—your job or role—but *who* you are. It is your own 'secret sauce' that helps connect you emotionally, intellectually, and even spiritually to others. Your personal charisma might be flashy or flamboyant. Maybe it's quiet and intoxicating or warm and witty. Once you identify yours and really own it, it can never be taken away.

"So with the help of these well-known ladies, let's look at what I believe to be the six main types of charisma:

"**POWER CHARISMA,**" she said, pointing to Sharon Stone, "is all about chutzpah. Sharon is shocking and fearless, and standing next to her you just might be a little intimidated by her energy and intensity, but you're also fascinated. Hillary and Condoleezza also have this kind of charisma.

"**HUMOROUS CHARISMA,**" Joey continued. "Whoopi is clever and disarming. She'll draw you in with her wit and amusing take on life, all the while making you laugh and feel at ease. Ellen DeGeneres has the same kind of power. There's nothing clownlike about this kind of charisma. Think about it. How high is humor on your list of what you want in a mate?

"No offense, but Whoopi Goldberg is not very sexy," Rebecca whispered, leaning over. "And Ellen is gay."

"Well, something's working for them, because they can pull some serious men—and women," Pia said, before returning her attention to Joey.

"Now, Angelina Jolie certainly personifies **SEXUAL CHARISMA.** Sex appeal and passion ooze out of every pore. Her sexuality permeates everything she does, and yet she's no bimbo. Her attire is elegant and refined and still enormously provocative."

"Jennifer didn't have a shot in hell," Julie joked from the back, setting off a roomful of titters.

"Jennifer Aniston is much like Reese," Joey continued through the laughter. "She's someone who is completely capable of taking care of herself, and yet people seem to want to protect her. Women with **CUTE CHARISMA** are friendly. They make people feel comfortable around them, and their appeal lies in the fact that they aren't intimidating, snobbish, or aloof."

"And aren't old enough to be pissed off at the world," Flo joked to those around her.

"Now, women who possess **SMART CHARISMA**," Joey continued, gesturing to Oprah, "are truly brilliant without the need to prove it. They listen and talk *to* you, not *at* you. They don't need to overwhelm you with all they know, but have the humble, unassuming ability to make you consider things in an entirely different light. Brooke Shields is another great example of smart charisma.

"And last, cool as a Coca-Cola, Halle Berry. Mystery is what makes a woman with **COOL CHARISMA** so appealing. Though she may be slightly aloof and you never quite know what she's thinking, her smile is as genuine as it is tempting, because it always implies that there is so much more to know and uncover. Charlize Theron is another cool customer.

"Each is different, yet each as seductive and sexy as the next, and most are a combination of several charismas. So, probably, are you. Let's take a moment to think about what kind of charisma you possess."

"Pia, you're easy. You've got cool charisma," Rebecca immediately declared. "You're beautiful and fashionable and there's a secret part of you that makes people curious."

"I can live with that," Pia agreed, visions of her own cool heroine, smooth and sexy jazz singer Sade, appearing in her head. "What about you, Florence?"

"Rocks don't have charisma. Not even sensible pet rocks," Flo deadpanned.

"Well, I want charisma like Angelina Jolie. She's so hot. Guys love her. But I don't exactly know how to do that," Rebecca admitted while waving her arm in the air.

"Joey," Rebecca asked, "if you don't know what kind of charisma you have, or don't have the kind you want, how do you get it?"

"By pinpointing the parts of your personality that are appealing and then working them to the max. Most people waste their time working only on their weaknesses. I say, strengthen your strengths," Joey advised.

"**TIP**: The things you are drawn to in other women are the hidden, undeveloped assets you possess but have yet to acknowledge. Study these women—and pull from their lives that which is you, but don't try to copy them. Imitation may be the sincerest form of flattery, but it's also the fastest way to look like an idiot.

"Now, enough lecturing for today—you have other exciting things to do. First, if you'd please turn to page seven to find your homework assignment for this evening," she said.

Pia and the others flipped to the pages.

EXERCISE: Identify three things: 1) your individual charisma; 2) the secret weapon you already possess but underutilize; and 3) what trademark icon you would choose to represent yourself. Write these down in your WMS journal with any thoughts or feelings that might accompany your answers.

"I don't get it. What exactly is a trademark icon?" someone from the back asked.

"An icon is merely a representation of something. In this case, *you*. Your trademark icon is something you can see and touch that connects you to your sensual, unique self and reminds you of the woman you are striving to be.

"Right now the bus is outside to take you on a very special shopping expedition. As you leave you will receive your shopping list. Sometimes it's the small and very personal things—shoes, jewelry, or fragrance—that make you feel sensually unique and become lingering clues to your inimitable personality. Now keep all these things in mind as you make your purchases.

"Your first stop will be a visit to my good friend Cosette. If anyone can make you feel like a true WMS, she will. I'll join you later at dinner. Have a sensual afternoon, lovelies, and by all means, take time to notice and smell the flowers along the way."

Chapter Five

Pia crossed the threshold and immediately felt a satisfying sense of homecoming. There was something about stepping into a lingerie shop that automatically brought a twist to her lips and put an adventurous gleam in her eye. Some women loved shoes. Others coveted jewelry. Pia adored expensive undies. For some, paying $125 for a brassiere and $65 for matching panties might seem excessive, but for her it was an investment in her positive state of mind. Fine lingerie made her feel attractive and desirable, feelings tough to hold on to when there was no one in your life reminding you.

"Holy Mary, Mother of Jesus. This is definitely not the bra section at JCPenney," Rebecca proclaimed in nervous awe as she eyeballed every satin and embroidered inch of their assigned destination.

Of course it isn't, Pia wanted to assure her. This was not a boutique for amateurs. The place positively reeked of feminity. And power. Erotic, sexual power. Even to the unindoctrinated eye, this was a sophisticated and elegant collection for those steeped in the art of seduction. Boudoir-style armoires lined the walls—each tastefully stocked with lace and silk-spun concoctions of sexy body armor, all designed to disarm and accelerate the fall of men.

Talk about your amorous arsenal, she thought, giggling to herself before a tide of pessimism swept over her. Despite owning an impressive munitions chest, Pia no longer possessed the confidence to wage an effective war. Perhaps Dee was right to dupe her into attending this workshop.

"*Bienvenue à Passionata*. Welcome to Passionata, ladies," interrupted an elegantly French-accented female voice. "I am Cosette. Your *pro-*

fesseur, Joey, has sent you to me this afternoon to teach you more about the power of the pretty things that surround you.

"Lingerie is a beautiful way for a woman to develop and explore her sense of identity. Pretty things like this or this," Cosette continued, holding up a black lace merry widow bustier and a delicate sheer white camisole as divergent examples, "are a special and secret manifestation of your personality, mood . . . or purpose," she added with a wink. "So let your most intimate apparel be the sign of how you feel."

Cosette's captive audience broke out in a chorus of flirty laughter. Power. Purpose. Pia almost felt sorry for the male population once these sex bombs in the making were released around the country.

"And never, never must you save these beauties for a special occasion. Every day is special, *non*? Put them on to clean your house, wear them to drive your *enfants* to school, to shop your groceries. If you choose to share with your lover, well, lucky him. But never do you buy just to seduce *him*. You must first seduce yourself. So every day when you pull on your panties, pull on a new attitude as well. What bubbles underneath radiates on top. *Non?*

"Ladies, enjoy the champagne. You will look and touch and find yourself here in Passionata. Now *mademoiselles* Marie, Aimee, and Jacquelin will begin to measure you, as fit is most important."

With a dramatic clap of her hands, Cosette's three assistants, clad in black smocks, pencil skirts, and stiletto heels, appeared and the fitting frenzy began. Pia walked over to Rebecca and the two were soon joined by Flo.

"Why do we need to come here?" Rebecca asked, thinking of her already sky-high credit balance as she curiously fingered a siren red garter belt. "Can't we go somewhere a little less expensive?"

"Because as Cosette said, proper fit is important," Pia explained. "Here, you'll get that. Buy what you want. It will be my gift to you."

"Really? Are you sure?"

"I'm sure, besides I'm not going to get anything. I have drawers of this stuff at home."

"Thank you," Rebecca said as she scooped up the garter's matching push-up bra and thong panties.

"I'm not tryin' to be your mother, Rebecca, but aren't those just a tad . . . well . . . risqué?" Flo asked. "How about a sweet little camisole that isn't so . . . red?"

"My mother would never let me wear anything red, not even a sweater let alone underwear like this. I've been sweet all my life. Now I want to be sexy like a Victoria's Secret Angel."

"Honey, there's not one thing angelic about these skimpy panties and brassieres. Those creations are the devil's work. And I am not talkin' about nothin' moral or religious, darlin'. I'm talkin' comfort. No underpants are supposed to disappear into the crevices of your body, and no nightie is supposed to be so full of hardware that it would stop you from gettin' on an airplane let alone gettin' a good night's sleep."

Pia couldn't stop laughing. Flo Chase was a natural comedienne. "Flo, in case you had any doubt, your individual charisma is definitely humorous, and I think that's your secret weapon as well. Now go on. The panty patrol is calling."

"Well, can't hurt to get a good fit," Flo said as Aimee beckoned her into a dressing room. "Maybe it'll keep my nipples from droppin' out my pant legs. Come on, Rebecca. You can try those on while I'm gettin' measured."

"*Mademoiselle?*" Aimee asked, gesturing to Pia.

"*Non, merci,*" Pia begged off, dragging out her high school French. "I'm just browsing today."

While her teammates headed for the dressing rooms, Pia decided to buy a gift for Dee and wandered over to the armoire of nightgowns and matching robes. "For Hector's homecoming," she decided, admiring a chocolate brown and lavender silk chemise. She'd just found Darlene's size when Rebecca's loud denouncement sounded above the background music and quickly steered Pia back to the dressing area.

"Absolutely not! It's supposed to be sexy. Pia, look at her. Tell her she looks like my grandma in that."

"Well . . ." Pia began softly as she viewed Flo standing in lingerie's equivalent of oatmeal—a sexless, shapeless, laceless cross-your-heart-looking number. "I've never seen Rebecca's grandma, but that's definitely not saying 'new attitude.'"

"Well, I guess a granny is what he saw too. It's no wonder . . ." Florence said, her words barely audible.

"You said that earlier today. If you don't mind me asking, it's no wonder what?" Rebecca politely inquired, curiosity winning out over protocol.

"No wonder why my husband, Dan, decided to walk out after twenty-six years of marriage. No wonder he moved clear across five states just to get away from me," Flo admitted before collapsing on the chair in the corner.

"I know yesterday I said I was here to refresh my marriage, but truthfully I think *save* is a better word," she softly revealed. "My friend Miriam gave it to me for a birthday gift and insisted I come out here—otherwise I'd be back in Texas still tryin' to figure out what exactly I did wrong. That test we took says I'm sensibly sensual and here I am standin' in a shop full of lacy tidbits, wearin' your grandma's boring beige *sensible* brassiere. And according to Joey Clements, when it comes to bein' a sexy, sensual woman, *sensible* is the last thing men want."

"Who knows what men want? I don't think they're even sure," Pia said, angry at a man she didn't even know for hurting a woman she'd just met. "Men leave for a variety of reasons. You didn't have to do anything to drive him away."

"I've been rackin' my brain over this, and I know I didn't do anythin' per se. I mean, I didn't have an affair or run up the credit cards or anythin'. Lookin' back, I'm sure he felt slighted for the past eighteen years or so, but the boys were a full-time job. In my mind, when the kids came our first priority was to be parents, and once they left to live their own lives we'd get back to being a couple. What I hadn't figured was that they'd all grow up and leave—Dan included."

"So he just up and said he wanted a divorce?" Pia asked.

"No, nothin' that definitive. Our youngest had just returned back to campus followin' Thanksgivin' break. Dan left two days later on a fishin' trip to Florida. Well, sometime between the flight down there and catchin' some big marlin, he decided he was bored and he wasn't gettin' any younger. Told me he needed to experience life. I hate that phrase, 'experience life.' What the hell has he been doin' the past fifty years? When he told me that I went down to the basement and took out all the scrapbooks I'd put together over the years. There were fifteen books just filled to the brim. How could he have that many memories and not have 'experienced life'? It makes no sense to me."

"I think that's one of those catchphrases people use when all of a sudden they look up and realize that there are more years behind them than in front of them," Pia offered. "Women may have their biological clocks, but men have these Big Ben timepieces that go off in midlife. It's their warning that their penises aren't going to stay hard forever so they better accomplish whatever they need to now to keep that feeling of youthful vitality."

"Well, whatever alarm clock went off, he called home and declared that he would not be returnin'. I managed to talk him into givin' it a little time before he files for divorce. So he's been livin' in Florida for the last five months and is due back next month. When he gets here we're supposed to figure out where we're goin'. The separation isn't official yet, but talkin' to him sure feels like it is."

"So you're taking this workshop 'cause you're about to be divorced?" Rebecca asked.

"Oh, no. I'm takin' it to keep from gettin' divorced, or at least Miriam thinks it might help. She said I should come here to become a sex bomb so I can blow Dan's mind. She figures that if the woman he left isn't the same woman he comes home to, then maybe his interest will be piqued enough to stay. I hope she's right. I don't know what I'll do if this doesn't work."

"It'll work, but if it doesn't, you'll know what to do to catch the next guy," Rebecca suggested supportively.

"But I don't want another guy. Dan is my life and I want him back. Even if it means shovin' these big ol' feed bags into a scratchy, overpriced brassiere."

"Feed bags? That's gross," Rebecca protested.

"Darlin', these are just baby feeders," she said, cupping her large breasts for emphasis. "I don't see what all the hype is about."

"Well, I'm sure Dan does. Now come on, let's find you something hot to wear for when he gets home. Something like that," Pia said, pointing to a poster of a femme fatale wearing an ivory and black push-up bra with lavish embroidery and a big satin ribbon.

"Honey, once you go from a thirty-eight C to a forty long, that kinda underwear just becomes silly. I'd look like a washed-up cathouse hooker wearin' somethin' like that."

"They do take getting used to, 'cause just trying them on feels nothing like the tightie-whities I usually wear," Rebecca said. "But you know what? I like it," she admitted with a lip-biting blush. "They make me feel . . . I don't know . . . different."

"Welcome to the world of lingerie. You have been bitten by the power of the panty," Pia said with a laugh. "But Flo's got a point too. You have to feel comfortable. So Florence, how about you get the bra you like in black with matching panties. Seductive but safe. And wait, I have an idea," Pia said as she ran back out into the store and to the nightgown display. She picked out a copper-colored silk gown edged in purple lace and a matching robe. It was elegant, age appropriate, and tastefully provocative.

"This should make you feel sexy *and* comfortable," Pia suggested, handing her the set. "Oh, my God—it matches your hair perfectly."

"Darlin', you're a genius. This feels amazin'," Flo said, touching the silk to her face. "Beats the pants off the PJs I got at home. Now, this could work. Aimee, honey, what else you got like this?"

Pia left her teammate in Aimee's capable hands to purchase Darlene's gift and some scented sachets. As she passed the freestanding floor mirror, her passing image made her pause. She smoothed her T-shirt over her breasts and pulled the fabric close, showcasing her bustline.

Will these ever be baby feeders? she thought, staring at her own cleavage.

Not if you don't pull on a new attitude with some new panties, Cosette's words reminded her.

"Aimee, *s'il vous plaît.* Can you bring me that Aubude Tulipes demi cup? Thirty-six C," Pia requested, catching Cosette's assistant on her way back to the fitting room.

In her mind's eye Pia could see the delicate scalloped edge combined with sensual white tulle in an exquisite tulip design. It was pretty, romantic, and perfect for making a baby.

With someone you love, not a sperm donor, an inner voice pointed out.

"Wait, Aimee—please, can you also bring me the Cabaret style as well," Pia asked. "In black." Sheer, sultry, tempting. Perfect for seducing a baby daddy.

Chapter Six

"Vanilla," Florence requested.

"This is Baskin-Robbins. Thirty-one flavors and you can't do better than *vanilla*?" Rebecca teased.

"Darlin', it's one thing to tinker with variety when it comes to your underpants, but there are times when plain and simple is just perfect. I'd suggest you remember that, Ms. Supersensual."

"Where's Pia?" Rebecca inquired as the two ventured back into the mall.

"She said she'd wait right here for us," Florence said, looking around.

"Here she comes, and she's got company."

Flo's eyes followed Rebecca's finger and saw Pia headed toward them with what looked to be a two-year-old boy in her arms. The pair appeared to be chums, with a glowing Pia singing and the child laughing.

"Sale at the toy store?" Flo inquired when Pia reached them.

"I found this cutie-pie wandering around by himself. I went into the center of the mall to see if I could find his mommy, but nothing. I'm taking him to the security office, but I didn't want to go without letting you two know."

"Whoa, he really likes you. He's grinning and laughing and he doesn't even know you."

"You're a natural," Flo remarked to her beaming teammate.

"He's sweet," Pia said, gently running her fingers through the toddler's curls. Her bittersweet smile was not lost on Flo. "Now let's go find your mommy," Pia said, touching her forehead to the child's. "I'll be right back."

Florence and Rebecca were just finishing up their ice cream cones when Pia returned. "The mom was already there in security. She was frantic. She said she turned away for a minute and he was gone. What a scary feeling it must be to lose your child."

"Good thing you found him and not some crazy," Flo said. "Now back to shoppin'. What else is on the list?"

"Well, we can check off number one: *Underneath* it all something that makes you feel beautiful," Rebecca said, quoting the shopping list Joey had given each of them. "Number two: A *scent*ual way to express yourself. I guess that's perfume."

"Or it could be scented candles or incense," Pia suggested.

"And three: a *tangible* indication of who you are or want to be. That must be the icon thing she was talking about. What aisle do you find that one in?

"I'm kinda confused," Rebecca admitted. "I get the underwear, but what's with the other stuff? I need some different clothes to go with my new lingerie, 'cause the closet I have isn't working."

"Clothes aren't as important as your mind-set. Joey's trying to get us to change our attitude, which, like Cosette said, bubbles from underneath. Everything on that list is about individual expressions that are related to our sensual personalities," Pia explained, becoming more impressed with her instructor's ideas. "I get it."

"Of course you do. Ever since we got started there hasn't been one darn thing that has you as confounded as the rest of us. If I didn't already like you so much, I'd have to hate you for bein' so damn together," Flo joshed.

Pia simply gave her a wink and a smile.

"So where do we do the fragrance thing?" Rebecca asked.

"How about there?" Pia suggested, pointing across the mall to a perfumery.

"I've been wearin' the Jean Natè all my life," Flo announced as they entered the store.

"They still make that?" Pia asked.

"Still sold at all your finest drugstores. It's the first Christmas gift Dan ever gave me and I've been wearin' it on special occasions ever since."

"Well, then you definitely need a change. Come on, I have an idea," Pia said, leading her over to the alphabetized fragrance wall. "Try this," she said, spraying a test wand with Chanel No. 19 and waving it under Flo's nose. "It's a classic, but it screams mystery."

"It smells good, all right, but you're the cool mysterious one. Why in the world would I want to be an unknown to my own husband?"

"Remember? Woman he left . . . not the same one he comes home to? Shake him up some," Rebecca prodded.

"Hmm . . . well, I guess I can try. You two are makin' me into a regular Mae West."

"I'll be back," Rebecca declared before making a beeline toward the celebrity display. "I'm going to check out J.Lo's new perfume. I want something . . ."

"We know . . . sexy," Flo and Pia responded in amused unison.

"And hot," Rebecca added, laughing.

"Does that girl have any other words in her vocabulary besides *hot* and *sexy*?"

"Apparently not, unless you include whoa. I hope Joey knows that she's creatin' a monster," Flo remarked in both concern and jest. "We need to shake a leg. We still have more shoppin' to do and the bus will be here to take us back to the hotel in an hour. What about you? Aren't you gonna buy anythin' here either?" Flo asked.

"Just these candles. I already have kind of a signature scent, Stella by Stella McCarthy," Pia declared as Rebecca rejoined them.

"Okay, enough already! You wear pretty panties *and* have a signature scent? Why are you takin' this workshop? You could be teachin' it," Flo asked.

"I guess I could if you believe the old saying 'Those who can, do; those who can't, teach.' Believe me, we have plenty of time left this weekend for my insecurities to surface. So, that's that. On to the trademark icon. What about charms?" Pia suggested.

"We passed a silver jewelry cart on our way here," Florence said, her curiosity piqued, but letting the topic go.

The three descended on the Silver Forest kiosk and began searching for a metallic representation of themselves. Pia immediately found what she was looking for among the Chinese symbols. Her fingers caressed the cool, smooth lines of the character for "mother." Even in unbending sterling silver, the calligraphy captured both strength and gentleness, just like the concept it represented. Did she dare buy it and own this state of being for her future self? She paused. Was she staking her claim or merely tempting fate?

"Is that the one?" Flo asked, her eyes scanning the tray from which Pia had made her selection.

"I think so."

"What's it mean?"

"Love," Pia replied, feeling as though she was only half lying. Weren't *mother* and *love* basically synonymous?

"Hmm. Really? Nice. Well, I think I'm settlin' on this," Flo said, holding a silver "cause" ribbon. "Bein' with you girls has led me to the belief that I am worth raisin' Dan's awareness over."

"Dan's or anyone else's," Pia added in support. "I love it."

"Whoa! Nicole Richie has a necklace just like this." Rebecca's excited voice rang out from the other side of the jewelry cart. "I'm so getting this," she declared, holding a charm of the iconic lounging mud flap girl.

"Honey, you want to be hot like Paris and sexy like Angelina, smell like J.Lo, and accessorize like Nicole Richie. Seems like you're tryin' to be everybody *but* Rebecca."

Hurt and bewilderment clouded the young woman's face, causing Flo to immediately regret her remark. "Don't mind me, darlin'. It's tough to decide on one thing that sums up who you are."

"Or want to be," Rebecca said sullenly. "I don't really know who Rebecca is. I never have. Not when I was in Iowa and certainly not since I've been in Chicago." She held up the charm and took a long look before sighing deeply and placing it back on the tray. "But the one thing I do know is, whoever she is wants to be someone very different."

"We all do at some point," Pia said, putting a protective arm around the girl. "You're young. Take it from us old chicks: other than the great body, the twenties basically suck, but everybody has to go through the confusion to get to the other side. You've got time to figure out who you are, and hopefully this weekend will help."

"It already has." Rebecca smiled, appreciating Pia's sisterly attitude. "Do you think they could make me a necklace that says Becca?"

"Not *Rebecca*?" Flo asked.

"Becca sounds more grown and . . . big city."

"It does sound a little less like you grew up in a cornfield or on Sunnybrook Farm," Pia said with a teasing giggle.

"I did not grow up in a cornfield," Becca shot back with practiced indignation. "I'm from Cedar Falls, which is right next to Waterloo. My dad is a high school science teacher and my mother is a nurse. We're not all farmers."

She hated the way people stereotyped her home state and the folks that lived there. Seems like her entire life had been spent peeling off the clichéd labels stuck on by other people.

"I'm sorry. That remark did sound pretty ignorant. Is Rebecca a family name? I only ask because you don't hear of many black folks named Rebecca."

"You're black?" Flo remarked. "I've been wonderin' what you are. I thought maybe Latina."

"My biological mother was African American and my biological father was white. I'm adopted." Pia and Florence listened intently as Becca conveyed her story.

Her parents, Chester and Mary Vossel, unable to have children of their own and tired of waiting in the long line behind other couples looking for healthy white children, emptied their savings account and headed south to the Window of Hope, a Christian adoption agency in Macon, Georgia. Three weeks later, six-week-old Rebecca Mary Vossel moved into the lovingly prepared nursery in her parents' modest three-bedroom home.

As the adopted daughter of devout, conservative Christian parents, Rebecca was raised to be obedient and God-fearing. Chester and Mary were strict but devoted parents, demanding good grades and community service at the church and allowing little social life. She learned quickly that her father's word was just as powerful as the Lord's, and she grew up toeing the line, learning to be seen and not heard. Naturally shy, she didn't find this difficult, and she actually preferred keeping to herself. It was the being seen part that she wished she could change.

Despite her name, she'd become the ultimate plain Jane, less by nature and more by parental design. No makeup, modest "proper" clothing, no flash, and absolutely no trash. As the years went by and the features of her African American mother emerged, it became impossible to disappear behind a veil of good behavior and the New

Testament. Amid all the corn-fed-looking girls surrounding her, Rebecca's honey-toned complexion and unruly hair made her stand out in all the wrong ways.

"That's why you said in session this morning that you spent your life trying not to get noticed?" Pia probed gently. "And why you want to change your name?"

"Yeah, pretty much. New identity, new life," she admitted, not sure if she could make them understand.

"My parents definitely loved me and they made sure I didn't get in any trouble growing up. They kept me away from alcohol, drugs, and wild parties, but the problem is they kept me away from *everything,* including boys. By the time I got out of high school, I just wanted out. I didn't know much about life or men and I still don't.

"When I refused to go to a Christian university they said that they were not going to pay tuition to a heathen school. So instead of going to college I worked for a few years in Waterloo until I moved to Chicago four months ago. Right now I'm working as a receptionist and trying to save money so I can get my degree."

"This workshop is very expensive," Flo remarked, her maternal instincts once again on alert. "Why would you go into debt for somethin' this frivolous?"

"I don't think it's frivolous. This is like a survival course for me. I'm tired of feeling as though I don't belong anywhere."

"I guess it's easy to feel out of place in a new city, but darlin', you're beautiful. You have such an exotic look about you."

"That's it!" Pia said, clapping her hands to the baffled looks of her teammates. "That's your weapon—the one you possess but don't utilize. Turn what you think is your negative into a positive."

"I don't get it."

"Becca, it's like Joey said today. Strengthen your strengths. You're exotic-looking. Play up the fact that you look different to your advantage. Don't try to cast yourself in a Hollywood cookie cutter starlet mold."

"I swear, I can't tell one skinny, blond, dog-totin' girl from the next, even if they are famous," Flo agreed.

"Oh, I don't want to be famous. I just want to mean something to somebody. To be *some*body's star instead of always feeling like a fish out of water."

"Well, then this should be perfect," Pia said, pulling a necklace from the display and clasping it around Becca's neck. "What are starfish but uniquely shaped fish. And where do you find starfish? Usually on the beach, out of the water. So whenever you feel like you don't belong, touch this and remember you're a one-of-a-kind star. Just presently undiscovered."

"You really think I'm a star?"

"Becca, I deal with so-called celebrities every day, and one thing I've come to realize is that whatever you believe you are, others will too."

Chapter Seven

Friday—Social Sensuality

After a morning dedicated to relaxing and sensual spa and aromatherapy treatments, followed by a sumptuous lunch of tasty bite-size cuisine, everyone reconvened in the Pacific Ballroom for day two of unearthing their inner bombshells.

"Good afternoon, lovelies! You're all glowing!" Joey remarked once her pupils were assembled. "And there's a new vibrancy in the air. Can you feel it? You all must be wearing your new lacy attitudes."

Happy laughter buzzed around the room. The sparkling energy was evident and contagious. It had even managed to warm Pia up to the idea of being there. Yesterday's lessons had obviously sunk in and were being fully applied this morning. Armed with a new confidence brought on by self-discovery and the emergence of self-acceptance, the weapons-in-waiting sat eager to absorb today's knowledge.

"Yesterday we began to discover our individual sensuality. You identified your personal signatures—the things about your personality, opinions, and choices that set you apart from every other woman in the room. Today we take the next step toward bringing out the sensual you in a social setting by learning how to interact on a joyfully flirtatious level.

"We were all born to charm. If you've ever watched a baby work the room with his or her sparkling eyes, irresistible smiles, and sweet coos, you already know that flirting is an inherent part of our DNA."

Like that little charmer in the mall, Pia remembered, smiling.

"And with practice, we can all be good at it. Flirting takes no special equipment and costs nothing. Your God-given attributes will do you just fine. A good flirt is merely a woman who has learned to revel in the power of being a woman, is determined to enjoy herself in the moment, and has a benevolent streak. Oh, yes, my lovelies, flirting is all about transferring your good feelings on to someone else, thus making someone else's day. So, as they say, 'It's all good.' "

"Excuse me, Joey." Florence raised her hand to interrupt. "I've been married over twenty years. Bowlin', I am good at. Flirtin', not so much. Just exactly how do you go about doin' it? Especially with a man who I haven't flirted with since *I was* a baby?"

"I agree that charming a stranger can somehow feel easier than charming a man who has experienced your 'natural loveliness upon awakening' and has come to accept your penchant for eating potato chips in bed. But flirting with your life partner is a crucial part of your arsenal. Flirting helps keep romance and playfulness alive in your marriage. It should not stop at the altar; neither should it stop at your twenty-fifth wedding anniversary.

"And here's another tip for you married ladies. Lightly flirt with other men when your husband is with you. Keep your flirtation mild and definitely don't tease—you don't want to start an argument. But by letting him see that other men find you attractive, you're revving up his competitive nature, which translates into him feeling pretty studly about himself and pretty damn lucky to have you.

"So whether with stranger or spouse, flirting begins and ends with feminine confidence. And it's this sensual strength that affects how you walk into a room, how you return a hello with your eyes, and how you come across as absolutely fascinating to both men and women. Exploit your charm and you will be surprised how people respond to you in all situations—and how often you get your way."

"That sounds kind of . . . manipulative."

"And phony."

"That's because you're thinking of flirting as if it's some kind of public performance with scripted pick-up lines, which is exactly what *bad* flirting is. Think of it as simply presenting the naturally charismatic and curious side of yourself. That's what true charm is about, and that's what people react positively to.

"But I always get stressed out because I'm worried that I'll look stupid," another participant revealed.

"Or desperate," Pia whispered under her breath.

"I wouldn't know where to start," Flo admitted.

"You start simply by **SELL**ing yourself using my four basic principles of flirtation: Smile, Eyes, Listen, Laugh. Let's turn to page thirteen in your Weapons manual." Joey paused the lecture while everyone pulled out the binders and turned to the correct page.

"With these basics—all tools each of you already possess—used in tandem with your personal charisma, your social sensuality can successfully step out into the public. So let's go over them now.

"**SMILE**: Often and naturally. We really don't pay much attention to how much we *don't* smile. And what's most amazing about that is, smiling is our most effective calling card, a free and easy spirit lifter, and a surefire antidote to negative energy. A genuine smile is power. With it you can change another person's entire mood and perspective. Let's try a little experiment. Close your eyes and smile right now. Stretch the corners of your mouth wide. How does your body feel?"

"Relaxed."

"Happy."

"Warm and kind of tingly."

"Where in your body do you feel it?" Joey probed. "In your chest and stomach?" Nods of agreement bounced around the room. "Now open your eyes, turn to the person next to you, and smile. Again, big and genuine. What happens?"

"They smile back."

"Exactly. Smiling is contagious. And in a flirting situation, we want to infect as many folks as possible. A smile makes you look friendly, confident, and approachable, and it puts the other person at ease. And if he's feeling at ease, he's bound to be more receptive and interested in you.

"**SELL TIP**: Even when you are flirting via telephone, have a smile on your face. The other person can feel and hear the difference in your voice. There is a warmth and friendliness that comes across with a grin.

"**EXERCISE**: For the rest of this week, pay constant attention to your facial expression and practice smiling. If you're waiting in a cashier's line, smile. When you pass strangers on the street, smile. Smile when you notice a beautiful flower or the clear blue sky. Make it a habit, and soon you will find yourself not only happier and more persuasive but on the receiving end with greater frequency.

EYE SMILE. Your eyes are your most important flirting tool. If you don't believe me, think of the ancient and yet still highly effective lessons of the Kama Sutra, where prolonged eye contact is a main tenet of this powerful sensual, spiritual approach to lovemaking. Think of belly dancers and their provocative sideways glances as they work the allure of the veil. Think Elizabeth Taylor and Prince—both masters of ocular seduction. Oh, yes, lovelies: The eyes definitely have it!

"In my younger days, my body wasn't quite so . . . so . . . voluptuous." Joey laughed, evoking a rush of "You got that right" around the room. "I depended on my body to attract men. And not once did I look into my basic brown eyes and see anything particularly special. That is, until I was nearly thirty and one very sweet gentleman—a master flirt for sure—told me that my eyes were the sexiest part of me. He said he loved the way he felt when I looked at him. His comment enlightened and empowered me. And from that day forward I stopped worrying so much about my body and began cultivating my 'looks' and other charming skills."

"I totally disagree. Men respond to sexy bodies," Juile argued with a convinced matter-of-factness only experience can bring.

"Trust me, lovelies, your breasts and bottoms will one day surrender to gravity, but when it comes to drawing a man over to your side of the room, a seductive set of eyes and a warm smile will rarely let you down."

"Julie's right. It's the sexy-looking girls who pull the guys across the room and home with them," Becca complained, getting plenty of support.

"It's no secret that men are visual creatures," Joey countered. "And I will concede that women who are considered more physically attractive do have a head start when it comes to *picking up* men. But let's be real here, lovelies: It's not really hard to pick up a man when everything about you is promising sex. You've got to know the difference between being sexy and looking and acting sexual.

"Flirting is not teasing. Teasing is used to *proposition sex*. Flirting is used to *entice interest*. And eye contact is a big part of getting and keeping his attention.

"And once you have it, use eye contact as your barometer of his interest. There is more direct gazing when people like each other and less eye contact when they don't. And should you lose eye contact, chalk it up to his loss, not yours, and move on."

"But then you haven't really succeeded," Julie goaded.

"When you go shopping, does every outfit you try on fit?" Joey asked, calmly making her point.

"How do you know how long to look? I mean, at what point does a look become a stare?" Rhonda asked.

"True, you don't want to scare him off by staring. Practice eye control. Give him a nice gaze and genuine smile for, let's say, no more than three seconds—long enough to let him know you're interested—and then look away. Follow up with occasional peekaboo glances to keep him on the hook and eventually reel him in," Joey suggested while demonstrating her technique.

"Another great eye smile is to catch his gaze, hold it for a second, and then let your eyes inspect his face and body for a few seconds. This lets him know you like what you see, which may be all the encouragement he needs to pursue you.

"Once you have captured his attention with your smile and have him locked into your gaze, let your eyes communicate all those things that you'd love to say but feel too silly or forward verbalizing. Let your glance dip to his lips and then back to his eyes as you mentally tell him how delicious his mouth is. Your facial expressions will translate the messages in your head. Drown him in unspoken compliments and he will start living to spend time in your gaze.

"**SELL TIP**: Your eyes and smile must work together. If one is smiling without the other, you'll appear bored and disingenuous.

"**EXERCISE**: Make eye play part of your morning routine. As you're getting ready, practice flirting with yourself. Look in the mirror and hold your own gaze. Practice complimenting yourself through eye talk. Smile and witness your mesmerizing effect. Keep practicing until flirting and smiling with your eyes becomes second nature.

"Next you must **LISTEN**. Your ability to listen effectively is the secret to coming off completely fascinating to men. The more you listen and ask questions, the more attractive, mysterious, and intriguing you become. Asking for more details proves you have been paying attention, and sends the message that you find him interesting.

"**SELL TIP**: Don't think too hard about what you're going to say—just really listen to what he is saying and respond naturally.

"And when she's not listening or talking, a WMS should be **LAUGHING**. Laughter and humor are also powerful armaments in your seductive artillery. It's almost impossible to flirt successfully and enjoyably without them. So don't be afraid of a little playful teasing.

"But remember, sarcasm and wit walk a very fine line. If telling jokes aren't your forte, don't. Let him do the telling."

"What if his jokes aren't funny?"

"Always let truth be your guide. Your best bet is to react naturally and sensibly. It's all in your delivery. A gentle, lighthearted grimace can be the bridge between a bad joke and an authentic shared laugh. And sometimes it's almost better if the joke does bomb, particularly if you can gracefully pull him out of a seemingly awkward situation. Repeating what I mentioned earlier, flirting is a benevolent act. It's about making a man feel good about being a man.

"**SELL TIP**: Stay away from giggling. Giggling translates to anxiety, and you are a cool, collected weapon of mass seduction, not an eighth-grader on her first date.

"Now let's quickly go over a list of three things you should definitely avoid.

"**DON'T TAKE IT TOO SERIOUSLY**: The most successful flirts are those who enjoy it and can flirt without expecting anything to come of it. Leave the 'must score' attitude at home or you risk looking desperate. Practice charming men you aren't interested in, and soon you'll be able to flirt with the one you adore and still seem casual.

"**FLIRT, DON'T TEASE**: There is a difference between innocent flirting and a full-court come-on. Avoid overtly sexual talk or touching. Be a little mysterious—show your interest by being friendly, but don't offer more than you intend to give. Consider this when you are choosing your attire for the evening. Suggestive and revealing clothing says less about you being a powerful, sensual woman and more about you being sexually available. Be clear what message you are trying to send.

"**DON'T BE UNKIND**: If someone you are not interested in approaches you, act appreciative and polite. Smile, ask his name, and thank him for coming over before gently discouraging further contact. Let him leave with his pride intact. Other men are watching to see what you do. If you laugh after he leaves or show visual disapproval, you are lessening your chances of anyone else approaching you.

"Now if you would please split into teams of six, we're going to do a little flirtatious role-playing in preparation for tonight's field trip."

As the groups divided up and began practicing making eye contact, smiling with sincerity and listening with rapt attention, Pia excused herself. Walking down the hallway toward the ladies' room, she could feel her entire body tighten up. Tonight's activity terrified her. These past five years of sitting at the singles bar of life, sipping a no-sex cocktail, had definitely taken a toll, and what used to come so naturally now felt like speaking a foreign language.

Damn, how does one say, "disaster waiting to happen" in Embarrassed Jackass?

Chapter Eight

Florence tapped softly at the door of room 1011, waited, and tapped again. Rebecca arrived and the two women stood several more minutes before a visibly flustered Pia, still in her short silk robe, opened the door.

"Darlin', since you're our team fashionista, we thought we'd come up here for inspection before headin' off to the cattle call."

"Uh, okay. Come on in. I'm having a little trouble deciding what to wear myself, which is ridiculous because this is just some flirting exercise and not the real thing," Pia rambled on.

Entering the room, it was apparent that a worry bomb had gone off. Clothes, shoes, and accessories were haphazardly strewn all over the place. Flo and Rebecca stepped through the modish land mines and migrated over to the small sofa while Pia fussed with her hair in the mirror.

"So what do you think?" Becca asked.

"Well, let's see," Pia murmured while conducting inspection. Becca, with her hair pulled back into her regulation ponytail, jeans, a white blouse, and a purple cardigan, looked like a perfectly cute, absolutely forgettable collegiate wallflower. And there was absolutely no hope for the shoes—matronly black pumps that in attitude would go fine with a grandma bra, but not with some fire red push-up. And Flo, in her blue knit dress and tan jacket, looked like she was running for PTA president. Her two-tone Ferragamo slingbacks were passable, but that colorful polka-dot scarf tied in a big bow around her neck and huge tote bag had to go.

"Be honest. I'd rather *you* tell us we look silly than some man we're supposed to be flirtin' with."

"Nothing that a little adjustments couldn't help," Pia said as she walked over to the dresser and retrieved her jewelry pouch. "Flo, great basics, but together they scream 'Excuse me,' not 'Meet me,' so off with the blazer." Flo removed her jacket to reveal a blank navy blue canvas on which to create.

"Perfect dress. The cut on you is fabulous. Now let's take this off," Pia said, confiscating her scarf, "and replace it with this." From her pouch she pulled a chunky bone necklace with a large silver disc and fastened it around Flo's neck before handing her a sterling cuff bracelet and tasteful hoop earrings. There was nothing she could do to Flo's sprayed-in-place hair, so she just smoothed her hands over it and let it go.

"Hmm, you smell great," Pia commented, sniffing Flo's new perfume.

"Whoa. And look about ten years younger," Becca said, impressed by Pia's quick transformation.

"And use this," Pia suggested, handing Flo a small silver metallic clutch.

Flo felt herself stand just a bit taller in her shoes. She had no idea that such a simple wardrobe adjustment could make her feel so young, and hip, even.

"Pia, will you take my picture?" Florence requested, handing her a digital camera. "I can't wait to show Miriam when I get back home."

"And maybe Dan?" Pia teased.

"My turn," Becca said, sliding in front of Pia once the photo session was over.

"I think all you need is a little more makeup and these," Pia said, bending down near the bed to pick up a bronze-colored pair of pointy-toed heels.

"Whoa. These are high," Becca commented, slipping into the shoes.

"They do take a little getting used to, but in my experience heels are a primo flirtation tool. They make your calves and legs look great and turn an ordinary walk into a major strut. You'd be surprised how many guys have shoe fetishes. Oh, and this would look great," Pia decided, taking Flo's discarded scarf and pushing it through Becca's belt loops before standing her collar upright. Pia took another five minutes to touch up the girl's makeup, defining and dramatizing her green eyes and full lips and pulling her ponytail up higher on her head, creating a sweet and sexy cascade of honey-colored ringlets.

"Darlin', you're lookin' like *Becca* now."

"Pia, could I borrow those?" Becca asked, pointing to a pair of crystal chandelier earrings and the small handbag that matched the shoes.

"Sure."

Looking like a new fawn taking her first steps, Becca happily negotiated her high-heeled self over to the mirror and put the glitzy earrings in her ears. Immediately she felt sexier and more sophisticated. Gazing at herself with her new makeup and hair, she practiced her rendition of Paris Hilton's head tilt and flirty smile, and suddenly Cedar Falls felt like a million miles away.

"Now I need to get myself dressed," Pia said, hurrying off to the bathroom. Fifteen minutes later she emerged looking lovely but just as nervous as when she'd answered the door.

"Ready?" Becca asked, reaching for her borrowed bag.

"Give me a minute. I want to change my skirt."

"Why? You look great. I love that outfit," Florence remarked, admiring Pia's simple but sophisticated slim black skirt, cap-sleeved silk sweater, and a cascade of chunky jet black beads.

"I feel overdressed. Maybe I should wear jeans," Pia said, trawling through what was left hanging in her closet. "I think I sprayed on too much perfume. They'll smell me a mile away."

"You look amazin' and you smell just fine. What's really goin' on, darlin'?" Flo asked as she snapped a picture.

"You wanted to see my insecurities. Well, here they are. The idea of going to a bar to flirt with a man makes me nauseous, even if it is just a class assignment. The fact is, I'm just no good at this anymore," Pia finally revealed before plopping down on the bed. "I want to . . . to start dating more *fully* again, but lately my dates seem to be one disaster after another."

"Darlin', we all have disaster stories. I think one of the reasons I got married so young was because I hated that whole datin' scene."

"It's more than just that. I decided to become celibate five years ago. I'm happy I did. I learned a lot about myself, but now it's as if a huge part of me is atrophied."

"Whoa. You don't look like a woman who doesn't have sex," Becca remarked, her eyes and mouth both opened wide with astonishment.

"You know the old saying 'Never judge a book . . .' " Pia said, not knowing how she could adequately explain her situation.

She still made it a point to dress and act in ways that made her feel sexy and desirable, as the last thing she wanted to lose was her sex life *and* her self-esteem. Men still regularly approached her, initially compelled by her mystery and appearance, but later they were turned off by her restraint. Eventually, to avoid the awkward explanations of why she wasn't having sex, she'd pretty much stopped dating, packed up her womanly wiles, and put them in storage with her libido and sexual confidence. So after twenty years of charming the pants off men, she was now in an exclusive relationship with her vibrator and a head full of sometimes nasty, sometimes romantic fantasies.

"Oh, come on, honey. You're beautiful, smart, successful, and have that cool charisma goin' for you. How bad can you be?"

"Well, I haven't had a second date in more than two years. That's pretty bad—so bad that after my last fiasco my secretary found it necessary to stage this emergency intervention."

"What happened?" Becca pressed. She was curious, and concerned that if a woman as fabulous as Pia Jamison could have trouble with men, she didn't have a chance.

"Let's just say that it was just the last in a long line of bad dates," Pia said, not wanting to get into all the embarrassing specifics. "My dating life has been a fiasco for years now."

"Haven't you ever been in love, darlin'?"

"Love and I don't seem to mix," Pia admitted. She could feel her barriers breaking down as she shared her sad dating history with these women. "There was this guy named Rodney," she began.

Pia winced with painful anger at the memory of Rodney Timble. Even after six years, his memory haunted her. God, she had adored that man. With Rodney, being in love had the same gooey, sentimental appeal that those lovesick romance novel readers gushed over.

And where had that gotten her? She'd given herself to him mind, body, and soul before finding out that she was not his first love but work was. When Pia confronted him, Rodney unceremoniously dumped her, making it clear that although he loved her, there was no relationship more important to him than his professional dream. The drummer, who was now on a world tour with Alicia Keys, had simply walked out of their apartment and life together with a dismissive wave and a "man's gotta do" all-attitude pass.

"That must have hurt," Florence interrupted.

"Is he why you stopped having sex?" Becca asked.

"Yes. At least at first," Pia explained.

Devastated and with no one waiting in the wings, Pia had not found celibacy to be difficult that first year. She was too busy grieving her lost relationship to care about sex. Year two had been a year of personal resolve. To push away the body cravings, Pia kept reminding herself that she didn't need a man to make her happy or whole. This resulted in the accumulation of a treasure chest full of sex toys and erotica and the occasional rendezvous where she allowed herself the pleasure of light kissing and gentle petting. But after far too many dates gone bad, she once again retired from the singles scene. The third year of her sexual fast turned into an exercise in spiritual cleansing and becoming one with her higher self.

Early that year she'd met Lamar, who became the first man who truly tested her resolve. He assured Pia that while he desperately wanted to make love to her, he respected her decision. Basking in the loving kindness of his understanding, she seriously contemplated giving up her celibate lifestyle until she discovered that his patience and sexual needs were being satisfied by a long list of women he met through an Internet sex site.

"Ewww," Becca commented.

"What a pig. Pickin' up prostitutes on his computer? That's just a new level of sleazy and lazy. I have to agree with you, darlin'; your man quest system needs a tune-up."

"I just shut it off. I'm done with grandiose ideas centered on men and marriage."

"I'd be mad as hell, but you don't seem bitter," Flo observed.

"No, just tired of the games and their emotional aftermath."

Unburdening herself from the need for men and taming her desires, Pia had put males on the shelf and gone to work on herself. Without a man's rude insertion into her life these past few years, she'd managed to climb from senior producer to senior vice president. For her hard work and impressive success record, she was compensated handsomely, her salary well into six figures. With only one mouth to feed, Pia was able to support herself in lavish style, from her apartment in pricey Chelsea to a to-die-for collection of vintage clothes and handbags to exotic travel wherever in the world she fancied. She'd become an even more fascinating, self-reliant woman and was happy living the exciting life she'd created for herself. Yet now, in an ironic twist, the only thing missing was the one thing she couldn't have without a man's assistance.

"So you want to date again 'cause you're ready to fall in love?" Becca asked.

"No, I'm not looking for love or a mate. Just a man to father my child. But because I've been off the market for so long, I don't have a clue how to make a guy call me back for a second date, let alone impregnate me.

"So you want to know why I'm here, well, there it is."

Florence and Becca sat in silent disbelief. Pia couldn't tell if they were appalled by her lack of social finesse or her plan to have a baby without a husband. The idea of being judged by these two women, who through a forced kind of intimacy had quickly become her friends, felt wickedly uncomfortable.

"Why don't you just adopt? Plenty of great kids out there need a home," Becca asked. "My parents did it. Tom and Nicole, Angelina and Brad, even did it," she added, as if a celebrity endorsement might help. "Plus, it might not seem so bad that you don't have a husband."

"I haven't totally ruled out adoption, but if I can, I'd really like to experience pregnancy."

"So what's your mama and daddy sayin' about all this?" Flo asked.

"My dad died years ago, and I figured I'd wait until I had something to announce before I said anything to my mom." Pia was not at all looking forward to that discussion, so it was definitely a bridge she'd cross only when and if necessary.

"Well, that explains the way you were lookin' at that baby in the mall," Florence said, her gaze directed at the charm around Pia's neck, "and your icon."

"What are you talking about?"

"I noticed the label on the tray yesterday didn't say 'love' at all. You picked out a symbol that stands for 'mother.' "

Pia lifted her hands to her neck and gently covered the pendant. Her silence was comment enough.

"Well, then, darlin', I may not agree with the whole no-husband thingie, but who am I to judge? Havin' three babies with Dan sure didn't guarantee he'd stick around. So put on whatever you're gonna put on and let's get out there and get you datin'."

Chapter Nine

Pia, Becca, and Florence, along with the other glammed-up WMS teams, stepped into Suede, a swank but currently empty restaurant and bar. Gleaming hardwood floors, exposed brick, subdued lighting, and inviting leather sofas trailing the serpentine walls provided a sensual mix of sophisticated textures and architectural lines. The velvety voice of the crooner Johnny Hartman and the great John Coltrane gave the environment a jazzy, romantic air.

The group was shuttled into the restaurant, where the furniture had been arranged into cozy tables for two. A single votive candle flicked at each setting, creating a warm datelike atmosphere and raising Pia's anxiety quotient a notch or two.

"Where is everybody?" As had become her custom, Becca voiced what everyone else was thinking.

"Patience, lovely. In the next fifteen minutes or so, the room will be full of men here to dash-date—which is exactly what it sounds like—dashing from one five-minute rendezvous to the next. By the time the evening is over, you will have had at least eight dates," Joey informed them.

"That's more than I've had all year," the woman standing next to Joey remarked. Several heads bobbed in agreement.

"It's bad enough tryin' to impress one guy in a night, but ten?" Flo remarked.

"Think of it like this," Joey suggested. "Just as frequent job interviewing can make you a better interviewee, these quick 'dates' will help improve your skills so that when the real thing comes along the meeting appears effortless. In five minutes you'll know if you two share that all-important chemistry."

"Some of the dates I've been on, five minutes felt like a lifetime," Pia whispered to Florence.

"A few last-minute tips," Joey coached. "The biggest mistake most people make is to try to start a *flirtation* instead of a *conversation*. Your best, most successful opening line will generally be 'Hi,' followed by an authentic smile. Of course, a compliment, 'You have a great smile,' or question, 'Is the special worth ordering?' can be a nice icebreaker as well. Simple. Spontaneous. Natural.

"Ah, I see the gentlemen are beginning to arrive. Now, my lovelies, why don't you take the next few minutes to affirm yourselves as the extraordinary bombshells you are. And don't forget your name tags."

"I'm kind of nervous. Do you think I look okay?" Becca's mouth asked while her eyes scoped out sexy Julie in her leg-enhancing miniskirt and cleavage-revealing camisole.

"Darlin', don't mind her. The way her breasts are always hangin' *outside* her blouse, you'd think they were afraid of the dark," Flo remarked. "You look adorable and you're a star. You remember that," Flo said, pointing to her necklace. "I have to tell you two, I'm not so sure about this dash-datin' business—least not without some courage in a glass."

"I'm with you, sister," Pia agreed. "Becca?"

"No, thanks, I don't drink."

The two women left their teammate and headed over to the bar, inciting a fair amount of head turning as they departed. "Darlin', the way these fellas are checkin' you out, I think if you can keep your long-term plans to yourself, you might just get your mojo back."

Pia turned toward Flo and her eye caught and momentarily held the gaze of an attractive, artistic-looking brother. Their look held, simultaneously pulling the corners of their mouths into a mutual example of Joey's all-powerful eye smile.

The rest of the weapons-in-waiting made nervous chitchat as the restaurant continued to fill up with the troupe of males recruited for the evening's speed-dating exercise. Each sex stayed congregated together, waiting for the starting bell, each checking out both the cuties and their competition.

Rebecca's eyes roved the room, inspecting the eclectic group of males. For this fishing expedition, Joey and her dash-dating partner had obviously tried to stock the place with men of all ages, shapes, sizes, colors, and wardrobe selections. She was immediately drawn to a tall, dark, and even handsomer version of Enrique Iglesias, wearing great-fitting jeans, a crisp white button-down shirt, and loafers sans socks.

"Whoa, he's so hot," she murmured to herself, doing her practiced head tilt and half smile. She focused her gaze on the man, hoping to catch his eye and as Joey had suggested lure him across the room. Finally he glanced in her direction and delivered a flash of white teeth and an acknowledging nod. Becca's half smile spread full-tilt across her face as she lowered her gaze, obeying Joey's three-second rule. She looked up again only to see Julie strutting her stiletto-wearing self across the room, breaking both the gender line and Becca's fragile confidence.

Rebecca watched in dismay as Julie, with her more-naked-than-clothed body and wild blond curls, unleashed a lusty smile and intoxicating glance on Becca's object of desire. His interest was obvious, though his eyes focused more on the top of her protruding breasts than her face.

So much for the power of eye contact, Becca thought.

Several other women, not wanting Julie to acquire any additional advantage, followed her aggressive lead and infiltrated the dating pool. Becca couldn't help but notice that they all had one weapon in common—blatant sexuality. Subtlety was not part of their arsenal, and by the looks of interest on their prey's faces, it was not required.

Suddenly, despite Pia's style suggestions, the urbane city girl she'd become morphed back into the shoes of her boring country cousin.

From their bar stools, Pia and Flo heard what sounded like the call for a hotel bellhop echo through the club. "You ready?" Pia asked, her nervousness slightly tamped by her champagne cocktail.

"Now, Pia, you saw those men. There are only two guys in the next room that are over fifty, and both of them look like perverts. How am I gonna look tryin' to flirt with one of those young boys? This isn't my spot to practice. For that we need to head out to the lo-cal retirement home."

"Florence, are you sure? You can't leave me alone in there," Pia said between chuckles.

"Darlin, one benefit of bein' fifty is knowin' your own mind. I'm gonna take some photos for my scrapbook and then I'll grab a cab back to the hotel. You go in there and get dashin'," Florence said.

"Here goes nothing," Pia responded as the *ding-ding-ding* of the organizer's bell called them all to attention.

"Good evening, everyone, I'm Cary Holley," announced the hostess, "and welcome to dash-dating. Each of you will have eight one-on-one conversations lasting five minutes each. After four dates we'll take a break and then finish up with four more."

"What if you want to meet someone who isn't one of your official dates?" Julie asked, twirling her hair and raising Becca's ire by winking at her coveted hottie.

"You may meet anyone else who catches your eye during intermission or after your eighth date," Cary informed them all. "Now, on your name tag you have your first table number. After each date ends," she said, ringing the bell for emphasis, "men, you'll move two tables higher. Ladies, you stay put and let the gentlemen come to you.

"It's as simple as that. So let's begin. Ladies and gentlemen, to your tables." At the sound of her now familiar bell, everyone scurried to the tables. Individual styles began to show immediately. Some men extended their hands in a gesture of gentlemanly gallantry, while others simply plopped down, ready to reveal their sparkling—or not— personalities.

From the moment he sat, Becca knew where her first date was dashing—straight to hookup hell. It became clear after the first thirty seconds of meeting Neil that her flirting skills would go untested. Becca quickly assessed him to be a friendly enough guy, just not particularly stimulating, and their ensuing conversation definitely matched his personality. He was from San Jose. Attended the University of Someplace in California. Was a big fan of George Lucas and the *Star Wars* trilogy and never missed the animated television show *The Family Guy*. Three minutes and fifteen seconds to go.

❧

"Hello, Pia. I'm Amir," an attractive Middle Eastern man with a distinct British accent announced after giving her a wide grin of approval.

"Hi. Based on your lovely accent, I'm guessing you're from England," said Pia, returning his with a genuine smile of her own.

"I grew up in London but I'm from Dubai. It's in—"

"The United Arab Emirates. I was there for work several years ago. It's a lovely city. The Souk Madinat Jumeirah. It's one of the most amazing bazaars I've ever seen."

With a world of common ground between them, Pia and Amir spent the next four minutes discussing the global music scene with great passion and mutual respect. Joey was right, five minutes was definitely long enough to realize if chemistry was present. Amir was attractive, educated, traveled, and highly interesting. The tragedy was that she was simply not attracted to him "that way."

Ding-ding.

Minutes into Becca's next date, she realized that her second encounter was also going nowhere. Danny, a handlebar-mustached, leather-vested motorcyclist whose best friend was Brutus, his pit bull, immediately dismissed her for being a B cup.

"Nothing personal," he said. "I just don't date women with small racks."

Nothing personal? He was rejecting her over the size of her breasts. How much more personal could he get? Seventy-three seconds of talk. Two hundred and twenty-seven seconds of silence. She felt like a prizefighter getting mercilessly pummeled and praying for the bell.

Unfortunately, Pia's next two dates weren't as successful as her first. Boyd, a handsome bisexual, quickly announced that while she was a fierce diva, he was only there to meet Morgan, a proclaimed heterosexual who Boyd was convinced was chin-deep in denial. Her third date, Rick, was a muscle-bound he-man who spent their date sharing all the gory details, benefits, and drawbacks, of complete colon irrigation.

Ding-ding.

"Hey, how's it goin'? Sam."

"Becca." *He's sort of cute in a Tobey Maguire kind of way,* she thought, hoping that her two-for-two losing streak was about to end. "Um, you have a little spinach in your teeth. Right over there, to the left."

"Damn," Sam said, sucking with enough force to pull in a small animal.

"So Sam, where are you from?"

"Thattle," he answered while rubbing his teeth with his tongue.

"I'm sorry, where?"

"Se-at-tle," he replied slowly, as if she were an idiot. "You gotta mirror?"

Becca rummaged through her purse, pulled out her lipstick case, and handed it over to her date. He flipped it opened and, stretching his mouth wide, peered into the narrow reflective glass. Becca's facial expression reflected her chagrin as she watched Sam run his tongue over his polluted teeth while turning on the incredible sucking machine again.

"Have you lived here long?" Becca asked, trying to ignore the nightmare happenings of three bad dates in the span of fifteen minutes. Boring old Neil was looking pretty damn good right about now.

"Shit. The hottest girl in the place is up next. I'll be right back," he said. Not waiting for or caring about Becca's reply, Sam went to the bar, returned with a toothpick, sat, and proceeded to engage in a little impromptu dental hygiene.

Becca felt her head and shoulders jerk back in astonishment. Her date was cleaning his teeth at the table in preparation for his next date? Could he be any less interested in impressing her? Her eyes darted across the room as she prayed that the others were too consumed with their own unbelievable circumstances to notice the tears welling up in her eyes and the word LOSER now tattooed across her nondating forehead.

Ding-ding.

She had one date to go before the break, but Becca had had enough. Instead of sitting for the next disaster-in-waiting, she pleaded personal emergency to her date and headed for the ladies' room. The sound of Julie's throaty laugh made her pause. Becca turned to see Sam the spinach man flashing his now pearly whites at her. She took note and watched as he melted under Julie's glaring, seductive heat. From the hair twisting to her Candies mule bobbing up and down like a fishing lure, Julie knew exactly how to use what she had to get what she wanted, and Becca was mesmerized.

The past two days, she'd listened to Joey and her teammates lecture her on the subtleties of flirtation. Maybe that's how old people flirted. But it certainly wasn't working for her. Joey was not teaching her how to be sexy. Julie's success was proof that, ultimately, men didn't care about eye contact, coy smiles, or interesting conversation. They wanted the promise or at least *possibility* of sex.

Joey Clements was not the only coach in the room, Becca decided as she departed to the ladies' room. A quick adjustment was in order before intermission.

⬿⤳

"You are even better-looking up close than from across the room," Mike, Pia's third date of the evening, announced as he sat across the table.

"Thank you. You have a great smile," she said, returning his compliment with one of her own. The man was a handsome, rough-around-the-edges edition of Owen Wilson, and Pia found herself feeling genuinely flirty. She crossed her legs before picking up her drink. Holding his gaze with hers, she took a slow sip and watched as Mike pursed his lips and started nodding his head.

"It's easy to smile when your eyes are feasting. So, what's a hottie like you doing taking some bullshit course on flirting? You seem to know what the hell you're doing."

His question shocked her. Pia wasn't aware, and neither were any of the other women, as best she knew, that their situation was common knowledge. As her interest waned, she swallowed her annoyance and gave Mike a quick closed-mouthed grin.

"Research. I'm a writer," Pia lied. "Why are you here?"

"I'm doin' the tourist thing around Frisco. My cousin runs the bar and he told me what was going down tonight, so I thought I'd check it out."

"Captured prey, as it were," Pia commented drily.

"Exactly. So what are you into?"

"Music, traveling, books."

"Nah, I mean what are you *into?* Sexually."

"I beg your pardon?" Irritation had now devoured her previously flirty disposition.

"Look, what do you say we just forget the rest of this bullshit and get out of here? I'll treat you to a nice dinner, and then later I can really give you something to write about. If you know what I'm sayin'."

"Sorry, Mike—you're really not my type."

"Don't tell me you're one of these Frisco dykes."

Pia's annoyance had turned into anger. "No, but given the alternative sitting in front of me, I'm considering the option."

"Frigid bitch."

Ding-ding.

"How the fuck dare he," Pia hissed under her breath as she angrily stood from the table and headed straight toward the bar. She was pissed. Her night was ruined because yet another egotistical male couldn't take no for an answer without calling her out of her name or making nasty and totally erroneous accusations.

Thank God it was time for a break. Another drink was in order to wash away the bad taste Mike had left in her mouth. Pia walked back across the entry into the bar and over to Joey, who was sitting on the couch, chatting with several of her students.

"Oh, my," Joey said, noticing the surly expression on Pia's face. "Something wrong?"

"Just some asshole. Nothing I can't handle," Pia assured her.

"Oh, *my*," Joey repeated with more urgency.

Pia followed Joey's stare and spotted Becca sitting at the bar with Mike in her face. Gone were the college coed looks. In her place was Becca—full-blown sex kitten. She'd given Pia's previous makeup application a big boost with more of everything and removed the white shirt, leaving on the clingy purple cardigan. The sweater hugged her tiny waist and emphasized her proud bust. She'd left it unbuttoned at the top to reveal cleavage uplifted by her new push-up bra and at the bottom to show off her flat stomach and, thanks to her now unbuttoned, folded-down-at-the-waistband jeans, a hint of her pelvic bones.

Catching Becca's eye, Pia waved her over. Becca excused herself and, fully aware that Mike's eyes were following her every step, made her way over to her friend and flirting coach with a tentative strut.

"You've got a new look," Pia commented after Becca reached her side, "and an entirely different sales pitch."

"No offense, but I tried it your way, Joey, and nothing was happening," Becca admitted, "so I thought I'd try another way."

"Julie's way?" Joey probed with disapproval.

Julie was like a zillion other women who wore their sexuality on their back. Judging from her clothes, her hair, and her attitude, the woman appeared to exude sexual confidence. But Joey had seen her type way too many times before. Julie tried everything she could to convince the outside world, and herself, that she was born to be wild, but Joey would bet her favorite rose crystal bracelet that when it came right down to it, she was anything but.

"Remember what we talked about today, Rebecca: the difference between flirting and teasing," Joey cautioned, as she excused herself and departed to find Cary.

"Be careful," Pia warned. "That guy is a real pig, not to mention way too old for you."

"Mike? He's nice, and *hot*. I like him," Becca said, mixing a little Paris Hilton and a couple of hiccups back into her act.

"Have you been drinking?" Pia asked, alarm bells going off in her head.

"Just a little bit. Mike bought me a rum and Coke. Said it would mellow me out. He was right. I feel *verrry* relaxed."

"But you said you don't drink."

"I know, but everyone else is, and I don't want to look like a kid. I'm legal, don't worry." Becca gave Pia a tipsy smile before meandering back to her seat.

Pia looked on with concern. These young girls had it all wrong.

It was clear that Becca desperately *wanted* to be sexy. In her head she had been going through the motions, overcompensating for her inexperience by assuming other people's sexual identities. Apparent now also was why despite her conservative upbringing and lack of sexual experience she'd picked all the supersensual answers on Joey's test; why she'd chosen the most provocative lingerie she could find; and why now she had added a walk, wink, and wardrobe that gave men what she thought they wanted.

Becca knew what sexy should look like but didn't have a clue as to what it felt like. If she did, she'd have already absorbed Joey's lesson that authenticity was truly the sexiest and most seductive state of all.

Cary's bell sounded, summoning them back into the restaurant. Pia watched as Mike extended his hand, helping Becca from her perch. She giggled as she stumbled slightly and leaned her body into his as they walked arm and arm out of the bar.

"Oh, hell, no," Pia uttered as she struggled through the crowd and into the other room. She zipped past her table, where her date sat waiting for her. Pia gave him a quick apologetic smile before turning her attention back to her search. Becca and Mike were nowhere to be seen. She checked the bathroom to no avail before rushing back into the entry. Pia's instincts were on high alert. *Becca wouldn't leave with him, would she?*

She stood near the hostess desk, trying to decide what to do next, when she heard an odd noise come from just beyond the front entry. Pia burst through the doors to find Becca pinned against the wall with Mike's hand up her sweater and mouth clamped on top of hers. It was obvious from Becca's defensive body language that this wasn't a show of mutual desire.

"Get off her," Pia said, rapping Mike on his back with her palm.

"What the fuck?" Mike said, disengaging and turning around to face Pia.

"Becca, get out of here," Pia ordered, still staring Mike in the eye. Becca, eyes wide with panic, made her escape back into Suede.

"What? Jealous? You decide you want some of this now?" Mike asked, slurring his words as he stepped toward her, grabbing his crotch with his left hand and her arm with the right.

"Not now or ever," Pia hissed as she tried unsuccessfully to free herself. Her defiance simply made Mike hold on all the tighter.

"Mike, what the hell are you doing?" a firm male voice demanded. Both Pia and Mike looked up and saw his cousin, the bartender.

"Nothing, man. Simple misunderstanding." Immediately Mike dropped Pia's arm. "I was just leaving anyway."

"Smart move. I'll check you later." The two watched as Mike's drunken legs carried him across the street and down the block.

"Thank you," Pia said, turning to give him a grateful smile. "My friend?"

"She was headed toward the ladies' room."

"Thanks again."

Pia bypassed all the dating activity that had resumed in the main restaurant and headed straight for the ladies' room. She found Becca in the toilet stall, throwing up.

"Ready to head back?" she asked once she'd gotten the girl a glass of water and helped clean her up.

"Yeah."

"Becca, I'm not your mom and I haven't been your friend for very long, but—"

"It's okay. Really. Let's just go." Becca was in no mood for Pia's sympathy or I-told-you-so lectures. Her head hurt, but as far as she was concerned, other than getting sick, the night had been a total success. Sure, Mike got kind of scary, but all guys weren't like him. He was older and drunk. She knew now to stay closer to her age and avoid the liquor. The important thing was that he'd found her sexy and desirable, and wasn't charming the cool off a man exactly what she'd come all the way across the country to learn how to do?

Chapter Ten

After getting Becca to bed, Pia headed back to her own room. Too wound up to sleep, she reached for the remote. She surfed channels for a few minutes before the talented cast of *Waiting to Exhale* captured her attention. As her eyes watched Robin try to shake off her no-good ex, Pia's mind replayed her evening.

So far, tonight had been a complete bust. First that idiot bore, Mike, followed by little girl lost, Rebecca. Surprisingly, Pia felt more disappointed than she'd have thought. Initially she'd been so apprehensive about going, and now she was upset that it had ended so abruptly. Now she would have to return to New York with all the cobwebs she'd arrived with still clogging up her dating game.

"You know the baby is going to have more than one mama, girl." The familiar line turned Pia's attention back to the movie. The characters were all gathered around a bonfire, raising a toast to the New Year and the new life Robin was about to bring into the world. The scene was a harsh reminder that Pia was in the uncomfortable position of needing the exact thing she claimed she no longer wanted.

"Screw this," she declared, turning off the television and grabbing her purse and hotel key.

Pia stepped into the elevator certain that the bubbles in her stomach alone could lift her to the penthouse bar. She was nervous. It had been an awfully long time since she'd been on the prowl, but Pia refused to leave California the same woman as when she'd arrived.

She could hear the pianist's cover of Sade's "Lovers Rock" as she approached her destination. *That's right,* she reminded herself, *slip into your cool charisma.* Pia walked into the bar and paused to scout out the place. Other than a group of what appeared to be beer-drinking sales-men, a few workshop-mates, and a couple engaged in private conversation in the corner, pickins were slim to none.

Pia approached the piano, returning the player's smile with a wide grin. *Did he just wink at me?* Pia wondered. As she passed, the song changed to "The Girl from Ipanema" and Pia glanced back to find the piano man looking directly at her as he sang the enticing story of the tall and tanned seductress.

"Hey, darlin', you're back. How did things go?" a Texas drawl called out, pulling Pia out of her musical flirtation.

Surprised to hear Flo's distinctive voice, Pia turned to find her friend sharing laughter and a plate of calamari with an attractive older gentleman. Apparently on the way back to the hotel she'd found a nursing home for the fine over fifty.

"Becca was in rare form," she said while the two engaged in an ocular exchange of *What's up?* and *I'll fill you in later.*

"Pia, this is Dr. Clay Bickford. Clay, Pia Jamison."

"Nice to meet you," he said, standing and shaking her hand in a gentlemanly manner.

"Clay is in town for a dental surgeons' convention. Pia's here at the WMS workshop with me."

You told him? Pia's eyes shot back.

"Perhaps you could help me. I've been trying to figure out what WMS stands for. My first guess was 'Women Making Sushi.'"

"Pathetic, right?" Florence jumped in. "I told him no self-respectin' Texan would travel all this way to learn how to roll up raw fish in some rice and seaweed. That's a meal for cats, not cowboys. I told him it was workshop on weavin' magic spells—"

"Which I'm inclined to believe, as this little lady has got me spell-bound," Clay said, raising his glass in a silent toast. Pia's eyes immediately locked on to his hand. No ring. No telling tan line. Perhaps the doctor was on the up-and-up. It was clear that he was interested. Clay was openly flirting, and Florence, blush creeping up her cheeks, was enjoying every second of it.

"Oh, darlin', that's just the Jack Daniels talkin', 'specially if you're callin' me *little,*" Flo insisted, downplaying his compliment.

Pia was surprised and thrilled by the flirtatious banter flying back and forth between them. Clay was giving Florence what neither she,

Becca, nor Joey could—confidence in herself as a woman. She could now go home and face Dan, buoyed by the fact that a handsome stranger in a hotel bar in San Francisco had found her attractive.

"So ladies, don't keep me in suspense. What does WMS stand for?"

"Women in Marketing and Sales. We're here for a . . . uh . . . re-fresher course," Pia offered with a sly twist to her lips.

"I'd say that about sums it up," Flo agreed.

"Please join us," Clay offered, though it was clear to Pia that he was just being polite.

"Thanks, but no. I don't want to interrupt. I just came up for a nightcap. Nice to meet you, Clay, and I'll see *you* at the morning session," she told Florence with a playful smile.

Pia took a seat near the window and waved over the waitress then gave the place another once-over while waiting for her drink. No other patrons had arrived, and even the piano man was gone. She glanced at her watch. It was already 11:25. Things weren't looking good.

Okay, cupid. Not looking for a keeper, just a playmate for tonight. Somebody to help me get back up on the bike and riding again. Please let him be sexy, polite, and, above all, patient.

Pia stared out at the city. It was a clear night and the city lights stretched out before her. There was something very seductive about this town. Or maybe it was just her mood.

"For you, pretty lady," an unfamiliar voice said, pulling Pia's attention from the view and her mythological request. As the piano player placed her champagne cocktail on the table, she noticed his smooth, well-manicured hands. She smiled as she stole a quick glance at his shoes, which were also well kempt. Experience had taught her that any man who took care of his hands and shoes generally applied that same attention to detail when it came to taking care of business.

"Thank you," she said, looking up to inspect his attractive chestnut brown face, lit by the bright shine of his dazzling smile. *Good move, Cu!* she congratulated, offering high fives in her head.

"I'm Argent," he said, smiling with eyes that said much more than hello.

"Pia."

"Short. Sweet. Difficult to forget."

Okay. Boy Toy has game. And up close he certainly did look young.

Were those puka shells around his neck? But there could be no deny-ing—the boy was a hottie. And for the first time in a long while, Pia's desires were such that toys and fantasies just weren't going to cut it.

"You're staring at me," Argent commented with a devastating grin. "What are you thinking?"

"Truthfully? I'm thinking you look way to young to . . . uh . . . to be working at a bar."

"I'm twenty-three and *completely* legal."

A quick calculation revealed their seventeen-year age difference. Pia was certainly old enough to be his big sister and in far too many neighborhoods his mother. Pia felt like the infamous Mrs. Robinson lusting after this young man, but tonight the pursuit of the forbidden was part of the thrill. And if she was to be honest with herself, with her rusty game seducing a young man was sure to be much less com-plicated—and ultimately more successful—than trying for an older, more experienced one. But still . . . twenty-three?

With Argent standing in front of her, Pia looked into his face as she crossed her legs, enjoying the way the rise in his desire caused a slip in his cool. She felt as if she were on a movie set. With her drink in one hand, all she needed was a cigarette in the other to complete this surreal seduction scene.

"Do you mind if I join you?" he asked.

"No. Please do," Pia replied, smiling into his eyes. "Thank you for the song."

"It seemed fitting. You do move like a samba," he replied.

"So, Argent, just why did you come over to me tonight?" Pia asked, curious to see how bold this young man truly was.

"Well, when you walked into the bar and we smiled, well, I thought we had this thing between us," he replied, nervously licking his lips.

"And do you still feel this *thing* between us?" she asked while try-ing to gauge her own interest. On a scale of one to ten, it was hover-ing somewhere around a very promising seven.

"Yes, ma'am, I do." Argent smiled while saying the one thing that turned her blossoming desire into lust lost.

Make that negative seven. Whatever sexy notions she had about taking this boy to bed and schooling him in the lessons of love had just been squashed and had morphed into the desire to take her *old* ass to bed—alone.

"You're very sweet," she told him, "and I am thrilled that you stopped by, but I'm really very tired. You know, jet lag."

"Oh. Yeah, right."

"This may not be our night, Argent," Pia said, leaning in close and whispering in his ear, "but know that for many years to come, you will be my fantasy." She kissed him slowly and sweetly on the cheek, stood, and walked away, leaving him there, hard as hell and feeling like a winner. Funny, she felt like a winner as well.

Damn! As much as she'd hated to admit it, and probably never would to Darlene, this workshop had been good for her. She was beginning to feel like the old Pia, and that was a very good thing.

Chapter Eleven

Saturday—Sexual Sensuality

OH THE THINGS I'M
GOING TO DO TO YOU!
HURRY HOME FOR
ONE RED HOT NIGHT.
THE FESTIVITIES
BEGIN PROMPTLY AT EIGHT.

"So, Missy," Flo said, meeting Pia in the hallway and giving her a thorough once-over, "anythin' you'd like to report about your evenin' out with the piano man?"

"Let's just say I wasn't quite ready to play Mrs. Robinson, but it was a successful seduction all the same," she replied. "And what about you? I seem to remember you and your beau still talking up a storm when I left."

"Clay's a real nice fella. Do you know what he did to celebrate his fiftieth birthday? The crazy man went sky-divin'. For his fifty-fifth he went swimmin' with the sharks. The man is a nut! We talked for hours. I even told him about Dan. He and his wife divorced four years ago and he gets what I'm goin' through. He gave me his phone number. Said to call him if I ever need a little moral support."

"But no boot knocking, huh?"

"The only knockin' takin' place was my scaredy-cat knees. He wanted to kiss me good night, but I didn't let him. I mean, I *am* still married, but it was nice he wanted to," Flo admitted with a shy smile. "Oh, Lord, speakin' of cats, look what just got dragged in."

With the telling signs of a morning hangover—sallow skin, puffy eyes, and the dead man walking shuffle—Becca joined them. Gone were last night's glam makeup, high heels, and party girl attitude, but remnants of the sex kitten still remained. Atop her blue jeans, Becca's white shirt was once again unbuttoned to allow maximum reveal.

The three walked into the Pacific Ballroom and took seats toward the front. To the left of Joey's podium, this time adorned with a cluster of bright yellow daffodils, was a beautiful carved screen.

"Good morning, lovelies," Joey's silky voice called out, greeting the sleepy but happy faces before her. "I have a few program notes before we get started. This morning we will explore *sexual sensuality* and then spend the afternoon in individual sessions. In these one-on-one meetings we'll go over your tests and address your questions and concerns about anything we've discussed these past few days.

"Tonight at our Isis Dinner we'll say good-bye but also celebrate the new sensual you. Sometime this afternoon you will receive instructions regarding your attire.

"Did everyone have a good time last night, working on your social sensuality?"

Joey's question was met with a mixture of cheers and groans.

"Well, through your dash-dating experience, you hopefully gained some insight into what about your flirting style works and what doesn't. As with everything else, with flirting, practice makes perfect. So when you leave here tomorrow, your training does not end. You should continue to flirt whenever an opportunity presents itself.

"Now it's time to talk about marrying flirting and seduction with sex."

"Woo-hoo!" A thunder of cheers and applause erupted, led by Julie and her team. Becca's robust cheers, momentarily replacing her malaise, were not lost on Pia and Flo. This was definitely not the sheltered, confused girl they'd met just two days ago. Rebecca was quickly morphing into her sexpot alter ego, Becca.

"Now, unlike yesterday's lesson, in which we made the very real distinction between teasing and flirting," Joey said, turning to look directly at Rebecca, "today we will discuss the art of seduction, which is an invitation to your lover to join you in a completely sensual experience designed to thrill and excite all of the senses.

"And to illustrate this, we will explore today some ideas on how to plan and execute a **RED HOT NIGHT**—a sensual evening meant to culminate in passionate lovemaking."

Again, the whoops and hollers interrupted Joey's lecture. It was clear that last night's flirtations had fired up today's expectations.

"Let me draw your attention to the short questionnaire in your workbook that actually provides the all-important foundation of any sensual entertaining. Logic dictates that if you are planning an evening with the sole purpose of turning you and your partner on, it's imperative to know exactly what kind of things . . . well . . . turn you on."

"So let's dive right in," Joey said.

Surprisingly, Pia was in complete agreement. After last night's successful reentry into the world of flirting, Pia was looking forward to adding new ammo to her arsenal.

"As any event planner will tell you, building your evening around a **THEME** can be very helpful. It allows you to stay focused as you choose elements that compliment your sensual style. Pick a theme that is unique to you and your lover. For instance, if you both love the beach, plan a passion picnic in your living room by creating the ocean ambiance through sensual accessories like surf sounds, ocean-scented candles, a seafood menu, et cetera. For today's example, I've chosen the theme **CHAMPAGNE AND PEARLS**.

"Your basic ingredients for this theme include champagne flutes and your favorite sparkling wine; several strings of faux pearls—toy store pearls are perfect; loose pearls from the craft store; rose petals—no faux petals, please; your favorite sexy CD; and candles.

"**INVITATIONS.** The primary purpose of your initial invite is to create a wonderful sense of *anticipation* and set the mood for what's to come. So go out of your way to create an invitation that is impossible to say no to, and then leave it in an unexpected place to be found. The element of surprise is all important here, so set everything up the night before. Here are a few suggestions," Joey said as she turned to her flip chart.

"Fill an empty champagne glass with pearls and tuck inside the details—a scented scroll tied with a satin ribbon. Leave it on the nightstand for him to find in the morning.

"Leave a seductive invitation on his cell or office phone. Again, do it the night before so he will hear it in the morning. Write your own or borrow a favorite poem or song lyric to recite and tag with your own message.

"Jot your invitation down in lipstick, complete with lip print, on the bathroom mirror or on a breakfast plate.

"You get the idea. The main thing is to be inventive and suggestive, and to incorporate the element of surprise.

"**RED HOT TIP**: Anticipation is everything. Continue to surprise him throughout the day. Drop a few pearls into his suit or pants pockets as a gentle promise of the evening ahead. He'll love it. Maintain the mystery and you'll surely maintain his interest."

"I can't wait to try this," Pia whispered to Flo. "Now I just have to go home and find a willing partner."

"*Willin'* bein' the key word here," Flo said while shooting her hand into the air.

"Yes, Florence."

"Joey, this all sounds wonderful, but my husband is much more a Budweiser and Mardi Gras beads kind of fella'. He'd laugh me out of the house if I pulled this on him."

"So make it a Mardi Gras evening complete with beer and colorful beads. Or apple cider or water—just serve it in a sexy glass with lots of attitude. It's not so much what elements you include; it's more about the mood, presentation, and mind-set. To be successful, any seductive entertaining should be tailored to fit you and your man's personalities.

"**RED HOT TIP**: Senses rule. Every aspect of your special evening should be planned according to your senses. Every sight, sound, smell, taste, and texture should be pleasurable.

"Now that the invitation has been extended, let's plan the menu for the rest of the evening."

On her signal, a member of Joey's staff removed the screen, revealing a luxurious picnic setting, with a chenille throw, several large pillows, flickering candles in jewel-covered votives, and a tray of various sundries, all designed in hues of burgundy, red, and tan. It looked sexy and inviting and was met with a chorus of delighted *ahhs*.

"Time for a little creative visualization exercise. Everyone close your eyes, take a few deep breaths, and relax. Now imagine this scene being played out by you and your lover.

"After hours of anticipation, your lover walks into a house flooded with soft, sensual music and candlelight. At the entry he finds a note telling him to follow the path of rose petals and wait for further instructions. The trail leads him up the stairs and into the bathroom, where he finds his **APPETIZER**, a warm bath drawn in a room and tub treated with candles, petals, and delicious-smelling bath oils. On a nearby towel rack hangs a pair of soft drawstring pants in his favorite color, but no towels. At tubside there is a glass of chilled champagne and a few yummy finger foods. There's also a note that instructs him to relax and unwind until further notice.

"He's intrigued.

"While he's relaxing, you're preparing the next course, and when everything is ready, you make your grand entrance, looking and feeling fabulous, smelling wonderful, and wearing your pearls. Because of your early preparation, those pearls unleash the desire he's been feeling all day. With a warm towel taken straight from the dryer, you help him dry off, take a seductive sip from his glass, and ask him to follow you.

"He's game.

"Are you all still with me?" Joey interrupted herself to ask.

A fragmented hum of "Yes," "Mmm-hmm," and "I'm with ya" was the reply. The entire room was lost in Joey's titillating daydream, and her breathy voice was the perfect tool to bring the scenario to life.

"You lead him back to the designated area for his **ENTRÉE**. Here you've treated the room with music, wonderful textures and scents, and candlelight. You invite him to recline among the pillows. On a nearby table sits a champagne bucket surrounded by loose pearls and rose petals and a tray of delectable yummies. He watches you pour his drink as you flirt with your eyes, and then you deliver it with a scorching kiss. Dinner is a slow, luxurious affair. He is no longer hungry but his appetite is far from satiated.

"He's on fire . . .

". . . and ready for **DESSERT**. You remove the string of toy pearls from around your neck and warm them and your favorite massage oil between your hands. He's curious. You ask him to lie back, and, using your hands and the pearls, as well as the back of your hands, your forearms, lips, even your hair, you caress and soothe your partner with a sensual massage. You use you imagination—and your pearls—for a second helping of dessert.

"He's impressed."

And totally whupped, Pia said to to herself, smiling.

"The things I could do with those pearls," Julie declared to those sitting around her.

"It does sound very sexy," Florence agreed, "but what about food? I mean, with all that drinkin' there'd be a lot more snorin' and a lot less sexin' goin' on in my house." Her humor helped break the sexual tension that had settled like a cashmere blanket around the room.

"I was just getting to the **DECADENT DINING** menu," Joey assured her. "On a red hot night, dinner is not just a meal, it's an experience. Mindful dining can be just as erotic as sex.

"Whatever food you serve," Joey continued, "should engage your senses and his through a complementary mixture of textures, tastes, and smells—sweet, juicy melon slices wrapped in salty proscuitto; spicy oysters served on the half shell, succulent sirloin chunks dipped in zesty, melted gorgonzola cheese—a meal of juicy, sexy foods served by hand, to your lover, bite by sexy bite. And whatever you eat, wait a minute or two between tastes to fully perceive and enjoy the food's flavors. Oh, and between each luscious course, cleanse your palate with sorbet or champagne."

"**RED HOT TIP**: Drown yourself in pleasure, not libations or food. You will negate all your hard work and satisfaction if you allow yourself or your lover to drink or eat too much.

"Let me interject a little day-to-day advice here. Food is one of the most sensual and satisfying pleasures we have, but most of us are so busy dieting or hurrying through our lives to truly enjoy eating. Eat healthily and watch your portion sizes, but don't shy away from the sensual pleasures of food. At mealtime, engage all of your senses—from your table setting to your meal—and find delight in the nourishment of your body.

"Now let's move on. On a red hot night, **DRESSING FOR SEN-SUAL SUCCESS** begins the moment you wake up in the morning. Put on your favorite, most flattering outfit during the day, and underneath wear lingerie that makes you feel beautiful. On your commute to and from work, listen to music that leaves you feeling loving and frisky and makes your imagination race. Apply your favorite scent or dab some of his on your forearm. Fondle your pearls throughout the day and evening to remind yourself of the pleasure to come. You can't successfully pull off a night like this if your heart isn't in it, so build the same anticipation in yourself that you are creating for him.

"Everything about you should be touchable. Your hair, your skin, and your attire should be inviting and be screaming to be caressed. Don't forget your manicure and pedicure, and in celebration do something different—maybe paint your nails, toes, and lips a flirty, come-hither red.

"What you wear is up to you, but make sure it's something comfortable and beautiful. Silk or cotton, risqué or demure, doesn't matter. Whatever turns you on will turn him on. Feeling positive about yourself determines how you give and receive pleasure from your mate. Your perceived body flaws and insecurities will evaporate as your partner responds to the sensually confident you.

"**RED HOT TIP**: To thine own self be true. At the core of a truly sensual woman is confidence in her authentic self. The evening you create should be driven first by your own comfort and enjoyment.

"Questions?"

Quiet all morning, Becca finally spoke. "I have one. What if it doesn't work?"

"In my experience, the one thing that will kill a red hot night every time is having too many expectations of yourself or your partner. Be flexible. Remember, one of the joys of living sensually is enjoying the moment and reveling in life as it comes. Plan your evening and then follow it wherever it takes you. Keep everything from your attitude to your menu light and flirty.

"One last thought. A red hot night is an amazing way to celebrate Valentine's or a birthday or anniversary, but what makes a night like this really hot is when it comes out of the blue for no reason other than to make your lover feel special."

"You should do a workshop for men," Tracy suggested, to unanimous agreement. "I'd love for my man to treat me to a red hot night."

"Something to consider. Well, lovelies, you have your scheduled time for our one-on-one meetings. I'll see you there and then all of you again tonight at our closing dinner. Enjoy your afternoon."

Chapter Twelve

"Whoa. This is hot. You should really be a fashion designer or stylist," Becca said as she and Florence watched Pia turn two ordinary hotel-issue bedsheets into on-the-fly haute couture.

"You'd be surprised what jobs fall under the title 'producer.' I've spent a lot of years being everything but talent on a music video set. Okay, let's add this brooch in the middle here, and voilà! Donatella Versace, eat your heart out."

Pia stepped back to view her handiwork. In the span of forty minutes she'd outfitted herself and her teammates in the three most stunning togas to make an appearance since Cleopatra set her sights on Mark Antony. Flo looked fabulous in her backless halter; Becca, recovered from her hangover, was more than pleased with her one-shoulder mini; and Pia too was happy with her sexy strapless gown—all created from bedding—wrapped, twisted, and tied together.

"I still don't get why we're supposed to wear sheets to dinner," Becca remarked as Pia adjusted the tie at her shoulder.

"Maybe we're supposed to represent Isis since the dinner is named after her," Pia offered.

"Didn't you all see the note that came with the instructions?" Flo asked before reading the letter. " 'For thousands of years the Egyptian goddess Isis has been held up and honored as the essence of feminine energy. Tonight our Isis dinner is about honorin' the great enchantress in *you*. Your attire is not a costume but rather a reminder that what makes an amazin' seductress is not designer clothes or expensive jewelry but rather the joy and confidence she exudes from within."

"She's got a point, and you have to admit, it is kind of fun," Pia said. "I've never felt this sexy wearing a sheet—at least not in a vertical position."

"Honey, after last night you'd feel sexy struttin' your stuff in venetian blinds," Flo teased.

"What happened last night?" Becca asked.

"Let's just say that I'm a proud graduate of the WMS workshop and once again a fully functioning flirt. So much so, I blew off my one-on-one today and went shopping. I felt the need for a second personal icon."

"So what new charm did you buy?" Flo asked.

"Well, it's not really a charm—more of an application." Pia lifted her toga to reveal a diminutive tattoo on the small of her back—three curvy letters reminiscent of prime womanly parts— *WMS*. The entire tattoo was a mere inch long, but for Pia, its power of suggestion was immeasurable.

"I love that. But why didn't you put it where everyone can see it?" Becca asked.

"Because it's not for everyone to see. *I* can't even see it. I got it as a little push from behind—a reminder that the art of womanly wiles is as entertaining as it is empowering. I don't want to ever forget that about myself again.

"I think the important thing I learned this weekend is that instead of cutting away such a huge part of myself, all I need is balance. And to remind myself of that, I also bought this," Pia said, flashing a new diamond right-hand ring.

"That's gorgeous, but how does that say balance?" Flo asked.

"It says balance because I say it does." Pia laughed.

"Well, I wish I'd skipped my session with Joey and gone with you," Becca said. "It was like getting a lecture from my mother."

"Really? I enjoyed my talk with Joey," Flo admitted. "I've learned a lot this weekend. She's really a smart cookie and a sexy ol' minx! Makes me feel like there's hope."

"So what did she tell you?" Pia asked.

"Joey said that I was a secret sensualist—meanin' I'm not fully connected to my sensual side. She said women like me squelch our sensual expression and hide behind what's proper and safe.

"She could tell I was feelin' apprehensive about all this sensuality stuff—stuff Dan would think was downright foolish," Flo continued. "She suggested that I try livin' in the moment and see if it brought me pleasure and expanded my view of life the way she knew it would. Then she said that if Dan couldn't accept this new part of me, then maybe it wasn't worth me acceptin' Dan—not if it meant rejectin' myself."

"Again, a sage point."

"Becca, darlin', I'm sorry. You had started tellin' us about your session and I just jumped in and interrupted."

"It was nothing. We just went over all my tests and talked about what happened at the bar. Joey just kept going on and on about how sexy started on the inside and radiated outward, not the other way around—whatever that means."

"Becca, I have to agree with Joey. Last night you were out of your league and, thanks to the alcohol, out of control."

"I agree I shouldn't have drunk so much, and that won't happen again, but I know that when I walked into Suede nobody was interested in me. I even had a guy clean his teeth at the table, getting ready for his date with Julie. I think that says a lot."

"I think it says that he's an asshole," Pia countered.

"All I know is that once I changed, the guys paid a lot more attention."

"Becca, darlin', I'm just gonna be blunt here and say it—sounds like they were payin' attention to your T and A, not Y-O-U—least, not the real you."

"You sound like Joey."

"Honey, I might be old like Joey, but you can't turn fifty-three without havin' picked up some sense along the way. I'm tellin' you, you've got what men want, so make 'em work for it."

"You'll figure it out," Pia said, giving Becca a warm, sisterly hug. "Just show more of the inside of Becca and less of the outside and you'll find the kind of guy you're looking for."

"I can't believe we're all leaving in the morning. I'm going to miss you both," Becca said, returning Pia's gesture with a tight hug of her own before repeating the same with Flo. "We're kind of like sisters now."

"So let's promise to get together again and catch up," Flo suggested.

"How about Columbus Day weekend? That's a little less than nine months away. Flo and Becca, do you think you can make it back east? New York is beautiful in October."

"I'm there, darlin'."

"Me too. I'll start saving as soon as I get back to Chicago."

"Don't worry about that. I have more than enough frequent flyer miles to get you to New York, and you can both stay with me. It will be fun."

"Okay, but let's promise to stay in touch in between," Becca suggested, to everyone's agreement.

"Ladies, we need to skedaddle. I'm starvin', and for once I'm wearin' an outfit that I can really eat in."

"Won't matter if Joey's just serving sexy finger foods again," Becca added, her smile returning. "I'm dying for a big old sloppy cheeseburger. One thing I learned this weekend—eating sensually will certainly keep you skinny."

"Wait, before we go, we need a picture together," Pia decided.

Florence retrieved her ever-present digital camera and set the timer so they all could be in the photograph. The flash went off, and they were a frozen moment in time. Pia studied the picture in the little screen. Even in a miniature image, the difference between the first day they'd arrived and this point in time was clear. Gone were the unsure, sensually tentative women Joey Clements had encountered just a few days ago. Under her tutelage, the proliferation of weapons of mass seduction had increased threefold. She had done her job and unearthed the sensual women within. Left unclear, however, was what, if any, threat-reduction measures were available to the poor defenseless men they were about to explode upon.

The

journey

is

as

important

as

the

destination.

Chapter Thirteen

"Pia, Grand Nelson is holding on line one," Dee said stepping into Pia's office. She'd bypassed the usual intercom alert, knowing her boss was going to need a little friendly encouragement before picking up this call.

"Oh, shit. What if he says no? Then what?"

"Then you'll find a way to convince him otherwise. Come on, *chica*, you can do this. You've been back from San Francisco three weeks. You're a trained professional now. You're the Jamie Bond of seduction—Double-Oh-Seven with a license to thrill . . ."

"Enough already," Pia said, giving Darlene a Can-you-get-any-cornier? look.

"Okay, how about this: Let's not forget that Grand Nelson has already seen you naked."

"I was sunbathing. I had no idea he was around."

"You were doing a lot more than sunbathing, *chica*."

"I should never have told you. Anyway, a lot has changed," Pia said, still blushing at the thought of Grand catching her literally with her pants down.

"Just remember all that phone flirting stuff you learned on the coast: You know, 'Smile, because the other person can feel and hear the difference in your voice,' " Dee encouraged.

"What did you do, read the manual?"

"I may have glanced at it once or twice," Dee admitted while nodding toward the phone.

Pia took a big You-can-do-this breath, plastered a huge smile on her face, and picked up the phone.

"Grand," she said in a soft tone she hoped he would find enticing.

"Pia Jamison. This is a great surprise," he said.

"I'm glad. It's nice to hear your voice."

"Yours too. You sound almost as good as when you were calling me Fin," he teased, referring to the name she'd called him during their marathon phone sex encounter.

"The Aruba shoot. That was a million years ago," Pia said, wincing as warm humiliation crept through her body.

"Maybe, but that call . . . hell, that whole weekend is still in the top ten of my life's highlight reel," he said.

Three years had gone by since the first time he'd laid eyes on Pia Jamison lying nude on the beach. She and their erotic time in the Caribbean was one fantastic fantasy he'd kept ready for instant replay over the years.

She looked over at Dee, who was shaking her head as she grabbed the Post-its and a pen from Pia's desk and furiously began scribbling notes.

FLIRT BACK!

"I confess, I think about that weekend from time to time myself," Pia replied.

"Is that why you're calling?"

"I wanted to talk to you about doing some more directing for SunFire . . ."

PLEASURE, NOT BUSINESS, with the word *pleasure* under-lined several times, was the content of Dee's next note.

". . . so I was wondering if we could get together and discuss the possibility of working together again. And to be perfectly honest, I'd like to see you," Pia added, heeding Dee's advice and adding some sauciness to her tone.

"I'd love to see you too. Like you said, it's been a million years. When's good for you?"

"When's good for me?" Pia repeated. "How about . . ."

FEBRUARY 21–23, read the note Darlene slid across the table.

"Either February twenty-first, twenty-second, or twenty-third would work for me," Pia replied, reading off the dates she would be ovulating.

"I am tied up all three days," Grand said, "but I could do the evening of the twenty-second. Would that be cool? Your husband won't mind?"

"No husband to mind, and the twenty-second is good," Pia said, making a mental note to cancel her Birkam yoga class.

"Great. How about we meet at the bar of the Royalton Hotel? Eight o'clock?"

"Perfect," Pia replied, giving Darlene the thumbs up and sending her across the desk to exchange a silent high-five. "Have a great weekend, and I'll see you in two weeks."

Pia hung up the phone and clapped her hands. The Grand plan was in motion. She was both elated and petrified. The prey was in her sights, but did she have the guts to pull the trigger?

☙

There was something about Pia's mission that made the unmarked door of the Royalton Hotel thoroughly appropriate. She entered and walked the long royal blue runway of a carpet, past the funky white chrome-legged chairs and sofas to the beat of the cranked-up techno lounge music, straight back to the bar and restaurant.

Pia perched on a stool at the far end of the bar to watch and wait. She'd purposely arrived fifteen minutes early to give herself time to settle down and prepare for the daunting task that was before her. Tonight felt like her last chance, and she didn't want to mess it up as she'd done in previous attempts.

"May I get you something?" the bartender asked.

Rehearsing for the main event, Pia threw a WMS eye smile on him, pleased by his return grin. "I'm sorry, your name is?"

"Steve."

"Steve," Pia purred, smiling and tilting her head. "I'd love a Bellini. In fact, make that two." She needed her courage fortified.

"My pleasure."

She turned away from the bar, crossing her shapely legs. As she perused the room, Pia was pleased to note that she'd caught the attention of several males, some with dates, others there to pick up someone else's. She was grateful for the appreciative stares and roving-eye appraisals. Pia smiled. If she could turn their heads, maybe there was hope for her with Grand.

"Here you go."

"Thanks, Steve," Pia said, lifting her glass and taking a sip.

"Excellent," she complimented before chugging down the first Bellini as if it were a shot of whiskey and starting on the second.

It boggled her mind that she was here in New York, waiting for the man who three years ago had been her mystery lover of sorts. Though they had never actually had sex, their stay in Aruba had been, bar none, one of the lustiest experiences in her life. Unbeknownst to her, Grand, there to direct the video, had happened upon her pleasuring herself on what she'd thought was an isolated stretch of private beach. Later that evening, he'd sent an anonymous note inviting her to be his fantasy lover. After a night of mind-blowing phone sex, they'd spent the remainder of the shoot in a sexual haze, enjoying both the pleasure and pain of a prolonged flirtation. But what went on in Aruba had stayed in Aruba, and after they returned to the States, the two lost touch. And now here she was, in full ovulation, waiting for this man to impregnate her without his knowledge.

Grand's professional attributes began parading through her head—intelligence, decisiveness, grace under fire, ambition, success. Immediately following behind were his outstanding physical traits—his five-ten frame, Boris Kodjoe looks, skin the perfect shade of mocha fudge, great hands and feet, and that impossible-to-resist, make-my-day, thousand-megawatt smile. Without a doubt, he was one of the sexiest, most sensual men she'd ever encountered in her forty-one years. He would make a beautiful baby, inside and out.

Pia's face broke out into a huge smile as Grand Nelson strolled through the door, drawing glances from all around. She sat unnoticed, checking him out as he looked around the bar. The boy still had *it*. Still lean, still bald and fine, and still strutting into the room like he owned it. It was impossible not to be both impressed and attracted.

The hostess motioned over to the bar and Grand approached, filling the room with his sunbeam grin. Pia, nerves settled by the champagne, returned his *I know a secret* beam with a welcoming smile of her own as she slipped off the bar stool and extended her right hand.

"Hey," Grand said, probing with eyes that revealed his delight. "You are still as beautiful as you were when I peeped you on the beach in Aruba."

"As are you," Pia replied. It was all she could manage to spew from a mouth busy trying not to form kiss-me lips.

"Come here, you," he insisted, taking Pia's outstretched hand and drawing her into a warm embrace. She stood there, her head resting against his hard chest, breathing in his heady cologne while experiencing the explosive inner mix of nerves, desire, and alcohol.

"Would you like something to drink?" Pia asked once they'd disengaged.

"Absolutely."

"Steve, could you bring my friend a vodka on the rocks with a twist? And I'll have another Bellini."

"You remembered," Grand said, impressed by not only her memory but by her physical beauty. Pia was even more gorgeous than he'd recalled. She looked delicious in her simple and sophisticated black sheath dress and necklace with one pearl dangling from a long gold chain down her back. Her black pumps with the high-cut vamp and stiletto heel were the perfect showcase for her toned and shapely legs. Everything about her screamed sexy twist on classic beauty. And judging by the admiring looks of the males populating the hotel bar, including the besotted bartender, he wasn't alone in his thinking.

"Mr. Nelson," Pia said, gripping her champagne flute with her thumb and forefinger and suggestively moving her other fingers up and down the stem, "there are a lot of things I remember about you."

"Glad to hear that," he said after gently clearing his throat. "I would hate to think I was reliving all those fantasies by myself."

"Fantasy lovers can be quite stimulating, don't you agree?" Pia asked, reciting a line from the note he'd sent her in Aruba. At the same time, she crossed her legs, and held Grand's gaze while taking a long sip of her drink. As predicted, her action caused a flash of teeth across his face.

Grand stood in front of her at the bar and the two proceeded to catch up on each other's lives. They talked about their respective jobs and travels, laughing and commiserating together about the realities of their so-called glamorous careers. In between, she sought the answers to questions that were vital to her mission tonight.

Are you married or in a seriously committed relationship? No. Apparently Grand Nelson and George Clooney had two things in common: a vow to remain forever single and a great love for the lake country in Italy. Finding out about the state of his health was a trickier proposition, and Pia drew that out in roundabout ways. As best she could tell, Grand exercised regularly, ate well, and was in general good health.

Pia continued the WMS SELL: smiling, making eye contact, listening closely, laughing, and lightly touching his arm when appropriate. Her actions had the desired effect, sparking and holding Grand's attention and piquing his curiosity. The sexual tension that existed between them in Aruba was still very evident, and with each passing minute and certainly every consumed beverage it became more and more prominent, eventually crowding out any semblance of a platonic evening.

"Why don't we go over to the round bar? It's a bit more private," Pia suggested, referring to a small, secluded bar area tucked in a quiet corner of the lobby. Grand helped Pia off her stool and followed her back down the blue runner to a sexy circular room, flickering with candlelight and, as luck would have it, still undiscovered by tonight's crowd.

Pia sat on the built-in leather banquette while Grand sat across from her on a leather cube. She leaned her head against the curved tufted-leather wall, flirting with Grand in silence. As she'd learned from Joey, she talked to him through her eyes and facial expressions, making it clear that she found him just as attractive today as she had three years ago and that if he was willing she wanted to finally end the celibate state she'd existed in all these years.

Grand moved from his cube and joined Pia on the bench. "Nice necklace," he said, fingering the pearls around her neck and leaning in for closer inspection.

"Thank you for noticing."

"Have you eaten dinner?" he asked.

"No, and come to think of it, I'm starving. No. Make that *ravenous*," she said before biting her lower lip, something she tended to do when she was feeling deliciously off-balance. The champagne cocktails were doing their job, lowering her inhibitions and fueling her bravado.

"I'll have them bring over the bar menu," he said, raising his hand to signal the waitress.

"Wait. I have a better idea," Pia said, reaching for his hand and lowering it into his lap. She gazed deep into Grand's sweet brown eyes, making it clear that food was actually nowhere on her mind. "Room service."

For the first time all evening, Pia saw some of Grand's studly cool melt. A flash of disbelief and uncertainty crossed his face. It didn't last long, but it was enough to leave Pia feeling uncharacteristically bold.

Close enough to see the gold glint in his brown eyes, Pia reached up and caressed his lips with her fingertips. "Do you know how many times I've fantasized about your lips?" she asked him. "All that talk in Aruba and I can't believe we never kissed."

"Well, it's not too late," Grand declared, allowing her finger to penetrate his mouth.

They both closed their eyes as he began to suck seductively. Pia tipped her head back, enjoying the rush of sexual currents spreading to every nerve ending in her body.

Pia felt drunk by both alcohol and desire. She replaced her finger with her lips and pressed her body closer to his. Grand's kiss became more urgent as his lips hungrily brushed her eyes, nose, ears, and neck before meeting hers. He passionately acquainted his tongue with the sweet recesses of her mouth. He ran his hands down her bare legs, momentarily stopping to tickle the sensitive area behind her knee.

"Do you know how many times I have fantasized about making love to you since Aruba?" he asked. "If your actions are half as convincing as your words, I might not be able to handle it."

Pia pulled away to look at Grand's eyes. Judging by their soft, dewy state, she was close to accomplishing the first half of her mission— getting him into bed. That realization spun her into a major good news, bad news scenario. The good news was that she really *wanted* to get him there. Beyond getting pregnant, the passion she had kept bottled up inside her for these past few years was about to blow, and her physical attraction to Grand was very real. The bad news was, she was having major second thoughts about not letting him in on her plans. Was it really fair?

"Well, it's not too late to find out," she said, echoing his sentiments and setting her future in motion.

"If you're serious, I can get a room," he told her.

Pia leaned in to deliver a deep, passionate kiss. And in case he had any doubt, she ran her hand across his thigh, bringing it to rest on the bulge in his pants.

"You *are* serious."

"A little bit," she said, smiling enticingly.

"Don't move. I'll be right back."

"Wait," she called out, stopping Grand's departure. He turned to look at Pia, his eyes pleading with her not to change her mind.

"It's just . . . well . . . bringing this up is such a mood killer, but . . . well, the whole safe sex thing," Pia said in an embarrassing jumble of words.

"Don't worry—I've had my shots and have a clean test record," Grand assured her.

"In that case, why are you still standing there?"

While she waited, Pia scanned her body, getting in touch with sensations she hadn't fully experienced in years. Yearning that came from lack rather than the thrill that came from a desirable partner was a monster of a totally different DNA. Tonight Pia's body was reminding her that there was no substitute for true passion.

Grand returned with key in hand and sweet expectation on his face. "Room fourteen-eleven awaits."

"Let me have that," Pia said, reaching for the key card. "You have another drink and then meet me upstairs in fifteen minutes." She leaned in and gave him a to-be-continued kiss before heading toward the elevator.

Once out of Grand's view, Pia set off like the wildwoman she was channeling to prepare for the games to come. Pia stepped into the elevator, willing it not to stop until it reached the fourteenth floor. Breathless after racing down the hallway, she threw open the door and began the task of readying not just the atmosphere but her attitude.

First, she threw the Royalton Hotel mix CD into the stereo. It was an eclectic collection of songs ranging from sexy Brazilian beats to smoky jazz and neo soul, perfect for a sensual evening of uncommitted lovemaking.

This was followed by a quick washup and gargle, and a spritz of her exotic signature scent. She took off her dress, leaving on her panties and bra, and pulled on the white terry robe hanging behind the bathroom door. Pia then turned off all the lights except the desk lamp. She dimmed it to its lowest setting and supplemented its glow by opening the drapes to reveal the twinkle of city lights. On such short notice, she had made the room look and smell beautiful.

Finally she sat down on the bed to catch her breath. Not a good move, as just a few seconds of inactivity was time enough to begin the second-guessing. After five years of membership in the Celibate Sistah Brigade, this is what it had come down to: sex with a familiar stranger whose earlier sexual experience with her had been all talk and no action. The mere thought sobered her. Pia was ready and willing, but was she still able?

What the hell am I thinking? Do you even remember what to do with a dick that isn't hot pink plastic and doesn't buzz?

Chapter Fourteen

Grand was seven minutes late, and Pia began to panic. She reached into the minibar and cracked open a bottle of Skyy vodka and chugged it, chasing it with one more for good measure. As she sat on the bed, enjoying the soothing effect of the alcohol, the neon light of the clock caught her eye. He was now ten minutes late. Had he changed his mind?

Time for reinforcement. Pia reached for her cell phone and called the one person she knew would talk her through this.

"Dee, where the hell are you?" she shrieked when her secretary's voice mail picked up. "Okay, I think I'm about to do *it,* but I think maybe I got stood up . . . He's late . . . Shit, I'm drunk and scared, but hell of horny. I don't know what we were thinking except he would make a *fine* baby . . . Can I really do this? Can I really fuck him and chuck him? Oh, that sounds harsh . . . but you'd be proud, 'cause I was flirting my ass off tonight and not once did the b-word come up . . . But now I think I should tell him, don't you think so? Anyway, we got a room and I'm here and I thought he was coming but he's late . . . I said that . . . Okay, I know I'm rambling but I just drank two mini vodkas to calm me down on top of the champagne and . . . actually I do have a lovely buzz. Oh, shit . . . someone's knocking . . . Okay, he's here, he came . . . We're going to make a baby! Should I tell him? I should tell him . . . Shit! I don't know. Okay, I'll call you later."

She heard the soft knocking again and took a deep breath before opening the door and releasing a double-flanked assault—the Brazilian Girls assailed his ears with a highly suggestive samba while Pia attacked his lips with an even more suggestive kiss.

"Damn, Pia, you look—" he said in a low voice that thrilled her ears and all areas south.

"Shhh," she demanded, holding her finger to his lips. Grand immediately stopped talking. His willing obedience swept away her anxiety and reconstituted her courage. It also sent a surge of POP, as Darlene would put it, power of the punani, running through her.

Pia, you can do this. Just close your eyes and go with the flow. Island Boy here is fulfilling his fantasy of being with you in Aruba. So let's give him a little of the WMS shock and awe.

Pia's breath became short as she clung to Grand with her arms and mouth. It had been so very long since she'd been kissed with such passion, and the act released her mothballed naughty girl. And though she'd dressed the set for seduction and lazy lovemaking, risqué lust and too many years of self-denial had overwhelmingly conquered any sense of decorum.

Pia pulled away and, resisting the temptation to simply rip the clothes from his back, swiftly began to unbutton his shirt. Grand, eager to assist, finished the job, and standing naked in one of the finest chocolate brown bodies she'd ever witnessed, quickly untied her robe to reveal her sleek torso adorned in Madame Cosette's sheer black baby-making demi bra and matching panties.

"Nice tattoo," he commented, eyeing the small dragon near her hip bone as he peeled away her panties and watched them drop to the floor. "And what's this one?" he asked referring to the WMS tattooed on her lower back.

"If you are a very, very good boy, I'll tell you later," she promised.

Pia smiled contentedly as he resumed his delicious ravishing. With unbridled enthusiasm, Grand directed his hot mouth down her neck and across her shoulders, bringing it to rest on one of her protruding nipples. He nibbled with surprising expertise until Pia heard a grateful moan escape her lips. Encouraged by her reaction, Grand lingered, causing a string of moans and *oh, shits* to fall from Pia's mouth. She could feel a delicious nagging sensation in her groin, causing her hips and pelvis to instinctively search for his rigid hardness and abandon all plans of being the do-er. Suddenly Pia was all for lying back and getting *done*.

With the bed on the other side of the room, and much too far away, the two crumpled to the floor, where Grand's mouth covered her body with a string of lingering kisses until his tongue expertly found the spot she was sure had atrophied after years without a man's touch.

Pia took a deep, satisfying breath. In the past she'd more often felt used than amused by the hurry-up-rip-my-clothes-off-and-do-me-NOW kind of sex. But this time, instead of being put off, she was totally turned on. At this moment, Pia didn't care about anything other than having a lusty spontaneous romp with this sumptuous black brother.

Grand slid his two fingers between her legs, lightly massaging her clitoris with his thumb. He fingered her urgently, following the rhythm of Pia's grinding motions. Her body moved with his hand, enjoying the sweet pleasure the friction was creating.

"I want you now," Pia demanded.

Grand gladly followed the first words spoken in the last twenty minutes by climbing on top of her and guided his rigid penis into her waiting body. He entered her with a slow glide toward full penetration. Pia, too willing and ready for full-on skin-on-skin contact, gripped his buttocks with her legs and pushed him deep into her fiending body.

"Yes, baby, oh, yes," Grand moaned.

Baby! The word stopped Pia cold in midthrust. A typical term of endearment spoken in any lovemaking session, it hit Pia's ears as an uncomfortable reminder that she was putting out for a purpose. Pia felt a slight tinge of guilt radiate through her belly. Was it right that Grand be tricked into impregnating her? No, she couldn't do it this way.

"What's wrong, baby?" Grand asked, confused by her mental lapse.

"A condom. We need to use a condom."

"My bad. I just got so excited." Grand found his pants and fumbled through the pockets, searching for a condom. Nothing. "I'm afraid I wasn't prepared for this," he sheepishly admitted.

"Not to worry. This is a full-service hotel," Pia said as she got up and headed to the minibar. There in the fully stocked drawer she found a choice of rubbers—Trojans for him, Elexa for her. *Girl power,* she thought, returning to Grand and handing him the condom made specifically for a woman's enjoyment. He quickly sheathed himself in latex and hungrily rejoined his body with Pia's.

Eyes closed and mouth open wide, Pia reveled in the almost forgotten joys of a man's touch. In between attempts to catch her fleeting breath, she moaned loudly, filling the hotel room with the undeniable sounds of approaching orgasm. Her body exploded, encouraging Grand to respond in a fury of syncopated thrusts. Together they bucked back and forth in a wild, passionate coupling as Grand felt himself swell and tighten before bursting inside her.

"Sorry, I couldn't hold it anymore," he panted, sliding off her body and onto the floor beside her.

"Not a problem," she assured him. The two lay together, enjoying the euphoria of their erotic union. Pia sighed with satisfaction. The drought was officially over. Oh, how she had missed sex! How had she let a series of unfortunate relationships with unfortunate men separate her from this amazing side of herself? She'd enjoyed feeling girly and flirty and *alive* again. She loved that she excelled in the art of seduction and was thrilled that she could still affect a man's mind as well as his member. But as glorious as tonight's sex had been, Pia's heart and soul were still hungry for some real lovemaking.

She allowed Grand to nap for a few minutes longer as she went to the bathroom and cleaned up. She was so grateful for and appreciative of Grand's role in her sexual rebirth. He had given her back the part of her soul and body she'd left languishing in layaway for much too long, and now she had one more life-changing favor to ask of him.

"Hey, sexy," Grand said, awakening from his brief nap. "You were everything I imagined and more."

"You too."

"Then why do you look so serious?"

"Because I have something serious to ask you. I need you to listen and hear me out, and then we'll talk about it. Okay?"

"Okay."

Pia took a deep breath and began her story. She told him everything, from her childhood days of playing mommy to her favorite doll, Minerva, to her disappointing record with men to her years of celibacy and pressing medical concerns. She even showed him the pendant around her neck and revealed its meaning. By the time she got around to asking the question, it was clear that this was no trivial decision on her part.

"I know you're a confirmed bachelor and are not interested in ever getting married. I'm not looking for that from you. I am financially independent. You don't have to be involved at all."

In a move Pia saw as promising, Grand, rather than turning her down outright, asked several questions, most of them queries she'd already heard before: Why not adopt or go to a sperm bank? Why me? She answered as honestly and thoroughly as possible and assured him that she would be the best, most loving mother to his child as was humanly possible.

"And I chose you because I genuinely like you. I like your looks, your intelligence and creativity, your sense of adventure. You're friendly and kind and I love the way you laugh. All attributes I'd like my child to have.

"Well?" she probed, hopeful that her case had been made successfully. "I'll understand if you need more time."

"One more question: Did you come here tonight with an agenda?"

"Yes, I am ovulating," she replied honestly, "but I decided that it wasn't fair to you and that's why I stopped and asked you to put on a condom."

Grand smiled. "That's the kind of honesty I'd expect from my child's mother. Look, Pia, I'm not interested in marriage, you know that, but like you I'm not sure if I want to leave this world without ever having a child of my own. At the same time, I'm not sure that I want to take on the responsibility of fatherhood. So I'll be honest with you. I'm willing to father your child if you're willing to leave the door open to any decision I make in the future as to being in his life or not."

"Absolutely," Pia said as a beaming smile crossed her face. "Thank so much, Grand," she said, hugging him tight.

"So shall we do it again and this time make a baby?"

"I'd love to," Pia said, melting into his arms.

"And let's do it right," Grand suggested. "We may not be in love with each other, but let's conceive this child in sweetness and light."

"I'm remarkable," Pia said, smiling wide. "I picked the perfect father for my child. You are kind and generous, and this baby will always know that about you."

"One last question. As the father of your child, I think I deserve to know: The tattoo . . . WMS . . . what's it mean? Some dude's initials?"

"No. It stands for weapon of mass seduction."

"Oh, yes, baby, your shit is definitely ballistic." Grand laughed as he scooped Pia up and carried her to the bed.

For the rest of the night, Pia and Grand had delicious sex, and with each orgasm they stopped and prayed that a baby had been made. By three A.M. they were both exhausted and fell asleep in each other's arms. At morning's first light they made love one last time before Grand had to leave in order to get home and catch a flight to Singapore. They parted friends and potential parents, agreeing that there would be no more contact between them until the child's first birthday. If Grand didn't hear from Pia he would assume that she had not gotten pregnant and they would both take it as a sign that their shared parenthood was not meant to be.

Pia saw Grand off and climbed back into bed, ready to sleep for a few more hours after such a long and ultimately satisfying night. Just as she was about to drift off, her cell rang.

"So, *chica*, please tell me you finally got laid and the Grand plan worked."

"I finally got laid and the Grand plan is a definite go. I guess we'll know in a few weeks if it actually *worked*."

"*A Dios gracias!* And you and your dusty *chocha* enjoyed it?"

"Thoroughly. Grand is an amazing lover, and, frankly, I still got it."

"I'm impressed. So what did you say?"

"I used the classic line: 'Hi, I've got the F, the C, and the K, now all I need is U.'"

"Listen to you—you finally get some and now you got jokes. So I guess this means you're not still mad that I tricked you into going to that seminar."

"I guess not. Funny enough, Dee, I kind of *feel* like a weapon of mass seduction now. It's great. I just wish there was something I could do to make this feeling last."

"Oh, shit. You're just like the damn government."

"What the hell are you talking about, Dee?"

"Give the bush a little power and it's ready to fuck the world. Just promise, *chica*, to use your power for good, not evil."

Chapter Fifteen

"Damn, just what kind of Mandingo man is this Grand Nelson?" Dee asked as she sat in Pia's office, staring her boss down in disbelief. "Besides fine, he's obviously virile as hell. So how far along are you?"

"I've missed one period and I'm late this month. I took another EPT this morning and it was positive."

"So are you going to call Grand and tell him he's going to be a daddy?"

"No. He doesn't want to know if I get pregnant, and if I do, other than a yearly update, I promised not to involve him unless he requests it. Dee, am I doing the right thing having his baby?"

"You're not having second thoughts because Grand doesn't want to be involved, are you? I thought that was the plan. You didn't fall for him or anything, did you?"

"Oh, no. Absolutely not. Grand is sexy as hell and we have an off-the-charts sexual chemistry, but that's where it ends. Neither one of us is interested in the other like that."

"Okay, then I don't get why you're questioning yourself. Ever since I've known you, you've always talked about wanting a kid. And even with all your plumbing issues, you got pregnant on the first try. This baby is meant to be."

"That is true."

"So, *chica*, what's next?" Darlene asked, leaving out all the smart cracks and putting a supportive arm around her boss.

"I'm going to see Dr. Montrae today at one and make sure that everything is okay."

"And then?"

"And then, I guess I'm going to have a baby," Pia declared softly before releasing a big sigh.

Dee, unable to contain her enthusiasm any longer, began doing the highly contagious happy dance, causing Pia to momentarily forget her queasy stomach and conflicting emotions and join in. She allowed herself to revel in the realization that after wishing on so many stars, fountains, candles, and turkey bones, she was finally going to be a mother.

"But you can't tell anyone. Not even Hector. At least not yet."

"I won't, but you're going to have to tell someone else."

"I know, and I'm dreading it," Pia admitted.

"You have to do it. You have to tell Maizelle."

"Despite the fact that my mother has been wanting and waiting to be a grandmother for years, she's going to freak out when she finds out that I'm pregnant by a man I have no intention of marrying."

"*Chica,* surely your mother is aware that you're not some teen pregnancy statistic," Dee teased.

"My teen years may be long gone, but that won't matter much to Maizelle. She's a traditionalist all the way. In my mother's eyes an unwed mother is an unwed mother—no matter what her age."

"In that case, you might want to tell her soon. She's going to need these next seven months to get used to the idea."

"You're right. I just have no idea what to say."

"Try saying, '*Mami,* the sad news is that I'm not getting married. The glad news is that I'm pregnant. And the best news is that the paramedics are standing by.' "

☙

Pia stared at the ceiling tiles and listened to the crinkling sound of her paper gown as she lay on the examining table. She winced slightly as the doctor spread the cool, clear gel across her belly in preparation for the ultrasound.

"This is just to help the transducer pass smoothly over your abdomen," Dr. Montrae informed her. "In just a minute, we'll be able to see the baby's heartbeat and make sure we have a viable pregnancy."

Viable. Pia ran through the word's definitions in her head. *Feasible, practical, doable.* Suddenly all the logical concerns she'd pushed to the back of her head came rushing to the forefront. *What the hell was I thinking? Have I lost my damn mind? How am I going to raise a child by myself? Especially with my work and travel schedule? And particularly when Maizelle is going to disown me for being a trollop and her grandchild for being illegitimate?*

The whooshing sound of the ultrasound drowned out her thoughts and forced Pia's attention back into the room. She was greeted by the fast, steady beat of a fetal heart. It was a beautiful sound that washed away all her doubt.

"That's it? That's my baby?" she asked, lifting her head to look at the grainy black-and-white image.

"Yes, Pia, congratulations. You are officially a mother-to-be."

Pia acknowledged the news with a weak smile and a deep sigh. "Hi, my miracle baby," she whispered.

"Let's see, today is April seventeenth. Judging from the date of your last period and the size of the fetus, I'd say you're about eight weeks pregnant. You can expect your little bundle of joy somewhere around Thanksgiving, give or take a week."

Still too stunned to speak, Pia simply shook her head. She felt strangely detached from this experience. It was as if her thoughts, emotions, and senses were muddled together, filling the room with a thick fog and keeping her from totally engaging in the reality.

"Are you okay with this? This is what you want, correct?"

"Yes, this is what I want. It just feels a little strange—in a good way."

"Because of your age, I'll be doing a few extra tests to rule out any chromosomal issues like Down syndrome," the doctor said as she wiped the gel from Pia's belly and helped her into a sitting position. "All routine stuff, so I don't want you to worry. Now do you have any questions?"

"The queasiness. That's normal, right?"

"Perfectly normal. Just keep your stomach from being empty by eating small meals and munching on saltines or rice cakes in between. That should help. Start taking your prenatal vitamins, and I will see you in a month. If you have any issues or questions before then, give me a call. Is there anything else I can help you with?"

Only if you can tell my mother that her grandchild was conceived in a rela-

tionship that was based on the endearing premise of Knock Me Up and Go Away.

"I'm fine, Dr. Montrae. See you next month, and thank you."

Pia dressed and minutes later stepped into New York's spring sunshine feeling unsteady and indecisive. It was a foreign sensation. But the fact was that in a few short months Pia's life was going to change forever. And crazy hormone fluctuations aside, she needed to get a firm grasp on her fast-changing world. And now was as good a time as any to get started. Conjuring up her deceased father's wise advice of 'Start it the way you want it to end,' Pia fished out her cell phone and dialed the number she'd been calling for the past twenty years. In the ring span of six seconds, Pia sent a prayer up to the heavens, asking God to fill her mother's heart with love and understanding and, if that wasn't possible, the ability to forgive in time to babysit.

"Hello."

"Mom, how are you?"

"Pia? I'm fine. Where are you?"

"Here in New York."

"Done globe-trotting for a while?"

"I wish. I'm leaving for London tomorrow and will be gone a week. I thought maybe we could have one of our legendary mother-daughter gabfests when I get back."

"I'd like that, honey—it's been a long time since we've had a chance to really sit down and talk."

"Me too. How about brunch on Saturday of next week?" Pia asked, knowing the majority of her mother's Sunday was taken up at the church. "I can meet you at eleven at Zoe's."

"My favorite restaurant? Okay, Pia, what's going on?"

"Don't be so suspicious, Mother. But something . . . well, I have some good news to tell you," Pia said employing Joey Clements's lesson of smiling while speaking on the phone. Hopefully her grin was filtering out the uneasiness from her voice.

"So tell me, sweetheart."

"I'll tell you when I see you."

"Okay, sweetie. Good news is always worth waiting for. I'll see you then."

Pia hung up the phone well aware that in this case, one woman's good news was another woman's *Lord, where did I fail?* nightmare.

Chapter Sixteen

"I thought you said you had *good* news," Maizelle remarked as she gently but purposely placed her spoon on the saucer. "You do realize that your father is turning over in his grave at this very minute. He loved you dearly, Pia, but he would be so disappointed in you right now. And I have to admit that I am as well."

Even though she could have written the script, Pia winced, crushed by her mother's dismay and the implied disapproval of her beloved father. She'd been a daddy's girl all his life, and the idea that he was out there in the great beyond unhappy with her hurt deeply.

"And what am I going to tell Mimi? Your eighty-three-year-old grandmother is going to be devastated. We just don't do this kind of thing in our family."

"Mom, calm down. I'm not giving birth tomorrow. Both you and Mimi have several months to get used to the idea," Pia said, wishing like hell she could have a glass of champagne to take the edge off this uncomfortable moment.

"I will never get used to this idea, Pia. How am I going to explain this to my friends? To Pastor Saxton? To God?"

"You don't owe your friends or pastor any explanation other than you're going to be a grandmother. And if they are truly in your corner, they won't judge you on the sins of your daughter. And as for God, I don't know, but I think ultimately it won't be you that has to make things right. This will be between Him and me," Pia added drily. Her outer stance might have been defiance, but inside she was shaking. Like most children—grown or not—she loved and respected her mother, and disappointing her felt painful and humiliating.

"Don't get smart with me. This is not how your father and I raised you, Pia Clarice Jamison."

"I'm sorry," she said, reaching for her mother's hand. Just as they made contact, Becca Vossel popped into Pia's mind. Her young friend was smack dab in the middle of trying to navigate the line between living her own truth and acknowledging her parents' values and expectations, and here she was, nearly twenty years Becca's senior, worrying about the same damn thing.

"Mom, I realize that for you this might seem disappointing and embarrassing, but let me try to explain it to you in a way that will hopefully make sense," Pia said softening her tone. "After last year's myomectomy to remove the uterine fibroids, my doctor made it very clear to me that time was running out and if I wanted to have a child, it was now or never. So I decided that I'd rather be a single mother than not be a mother at all.

"I would like nothing better than to marry some amazing man and raise a baby together like you and Daddy did, but it's just not meant to be. I'm not in a serious relationship—in fact, I'm not even dating anyone at the moment."

"Pia, you're pregnant. You must be in some kind of relationship. Who is the father? Is there no chance you two could make it work?"

Damn. The one question she was hoping to avoid was now on the table, but Pia had no intention of making an already bad situation worse by revealing the entire set of facts.

"No, there's no chance for us to be together. I used a sperm donor," she revealed, settling on the basic truth in hopes that it would sound more acceptable to her mother's ears.

"I'm going to have to pray on this. I just don't understand how you could do something like this."

"I realize that this is a difficult concept for you to wrap your head around. I've spent most of my adult life looking unsuccessfully for the same kind of loving relationship you and Daddy had. But I've given up looking. I've decided to let him find me. But the reality is, he may not come looking.

"But Pia, you're already forty-one. Soon you'll have a baby. What man is going to want you even if he does find you?"

"Hopefully, a man who truly loves me. I know what you're saying, and maybe if it wasn't a now-or-never proposition, I'd wait longer—

wait to do it the way I'd always intended . . . the way *you* intended. So maybe we won't plan the wedding together, but how about a christening?"

"I don't know. This is all too much. This is not what your father and I wanted for you."

"Just know that I love you very much and want you to be happy about your grandchild. I need you to help me get through this now and in the years to come, because there is no other woman who can give me better advice on being a great mom."

"Being a great mom begins with doing what's best for your child. Are you sure this is what's best?"

"It is for me and it will be for the baby. Now, I'm sorry, but I have to go. I have to get to the studio," Pia said.

"It's Saturday. Did you ever consider that maybe if you weren't always traveling and working on weekends, you could find a proper husband and move that right-hand ring over to the left?" Maizelle remarked, eyeing Pia's new diamond band.

Pia felt herself cringe. They'd been down that road so many times before in the past ten years, she had no intention of retracing her steps. It seemed as if two minutes into Pia's thirtieth birthday, Mai had begun the drumbeat that is the angst of every unmarried woman over twenty-nine. When are you getting married and having some grandbabies?

Instead of replying to a remark she'd heard too many times before, Pia reached over and hugged her mother. And for the first time since she had been caught shoplifting a Jackson Five T-shirt on a dare, severe disappointment buffered her body, insulating Pia from the warmth of her mother's love.

"I love you," she said, a tear threatening to fall.

"I know you do, Pia."

Her mother's lack of return affection cut the same way it had decades ago when she was standing in the department store's security office. And just like that shunned thirteen-year-old, grown-up Pia was feeling ashamed and alone and left wondering if her actions had been worth it.

Pia and Darlene sat in the edit bay with the editor, sorting out the order of appearances for Hector's "shout out reel." Months ago, Dee had arranged with Pia to have various singers, rappers, and celebrities record short messages to be sent to Iraq as a surprise for his twenty-seventh birthday.

"So should we end with Ashanti singing 'Happy Birthday'?" Dee asked, sorting through the cut list. Pia, sitting with her head in her hands, trying to ride another wave of nausea, could only reply with a low moan.

"Why don't we start with Ashanti and close with you. That way you'll be the last thing on his mind when it's over," the editor suggested.

Pia lifted and gestured her agreement with one hand before resuming her ailing position. She really was feeling horrible—not only nauseated but dejected and dog tired as well.

"Are you okay?" Darlene asked.

"Mommy pains—in all meanings of the word," Pia whispered, trying not to share her business with the rest of the production crew.

"Can I get you something?"

"No, I'll be fine. I'll just munch on some more rice cakes and sip on my ginger tea and try to remember that my mother would never disown her only child, even if she thinks I'm a terrible daughter."

"It could be worse. My mom plans to exact her revenge on me by moving in when she gets old and refusing to wear clothes."

"Don't make me laugh. The shaking makes the nausea worse."

"So Darlene, if you're ready, we can tape your close," the editor interrupted.

He and Dee slipped into the next room, leaving Pia to rewind the mental video of this morning's brunch. While it had gone pretty much as she'd expected and Maizelle's disappointment weighed heavy on her, most surprising was the battle waging inside. Traditional, righteous, good girl was warring with independent, modern, ain't-nobody's-business-if-I-do girl for rights to her peace of soul.

Pia Clarice Jamison had been trained to be a good girl in a household where traditional family values were touted and instilled long before the idea of "family values" was a political lightning rod.

For the second time today, Becca Vossel popped into her head. When you took away the race and adoption issues, their upbringings weren't all that different. Both were brought up in God-fearing middle-class households where dignity, respect, and a daughter's reputation were paramount issues. Pia's late father, Charlie, was a man who respected women but also expected those same women to respect themselves. The avoidance of parental disapproval became Pia's internal police force and moral guidance system.

Pia, determined to respect both her wants and her parents' rules, unconsciously took on a passive-aggressive approach to her teen years. Pia had spared Maizelle and Charlie the stress of any true teenage rebellion and she'd experienced enough life on her terms to feel as though she hadn't missed a thing.

Despite Maizelle's doctrine, Pia marched to her own truth and lost her virginity to her first love the summer before going off to college. Pia had been pleased that her initial sexual experience had taken place in the context of a loving (though not marital) relationship, and she had been responsible enough to get herself on the pill, which was how Maizelle had discovered she was sexually active. Her mother had been upset and "disappointed" that she hadn't waited until marriage, but eighteen-year-old Pia, in love and intoxicated with innocent lust, had stood her ground. But later, in college, when love moved on, Pia was left dealing with the contradictory pull of her physical urges and her parents' morals. Fifteen years of tiptoeing through those sexually and emotionally explosive mine fields had left Pia confused and eventually celibate. And now, at forty-one, sex, love, reputation, and parental approval were still causing her conflict and muddying her self-image as a sexual being.

"Hector is going to love this," Darlene exclaimed, interrupting Pia's thoughts as she burst back into the room. "Thank you, *chica*, for making this happen."

"No problem. We'll send a bunch of CDs along for him and the rest of the unit."

"I miss him so much. I hate that I can't be with him on his birthday or Christmas or our anniversary," Dee revealed in an uncharacteristic moment of vulnerability.

"One year goes by fast," Pia said, trying to comfort her friend. "And you'll to be so busy playing *Tia* Dee that before you know it Hector will be walking through the door, safe and sound, and you two will be making a baby of your own."

"I hope so. But until then, don't get any crazy ideas. Don't think you're going to be dropping little Pomegranate on *Tía* Dee all the time . . ." Darlene said, reverting back to her usual cheeky self.

"Pomegrante? Where the hell did that come from?"

"Because right now it's a little seed, and it's also *muy* Hollywood."

"Darlene, you are certifiably nuts," Pia pronounced.

ॐ

The stroll to her apartment helped to quell Pia's morning sickness. Maybe it was the fresh air, but by the time she walked through the front door, she was feeling better.

"Hi, Paolo," Pia said, throwing her doorman a saucy grin as she strutted toward her mailbox. Since the workshop and rejoining the sensually and sexually active, Pia definitely felt more like a total woman again. And practicing her flirting as Joey had suggested had become a fun part of her day.

Once inside her apartment, Pia went about her usual routine of turning on her water fountain, lighting the candlescape in the fireplace, and flipping on her current favorite CD, *Putayamo Presents: Asian Lounge*. It was a homecoming routine she'd adopted years ago in the first few months of working in the hectic and very loud music video business. After a long day of dealing with booty-shaking music and the fragile egos of the artists who create it, the soothing sounds of water and soul-satisfying rhythms was a salve on her weary spirit.

Her last task was changing her daily inspiration card. Dee had given her the Inspire and Affirm box for her birthday last year, and selecting daily words to live by had become part of her evening ritual so that each morning she could wake up with fresh positivity. Considering today's baby and mama drama, Pia chose a quote from Louisa May Alcott to display: "I am not afraid of storms, for I am learning to sail my own ship."

Now if I can just avoid running the damn thing aground, I'll be okay, Pia thought with a twisted smile.

Usually she'd sip a glass of champagne or a good merlot to take the edge off a tough day, but that part of the ritual was over—at least for a while. She'd have to settle for more herbal tea, Pia decided as she strolled through her sand-colored living room and into the kitchen.

Pia stopped by the eat-in counter to read her mail. She rummaged through the bills and junk mail disguised as "important, time-sensitive" documents before picking up a small manila envelope with the words PHOTOS: DO NOT BEND scribbled several times across the front and back. A quick check of the return address made her smile. It was from Florence Chase.

She filled her mug with water from the hot water dispenser on her sink, dunked a chamomile tea bag inside, and sat down. Pia opened the package to find a letter wrapped around another envelope filled with photos. Pia picked up the photographs and quickly flipped through, smiling at the memories they invoked.

She put the pictures aside and opened the letter, eager to find out how things were going in Texas.

Hi there, sugar. Sorry to be getting these to you so late, but things have been really busy since I got back to Dallas. First off, Joey inspired me to re-decorate my boudoir in a much more sensual way. Before Dan came home, I got rid of all my bedroom furniture and created a suite that was more be-fitting a hot mama like myself (smile). I got new sheets, Egyptian cotton, 800 thread count, which is about 738 more threads than we're used to. And can I tell you, you can rightly feel the difference. I tried sleeping in the altogether and they did feel really nice on my skin. I even sprayed the pil-lows with some of that Chanel 19. I have to admit, honey, I like this sen-sual stuff. Joey was right. It does make you feel real good and real girly.

Dan's been home more than two weeks now. Things are moving a lit-tle slow. It's like we're trying to get to know each other again. Honestly, I feel like we're like roommates—sharing a space but not really a life. Maybe we've been like this for a while and I just haven't noticed. I've been wear-ing my perfume but haven't taken the underwear and the nighties out yet. I know the woman from the lingerie shop said not to wear them just for him, but I haven't really felt like wearing them for me either.

Haven't been doing any flirting. I tried practicing in the mirror, though to be honest, I feel a little bit stupid doing all that eye talk jazz. Dan's birthday is next month, so I thought maybe I'd try some of that red hot night stuff. We've got to break the ice sometime, right?

Enclosed are pictures from the workshop. We all look pretty darn good wearing those sheet dresses you whipped together, and I framed the one from the night you fixed me up (same night I met Clay). And no, I haven't mentioned Clay to Dan and I won't. I like having him as my secret memory. It's silly, but it makes me feel good knowing that he thought I was attractive enough to want to kiss. Sugar, at my age (and weight class), that's a Vatican-sanctioned miracle!

How's the daddy hunt going? So have you met anyone who's put the swing back into those hips of yours? Hope you're givin' those New York fellas hell.

Call me sometime so we can properly catch up.

Love, Flo

P.S. Have you heard from Becca? Somehow, I don't think Chicago will ever be the same!

Chapter Seventeen

Pia sat in Harmon Goldstone's outer office, hoping like hell that Dee was downstairs pulling off the impossible. This sudden request for a meeting by the new boss had thrown her schedule totally off. It had taken her months to be granted a workout with Benita Perkins, the most sought-after celebrity prenatal yoga instructor in the business and a woman Pia had been trying to hire since her first sonogram. Hopefully Dee was able to reschedule their session for tomorrow.

After Pia scanned through *VIBE, Source,* and *Rolling Stone* magazines, Harmon's secretary finally waved her into his office. She sat another five minutes, waiting for him to finish his phone call and acknowledge her presence. While she waited, Pia studied her new boss. He was definitely a suit, and rumor had it that he'd been brought in to pump up the profit margin so the company could be sold.

"Pia, sorry to keep you waiting," he said, hanging up the phone and giving her a handshake and matching smile. Neither looked or felt totally sincere, but Pia did not take it personally.

"Harmon, welcome to SunFire. Nice to finally meet you."

"Have a seat. I'm sorry that our first meeting has to be under such . . . well, under these circumstances. No, don't worry," he said, reading the concerned look on her face. "I've heard only great things about you and your department."

"Thank you. So if things are great in my department, what circumstances are you're referring to?"

"You are aware that the midterm congressional elections are coming up?"

"Yes, but how does that relate to what we do here?" Pia asked, trying to keep the What-the-hell-are-you-talking-about? look off her face.

"You are also aware that Valen Bellamy is challenging the Democratic candidate Betsy Franklin for her Senate seat."

"Yes. Mr. Bellamy is a black moderate from New York who is being touted as the Republicans' newest darling," Pia again affirmed, still not sure why she was sitting here going through the state's political landscape.

Oh, God, please don't tell me we're going to start producing campaign videos, Pia thought as she began running through numerous reasons that this would not be a good idea. *Damn that Diddy and his Vote or Die campaign.*

"Exactly. Bellamy is running on a platform emphasizing inclusiveness and tolerance. His campaign is calling for the end of 'contrary and destructive' images of women, blacks, and Hispanics in the media—including music and videos."

"Youth, blacks, Hispanics, *and* women—well, he's got all the bases, or shall I say voters, covered. Surprised he can't find a way to fit the NASCAR dads in there."

"Democrat, are we?"

"Little bit." Pia smiled. "Shall I conclude that we're being targeted as a provider of these negative images?"

"The entire industry, not just SunFire. Mr. Bellamy is meeting with several companies and individuals to form a committee of experts. His goal is to become educated on the issue so he can better form his opinions and campaign. I called you up here because we'd like you to represent SunFire on this committee."

"Why not send Suzy O'Brien in PR? This seems right up her alley."

"I don't want to come off as if we're trying to put a PR spin on a very explosive issue. The fact that you, a black woman, are actually responsible for the production of positive imagery sends a better message. It says we at SunFire take this all very seriously."

"I try, but let's be honest. Not all of my work can be held up as a shining example. I've produced my share of questionable videos."

"As long as it's only a share and not all, I'm satisfied."

"But I'm a Democrat—a *very* liberal Democrat. I'm not sure Mr. Bellamy will appreciate some of my positions," Pia responded, trying desperately to get out of this undesirable assignment.

"To his credit, the man appears to be interested in all sides of the debate."

"Of course he appears to be. It's election time."

"He's holding an information-gathering meeting tomorrow at two o'clock at the Marriott Marquis. It's no big deal. Let him pick your brain and give him some suggestions on how to improve things within the industry. Hopefully we'll get some positive press coverage and it will end there. Pia, I need you to understand something. We do not, I repeat, *do not* want SunFire to receive any negative press on this. We want nothing that is going to tarnish our reputation. Is that understood?"

"Clearly," Pia replied.

The two chatted strategy for several more minutes before Harmon was called away to take another phone call. On her way back to her office, Pia thought about what she'd just been volunteered to do. On one hand, the idea of getting involved, however peripherally, in a political campaign was something Pia had neither the time nor the inclination to do, but political ideologies aside, she had to admit that the thought behind Bellamy's campaign was solid. If women and people of color wanted respect from others, they must first demand it of themselves.

Still, Harmon's zeal in insisting she not screw up made it clear that the rumors to sell the company were true. Just as clear was the fact that there was an awful lot riding on her performance with this Bellamy character, adding pressure she did not need right now.

Pia turned the corner toward her office when it dawned on her that she now had to reschedule her rescheduled appointment with her yoga instructor.

"Dee, I need you to beg, plead, and barter with Benita to once again reschedule my appointment. Tell her we'll use her in Pharrell's new video, tell her anything, but don't let her drop me before I even get started."

"Okay. But damn, getting you pregnant was easier than scheduling time with Benita Perkins. And just so you know, stuff like *this* is why you pay me the big bucks."

"This time I agree with you. And please get me a bio on the congressional candidate Valen Bellamy. Meeting with this political wannabe had better be worth my risking *pre*partum depression. Pregnancy and hormonal bitch syndrome is a truly unsightly combination."

᠀᠀

The next day at 1:55 P.M., Pia was sitting in a conference room at the Marriott Marquis Hotel with four others, all from different areas in the music industry, waiting for Valen Bellamy. They spent the next twenty minutes chatting together about the latest gossip swirling around their business, but when the conversation moved to athletes turned rap stars, Pia politely bowed out, turning her attention to the hastily obtained biographical information Darlene had pulled off the Internet.

The fifty-two-year-old Valen T. Bellamy had earned both his undergraduate (international relations) and law degrees from Georgetown University. He also attended Britain's Oxford University on a Rhodes Scholarship. Currently serving out his term as New York State comptroller, Mr. Bellamy had been heavily recruited as a poster child for the new Republican party.

"I am so sorry to keep you good people waiting," a voice with notice-me impact rang out. The man behind it was tall and handsome and had an unmistakable aura of power surrounding him. With him was a woman, obviously an assistant, carrying a stack of black binders.

"Forgive me, but I had a last-minute phone call from my son with some wonderful personal news—looks like I'm going to be a grandfather," he explained as he circled the meeting table, clutching an accordion folder under his left arm and shaking hands with the right.

As the others offered their congratulations, Pia sat mentally doling out brownie points while waiting for him to reach her. It was obvious he'd also been briefed on everyone's title and company, which lent a natural, friendly air to his greetings—definitely a political asset. And his good looks didn't hurt either.

"Thank you for coming. I'm Valen," he said, offering an orthodontic masterpiece of Crest Whitestrips teeth as he extended his hand. No surname. Just his first, delivered in a quiet-storm voice that vibrated deliciously through various zones of her body. Pia was surprised by her strong physical attraction to this man. Though she'd returned to her celibate state following her encounter with Grand, apparently the floodgates had opened up.

"Pia Jamison."

"I unfortunately don't know your work firsthand, but I'm told you enjoy a stellar reputation." His charm was thick but genuine. No wonder his political future was on the fast track.

"Thank you," she replied as she studied his brown face framed by short salt-and-pepper hair. She found herself mesmerized by this grandpa-to-be's cute crow's-feet crinkling around the corners of his smiling gray eyes. Why were the same fine lines that sent women in frantic search for Botox needles so damn sexy on men? Life just wasn't fair.

She tried not to gawk as Valen pulled out his notes and hastily prepared for his meeting. Once settled, he introduced his assistant, Melody, to the group and announced that she'd be taking notes.

"Thank you all for coming this afternoon to discuss a crisis that has hit our communities as hard as obesity, high blood pressure, black-on-black crime, and HIV/AIDS. Along with the supersizing of our fast food meals has come the supersizing of our appetites for hyper-sexuality, violence, and a blatant disrespect for ourselves and each other.

"Rappers boast about being the 'spot smacker and favorite macker' while proudly promoting the image of the pimp as a flamboyant beacon of power and wealth. In bookstores, displayed beneath signs marked African American Literature, are titles like *Ghetto Azz, Thug Livin',* and *Toxic Ho.* In millions of PlayStations and Xboxes are games where kids can watch strip shows, carjack soccer moms, and kill police officers.

"Our young people are experiencing a triple whammy of 'entertainment' sources that glorify violence and dangerous sex practices to the detriment of our collective sense of self-respect. And this is why I've asked you all to join me today.

"This is a fact-finding mission to gather ideas and information to shape my campaign platform: 'Respect Yourself, Be Respected.' My hope is that through awareness we can begin to reverse the negative cultural trends that are having an impact on our daily lives, for example, making heroines of women who make a living shaking their booties and servicing 'gangstas' who refer to them as 'tricks,' 'bitches,' and 'hos.' "

"Excuse me. I'm not a whore. I'm an actress," argued Jalese Chantal, a successful video girl. "Videos pay the bills while I advance my acting career."

"Man, we're selling a product . . . and everybody knows that sex sells everything else from cars to cameras. Why not music?" the hip-hop artist Playadoh added.

"Crack cocaine is a product. Shouldn't we be policing ourselves when it comes to all questionable and potentially harmful 'products'?" the candidate queried.

Pia could see that Valen Bellamy was quickly losing his congenial charm as he delved into this issue. It was clear that he was impassioned by the subject, but his passion was putting his audience, including Pia, on the defense.

"Let's not forget that we're in the business of producing and selling fantasy and entertainment," record producer Alison Black replied.

"The key word being *business*—and one that follows trends," video channel executive Tourè Peterson added. "So if our consumers like what's being supplied and keep asking for more, who are we to stop giving it to them? And by the way, I think this whole hypersexuality thing will eventually burn out once a new trend emerges."

"And while we wait for the trend to burn itself out, what about all the damage it's causing now? Ms. Jamison, you're in the business of producing these videos. What's your take on the subject?"

"My take is that the issue goes so much deeper. It's about how we raise our kids. Accountability and positive self-imagery starts at home."

"Which is why family values must be resurrected in our community," Valen inserted.

At the sound of that loaded phrase, which now felt like a personal attack on her own morality, Pia could feel her liberal sensibilities surfacing and could not resist turning the discussion political.

"Despite the fact that politicians like yourself have tried to co-op and turn the idea of 'family values' into a narrow discussion of conservative sensibilities, the root of the problem is not how we are portrayed on videos or in books, but how we each portray ourselves on a daily basis."

"And I don't see how you can tell me that what our children consume as entertainment on a daily basis does not affect how they behave," Valen shot back.

Was that a smirk? Did he just smirk at me? Pia wondered, feeling her ire rise. In her head, she heard the screeching sound of the brakes bringing an immediate halt to her initial attraction to this pompous ass.

"Around this table you have gathered together five black people, as if to say that respect or lack or respect is a problem only in our community," she continued.

"It cannot be disputed that the black family is in crisis," Valen argued. The others in the room were struck by the escalating debate between the two and sat back quietly, watching the drama unfold.

"Mr. Bellamy, the entire *American* family is in crisis. And as you pander to the black vote by simply drawing more attention to our problems but with no plan of action or budget to help solve them, I find it difficult to see you as anything more than an opportunist. Without action and money behind it, 'Respect Yourself, Be Respected' will prove to be just as *ineffective* as that last Republican-backed slogan-only campaign, 'Just Say No.' "

There's that damn smirk again. He thinks I'm funny?

"It may not be perfect, Ms. Jamison, but it is a start at taking back the demeaning images and destructive lifestyle choices disguised as art. Because until we start respecting ourselves, we will never be respected as a people and never be given the opportunities and credit we deserve for being contributing world citizens."

"That's something for *all* Americans to be concerned about. When is the GOP going to stop trashing America's image and its people so we can be respected by the rest of the world again, and not because we demanded it by pointing a gun in someone's face, but because we earned it by doing the world good?" Pia countered angrily.

"That is an entirely different discussion, Ms. Jamison. One I will gladly debate at another time. But as we are here to discuss specifically images in the media, I'd respectfully ask you stay on topic."

"It is clear, Mr. Bellamy, that you are here not to listen to our opinions but to merely give us yours. So, if you will excuse me, I must get back to work. Know that our discussion today has given me cause to think about how I can better do my part on this issue. So perhaps this afternoon was not a *total* waste of *my* time."

Pia gathered her things and quickly exited the room. Damn. It was truly disappointing to meet such an attractive and intelligent man and watch him turn into a total asshole because of his political views. If Valen Bellamy was the personified cliché of sex and politics making strange bedfellows, thank goodness she was back to being celibate.

Chapter Eighteen

Just to be sure, Becca took another long glance in the mirror. She barely recognized herself. If not for the familiar though astonished green eyes staring back at her, she'd swear she was looking at a stranger—a very *hot* stranger.

Gone were the frizzy curls that more often looked like a hair-don't than a hairdo. In its place were bone-straight locks cascading down her back, framing a more polished and dramatic face. All thanks to the wonder of the modern beauty industry—a transforming combo of relaxer and a ceramic flat iron; waxed and reshaped brows; and two hours spent at the Mac cosmetic counter, learning how to apply makeup like a pro.

Also abolished for the evening were her usual work clothes. Instead of the efficient receptionist uniform Rebecca donned each day—slacks and a top—*Becca* had her party clothes on. The outfit she'd chosen for her official WMS launch was a figure-skimming dress with a seductive twist shoulder and plunging neckline that attractively showcased her breasts and trademark starfish necklace, and a flirty, leg-enhancing asymmetrical flared skirt. It cost more than she could afford, but it was well worth the investment. Its color, that of Caribbean blue water, set off her natural golden tan, showcasing her exotic looks and burgeoning "sexual charisma." Gone too were the matronly pumps, replaced by the Pia Jamison–sanctioned strappy high heels.

This new look had been a work in progress since Becca's return from San Francisco. She'd come back to Chicago buoyed by her suc-

cess at the dash-dating event and ready to put her new flirting skills to
the test. Her first weekend home, she and her best friend, Cris Yang,
had hit Crème de la Crème, the favorite see-and-be-seen spot of the
young employees at the Bonaire Advertising Agency. She'd dressed in
the same jeans and tight sweater ensemble she'd worn to Suede, but
as usual, it was the Julie type hottie magnets who had commanded the
place and the attention.

After that less-than-successful evening, Becca had decided to tem-
porarily withdraw from the social scene. Largely fueling this decision
was the need to recuperate financially. The workshop in San
Francisco had drained her bank account, and she didn't have the
monetary resources to fund a proper social life. Not when drinks
were upwards of ten dollars a pop and her initial foray into Crème
had proven her wardrobe to be way less than effective. Now, several
months later, and after working all the overtime hours she could
manage, the monetary sinkhole she'd created by going out west had
been reduced to a more manageable pothole. And after hours poring
over fashion magazines, and with the help of Cris and his talented
friends, Rebecca's transformation was complete and Becca was ready
to roll.

"Rebecca, let's go," Cris prompted through the ladies' room door.
"Happy hour doesn't last forever."

"I told you, it's *Becca,*" she corrected Cris as she stepped past him.

"My bad. Give the girl a little fresh air and it's good-bye corn-
fields," he teased.

"Not every Iowan grows corn, you idiot."

"Touchy, touchy. Come on. If you're finally going to unleash all
that explosive weaponry across the Windy City, we'd better get a
move on."

Twenty minutes later they arrived at Crème de la Crème at the
peak of Friday's happy hour. As was the plan, both went their separate
ways. Becca walked into the sea of big-city sophistication and for the
first time ever, felt like she belonged. Her new look was attracting a
lot of coveted attention—from men and women alike—and she felt
her confidence level rising through the roof.

Smile, eyes, laugh, listen, she reminded herself, planting a slight smile
on her face as she began her slow trek around the room on her way

to the bar. The trail of eyes following her moving tail felt incredible, and for the first time in her life, Becca Vossel felt sexy, seductive, and powerful.

"You look like a girl who would like silk panties," a male voice suggested. Becca turned to find a young Sean Penn look-alike smiling coyly in her face.

Okay, that's real subtle, she thought, though she was oddly flattered. Preppy in a surfer dude kind of way, he wasn't really her type, but he was cute enough for Becca to practice on, to work the kinks out of her flirt game until something more interesting came along.

"Whoa. That's kinda personal, especially since I don't even know your name," Becca said, giving him Joey Clements's suggested three-second glance and closed-lip smirk.

"Gil," he said. "I didn't realize cocktail preferences were so personal—silk panties is a drink. Wait, you didn't think I would actually use such a cheesy pick-up line, did you?" he asked, his voice perfectly pitched between irony and sincerity.

Becca's response was delayed by a laugh and an exaggerated shoulder shrug. "I'm Becca."

"Pretty name for a pretty girl. So what can I get you to drink, Becca?"

"I'll have a ginger ale."

"Ginger ale is for kids, not sexy women. Come on, let me buy you a real drink," Gil pressed, winking at her.

"Okay," Becca relented, not wanting him to think she was neither grown nor sexy.

"Jimmy, a pair of silk panties."

Gil continued to stand beside her stool while they waited for their drinks. Becca could smell his woodsy cologne as she studied his one hand extended across the counter. He tapped his index finger, adorned with a thick sterling silver band, to the beat of the piped-in music.

"Whoa. I like your ring," Becca said. "What is that design?"

"Flames. Here, take a look," he said, putting his finger in his mouth and slowly removing the ring as he looked into her eyes. It was a move as seductive as it was sleazy, and Becca marveled at his audacity.

"Nice." Becca was saved from making any further comments by

the arrival of their cocktails. She was careful to sip her drink, but as had happened at Suede, within fifteen minutes the sweet drink of pure alcohol rushed straight to her head, leaving Becca feeling tipsy.

"So, sexy Becky, it's getting awfully noisy in here. I have access to the VIP lounge. Would you like to go upstairs so we can talk?" Gil asked, taking her right hand and running his left up her arm.

"Where?"

"Upstairs," Gil cut in, taking advantage of the noise and Becca's slightly altered state. "Now come on, sexy, let's go upstairs and be VIPs." Gil pulled her from the chair. "A hot girl like you shouldn't be down here with all the regulars. You're a superstar. You deserve special treatment."

Gil had said the two magic words—*hot* and *star*—that bent Becca's will and allowed her to acquiesce. The two climbed the stairs to the VIP lounge and were stopped by a velvet rope blocking entry. Gil flashed some kind of card and the bouncer pulled back the rope, giving them access to the dark and smoky private room. Scattered around the place were various conversation areas, occupied by couples and threesomes—some talking, others communicating in much more personal ways. Techno lounge music filled the space, and Becca could feel the pulse of the beat in her chest.

Gil led her over to a vacant love seat and ordered two more drinks. "Come closer so we can talk," he insisted. Becca smiled and scooted over until their hips were touching.

"Mmm, you smell good, like vanilla and chocolate," he said, brushing the hair off her shoulder and nuzzling her neck. "Makes me want to lick you," he buzzed in her ear. The pleasurable sensations that ran through Becca's body were also unsettling—as if her body shouldn't feel like this with someone she didn't know. "What kind of perfume is that?"

"I thought we came up to talk," she insisted in a soft voice, and accompanying her words with a gentle push.

"We are talking. I asked you a question."

"It's from Jessica Simpson's Desserts."

"Yummy," Gil said as he fiddled with the starfish dangling in her cleavage. His fingers made light contact with her breasts, sending more logic-blocking waves to her head.

"So, Gil, what do you like to do?" Becca asked, fighting to stay in control.

"Kiss pretty girls," he said as he leaned forward and covered her mouth with his. Becca was initially shocked by his action, but the part of her coaxing her to pull away was being out muscled by another insisting that she enjoy the moment. Her resistance soused, Becca had no choice but to relax and soak in the experience.

Uninvited but not spurned, a drunk Gil continued to explore Becca's mouth with a heavy tongue. His kiss was penetrating and very wet, and Becca found herself wanting to reach for a cocktail napkin. She tried to discreetly wipe the saliva from her chin with her hand as Gil began to kiss her neck and nibble her earlobe.

"You've got me so fucking turned on, Becky. Check it out," he suggested as he took her hand and placed it on his crotch. Becca felt Gil's erection through the denim and quickly removed her hand.

"I think I'd better go home now," she told him as she tried to will herself sober.

"Oh, Becky, please, no. I am so fucking hot right now. You did this to me," he said, cupping his hard dick. "You have to stay, please. Let's have a little fun. You are so amazing. Please. Don't leave now." There was a desperation in his voice that intrigued her. As she had all evening, Becca felt two disparate emotions—annoyed because he kept getting her name wrong but assumed she wanted to touch his crotch, and powerful because she had managed to excite a man to the point of begging. The idea had her curious, and she leaned in to Gil's body and delivered a long, passionate kiss, feeling him melt under her influence. Becca practiced kissing, experimenting with depth and intensity, judging their effectiveness by Gil's reactions. She allowed him to fondle her breasts through the fabric of her dress, thrilled not only by the arousal rising between her legs but the power blooming there as well.

It was as if she were having an out-of-body experience. As Becca sat on the couch in a public place, making out with a man she didn't know, Rebecca looked down, studying her technique, her body's reactions, and her basic state of mind.

"I gotta go," she insisted, pushing away after Gil's hand migrated beneath her dress.

Becca had had enough practical weapons training for today. It was time to go home. She'd come tonight to test her WMS skills, but through her encounter with Gil had found a new part of herself. This part was sexy and daring. This part could make a man beg. This part of her deserved further inspection, but with a man she wanted to kiss, not with one who simply took the liberty. Someone special.

Chapter Nineteen

"Flo, hi. It's Pia."

"Mornin', darlin'. What a great surprise."

"I wanted to call and say thanks for the pictures and see how you were doing."

"I'm fine, though goin' crazy right now. It's Dan's birthday and I'm doin' my red hot number tonight."

"Really?" Pia replied, her surprise evident. "I thought Dan wouldn't go for such a thing. What did you call him? A romantic Neanderthal?"

"I'm takin' a chance for sure, but I took Joey's advice and planned things more to his tastes, and there is nothing he finds more tasty than the Dallas Stars."

"Are they like the Cowboy cheerleaders?"

"No, darlin', the Stars is our pro hockey team."

"Red hot seduction and ice cold hockey. This just gets more interesting by the minute! All right, girl, let's break it down."

"Like I said, Dan loves the Stars. So for his birthday I rented out an entire suite at the American Airlines Center. It'll be just me and him and his favorite eats—or should I say, a more upscale version of them."

"Sounds like a perfect setup for a little one-on-one pucking—pun absolutely intended."

"Sugar, let's hope so."

"My, my, Ms. Flo. I thought Becca was the monster Joey created."

"It's like I told you in my letter: I'm gettin' a kick out of all this sensuality stuff. Joey was right, it's fun. It's like every day you wake up to a scavenger hunt, just lookin' for all the goodies the Lord and Mother Nature left for you to find. And what about you? You been spreadin' some of that cool charisma around the Big Apple?"

"In a manner of speaking. I did meet one interesting guy—a politician, but, well, nothing there. He's a bit of an asshole."

"Darlin', I thought you'd go back home hotter than a honeymoon hotel."

"Funny you should mention 'hot' and 'hotel,' " Pia hinted.

"Uh-oh."

"I wanted to wait until I was sure, but, well, I'm almost three months pregnant." Pia went on to tell Flo about Grand and their evening together and agreement to become parents. "At first I was a little freaked when I found out, but now I'm really happy."

"Well, pregnancy will do that. So what does this Grand fella think?"

There was a pause on the other end of the phone while Pia played with her necklace and tried to figure out how to break the news to Florence.

"He doesn't know. And you don't plan to tell him," Flo answered for her.

"Correct. But it's not like I tricked him or anything. We made an agreement that includes no contact until the first birthday, and then every birthday after, I'll send him an update. He can opt in at any time, but right now he's opting out, which is fine by me."

"This newfangled kinda parenthood takes some gettin' used to."

"I think it worked out in the best possible way."

"Darlin', this is a lot to digest in one day—particularly when I'm supposed to be fillin' my head and belly up with sensual and seductive things. How about I call you tomorrow and we'll discuss all angles of this then. But right now, I got a load of work to do to get ready for tonight."

"Oh, yeah, of course. But Flo, I'm doing the right thing, aren't I?" Pia asked, anxious for some positive maternal feedback, even if it was from a friend.

"Sugar, only you can decide that. But if this is what you want, I'll back you a hundred and fifty percent."

"Thanks, Flo. That's all I needed to hear. We'll talk soon. Enjoy tonight. Don't hurt Dan too bad."

Flo hung up the phone feeling as through Pia had gotten herself in one big mess. But there was no time to dwell on that now. She had to focus on herself and Dan and cleaning up her own muddle of a marriage.

Happy Birthday, Sugar!

Please Join Me
For a Starry Evening of

Sweets on Ice

To Celebrate 56 Years of
Living, Laughing, and Loving

Friday, May 19
Location to Be Announced

"Is the blindfold really necessary, Florence?" Dan asked for the umpteenth time.

"It's a surprise. Just go with the flow, man."

"I look like a jackass walking around the streets wearin' this thing."

"Darlin', you can't see how you look, so how would you know? Now, I can gag you too if you'd prefer," Flo suggested with a laugh. Even though her husband had complained since leaving the house, they were both enjoying her mysterious behavior.

"So I'm bein' kidnapped on my birthday?" Dan asked as he unknowingly walked through the private concourse of the American Airlines Center toward their suite.

"Yep."

"Can you at least give me a hint where you're takin' me?"

"Oh, absolutely I *can,* but I won't," Flo replied, continuing her playful torment. "I would suggest that if you stop complainin' and live in the moment, you might be able to deduce a few things for yourself."

Florence made the statement knowing it would be nearly impossible for Dan to figure things out. She'd arranged to have dinner served ninety minutes before the start of the hockey game so there would be few noises, smells, and other obvious signs pinpointing their location.

"Oh, there you go with that flower power talk again. I still don't get who's puttin' all that new age stuff in your head. Always talkin' about enjoyin' the world through your eyes and nose."

Flo brushed off his comments, not sure if they had crossed the line between teasing and complaining and not wanting to risk ruining her red hot surprise by guessing wrong. She knew that surprises were as popular with Dan as liver popsicles, but this was a special occasion and hopefully the start of a lot of new things.

"All right, I guess we can remove the blindfold and let you see where you are," she said as she led him across the threshold into the luxury box. Before Florence could react, Dan whipped off the black satin sleep mask she had purchased as part of their red hot night.

"What is all this?" Dan asked. A wide smile broke out on his face as he surveyed the party decorations and a small table set for a romantic dinner for two. Flo had supplemented the green, gold, and black balloons—the official Dallas Stars colors—with tea lights and yellow rose petals scattered around the suite. Each of the monitors in the sky box also had the animated words "Happy Birthday, Dan!" exploding across their screens. It was a mix of seduction and sports that managed to have mutually satisfying appeal to both husband and wife.

"Happy birthday, sugar," Florence shouted as she delivered a warm hug. Dan was not a man prone to expressing his emotions, but she could see that he was not only surprised but touched.

"Woman, what have you done?" he asked, smiling broadly as he continued to look around.

"It was all spelled out in the invite. Sweets on ice . . . starry evening . . . You're here in this lovely, *very private* luxury box to watch the Stars in their first playoff game and celebrate *any way* you see fit, darlin'. The night belongs to you."

"This is amazin'," Dan said as he gazed down at the now empty arena and ice rink. "You can't miss a thing from up here."

"Here you go," Flo said, joining him with two pilsner glasses, each filled with a shandy cocktail. She looked Dan straight in the eye and tried to hold his gaze as she'd learned. Dan smiled and quickly looked away, finding it more comfortable to put his attention toward the smoked oyster roll appetizer.

"A toast: Dan, may tonight be not only a celebration of your birth, but the birth of a new beginnin' for us as well. I love you, darlin'. Happy birthday." The two touched glasses before drinking.

"Whoo-wee. What is this?"

"Lemonade and lager beer. It's called a shandy. What do you think?"

"Interestin', but if you don't mind, I think I'll stick to straight beer."

"It's your night—you can have any darn thing you desire," Flo said, hiding her disappointment and anxiety behind a smile.

Well, that went over like a skunk at a picnic, Florence thought as she walked over to the bar area to replace Dan's drink. Apparently beer cocktails were all the rage, and she'd gambled on Dan's taste buds and lost. Hopefully dinner would be different. She'd worked closely with the chef to create a sumptuous and more sophisticated meal catering to her husband's tastes and comfort level. Tonight's seafood menu included shrimp and avocado quesadilla appetizers; a dinner of lobster tacos, yellow tomato salsa, and jicama salad; and for dessert a sexy fresh fruit and chocolate fondue—all foods Dan loved, but prepared with a more sensual twist.

"Here you go, sweetheart," she said, following her script for a red hot night and taking a seductive sip before handing the pilsner glass over to Dan. He gave her a brow-furled smile, which Flo decided was a cross between intrigue and surprise, as she'd never before had the audacity to drink from his glass. "Come with me," she cooed, taking his hand.

She led him over to the dinner table and, while trying to maintain eye contact, unfolded his napkin and placed it in his lap. She went back to the kitchen and plated their food, careful not to serve too much. Florence placed dinner on the table and before returning to her seat gave him an enticing kiss on the mouth.

Dan, feeling his penis stir, once again smiled with question marks in his eyes. In a surprising move that caught his wife totally off-guard, he raised his glass in a toast. "You know, I'm not really good at this kind of thing, Floey, but thank you for all of this. It's really nice and very special."

Florence tapped her glass against his, thrilled that he'd acknowledged and was touched by her effort. Dan's words set the tone for
harmonious dining. At first, she tried to use her WMS tricks—from
flirting to playing footsy—but stopped when it became glaringly apparent that Dan still didn't know how to relate to this unseen side of
his wife. Reminding herself to remain patient and flexible, Flo put
their red hot night on simmer and eventually they settled into amicable conversation. They covered everything from talking about the
boys to gossiping about the neighbors to trying to figure out what
model SUV they should buy next. With the help of good food and
drink, talk turned into laughter and laughter into hand-holding.
Florence sat back, happy that they'd returned to their comfortable old
ways, but also disappointed that Dan was not responding to her new
sensual side with the interest and vigor she'd hoped for.

Down below, they could hear the noises of the arena coming to
life. It was still forty minutes until the face-off and before Dan's attention was totally turned to his beloved Stars, Florence decided one
last time to try to engage his senses and his imagination.

"Time for birthday gifts." Flo walked over to the closet, where
she'd had the staff stow Dan's gifts. She removed from its hanger the
sinfully soft cotton bathrobe.

"Why don't you put this on?" she suggested, holding the robe like
a valet.

Dan, tipsy and willing to oblige his thoughtful wife, stood up and
turned his back to her, ready to slip his right arm through the sleeve.

"No, I mean, why don't you take your clothes off and slip into this.
You'll love the way it feels—like wrappin' up in a cloud," Flo said as
she reached up and began unbuttoning his shirt.

"Flo, I do not know what's gotten into you. I do appreciate all this,
but let's wait till we get home and take care of business properly. You
know, I'm just not built for this kinky kind of stuff. I don't want to
hurt your feelin's, but this is all kinda new for me," he added, reading
the rejection on her face.

"New and you like it, or new and you don't?" Flo harnessed her
courage to ask.

"I don't know—it's gonna take some time to get used to. You've
been actin' kinda different since I got home."

"Is that bad?"

"Not bad so much as different. It's given me cause to rethink my decision to leave. Hell, I don't think I'm cut out for the bachelor life anymore. Been married way too long."

"But you left because you said you were bored. We can't just ignore that. We have some things to work on. So maybe we should try startin' over," Flo suggested. "Start datin' each other and revisit everything in six months and see where we stand."

"I'm up for baby steps," Dan agreed before giving his wife a quick hug and a kiss.

The commotion of team introductions down on the ice pulled them apart, and Dan moved away from her to his front-row seat. "Floey, could you grab me another beer?"

Flo exhaled softly before heading over to the bar. She couldn't deny that she was disheartened that her intended evening had been more lukewarm than sizzling, but progress had been made. Dan had noticed the changes in her, and though he hadn't embraced them totally, he didn't seem to be totally put off by them.

He's right, we'll have to take it slow, she reminded herself. She would take the baby steps necessary to put her marriage back on course, but this time Florence Chase, now a weapon of mass seduction, would be stepping out in heels.

Chapter Twenty

Pia picked up line two, expecting to hear Florence's comical report of her evening out, but instead her ears were surprised by the sound of Valen Bellamy's voice.

"Good morning. I think it's time we finished up our discussion, don't you?"

"I thought we had done that," Pia replied. "Can you please hold for a moment?"

Pia put him on hold and picked up line one, let the location scout know she'd have to call her back, and counted to five before returning to Valen. She was pleased to hear from him, but only because she'd spent the past three weeks waiting for the call from her boss firing her for jeopardizing the company's future.

"I'm sorry. You were saying?"

"I was saying that I was very impressed with you and your insights on the topic we were discussing and I wanted to continue the dialogue."

"I see, though I find it interesting that based on our last meeting a man of your political leanings would find anything I had to say insightful."

"Well, sometimes the messenger can make the message much more palatable."

Okay, does he actually have the nerve to be flirting with me?

"Or cause a good message to get lost in a bad delivery."

"I suppose I deserve that. I apologize for what seemed to be an attack on you and your colleagues. But in all fairness, that was a fact-finding mission. I didn't have all the components in place, but I do now and I'm willing to fall on my sword, because I really do need you."

I need you. Pia hadn't heard those words from a man in a very long time, and they gave her an odd sense of satisfaction.

"I thought you made a great many sensible points, and as my campaign is about to be launched, I'd like to get your take on my ideas. How about it?"

"Wouldn't you rather your staff do that for you? As you learned at our last meeting, I have a tendency to tell it like I think it is."

"And that is one of the many things I already like about you. In my business there is an overabundance of yes-men. I don't need another. Come on, Pia, political parties aside, we both want to help our people, so please join me for breakfast tomorrow at eight."

A hundred different excuses for why she couldn't meet with him ran through her head, each batted away and discarded by the fact that her boss would be very unhappy if she said no.

"Well, Mr. Bellamy, when you campaign that effectively, how can I say no?"

"I'm not sure what I said to enlist your change of heart, but obviously it's something to figure out and remember when I'm stumping. I'll have my secretary call you with the address, and I will look forward to seeing you tomorrow."

"Okay. See you at eight."

"Pia?"

"Yes."

"Mr. Bellamy is my dad. Please call me Valen."

❧

Pia stood midblock on East Fifty-first Street, next to the Sutton Synagogue. She was confused. Valen's instructions, relayed through Dee, were to meet him at Greenacre for breakfast, but instead of a restaurant she walked into a pocket-size emerald green sanctuary. With each step forward, Pia's smile widened. Immediately she was drawn to the park's focal point—a huge waterfall cascading down the granite back wall. The falling water created a soothing barrier to the city sounds, eliciting a sense of solitude and privacy.

She stood mesmerized under a grove of honey locust trees, their fragile leaves forming a protective sunscreen and projecting lacy shadows across the stones underfoot. Hedges of fuchsia rhododendrons and white azaleas, supplemented by gorgeous blue and purple hydrangeas in big pots scattered around the park, provided bursts of color. The upper and main tiers were empty but for two singles, one reading the newspaper, the other meditating, both enjoying themselves in this awe-inspiring city oasis.

"It's beautiful, isn't it?" Valen asked, walking up beside her. "This is my favorite spot in the entire city. If you close your eyes, smell the flowers, and listen to the waterfall, you can almost believe that you're in some tropical paradise."

"You really do believe in serving the public, don't you?" Pia asked, begrudgingly impressed by Valen's sensual nature.

"Meaning?"

"Meaning that only a man dedicated to the public good would be willing to share something so beautiful. I've lived in Manhattan for years and never knew about this place. And now that I do, I'm not telling a soul. I'm keeping this amazing secret to myself."

"And you call yourself a Democrat," he teased. "Come, let's sit. I promised you breakfast, and as I aim to do with all my campaign pledges, I shall deliver." Valen led her past the small concession stand and toward the back of the park, then down a short flight of roped-off stairs. There behind the hedges and next to the waterfall was a table—the only one in the small park set with white linen, china, and silverware. At each place setting was a glossy white box tied with a red and white gingham bow.

Pia was stunned. This looked like a setup for a romantic date, not a business meal. Pia was savvy and experienced enough to know that any man who went the extra mile like this did so not because he was interested in a woman's ideas but simply because he was interested in the woman.

"You did this for me?" Pia asked as Valen helped her into the chair.

"You know how we politicians are—anything to get a vote. But in all truth, I do some of my best thinking here, and yes, I did want to share this with you. Mimosa?"

"Uh, no, thank you." Pia was confused and oddly touched that he'd wanted to share his favorite place with her. Where was the man she'd spent the afternoon sparring with not so long ago?

"You don't drink?"

"Not much lately. Watching my waistline," she offered. It was the truth, though for reasons other than Valen suspected.

The way he pursed his lips, it was clear to Pia that he had just swallowed a flirtatious comment. And though she was curious, it was probably for the best that she not know what he was thinking. If his thoughts were running parallel to hers, the idea of sharing a romantic breakfast in this beautiful setting should be sending the same uneasy chill down his spine that was currently zipping down hers.

Pia quickly tried to assess her feelings. It wasn't fear that was confusing her; it was something much more dangerous—the delicious agitation caused by the potent mixture of intellectual interest and overwhelming physical attraction to the wrong man.

"I think I owe you an apology," Pia said, commanding her brain to focus. "I was pretty rude walking away from your meeting like that."

"Apology accepted. And I offer the same. Sometimes passion can get the best of you," Valen said in a voice equal parts sincerity and innuendo. So equal, Pia wasn't sure whether he was once again flirting.

"So that's why you . . . well, you smirked at me."

"Smirked?"

"Yes. Smirked. Every time I said something you got his look . . . a smirk . . . on your face, as if what I was saying was so totally off-base that it was . . . cute or something."

Valen's face broke out into a crooked smile.

"That's it! That's the smirk!" Pia declared.

"I don't know what my face is showing, but my mind is and was thinking, *This is really a bright and interesting woman.* So any smirking was strictly complimentary."

Okay, he's flirting, Pia thought through her grin.

"May I ask you a question?" she said, choosing to reside on the side of mystery and ignore his comment altogether. "Why politics?"

"I think it was my mother's influence above all else. Whether the Boy Scouts or PTA or Jack and Jill, she was always involved in some sort of leadership position. She said by leading she was sure to make a difference."

"So what kind of difference do you want to make?"

"I want to give our people options beyond political parties—real options. We need to teach our folk that choice goes beyond someone holding out their hands and saying, 'Pick one.' And Easter Elizabeth Bellamy was all about creating options."

"Easter?"

"She was born on Easter Sunday and my grandmother thought it was the perfect name. My mother decided to continue the holiday tradition with me."

"So Valen is short for Valentine?" Pia asked, drawn again to the gray eyes behind his glasses.

"Yes. My birthday is February fourteenth."

"Well, it could be worse—she could have named you Cupid. So you don't have any other siblings named Christmas or Cinco de Mayo, do you?" Pia asked, smiling broadly.

"No. I do have one sister named Tina. She was unfortunately born on a regular old Tuesday."

"And your son?"

"Well, he in fact was born on Arbor Day. So in keeping with family tradition, he's named Spruce Sapling Bellamy."

Valen's delivery was so deadpan, Pia didn't know how to react. It wasn't until he burst out in warm laughter that she realized he was joking.

"His name is Robert. Maybe we should eat before this gets cold," Valen suggested, with a chuckle.

"This is all very thoughtful," Pia commented as she untied the gingham ribbon and opened her box to find a gourmet breakfast of a shrimp and crab burrito and fresh fruit.

"I hope you don't mind. I took the liberty of ordering for you."

"Not at all. It's wonderful . . ." A briny whiff of seafood hit Pia's pregnant nose with a vengeance. She quickly closed the box, hoping to stop the smell and the swell of nausea creeping up on her.

"You don't like shrimp?"

"I'm allergic to shellfish," Pia fibbed, hating to lie but feeling she had no other option. It was rare enough that a man made this kind of effort, and she hated to crush his enthusiasm. "But it looks lovely, and I do so appreciate your thought."

"Thoughts are nice, but they won't feed you," Valen said, obviously disheartened. "Looks like I've got two strikes already—you don't drink and you don't eat shellfish. My batting average is looking pretty dismal this morning."

"Do you think the concession stand over there serves tea and maybe an English muffin?" she asked, trying to salvage his ego and her stomach.

"I'll go check."

Pia closed her eyes until the wave of discomfort passed. Then she concentrated on the park sounds, merging her thoughts with the rumble of falling water.

She was impressed that Valen hadn't done the typical restaurant thing. She liked that he had instead exercised his creativity and sensual side when picking out this tiny paradise to share with her. His attention to detail said a lot about him, and it was telling Pia that she definitely needed to know him better.

Valen Bellamy was smart, attractive, sexy, creative, attentive, and caring. Did it get any better? She had definitely misjudged him following their first meeting. After this morning's conversation, it was clear that despite the differences in their political leanings, at the core they both cared about their people, their country, and their world—so why was he unattached and a Republican?

Stop. Not an option. He's a conservative man running for office and you're a liberal single woman having a familiar stranger's baby. You're oil and water. Chocolate and beetles. Santa Claus and Chanukah. Two entities that do not mix.

Valen returned with her requested order. Once they'd eaten a few bites in companionable silence, Pia felt the need to learn more about his personal side.

"So, are you excited about becoming a grandfather? This is your first, right?"

"Yes, Robbie is my only child and he and his wife are expecting in late November."

Me too, Pia informed him through her eyes.

"Your wife must be really excited," despite his open flirtation, Pia had to know.

"Ex-wife. I've been divorced for twelve years."

"And never remarried?"

"No. I ended a long-term relationship with a lovely woman about three years ago. We were good together, but marriage wasn't in our cards. She wasn't interested in my political ambitions. Didn't want to be caught up in the scrutiny of politics. I came to learn later that she probably did me a favor."

"If you don't mind me asking, why do you say that?"

"Let's just say that there were things in her past that didn't mesh well with a public life. And I know that sounds harsh, but unfortunately, in the current political climate it's one of the things a politician has to think about."

Valen's answer sent a blast of discomfort through her.

"What about you? Ever been married?"

"No. Guess I've been too busy with my own career aspirations. My kind of job—irregular hours, lots of traveling—doesn't lend itself to the traditional lifestyle."

"I know that feeling well. No desire to ever have a husband or kids?"

"Never say never, right?" Pia said, deciding to dodge that hot topic and redirect their discussion. "So, Valen. You've explained your passion for politics, but why—"

"Am I a Republican?"

"Well, yes."

"Because it's political suicide for all of us to be in one party. For all the decades of support that black folks have thrown blindly at Democrats, what have they gotten in return? We still rank at the bottom of everything, from education to employment to life expectancy," Valen stated in a voice that let her know he'd been down this line of questioning many times before.

"But what about GOP politics do you find attractive?"

"Fighting terror, strong family values, empowering the individual. It's more important to teach a man to fish rather than give it to him on a plate in some soup kitchen."

"But it seems that under the banner of 'individual empowerment' your party seems content to make political decisions based on what's good for the one and not the many. They forget about the rest of our folks languishing at the bottom or struggling in the middle," Pia said, her indignation rising.

"Pia, just because I am a black Republican doesn't mean I stopped caring about black people. If things are going to change, sometimes the fight has to come from the inside as well. My goal is to engage our people in such a way that everyone benefits. Hopefully I'll be one more nonpartisan voice trying to do the right thing."

"But . . ."

"Why don't we agree to disagree and leave politics alone for a minute? Is that okay?" Valen could feel the conversation about to explode into a repeat of their last meeting, and it was the last thing he wanted to happen today. He needed to change the topic and change it fast.

"Okay," Pia agreed. It was much too beautiful a day to spend it arguing over political ideologies. "But you did want to talk about your program."

"And we will, but first, do you mind if I ask you a couple of personal questions?"

"Okay," Pia said, hearing the hesitation in her voice.

"Who's your favorite singer?"

"Sade."

"Good choice. Very sexy and elegant." *Like you,* he wanted to tell her, but he kept that to himself.

"What is this?"

"Just a quick way of knowing you better."

"Okay. Yours?"

"I'd have to say Stevie Wonder."

"*Have* to? As if you could go wrong with Stevie Wonder. The man is a musical genius. There is no better album than . . ."

"*Songs in the Key of Life,*" they said in unison.

"What's your favorite cut on the album?" Pia asked.

" 'Knocks Me Off My Feet' and 'As,' but I like them all."

"I can't disagree."

"Okay, we both have great taste in music. Now, this is important. What makes you smile?"

"Um, lots of things, but I guess I'd say natural beauty—both inner and outer. That and a seventy-five percent off sign in the Jimmy Choo store window. What makes you smile?" Pia asked, suddenly very curious.

"Blue, blue ocean water."

"Any ocean in particular?" Pia asked.

"The Indian Ocean. I am very partial to the waters off the Maldives. There's a resort there called the Reethi Rah where every view is just breathtaking."

"Hmm," Pia murmured, imagining herself there. "Where are you getting these questions?"

"Do you know how many interviews I've given over the years? I've been asked everything from my positions on Iraq and Iran to 'Boxers or briefs?' "

"So?" Pia asked with a mischievous glint in her eye.

"So, what?"

"Boxers or briefs?"

"Sorry. That's classified information," he joked back.

"I have a question," Pia declared. "What surprises you?"

"Unfortunately, not much surprises me these days. How about you?"

"The way my clothes shrink just hanging in my closet."

"Funny, girl. Anything else?"

"I guess how fate works," Pia said, thinking about the way her life was unfolding.

"Here's a question a reporter asked me last week. Answer with just one word. A man is powerful when he . . . ?"

Pia took a moment to think before replying. "Listens, though—no offense to your gender—it's tough to find a man who really listens. He may hear you, but it seems that rarely does he *listen*."

"Listens would be my answer too."

Without thought or provocation, Pia playfully reached over and punched Valen in his upper arm. It was an involuntary reaction, stored muscle memory from junior high, where every girl slugged her crush. "Get your own answer. You're just saying that because I did," she accused him, her entire body suddenly in automatic flirt mode.

"No, really. We just happen to once again agree. Think of it as a happy bipartisan moment. Okay, when is a woman powerful?"

"That's a tough one," Pia said, taking time to think. "I'd have to say when she's natural and doesn't try too hard. When do you think a woman is most powerful?"

"When she loves," Valen said, briefly looking into her eyes before dropping his.

There was no doubt that something was happening between them. Despite his untenable political leanings, Pia was beginning to like this man, and the idea was making her extremely uncomfortable. He was a refreshing change from the usual characters she knew. And he was giving every indication that he liked her back. Suddenly the comfortable, playful feeling she'd had earlier was gone, replaced by the need to vacate this beautiful place and the company of this far too interesting and handsome man. Attracted as she might be, Pia saw no reason to explore a potential coupling that had DOOMED stamped across its welcome mat.

❧

"So let me get this straight," Dee said, dropping a folder full of information on Valen's campaign that they'd never gotten around to discussing. It landed on Pia's desk with a thud that seemed to accentuate the mood of their conversation.

"You were having a great time, best date you've had in years, and you decided you simply needed to bolt."

"Yep," Pia said, pretending to be too preoccupied with work to have this conversation. She hoped in vain that Darlene would get the hint and skedaddle.

"*Plus* you think he's an all-around great guy and a major catch."

"Uh-huh."

"*And* he gave you the distinct impression that he'd love to get to know you *a lot* better, like up close and real personal, but you want me to screen all his calls. No phone, no e-mails, no communication of any kind."

"Yep."

"*Chica,* I do not get you. You ace the workshop, finally start acting like a girl again, get asked on a second date—and by some rich, successful guy, mind you—but you have no interest in him. Just tell me one more time—why?"

"It's not so difficult to understand, Darlene. I accomplished my goal, which was to get pregnant, but that's it. I'm not interested in hooking up with anyone, at least not now. And particularly not with a man who is running for the U.S. Senate on a Republican platform that touts a bunch of conservative viewpoints including strong 'family values.' "

"So that's it. You just give up?"

"Yep. Better to quit now while I can."

Chapter Twenty-one

"What exactly are you searching for?" Cris asked as he trailed Becca at the Golden Pagoda jewelry counter.

"I'm looking for a cool ring. Something that's interesting and draws attention," Becca said, continuing to inspect the tray of rings.

"Like this?" Cris asked, handing Becca a gold band.

"Whoa—this is beautiful. It's like a piece of sculpture," Becca said, immediately falling in love with the piece. Cast in gold was a nude, three-dimensional woman stretched luxuriously across the band, smelling a bouquet of flowers.

"It's perfect," she cooed, slipping it on the middle finger of her right hand. There was something magic about this ring that suddenly made Joey's whole trademark icon explanation make sense. The artsy band of gold immediately made her feel connected to her sensual self, and just viewing it on her hand reminded Becca of the woman she wanted to be. "It's also a hundred and fifty dollars," Becca said, sneaking a peek at the price tag.

"Marked down from three hundred," Cris pointed out. "Get it. You'll never see anything like it again."

Cris was right. It was unique and sexy—just as she aspired to be. Becca really couldn't afford it, but it was too perfect and made her feel too good to leave behind.

"I wish you were coming with me tonight," she said as they waited for the clerk to approve her credit.

"I know, but it's Phil's birthday, and he's got his heart set on celebrating at Rumba's. I still think you should go with Heather or Angelique. Why go by yourself?"

Because I don't need the competition, she wanted to inform her friend, but didn't. "I'll be fine."

෨৯

Becca, dressed in her supersexy blue dress and sporting her new jewelry, purposely arrived at the opening of Uptown fashionably late. She'd learned from the comings and goings of all her celebrity idols that no socialite worth her one hundred pounds would ever come to an opening on time. Outside the door, trapped behind a velvet rope and a burley bouncer, was a crowd of folks clamoring to be admitted.

"If you don't have an invitation, you're not getting in," the bouncer's voice boomed over the throng. At that, several people gave up in defeat and walked away, thinning the crowd enough for Becca to make her way to the front with minimal effort. Pulling out her best imitation Paris Hilton smirk and Naomi Campbell vamp, Becca strutted up to the bouncer and gave him a bold wink.

The door man gave Becca an *I'd like to tap that ass* once-over, licked his lips, and unclipped the rope, allowing her access. Becca could hear the disappointed smacks and lust-hungry moans of those left on the sidewalk. Funny, before the WMS workshop, she would have been standing among them. But now, after her experience with the sweet power of whip appeal, there was no stopping her.

Walking through the crowded club, Becca enjoyed but ignored the looks and suggestive comments as she made her way to the bar, which was jammed with women of every color and size.

Must be ladies' night, she decided before her mouth gaped open when her eyes got a look at the reason these chicks were all jockeying for position.

Nico Jones—obviously Chicago's sexiest bartender—was Eve's restitution to all the women she'd kept out of Eden for trying to sauté Adam's apple. He was handsome and charming, and, unlike the first man on earth, he thrived on temptation—as witnessed by the constant flow of propositions he was receiving.

It wasn't his tight muscular frame, built up to medium height and dipped-in-chocolate brown skin, or his flowing shoulder-length locks that were most appealing. It was Nico's charismatic display of boyish (*I need your doting mother-love*) charm and manly (*as long as you're a*

MILF) sex appeal that was such a damn turn-on. That and his eyes, which tilted downward and could read sad and needy when his sparkling white smile was not on display. That body, that charm, those eyes—you just wanted to draw him to your breast and perform the most unspeakable acts while he was there.

Becca stood shrouded in the shadows, studying the bevy of sizzling chicks surrounding this magnificent specimen. They were a rainbow of races and colors and with various body types, all trying to command Nico's attention.

Becca suddenly felt all the air rush out of the room when the object of her obsession turned, flashed his heavenly grin in her direction, and began walking toward her. Becca felt the contents of her stomach drop and with it all her earlier confidence.

Oh my God, he is beautiful. Don't blow it. Remember lessons learned. Be cool. Sexy, crazy, cool. In the few seconds it took for him to reach her, the combination of thoughts, instructions, and advice flooded through Becca's mind, overwhelming her speech center. They were finally face-to-face, and all she could manage was a nervous smile.

"So what's your pleasure?" His rich baritone voice melted over her.

Becca tried to sneak a deep breath before answering. Sucking in renewed confidence as well as oxygen, she replied, "Silk panties," then watched in silent glee as her answer caused a noticeable twitch of Nico's full, luscious lips.

"Nice," he replied, a wink in his voice, before walking away to mix her drink.

Becca took the time to breathe and regroup. Another new discovery: Self-assurance was easy to manufacture when the man in question wasn't relevant. But when he mattered, confidence was more of a hide-and-seek proposition.

She watched as he mixed her cocktail and then became distracted by the throng of partyers looking to get their buzz on. Becca checked her watch. It was twelve-thirty. Hopefully the crowd would soon begin to thin and she'd have an opportunity to talk with Nico.

"Sorry for the wait. It's crazy tonight," Nico shouted over the pulsating music and noisy hubbub of voices as he delivered her drink.

"It's okay. I'm Becca," she said loudly, leaning over the bar and giving him an unobstructed view of her cleavage.

"Nico Jones," he said, nodding and smiling. "Don't go away. I'll be back."

Nico returned to his bartending duties, leaving Becca plenty of time to watch, fantasize, and nurse her drink. Every now and again, she'd catch his eye, smile, and manage to hold his attention until it was needed elsewhere. They played this game of peekaboo for about twenty minutes until Becca noticed some other woman holding Nico's attention for longer than she found comfortable. She had to do something.

Becca watched and waited until Nico looked back in her direction. As she waved him over, she had no idea what she was going to say or do, but getting him away from the redhead and back to her side of the bar was paramount. Once he was there, she'd figure something out.

"What is your pleasure?" he asked. At that moment, Becca was glad he could not read her mind.

"A glass of water, please," Becca requested while running her finger around the rim of her cocktail glass, just as she'd seen Julie do.

"Nice ring. Is that a panther?" he asked, taking her hand.

"No—here, take a closer look," she suggested as her next move revealed itself. Becca gently extricated her hand from his grasp, put her finger between her lips, and, looking squarely in his eyes, pulled the ring off in her mouth. Reaching for his hand, Becca plucked the band from her tongue and placed it in Nico's palm.

"Nice," Nico repeated. Becca wasn't sure if he was referring to her jewelry or her antic. "And very sexy," he stated, placing the ring back on her finger while lightly caressing her palm. His touch released an icy hot shower of desire throughout her body, causing her to inhale sharply.

"Thanks," she said, unable to think of a clever reply.

"So, um—"

"Becca."

"Right. I'm almost done here. Why don't you wait for me," he said.

It took every bit of willpower Becca had not to jump over to the other side of the bar and scream, "YES!"—especially after noticing the jealous eyes and ruffled feathers around her. So many times she'd been the owner of those envious eyes—to be the one being envied felt golden. Tonight Becca had the chance to be the hot girl who left with the hot guy. But the avalanche of voices that suddenly overwhelmed her head dampened her delight.

There's a difference between flirting and teasing, Joey's voice rang out in her head.

You've got a new look and an entirely different sales pitch, Pia's added.

Even Mike from Suede made an appearance, his pushy, up-against-the-wall come-on rushing to her memory's forefront. He had refused to take no for an answer, sure that "No" meant "Try harder." Would Nico be the same way?

Maybe she was a little out of her league, and certainly she was not as experienced as her actions would imply. Becca needed to slow this train down a bit, but the line behind her waiting to board was long and full of eager riders. Would there be a second chance if she declined?

Nico returned, his eyes full of promise and expectations. "So, are we going to hook up?"

"Hmm—Nico, I wish we could. But I actually came with somebody."

"You're sure?" he asked, tucking his bottom lip behind his upper teeth, a nearly impossible-to-resist gesture.

"Yeah, but here's my number," she said, writing her cell phone number down on a cocktail napkin. "Call me and we'll hook up soon," Becca said, sliding the paper toward him.

Nico took the napkin, folded it, and put it in his pocket.

"You'll call me, right?" Becca asked, hoping she didn't sound desperate.

"Sure." Nico Jones winked and walked away, leaving Becca high on a cloud of silk panties and great expectations.

Chapter Twenty-two

"Downward-facing dog is a perfect pose to help with overall energy," Benita said as she gently lifted Pia's hips toward the ceiling. "I do not, however, recommend this once you're in the third trimester."

On all fours in the middle of her office, Pia tried to calm herself by breathing deeply and silently pushing away her anxieties. Switching into child's pose, she sat on her legs and with torso and arms stretched over her head, rested her body and tried to figure out how she'd gotten into the uncomfortable position of being the company mouthpiece for issues important to Valen Bellamy.

Harmon Goldstone's request—rather, demand—prior to Benita's arrival was really putting a strain on her so far successful attempt to ignore Valen Bellamy's advances. Until now, things had gone fairly smoothly. In her two meetings with the candidate, she'd represented herself and the company well, so well that following their breakfast in Greenacre Park a spray of every purple flower in Mother Nature's garden arrived. A secretly thrilled Pia, touched by his thoughtfulness, did not want to encourage his attention. It killed her to send an official note thanking him and requesting that he cease sending gifts. And after two weeks of her refusing to answer any of his calls or e-mails, Valen finally got the message and ended his campaign for her attention while escalading his bid for the U.S. Senate.

Just because she refused to see him didn't mean that Pia had not been actively following Valen's stumping. In the latest poll, just five months away from the midterm election, he was still trailing behind the popular Democratic incumbent by twelve percentage points, but he was making steady progress. His campaign speeches extolling the benefits of four of the five pillars of the Bellamy Plan, which called for fiscal responsibility, energy independence, and education and health reforms, were gaining impact throughout the state. Pia had been waiting to hear the announcement regarding his family values tenet, but no public unveiling had been forthcoming. She now knew why.

After nearly a month of hearing nothing further on the issue, Harmon Goldstone was back to unwittingly pushing the two of them together. And this time he'd upped the pressure significantly.

Reston T. Walker, a staunch Republican and New York media mogul, was keenly interested in not only the purchase of SunFire but also the success of his party's candidate. Now, in a move instigated by Walker's office, the SunFire PR department had decided to coordinate an event, a VIP fundraiser hosted by Pia, at which Valen Bellamy would announce his "Respect Yourself, Be Respected" campaign. The only hiccup in the plan was Valen's refusal to participate. Harmon's phone call this morning had been a direct order for Pia to persuade him to appear.

Now, after totally blowing off Valen Bellamy—both his thoughtfulness and his politics—Pia felt as if she were dangling from the high wire by her big toe, and she was hoping like hell that the man would at least agree to see her.

"Keep breathing," Benita said as Pia struggled to maintain her form. "Okay, let's get into your relaxation position," she then instructed. Pia lay on her left side and tried to clear her mind and simply relax into the moment. God knew she was going to need this calm to take her through the rest of the day.

Twenty minutes later, Benita was off to her next client and Pia was back at her desk, going over budgets for the Pharrell shoot. As usual, the phone was ringing nonstop, and each time it rang Pia tensed, reminded that she really needed to place *the* call.

She pulled from her desk the card with Valen's private cell number. She stalled another few minutes, keeping herself busy by turning the card over and over again in her hand. The buzz of the intercom interrupted her mental preparation.

"Yes?"

"*Chica,* just call the dude," Dee's voice insisted.

"What are you doing? Watching me through the walls?"

"Yeah, so watch what you're doing under your desk," Dee ribbed.

"Nasty freak," Pia responded, laughing.

"Celibate chicken. Just call him."

"I will, and for the record I can't be so celibate. I'm thirteen weeks pregnant and my name is not Mary."

"And how do I know this for sure? You're not showing. For all I know you cooked up this story to make me believe you finally had sex."

"You're nuts. Stop bothering me with your insanity. Don't you have work to do?"

Pia turned off the intercom and before she could talk herself out of it dialed Valen's phone number. It rang twice before she hung up. She got up and crossed the room to the water dispenser and filled her glass before the buzz of the intercom called Pia back to her desk.

"Yes, Darlene."

"Valen Bellamy is on line one."

"But how? The phone didn't ring."

"I know."

"Why did you call him?"

"Because you were being such a weenie about it, and if this doesn't happen then Harmon is going to fire you, and if you get fired I lose my job and then Hector won't get the car I've decided to buy him as a welcome home gift. So, I repeat: Valen Bellamy is on line one."

"Tell him I'll call him back."

"I can't do that. *You* called him. Now, for once in your sorry, no-dating life, pick up the phone and talk to him. If you don't, I'll tell him you can't come to the phone because you're having a hysterical pregnancy."

"You are so fired," Pia said, shutting off the intercom and taking a deep breath. She counted to three and picked up the extension. "Hello, Valen."

"I was beginning to think that you'd called and put me on hold just to reiterate that you weren't speaking to me," he said. Pia's brain went into overdrive trying to decipher his tone. She couldn't tell if he was pissed or disinterested, but either one could be a death knell to the mission at hand.

"Sorry about the wait. I had to deal with someone in my office. How are you?"

"Confused," Valen said, not giving an inch.

"And you have every right to be. That's why I'm calling."

"Really?" he said, his voice thawing ever so slightly.

"Yes. You were so thoughtful about sharing your favorite spot in New York with me. I thought I should at least reciprocate."

"I'm listening," Valen said.

"Will you meet me tomorrow night?"

"What's tomorrow? May twentieth? Sorry, I'm in Buffalo."

"Thursday? Any time is good for me."

"I'm on campaign stops in Westchester County all day, and then back in Manhattan for a black-tie fundraiser at the Metropolitan Museum of Art. My schedule is out of control for the next two weeks—make that five months."

Pia hadn't fully recognized his scheduling constraints, and time was running out. If she didn't get him nailed down quickly, the date would be gone and so might she.

"What time is your event at the Met over?"

"Probably around eleven."

"How about you meet me afterward?"

Pia's suggestion was met with a sigh and an elephant-size pregnant pause. A thousand reasons that he might turn her down ran through her head. She was trying to decide between spite and another woman when his voice, turning from professional politician to scorned suitor, assaulted her ear.

"You know, Pia, the truth of the matter is that I'm no longer interested. I appreciate all of your help, and I wish you the very best. Take care." And with that he was gone.

"Damn" was all she could say as she hung up the phone. She was embarrassed by his rejection but at the same time more determined than ever. Yes, her job may be on the line, but now so was her pride. As far as she was concerned, Valen Bellamy had just issued a challenge, and immediately Pia decided on her strategy. He might be pissed and his ego bruised, but he liked her and she would make full use of her tactical advantage. Pia intended to pull out and dust off every last one of her feminine wiles and use them to bring Valen to his knees.

*Okay, Pia Jamison, weapon of mass seduction, it's time to get your flirt on.
And Mr. Bellamy, find your white handkerchief and hunker down, 'cause
brotha, it's on!*

She swung her chair around to her computer and went online.
Within minutes, she'd found the perfect image.

"Dee, come here," she requested.

"What's wrong?" Dee asked, scurrying into Pia's office.

"Nothing's wrong. I need you to take this to the art department
and tell them I need an eight-by-ten by five o'clock," Pia said, handing her the computer printout.

"This is beautiful. What's this all about?"

"We've just declared war on Valen Bellamy."

"You two just get more interesting by the minute. Oh, Becca
Vossel is on the phone. She says it's personal," Dee informed her.

"I was just talking about her last week. Ask her to hold a minute."
Pia wanted the time to decide whether to reveal her big news.

Why not? she decided.

"Hi, Becca, sorry about the wait. I was in the middle of something."

"Do you want me to call back?"

"No, girl, this is actually a perfect time to chat. I don't have to be
at a lunch meeting for another half an hour. How are you doing?"

"I'm good. How about you?" Becca asked.

"I'm pregnant. Due in November and really happy."

"Whoa. I guess that workshop worked for you after all."

"It did. How's it working for you?" Pia asked, ready to move the
conversation forward.

"Okay, I guess. I just need a little advice. I met this bartender, Nico
Jones," Becca said, telling Pia the story of their meeting while leaving
out most of the sordid details. She knew Pia wouldn't approve of the
silk panties drink or the ring trick, thinking they were seedy manipu-
lations designed to lead Nico down a road that Becca may not be
ready to walk. But they got her noticed and brought home one very
pertinent point that Pia refused to consider: Guys her age—guys like
Nico—weren't sophisticated gentlemen looking for sophisticated
ladies. They wanted hot women who loved to party. "He's amazing
and I thought he liked me. I gave him my number, but he hasn't
called me and he said he would but it's been three weeks and I haven't

heard a word. I don't know if I should call him or not. So what did I do wrong?"

"Well, sorry to say it, but if a guy hasn't called you three weeks later, he's not going to. You have to chalk that up to one of those heat-of-the-moment things."

"That's what Cris said. He started quoting that stupid book, *He's Just Not That into You*."

"How can he be? You two just met. He barely knows you."

"But he seemed to really like me—you know, all the eye contact and smiling back," Becca insisted, refusing to follow Pia's logic. "And Pia, he's amazing."

"You keep saying that, but you never say what exactly is so amazing about him. I mean, how much time have you spent with him? Alone?"

"Not much. But I love the way I feel when I'm around him. When he looks and talks to me, he makes me feel like I'm the only girl there."

"He's a bartender. It's his job to flirt with the girls and buddy up with the guys. You said he wanted to hook up and he took your number but still hasn't called. It sounds like Nico was just trying to get into your panties."

Pia's words made something inside Becca snap. "And what if he is? And what if I just want to get into his?"

"If that was the case, why didn't you just stay and wait for him?"

"Because I didn't want to then. But what if I did? What's so bad about liking sex? And about wanting it even if you aren't in love? You sound like my mother: 'Only bad girls have sex outside of marriage, and the worst of them like it,' " Becca mocked. "Well, I don't want or need that kind of advice. I've had enough of that lecture to last a lifetime."

Becca's angry response put the brakes on Pia's preprogrammed speech on sex and morality. How many times in her two decades of having sex was irresistible lust the reason she'd dropped her drawers and her inhibitions? How old was she before she began supplementing her romance novels with erotic literature in a quest to balance out her good girl values with her bad girl desire? And how many years had it taken—celibate or otherwise—to realize that being a bit of a naughty girl could be a very nice thing?

Becca was right. She didn't need more lectures on how to preserve her saintly self; but rather, she needed to hear how to grow and maintain her sexual self in a healthy, responsible manner. The last thing the world needed was one more mixed-up woman whose sexual curiosity had been muted and turned into guilty timidity or, worse yet, raging promiscuity.

"Becca, you are so absolutely right. Girl, it's taken me twenty years to know what you're already beginning to figure out. You've got to live your own truth—not your parents', not your preacher's, and not some conservative political movement's. Ultimately, it's your life, and at the end of it you want *your* choices to be the ones that you lived to love or regret.

"So, here's my advice to you. On top of everything that you learned from the WMS workshop, here are two more things that you may find valuable: One, always trust your gut. If it doesn't feel right at decision time, it probably never will, so when in doubt . . . pass. And two, it's better to regret something you did than something you didn't do. If you remember the first, the second will usually work out."

"But what about calling Nico?"

"I still say no. Not a good strategic move. Go back to the bar and get him to notice you again. Keep some mystery about you. Men like a chase as long as they feel encouraged."

"Thanks, Pia."

"If Nico is what you want, go for it. Just always respect yourself and be clear about what you're getting into. Don't have too many expectations. And above all, Becca, safe is sexy. Be smart. These days lust can do more than change a girl," Pia said. "It can kill you."

Chapter Twenty-three

"Pia, Valen Bellamy is on the phone. What should I tell him?"

"Ask him to hold on for a minute," Pia instructed. While Valen held, she did a modified, seated version of the victory shuffle. It had taken him two days to respond, but she knew he wouldn't be able to resist her gesture.

"Pia Jamison," she answered, shutting down the glee and putting a little seductive edge on her tone.

"Okay, it worked. I'm smiling," Valen said.

"Well, you just sounded so grumpy the last time we talked, I had to think of something foolproof. So the photo of the Indian Ocean taken from your favorite resort is my peace offering to you."

"Like I said, it worked. Every time I look at it, my stress just melts away—at least for a second or two."

"It is beautiful. I just might have to go see it for myself."

"Well, it was a very gracious gesture. Was I really grumpy?" Valen asked.

"Oh, yes. Grumpy and cruel. You hurt my feelings, Mr. Bellamy," Pia said with just the right touch of coyness.

"Then I must find a way to make it up to you."

"Well, with your crazy schedule, I know it'll be weeks before you're available, so why don't we just call it even," Pia suggested, crossing her fingers while applying a little reverse psychology.

There was a beat of silence before Valen, unwittingly taking her bait, asked, "What are you doing tonight?"

"Nothing, actually, but I thought you had some fund-raiser to go to," Pia responded in a tone that held secret her glee.

"I know it's really short notice, and I apologize, but would you consider joining me? At least for a short time."

"You have somewhere else to be?" Pia asked.

"Hopefully. If I recall correctly, you extended an invitation for me to see your favorite city spot. Maybe we can slip out and you can take me there," he suggested, upping the ante.

"Well, I don't know. That invitation was extended before I saw your grumpy side," Pia teased.

"I promise, Ms. Jamison. My grumpy days are gone. So is it a date?"

"Yes, it's a date," Pia confirmed, though strangely uncomfortable saying the word. "What time and where shall we meet?"

"I have to jump, but Melody, my assistant, will get back to you. Pia, thanks again for the photograph."

"You're very welcome," she said, her broad smile proving she meant it. Though it had been a ploy for attention, she was glad he truly enjoyed her gift.

Chalk one up for the girls' team, Pia congratulated herself, hanging up and swirling around in her chair.

"Dee," she said, leaning into the intercom. "Can you please get me Carmen Grey, the PR and special events coordinator at the Empire State Building? She's in the file. We've worked with her before, on the Fantasia video. And then look up Nina Horton's number. I'm going to need her too."

Pia sat and waited for Darlene to inform her that the call had gone through. She put her hands behind her head and with her feet on her desk leaned back in the chair, smiling wide and very pleased with herself. Valen Bellamy wasn't the only one who could campaign hard when need be. And he certainly wasn't the only one who could plan one hell of a surprise.

❧

"Hello?"

"Hey, darlin'."

"Flo! Girl, how are you? That red hot night must have caught fire. I thought you were going to call me the next day. So how did it go?"

"Good, all things considered."

"Any hot pucking?" Pia asked, repeating her joke.

"No. Old Dan just wasn't quite ready for anythin' that kinky . . ." She paused, not sure she was ready to admit the defeat she was feeling.

"And?"

"And I think he was more excited by the hockey game than bein' with me. When it came time for the red hot part . . . well, let's just say the night cooled down considerably."

"I'm sorry, Flo. I know how much you were looking forward to it."

"It wasn't a complete bust. We agreed to start datin' again and see where we stand at the end of the year."

"Sounds like progress. Have you started yet?"

"Well, we went to dinner and a movie this past Tuesday. We had a good time, considerin'."

"There's that word again. Considering what?"

"Considerin' nothin' went as planned. I thought we'd try somethin' different like Thai food and then go see that Reese Witherspoon movie."

"Sounds fun so far. It's hard to go wrong with pad Thai noodles and Reese."

"Well, Dan decided he wanted to eat Tex-Mex—*again*—like he doesn't eat *that* six out of the seven days in a week. But I figured it was more important to have a good time than argue where my next five pounds were comin' from, so I agreed."

"Sounds reasonable," Pia replied.

"Yeah, 'cept he farted nonstop through the movie, but then that stunk too, so they kinda worked together."

"That movie got great reviews," Pia remarked between giggles.

"It did, but we didn't see it. When we got to the cinemaplex, Dan saw the new Nicholas Cage movie was playin'. He begged me to see that instead of 'some chick flick.' By that time I was too miffed to care. But the popcorn was good and Nicholas Cage is cute, even though he's more than a few macaronis short of a mosaic."

"I don't know what to tell you, Flo," Pia said, hoping her uncontrollable laughter didn't make her seem insensitive and uncaring, but Florence was damn funny.

"Darlin', there's nothin' to say except that's marriage to Daniel Jeb

Chase. At least we're spendin' time together. So enough about me and my sizzlin' love life. What about you? How you feelin' these days?"

"Good. The morning sickness has settled down, and even though I'm three months along, I'm still wearing my own clothes."

"The first time around, I was nearly seven months before I had to make the switch. By the third kid, I went straight from peein' on the stick into the cow clothes.

"And speakin' of keepin' things hidden for as long as you can, how's your politician doin'? Any more dates in the park?"

"No, but I'm seeing him tonight."

"So you two are datin' now."

"No. I mean, I like Valen. He's a very interesting man, but the only reason I'm seeing him again is because my boss stepped in and insisted."

"Your boss? I don't think so, sugar. Make no mistake, that was fate doin' the high steppin'."

❧

You're not even showing. Dee's words echoed through Pia's head. She was grateful for that fact, particularly now, as she zipped up her evening gown. She'd chosen an emerald green Grecian-styled empire waist dress for her night out with Valen. It was the perfect design, not only because it was fabulously fashionable but because of the way the silky accordion pleats flowed over her body, camouflaging any questionable bulge. Strappy high-heel sandals and a crystal-studded headband completed her ensemble. Pia smiled. She was pleased. She looked appropriately dignified and yet sexy.

After a quick touch-up to her makeup, she grabbed her purse and wrap and the brown envelopment tied neatly with a bow and bearing a tag with Valen's name on it. She'd worked hard to create the hand-made invitation, wanting it to look and feel special. Pia tried to convince herself that this was all about saving Reston Walker's event, but deep down she knew this was also about impressing a man who seemed so thoroughly impressed with her. It had been so long since Pia had experienced romance in her life that her soul was starved for the sweet thrill that came with such feelings. She knew it was only temporary, just for this one Cinderella night, but Pia was determined to savor every delicious moment this evening might bring and not worry about tomorrow until tomorrow arrived.

Pia headed downstairs to hail a cab. She climbed in and settled into the worn leather of the taxi seat. She could feel her stomach bubbling up, and for once it wasn't nausea. This was pure, unadulterated excitement causing her stomach to flutter. As much as she claimed the opposite to both Dee and Florence, she was looking forward to seeing Valen again. If everything went as planned, tonight was definitely going to be memorable.

The GOP candidate for the United States Senate had no idea what he was walking into later this evening. Thanks to some mighty string pulling, Pia was planning to top their breakfast at Greenacre Park, lovely as it was, in a big, big way. Pia was determined to make their one night together the best, most romantic *almost* affair to remember.

By the time Pia arrived at the Metropolitan Museum of Art, its majestic lobby, with its sky-high archways, impossibly tall ceilings, and stately columns lining the room, had been transformed into a cool and charismatic summer venue. White linen curtains, gently caressed by artfully placed fans, fluttered along the room's perimeter, brushing along the grove of palm trees that had been shipped in for the event.

It was nine-forty. She'd agreed to meet Valen at nine-thirty, but in a space teeming with designer-clad lawyers, financiers, businessmen, and other such power brokers accompanied by their bright and shiny escorts, it was difficult to immediately pinpoint Valen's location. Pia watched this multicultural crowd of semiprofessional philanthropists merrily talking, dancing, and drinking and suspected that this was probably the second or third such event they'd attended this week.

She found her way to the bar and requested a ginger ale and lime. Then a commotion drew her attention away from her people watching. Turning to the source of the bustle, Pia saw Valen and his small but obvious entourage enter the party. From the moment he stepped through the door, Pia watched him work the room with his campaign manager. Guided by Ed, Valen made the rounds, shaking hands, smiling brightly, laughing appropriately, and charming his supporters and potential voters. Ed would run interference, directing Valen toward those he had to speak to and away from others he perceived to be trouble. Eventually they made their way to the bar, and the sight of

Valen Bellamy walking toward her, with his suave, confident stride, made her stomach lurch with the kind of excitement reserved for kids on Christmas Eve.

Pia, remember what you're here for. Keep your eye on the prize.

It was impossible not to. The up-close view of Valen Bellamy was spectacular. While it was difficult for any man, no matter how unattractive, to look bad in a tuxedo, Valen wore the uniform exceptionally well. He looked as if he'd just stepped off the page of an Armani ad.

It was obvious the moment he spotted her. Pia watched as his tried-and-true candidate's smile grew wide into authentic personal delight.

Oh, this is going to be big fun, Pia decided. She took a deep breath, eliminating any nerves and revving up her flirting machine.

"Valen Bellamy, so glad to see you," a rough voice with a Don't-mess-with-me edge called out, interrupting their reunion.

"Reston. How are you?" Valen asked, returning his benefactor's hearty handshake. He glanced over the man's shoulder and was pleasantly unnerved to see Pia's eyes glued to him as she sipped her drink. He gave her a nearly indiscernible wink before turning his full attention back to his conversation.

"We should talk about the Bellamy Plan," Reston Walker said, clinging to Valen's hand for dear life. "And the big announcement coming up. We need to nail things down."

"We will. But not tonight. Please speak to Ed here and give him your ideas," Valen said, reclaiming his hand. "We'll chat very soon." Pia watched as he deftly stepped aside and behind his staffer, using Ed as a buffer so he could make a graceful exit. It was a skillful pas de deux the two had obviously performed countless times before.

With a head nod, Valen signaled to Pia to cross to the other side of the room. She joined him and for a frozen moment in time the two stood in a pool of mutual admiration, inspecting each other. Valen's eyes devoured Pia, starting from her sparkling headband to the red-tipped toes peeking from underneath her gown. Accompanying his gaze was a warm smile that was a mixture of manly appreciation and boyish delight.

"You look stunning," he told her, continuing to treat his eyes to her form.

"So do you."

"Thanks. I'm so glad you could come on such short notice," Valen said, reaching out to shake hands. It was clear from way he gently cradled her small hand with his larger one that this handshake was simply about protocol. She had the distinct impression that had they been alone his greeting would have been very different.

"I'm so glad you asked. It's interesting to watch you work, Senator."

"Not yet, but I'm glad you're thinking positively," he said, smiling again. At that moment flasbulbs went off, capturing the two of them on film. Valen graciously posed but gave a quick signal, and from seemingly nowhere Ed appeared and politely shooed the media away.

"Sorry. Occupational hazard."

"No problem. May I speak to you for a minute before you have to get back to work?"

"Sure."

"I need a favor."

"I don't think there's much I could deny you while you're wearing that dress," Valen flirted. Pia felt herself blush as she tucked her lower lip behind her teeth to keep her smile from floating off into the decorative breeze. It had been so long since a man had looked at her with such glowing intensity that Pia found herself savoring the attention.

"My company and Reston Walker are hosting an event in two weeks where they are hoping you will announce your 'Respect Yourself' campaign. I'm told you've refused to participate, and, well, I wanted to make sure you didn't say no because you were angry at me, because, well, you know—"

"Wait," Valen said, stopping her in midsentence. "You are beautiful, Pia Jamison. Beautiful and smart, sexy, and *real,* and those are all things I covet in a woman. But as attractive as I find you, I would never pass up such an important event just because my ego got bruised. If I did that every time someone shut the door in my face, I'd be in another line of business."

"So why did you say no?"

"I'm not really sure that I did. My staff may have been weighing other options. I can't honestly tell you," he explained. "I can tell you that if you're going to be there, I'll make it happen."

"Thank you, Valen. I can't tell you what great news this is," Pia replied. She knew his agreement would please Harmon and Reston, but Pia was surprised by the level of delight it brought her to know that another opportunity to see Valen awaited her.

Once again, a knowing tension took over the conversation, leaving them to communicate through their eyes and facial expressions. "Well, you have flesh to press and votes to win, so I'll leave you to your work," Pia said, breaking the silence.

"Have I won yours?" Valen asked with an *I dare you to say no* grin.

"That remains to be seen, Mr. Bellamy. There you go again."

"What?"

"You're smirking."

"Sorry," he offered, only smirking more.

"So, I'll just mill around here for bit longer and then go."

"But we haven't danced together yet," Valen said, not wanting to give up an opportunity to hold this captivating woman.

"Another time."

"We're still meeting later, right?"

"Of course."

"You haven't told me where."

"This will explain everything," Pia said, handing Valen the hand-made invite. "Put it in your pocket and promise not to read it until you're sitting in the back of your car."

Valen reached for the invitation and placed it in his breast pocket without breaking their gaze. "You're sure I can't open it now?"

"Absolutely not. It's all about the anticipation, Senator," Pia said looking away and once again biting her lower lip, a telling sign that Valen was getting to her. "I think you'd better go. Ed looks as if he's about to come drag you off by your hair."

"He's tenacious, but not so tough," Valen said, making them laugh and dispersing some of the energy engulfing them. "I'll see you soon. And Pia, once again, you're right."

"About?"

"The anticipation. It's killing me."

Chapter Twenty-four

Ninety minutes later, at 11:49 P.M., Valen climbed into the back of his black town car and closed the door, effectively shutting out the crazy world of political campaigning. He could not remember when he'd looked forward to the end of a party so much.

Since last October when he'd announced his run for the Senate, Valen's life had become a nonstop series of meetings, appearances, parties and powwows. As state comptroller, his schedule had been rough as well, but campaign life had definitely kicked the concept of all work and no play into a much higher gear. Tonight he wanted to play, and he wanted a playmate who intrigued and excited him. Pia Jamison was that woman. It was as if he'd been waiting forever for her to come into his life and fate had decided that now was the time, and tucked safely in his pocket was the place.

Valen reached into his jacket and retrieved Pia's invitation. He took a moment to examine the presentation. With its chocolate and blue satin bow and name tag, it looked more like a gift than an invitation. Little did she know that time away from the rigors of his dreams and responsibilities was the most precious present she could ever extend. Smiling at her thoughtfulness, Valen slipped the tie from the envelopment and opened the four flaps to reveal his destiny.

Thursday, May 21

"There must be something between us,
even if it's only an ocean."
—*Terry McKay,* **An Affair to Remember**

Your presence is
requested in the eighty-sixth-floor observatory
of the Empire State Building
350 Fifth Avenue
at midnight
for an evening to remember

"An evening to remember, indeed," Valen murmured, noting the date. "Mr. Lee, to the Empire State Building. And please, drive carefully."

On the ride over, Valen studied Pia's invitation, reading between every line to garner any hint about her feelings. *"There must be something between us, even if it's only an ocean."* Pia had chosen the perfect quote to describe his mind's ponderings. There was something solid but currently indefinable about what was happening between them, but whatever it was, it had definite possibilities. Were those possibilities ocean deep? Only time would tell. But right now Valen was ready and willing to wade out into the surf to find out.

He arrived at the New York landmark and to his surprise found the elevator door open and a glass of champagne awaiting his arrival. "Eighty-sixth floor," Valen requested, though he had the feeling the elevator operator already knew. Free from the constraints of public scrutiny, he gulped down the sparkling wine, hoping to sedate his nerves. He wasn't sure what awaited him, but whatever it was, Valen was already having a great time.

The doors opened and Valen stepped out into the warm night air to find a silent and completely deserted observatory deck. He checked his watch. He was only minutes late, so certainly she hadn't left. Perhaps she was running late. Valen stood paralyzed by indecision. Should he return to the lobby or wait for her here?

A flash of the movie on which this evening appeared to be themed ran through his mind. Would he be like Cary Grant, waiting in vain for a lover who never arrived? While Valen's logic didn't play out the whole cab accident scenario, he had to wonder if Pia, skittish as she'd been in the past, had changed her mind.

Off in the not too far distance a fluted rendition of Stevie Wonder's

"Knock Me Off My Feet" caught his ear. Valen turned and slowly walked toward the pleasantly haunting sound. Another wave of luscious anticipation swept over him as he approached the curve that led to other side of the deck.

As Valen made the turn he saw her standing at the rail, looking absolutely stunning, gazing out into the city lights. Through the miracle of connected friends, Pia had managed to turn the back corner of the observatory into a private and very romantic stage set for a lovely night of city gazing.

Nearby, a single, high bar table topped with flickering tea lights and flanked by two stools sat as focal point of this enchanting setup. The stools sat high enough to see over the rail and out into the impressive Manhattan skyline. Nina Horton, a popular jazz flautist and a friend of Pia's, sat in the shadows, physically removed from the scene, her music filling the spaces between conversation and the faint night sounds of the city below.

"I thought this would be a nice place for a nightcap," Pia said as he approached.

"This is your favorite spot in New York?" Valen asked, feeling his smile stretch wider than it had in years.

"It is tonight."

"Well, Ms. Jamison, you have managed to do something that nobody has done in a long time."

"What's that?"

"Surprise me."

"Good. Then maybe this really will be a night to remember."

"How did you manage all this?"

"You aren't the only one in this town with connections. The only caveat is that we have to be out of here by one o'clock, but that gives us nearly an hour to enjoy the view."

"And each other," Valen added.

"And each other," Pia repeated. "More champagne?" she asked, reaching into the wine bucket standing nearby and filling his empty glass.

"Thank you. Are you joining me?"

"Sparkling wine for you, sparkling water for me."

"It is so beautiful and peaceful up here," Valen remarked. "Thank you, Pia. This is such a needed respite. It seems I never get the chance to do anything normal people do anymore—go to the movies, read a good book, play Scrabble—you know, stuff that pals do together. You have no idea how much I appreciate your thoughtfulness."

And it was true. Pia could not know that there was nothing he coveted more these days than privacy. Most of the women he'd dated of late would have surprised him with dinner or drinks at some major Manhattan hot spot—more for the opportunity to see and be seen with him than to enjoy each other's company. Pia's planning of this quiet evening meant for just the two of them, away from the prying eyes of the public and press, made this night, and her, all the more special.

Pia smiled, pleased that he was pleased. The two once again lapsed into companionable silence, taking a moment to enjoy "I Am Singing," another Wonder selection from his favorite album.

"I'd be happy to pal around and do some normal stuff with you," she offered.

"I would like that very much. So, buddy, would you like to dance?" Valen asked, extending his hand.

Fifteen minutes into the next day, Valen Bellamy finally got what he'd been aching for since walking into the Metropolitan Museum several hours ago—to hold this lovely lady in his arms.

"Nice touch," he whispered in her ear.

Pia closed her eyes and took a second to enjoy the tickle of his breath on her ears.

"Can't go wrong with Stevie. Plus, I was feeling very competitive when I was planning this. You did such a lovely job with breakfast in the park that I had to step up big-time. Very impressive, Senator."

"Apparently not impressive enough, as instead of creating intrigue and interest, it seemed to cause your avoidance. What were you running from?"

Another pause while Pia contemplated her answer. Should she tell Valen the truth? That while her physical attraction to him had been immediate and strong, she'd chalked those feelings up to her parched libido? That she was not interested in falling for any man at this time, particularly one she knew she could never have? And that tonight was simply about achieving a professional goal while having a little personal fun?

Valen stopped dancing and widened the space between them so he could look at her. Tenderly lifting her face with his hand, he brought her eyes to his. "Pia, I asked you a question. What were you running from?"

Influenced by this fantasy environment and the warmth of Valen's embrace, and thoroughly enjoying the close proximity of his manly smell and body, Pia opted for the truth . . . or at least most of it.

"This," Pia replied in a barely audible whisper before reaching her lips toward his. Valen responded by once again closing the gap between them and returning her kiss with a light, sensual one of his own.

Looking deep into her eyes, he gently parted her lips with his tongue and began to tenderly explore the sweetness of her mouth. With just the right amount of pressure and speed, their tongues and eyes danced a sexy tango that sent quiet explosions of desire through Pia's body. In another example of expert timing, Valen withdrew, and his lips began a slow, seductive march down her chin across her shoulders and up her neck, landing on her ear, where his tongue and teeth took over. He nibbled and gnawed until Pia felt her knees and defenses go weak.

"Pals don't kiss like that," she said with a breathlessness that Valen found irresistible. "How could you know?"

"How could I know what?" his mouth once again returned to her ear to ask.

"You kiss me like you know me," Pia told him, enjoying the caress of his hand down her back. "Like you've been doing it for years."

"Maybe I have. Maybe we were great lovers in another life and have returned in this one to find each other." Inwardly Valen smiled, intrigued by the idea.

"Senator, you sound like a Democrat. A new age Democrat, at that."

"Just another amazing effect you've had on me," Valen admitted before pulling Pia back into his arms and devouring her mouth with his. This time his kiss was hungry and possessive. It was a kiss that crossed the line between interest and possession. A kiss that both scared and seduced.

"It's almost one," she said, pulling away, both relieved and disappointed by that fact.

"Okay, Cinderella. I don't want you to miss your pumpkin. But I would definitely like to see you again."

"I'd like that," she agreed.

The truth, Pia finally admitted to herself, was that she was lonely and enjoyed Valen's company. And the pal thing she could do. It was perfect. No commitment, no nasty breakup when the time came, just two friends spending time together.

Two friends that are obviously very attracted to each other, Pia's brain commented, sending a shiver down her back as a quick reminder of his kiss.

True, dat, she agreed. *This definitely cannot be a friends with benefits situation.*

"But . . ."

"But what? I promised I wouldn't be grumpy."

"There is something you should know about me before we proceed any further." Pia looked at his handsome face and took a deep breath. This would be a tough admission. "And I won't hold any grudges if you decide to just walk away now."

"Okay," Valen said, convinced that there was not much she could say that would deter him.

"I'm . . . celibate," she said, at the last minute opting to go for the secret she already had years of experience revealing. It was so much easier than confessing that she was pregnant. Besides, it was the truth. Since her night with Grand, she had not had sex and had no intention of partaking again until after the baby was born.

"That's not something you hear much these days," Valen said with a poker face. "How long?"

"Five years." The number automatically slipped out of her mouth and Pia didn't bother to correct herself. What was she going to say? Five years except for one night four months ago?

Valen was shocked and disappointed but at the same time impressed. Celibacy was not an easy state to exist in these days, which he knew from his own experience. "Well, I respect that."

"Thank you."

"And it doesn't change my desire to see you again."

His words caused Pia's face to break out into what must have been a contagious smile as Valen returned hers with one of his own. "I still like to kiss, though," she admitted. "And hug."

"Well, then, I think we're going to be *best* friends," Valen said pulling her close.

Chapter Twenty-five

Florence noticed his stare almost as soon as she walked in the room. She could feel his eyes following her as she continued to stroll through the Lobby Living Room of the Hotel Adolphus and to the floral-covered couch where her best friend, Miriam, sat waiting.

"Does this hat make my ass look big or somethin'?" she asked before even saying hello.

Miriam took a minute to inspect the wide bell-shaped hat adorned with a huge white flower, which matched Flo's navy suit to perfection. "No, it's adorable. Very *Breakfast at Tiffany's*." Miriam replied. "Why?"

"Because that man over there—for chrissake, don't look—keeps starin' at me."

"Honey, he's not watching the hat. He's more interested in what's shaking underneath it."

"Oh, please. Stop bein' so silly. Now let's just order and get to gossipin'."

"May I bring you some tea?" a tall, elegant black waiter asked as another set down a three-tiered plate stand filled with open-faced finger cucumber sandwiches, English scones, and mini-croissants with grilled chicken salad.

After ordering the orange jasmine tea, the two women enjoyed the performance of the classic pianist. Florence took the opportunity to sneak a peek across the room. Her admirer was still there and had been joined by another stately-looking gentleman. For some reason,

Clay, the dentist she'd met in San Francisco came to mind, causing Florence to smile.

"He is very handsome," Miriam stated, mistaking the reason for Flo's grin. "So is his friend."

"He looks nice enough," Flo answered, reaching for a scone.

"Florence, you know the birthday gift I gave you?"

"You mean the Women in Marketin' and Sales workshop?" Flo asked, remembering how she and Pia had teased Clay.

"Funny. Yes, that birthday gift."

"What about it?" she asked before nibbling on her scone.

"I'd like to see what you learned. I've been hearing about it for months now. I want to see you in action. I want you to go flirt with those gentlemen and get them to come over here."

"Miriam, I'm married."

"But I'm not. And I'm shy and divorced and happen to have a best friend who is a certified flirty mama."

"So that's the real reason you gave me that workshop. Not to try to save my marriage, but so I could be your pimp?"

"You got it," Miriam said with a laugh.

"Okay, fine. You know what this prissy tea needs?" Flo asked, suddenly feeling up to the challenge.

"What?"

"Champagne. I'll be right back." Florence stood, smoothed the wrinkles from her skirt, and did her best not to trip as she sashayed across the lobby. *A genuine smile is power,* Flo thought, remembering Joey Clements's words. She broadened her grin as she approached the two men and noted with satisfaction that her smile was met with two others just as friendly and just as wide. They both stood as she got closer, and Florence was impressed by their gentlemanly show of manners—a rarity these days.

"Excuse me, gentlemen. I'm Florence, and I'm sorry to disturb you, but I was wonderin' if one or both of you could help me out," she said, extending her hand.

"Steve," the gazer revealed, clasping her hand.

"Tom."

"How can we help you?" Steve asked once the introductions and handshakes were finished.

"My friend, Miriam—that's her sitting there," Flo said as both men turned to look, "insists that the song the pianist is playin' is Beethoven. I say it's Brahms. Any clue as to who's right? But be sure, because there's a whoppin' five bucks ridin' on your answer."

"Well, with a wager that big, I'd hate to guess," Steve said, chuckling. "Tom, any idea?"

"Brahms's Waltz in A-flat."

"How brilliant are you, Tom," Flo said, touching his upper arm and delivering a huge smile. "Now, could I ask one last favor? Would you two mind comin' over and tellin' Miriam the news. I think she's more apt to believe it if it comes from an impartial party."

Miriam smiled as she watched a grinning Florence return with the two men in tow. Never in the eight years they'd been friends had Flo done anything so bold.

"Miriam, please meet Steve and Tom. I'm afraid Tom has some bad news for you," Flo said as the three shook hands.

"Bad news?" Miriam asked, looking at her friend for some kind of clue as to what was going on.

"Yes, I'm afraid Florence was right. The song being played is Brahms's Waltz in A-flat."

"I see. Florence, you got me again," Miriam said with a conspiratorial smile.

"Yes, I did, and I am expectin' my five dollars."

"Well, Tom and Steve, since you got dragged over here and placed in the middle of our silly bet, would you like to join us?" Miriam asked.

"Thank you," Tom said, taking a seat next to her on the sofa. Steve and Florence sat in the two armchairs directly across from them.

"Would you ladies care for anything? Champagne, perhaps?" Steve asked.

Miriam's eyes immediately sought out Florence's in amused congratulations.

"Sure. My treat, though. Thanks to Mir, I just came into a truckload of money."

Flo's comment set the foursome off into laughter and fixed the tone for the rest of the afternoon. They discussed everything, from politics to sports to favorite vacation spots, with Florence front and center, entertaining them with her comical stories and witty insights.

Miriam noted the changes in her friend, which were nothing short of remarkable. Sitting there laughing, flirting, and entertaining Steve and Tom, Florence had never looked happier, lighter, or younger. It seemed that Florence had gotten in touch with a place deep inside her—a place where the simple joy of being became a daily celebration. And in an I-want-some-of-what-she's-having moment, Miriam decided it was time to follow her friend's example and unearth her own inner bombshell.

Teatime turned into cocktails, and they moved their party into the hotel lounge, where the budding interest between Tom and Miriam continued to blossom. The hours flew by, and at nine-thirty Florence informed the group that she must put an end to their lovely visit and get home to her husband.

Good-byes expressed all around, Florence got into her car and started the drive home. It had been such a lovely afternoon. Tea with Miriam had never been this much fun before. In fact, Florence couldn't remember having this much fun since her evening spent with Dr. Clay Bickford.

I wonder how he's doin'? she thought as she merged onto the highway. Florence relived their encounter in San Francisco all the way home—reminiscing over the interesting conversation, the shared laughter, the unacknowledged mutual attraction. She also remembered fondly Clay's boyish enthusiasm when he talked about how much he loved to fish, his love for the city of Barcelona, Spain, and the desire in his eyes when he looked at her.

Thirty-five minutes later, Florence pulled her Lincoln Navigator into the garage. Stepping out of the car, she felt a surge of energy throughout her body, leaving in its wake an ache she hadn't felt in years. Florence couldn't pinpoint the feeling. She wouldn't describe it as pain, exactly, but it was definitely uncomfortable.

Flo walked into the house and through the kitchen, reaching the foyer near the stairs when it hit her. She was aroused. And not just any aroused, but "Let's Get It On," "Sexual Healing," Marvin Gaye horny.

A tickled and energized Florence nearly ran up the stairs to her bedroom suite. She slowly opened the door, first hearing Dan's soft snore and then witnessing his sleeping body buried under the covers. She stood and watched him slumber, smiling affectionately at the sight.

Flo walked into her dressing room and went straight for the third drawer from the top of her bureau. After opening the "Passionata" drawer, she pulled out the copper-colored silk gown and the matching robe that Pia had picked out for her. Though totally against the WMS credo, she'd been saving it and all her other purchases for months, waiting for a special night. Well, tonight was the night.

She took another fifteen minutes to freshen up, dress, and apply an appealing spray of perfume. Before leaving the mirror, Florence took a long look. She fluffed the hair around her face, smiling as she wondered for the first time about how a different cut and color might bring out the hazel in her eyes. *You have great eyes,* she complimented herself.

Flo took a moment to hold her own gaze and flirt with herself in the mirror, silently complimenting herself through eye talk as Joey Clements had suggested. Funny, the first time she'd done this she'd felt stupid. But now, in her agitated state, it turned her on. Flo smoothed the silk gown taut, revealing the ripples and waves that had become her fifty-three-year-old body. Yes, she could stand to lose a pound or twenty, but she was still beautiful and sexy, big ass and all.

Pulling a rose from the vase and awash in sensual confidence, a hot and bothered Florence padded softly back into the bedroom to wake her lover. She sat on the side of the bed and pushed the covers back enough to reveal his sleeping face. Smiling tenderly, she took the flower and lightly ran its soft, velvety petals across his face. Dan twitched and snorted, making Florence chuckle. She bent over and softly retraced the rose's journey with her lips before resting them on top of his. Once their mouths made contact, the dam burst, releasing Flo's pent-up passion. Dan's eyes flew open, and after a few seconds of getting his bearings, he pulled away.

"Floey?"

She didn't have an answer to the questions in his eyes, so she simply reached under the sheets and began stroking him. Now fully awake, Dan repositioned his wife onto her back. Florence raised her body enough so he could lift her nightgown to reveal the treasures he sought. Not bothering to hoist the silk any farther than her collarbone, he hungrily devoured her breasts while reaching down to guide his penis into her body.

Flo lay back feeling like a human all-you-can-eat buffet as Dan ignored her and pleasured himself. He bucked back and forth in exact rhythm to his grunts. Ten minutes later, his series of grunts became one long, guttural rumble and he collapsed on top of her.

"That was great." Having announced his satisfaction, Dan rolled off and flipped onto his stomach with his head turned to the wall. Florence lay there, not knowing whether to laugh or cry. She'd just been screwed by a husband who couldn't have cared less if she was a blow-up doll. Dan had neither noticed her appearance nor cared that other than her initial kiss their lips had not touched.

Is this what sex is supposed to be like? When she looked back at the last fifteen years, their lovemaking—with subtle variations and occasional bursts of passion—had certainly had been pretty much like this. Florence didn't know what to think about the irony of her situation. Here she had been bitten by the sex bug, causing a breakout of passion and lust, and a ten-minute poke and stroke by a man who didn't even bother to kiss her was supposed to satisfy her?

Flo eased out of bed and back to the bathroom. She took off the nightgown, washed up, and pulled on this week's version of the cotton pajamas she'd been wearing for the last thirty years. Listening at the door for Dan's steady breath and snore, she went into her dressing room and opened the Passionata drawer. Her hand rummaged around until it landed on a small silk pouch. She unsnapped it and lifted from it a cocktail napkin folded in quarters. With slow reverence, she unfolded it and breathlessly recited what was written there: *Clay Bickford, 678-555-4859.*

Flo stood alone in her dressing room, staring at the paper and running her fingers across the strong, forceful black strokes. After several minutes, she refolded the napkin and returned it to its hiding place. She then clicked off the light and headed back to bed, but stopped just outside the bathroom door. There in the darkness, unbeknownst to her husband, Flo stripped off her pajamas until she was butt naked in the moonlight. In a moment of sheer defiance, she did a little dance before returning to the dressing area and retrieving her nightgown.

"Wear it for yourself," she whispered as she returned to the bed. Now properly dressed, she would perhaps in her dreams find the love and passion she craved.

Chapter Twenty-six

It took another two weeks for Valen to schedule a free evening to spend with Pia. Once she'd been given the go-ahead on a date, she began scouring her imagination for ways to make his time off both fun and memorable. Pia had now seen first-hand how busy Valen was and how the normal pleasures most people took for granted were forgotten treats for the man who would be senator.

She decided on a private book club meeting and sent him another handmade invitation, inviting him to join her at her apartment for a reading of *Rose Water*. It had been on the WMS book list and she'd been wanting to read it for months, as it was touted for intelligently exploring the intrinsic nature of love and sex and the many demons around the subject.

At eight o'clock on Sunday evening, Valen arrived with a bottle of Sancerre for him and a bottle of sparkling apple cider for her. He kissed Pia lightly upon arrival and walked into her home, tantalized by the yummy aroma swirling around the room.

"Something smells awfully good in here," he commented.

"Glad you think so. Since the novel is set in Brazil I've ordered several popular dishes."

"Ordered? Are you telling me you can't cook?" Valen teased.

"Oh, I can *cook*, Mr. Bellamy," she said, letting the sexual innuendo linger. "Now, as I was saying, I have *ordered* chicken and shrimp empadinhas, sweet plantains, and black beans and rice. They are warming at the moment, so may I get you a cocktail? I can open the wine or I can mix you a mojito."

"Well, when in Brazil . . ."

"Come in the kitchen and keep me company while I get things ready."

The two sat in the kitchen like old friends, talking, laughing, and catching up on their lives. There was a real comfort between them that both Valen and Pia appreciated. This being pals thing was working out well for both of them.

"It was sad, to hear this girl talk about losing her father and the family not having the money for a proper funeral," Valen told her. "I wanted to give her the money right then, but if I wrote a check for every story I hear like that I'd be broke."

"I lost my dad when I was eighteen," Pia said, surprising herself. "It was so sudden that I think it made everything even worse."

"I'm sorry. How did he die?"

"Freak accident. I was coming home from college for a long holiday weekend and he insisted on cutting fresh roses for my room. He got stung by a bee. He'd never been stung before so we didn't know he was allergic. My mom was at the store, so by the time she found him it was too late."

"I'm sorry," Valen repeated.

"Me too. I was his stereotypical apple. Daddy died trying to do something to please me. But instead of being grateful, I was angry at him for a long time for leaving me and my mom."

"That's not uncommon," Valen said, placing a comforting hand over hers.

"Guess not. But it still doesn't seem right.

"How did we get on this gruesome subject? I think the food is ready," Pia declared jumping up to get out the plates and silverware.

The two filled up their dishes and brought them out into the living room. They sat on the couch to eat while continuing to laugh and talk. The conversation between them flowed smoothly. They talked of Valen's devotion to the NBA, and he admitted that his favorite team was the Miami Heat and not the New York Knicks. He forced her to pinky swear not to tell, insisting that such an admission would surely derail his campaign.

"So any deep, dark secrets you'd like to divulge?" Valen asked with a grin.

"I have two tattoos," Pia responded, made uncomfortable by his question and feeling pressed to admit to something. "I'd show them to you, but I believe it's time to get our meeting started," she announced, jumping up to get the book and changing the subject.

"Something to look forward to," Valen quipped under his breath as he cleared the dishes. He returned and stretched out on the couch, laying his head in Pia's lap. There was no discussion as their bodies seemed to naturally assume the intimate position.

They took turns reading to each other, both clearly moved by the subject matter and the personal method of consumption. After ninety minutes they stopped, their reading voices exhausted, their interest in the story piqued.

"We must do this again. I have to know how the story progresses," Valen said. "But my schedule is so forbidding."

"Why don't we make a phone date at least once a week. We'll take turns reading for thirty minutes," Pia suggested.

"I'd love that. You'd really do that for me?"

"Well, yes, but I'm being selfish. I enjoyed this myself."

He reached down and covered her lips with his in response. Valen's kiss was sweet and endearing, and Pia's was warm and receptive. The two sat on the sofa, making out like high school sophomores and stimulating the desire between them to combustible levels.

"I should go," he said his voice gruff from sexual arousal.

"Okay," she agreed, knowing if she didn't stop now, she wouldn't.

"But there is something I need to say first. I'll admit that I was initially apprehensive about calling you after receiving the photograph, but I'm so happy I didn't listen to those negative thoughts. These past couple of dates have been magic for me, and I can only hope you feel the same," he told her, punctuating his statement with a soft fingertip caress of her lips.

Pia chose not to respond, only to listen. The fact was, she didn't know if she could speak as fighting back the tears was commanding much of her attention. Damn those hormones.

Valen, slightly taken aback by her silence, pressed on.

"Your invitation to the Empire State Building contained the quote 'There must be something between us, even if it is an ocean.' I take that to mean that you also feel the incredible pull between us. It's chemical and spiritual. It's nothing but it's everything. It feels like a fantasy, but it exists in my heart with an astounding reality.

"So I am asking you to confirm what I *think* I already know. There is something happening between us that shouldn't be denied. I don't want to ignore it. I'm not sure I can. Can you?" he asked, searching for confirmation in her face.

"Please, Pia, you have to say something, because I am beginning to feel like I am giving a campaign speech here," Valen quipped, hoping to cover the growing dread that was seeping into his heart.

Pia's face remained expressionless, but her passionate brown eyes revealed all. Slowly the tears slid down her cheeks, hanging momentarily before falling to her lap.

It was an agonizing rain that broke his heart. It was clear his interpretation of her actions and words had been way off. Had he read wrong the passion and desire in her kiss? Apparently the intuitive insight he prided himself on had been all wrong, and wrong at a time when the one thing he wanted most in the world was for it to be right.

Damn it, Pia thought, cursing her overactive hormones. Valen had totally misread the reason she'd used that particular quote from the movie. She'd meant it to be quippy, thinking he'd read it as a shared interest in the Indian Ocean or even as the ocean of political differences between them. But in Pia's mind, it wasn't politics but the current realities about her life and her ideas on relationships that separated them.

At fifteen weeks, this baby she was carrying might have measured only four and a half inches from crown to rump, but it was as big as an ocean when it came to crossing the barriers that divided them. And more than that, Pia was in this simply for the romance. She enjoyed the reawakening of her sexy, sensual side that had taken place in San Francisco and she didn't want to give that up again, but she was not interested in falling in love. Friendship was all she was willing to give Valen. Frankly, it was all she knew how to give him. Pia couldn't afford to allow herself to get in any deeper than the flirting and kissing she was currently enjoying with him.

"I can't make any promises to you. Your life, my life . . . it just wouldn't be fair." she said as he gently wiped the tears from her face.

"Understandable. My lifestyle and schedule are a lot to take on, even for the most patient of women," Valen responded, feeling slightly more encouraged than he'd been just a few moments ago. At least Pia wasn't giving him a flat-out no.

"Let me suggest we just take this thing slow and see what happens. In fact, the reality is, we have no other choice. My schedule leading up to the election will be grueling. So we'll talk on the phone, send e-mails, and finish reading our book. Slowly we'll figure this thing out, okay?" Valen said, drawing her back into his arms.

Pia went willingly into his arms but didn't have the heart to tell him that since the day they'd met everything had already been sorted out between them.

Chapter Twenty-seven

It was him. She was sure of it. Like the Greek god Triton, there was Nico Jones, rising from the waters of Lake Michigan. Becca sat watching his near-naked body, mesmerized by the sheer he-ness of him. His sun-kissed, cocoa-colored skin gleamed as water dripped from his hair and clung to his oiled and buffed body like diamond drops.

Oak Street Beach at Lake Shore Drive—Chicago's version of the famed Venice Beach—was billed as one of the city's sexiest summer-time hangouts, and the presence of Nico Jones merely added truth to the notion. From sun-worshipping bikini-clad beauties to meeting-weary businessmen walking the beach with their pants rolled to the ankle, from happy tourists to Rollerbladers and cyclists, Oak Street Beach was *the* gathering spot to see and be seen. And this third Sunday in June was no exception.

"Hot damn!" Cris exclaimed sitting up and removing his shades for a better look.

"Whoa. Oh my God, that's Nico," Becca informed him, gripping his arm tightly. Neither one of them could take their eyes off the shoreline.

"Your Nico?"

"Yep. *My* Nico," she said with a pride of ownership she didn't really deserve.

"Damn," Cris repeated, his words changing from enthusiasm to concern. "No wonder you were bugging."

Nico stepped through the people-littered sand to his staked-out territory, just a Frisbee throw away from Becca's adoring eyes. Instead of toweling off, he lay down on a large blanket to air dry. She was relieved to see that the beauties surrounding him were of the toddler variety. At least today, she would have him all to herself.

"How do I look?" Becca asked, scrambling to find her purse and cosmetic kit. Why hadn't she worn the yellow bikini instead of this totally unremarkable tank suit?

"You look great. Just throw on some more gloss and big attitude," Cris suggested.

Becca straightened up her ponytail and put on her skirt and over-size sunglasses before taking a deep breath and venturing over. She stood, unnoticed, looking down at him, taking a moment to admire his beauty. Nico lay on his back, his arm crossed over his face to shield the late-afternoon sun from his eyes. Had biceps ever been so beau-tiful? From the slow rhythm of his breath, it was apparent that he was napping. As she debated whether to disturb him or not, Becca had to fight the urge to lie down and snuggle up beside him.

"Nico?" she asked, hoping she sounded as surprised as she was pretending to be. Becca watched as he slowly opened first his eyes, then his lips to smile. "What are you doing here?"

"This is one of my favorite spots," he informed her, sitting up. The way he studied her face and torso, it was clear that he had no idea who she was.

"Can I get silk panties here?" she asked, smiling and hoping he'd get the clue and remember their first encounter.

Becca could see the pages of his memory turning as he tried to re-member. "Ah, sexy ring girl. How are you, gorgeous?"

"I'm good, but, well," she said, smiling nervously, "you said you would call."

"Oh, don't put it on me. I waited for you to call me at the bar. When you didn't I figured you'd just blown me off for some other lucky dude," he said, tagging his on-the-fly explanation with an irre-sistible smile.

She tried, but Becca was unable to keep a poker face. She knew there had to be a plausible explanation for Nico's not following through on his promise to contact her. She was delighted that he'd wanted to talk with her and mortified that she'd screwed up so badly. Yet fate had happily extended them a second chance.

"So, gorgeous, what do you say we have that hookup we never got to have?"

"Whoa, now?" Becca asked, feeling her eyes go wide with excitement.

"Absolutely. I don't want to wait another moment. I know it's short notice, so if you already have plans—"

"No, now is perfect," she admitted, a bit too quickly. She knew her overeager response had just cost her many cool points, but Becca didn't care. Nico Jones was so eager to see her that *now* was not soon enough.

"Okay. Um, could you . . . don't go away . . . 'cause I have to . . . I'll be right back," she rambled on nervously. Becca took several steps backwards, unable to tear her eyes away from her good fortune. It wasn't until she tripped slightly that the spell was broken and Becca hurried back to Cris.

"He wants to take me out," she reported as she began frantically gathering up all her beach apparel.

"Okay, but did you find out why he didn't call you?"

"He said he was waiting for me to call him."

"And you believe him?"

"I don't know. Maybe. But he's here now," Becca admitted with a giggle, "and he wants to hook up with *me*."

Becca turned and took two steps, then turned back around to Cris. "I'm nervous," she admitted, hugging her belongings to her chest.

"You'll be fine. Just play it by ear. Here, take this," he said, finding his batted-up jeans and reaching into the pocket, pulling out a condom. "And call me as soon as you get home. I want details. Every last juicy one!"

❧

"So who do you thank every night for those sexy green eyes? Your mom or dad?" Nico asked as they sat outside of Oak Street Beachstro, finishing up a Chicago-style deep dish pizza smothered in hot pepper flakes.

Even after all these years, the question still caught her off-guard. Becca had no idea whose eyes she'd inherited.

"My dad," she told him, falling back on a fifty-fifty guess.

"I bet he has no idea what an exotic and sexy gift he gave the world," Nico said, sliding his fingers between hers.

Both his words and touch caused Becca to blush. "So why did you become a bartender?" she asked, wanting to know but also wanting to turn the conversation away from her parentage.

"Because one day I want to own my own bar. No, make that several—first here in Chi-Town, and Vegas, then L.A. So I'm learning the biz from the ground up. Besides, I love bartending. Mixing cocktails is an art form—kind of like cooking. I like coming up with new recipes and drink presentations, though silk panties wasn't my recipe," he said, shooting her a devastating grin.

"That's a crazy name."

"Yes, but a memorable one. There are a lot of drinks with sexy names."

"Tell me some," Becca insisted, enjoying the spicy taste of both the meal and their conversation.

"Well, there's the slow comfortable screw. That's vodka, Southern Comfort, sloe gin, and OJ. And who can forget a screaming orgasm, which is amaretto, Bailey's, and Grand Marnier," Nico informed her with a sly smile while lightly caressing her hand. "And then there's my favorite, sex on the beach."

"What's in . . . uh . . . that?" Becca asked, her words momentarily catching in her throat.

"It's delicious," he said, gazing into her eyes. "Vodka, melon and raspberry liqueur, and pineapple and cranberry juice. Everyone should try it at least once."

Becca giggled nervously, not knowing how to respond to Nico's sexual innuendos. The two sat staring at each other for several moments before Nico abruptly stood. "I can't take those eyes any longer, and it is getting hot as hell in here."

"But we're outside."

"Which says a lot about how you affect me. How about we get out of here and go enjoy the beach. I know the perfect spot. You haven't lived until you've watched the sunset on the lake. Wait here for a minute," Nico told her as he disappeared into the bar area. He reemerged five minutes later with a bottle of white wine and two plastic cups, thoughtfully uncorked by his fellow bartender.

Nico reached for her hand as they departed the restaurant. Becca smiled joyfully in the dusky light as she actively refrained from breaking into a skip. Here she was, walking hand in hand with Nico

Jones as if they were a couple. Could life get any better than this moment?

Dialogue was sparse, but Becca didn't mind. She was far too starstruck and dumbfounded by her good fortune to make any kind of decent conversation. Shoes in hand, she followed Nico through the sand about a quarter mile onto a concrete jetty that jutted out over the lake. It was a more private location away from traffic and beachcombers and provided a spectacular view of Lake Michigan. Nico pulled the blanket from his backpack and spread it out across the jetty.

"This is the hottest spot in the city," Nico declared. The two sat shoulder to shoulder, sipping their wine and enjoying the colorful spectacle of the setting sun. After two glasses, Nico put his arm around Becca and stroked her neck as they watched the violet blue sky turn dark over the lake. Becca sat in blissful awe, luxuriating in Nico's presence and listening to the soothing lap of the lake waves. It was the perfect sensory blend of touch, sight, and sound, and Becca had never seen, nor could she have imagined, such a perfectly dreamy setting.

"So, gorgeous, I've been wanting to tell you something all night," Nico said, turning to face her.

"Yes?"

"Those lips of yours are driving me crazy. May I?" he asked, leaning in so their foreheads touched but progressing no further. She could smell the wine as his warm breath gently misted her face. She grinned, knowing right then that he was special. Unlike Gil or Mike, Nico had asked permission to kiss her. He hadn't simply assumed it was okay, and Becca was touched by his thoughtfulness.

In lieu of a verbal response, Becca brought her lips to his, timidly kissing him, hoping she was doing it right. Did lips have muscle memory? She tried to recall the kisses she'd shared with Gil at the Crème de la Crème. Becca mimicked his movements, and added a few of her own.

He returned her kiss with the practiced expertise of a sexual vagabond. Nico showered her face with soft, fluttery kisses as he pulled the elastic band from her ponytail, freeing her hair. He pulled away long enough to entangle his hands in Becca's mane, using his fingers to comb gently through her hair.

Brushing a wayward lock from her face, Nico began nibbling at her ears and neck. Using his body weight, he gently pushed her back on the blanket, positioning their torsos until they were on their sides, lying belly to belly. The concrete was hard, but after Nico's long, toe-curling kiss Becca felt as if she were floating and ceased to notice. His kisses continued to release the tension in Becca's body, leaving her increasingly relaxed and receptive.

"You really are beautiful," he whispered, his breath on her ears feeling like butterfly wings. "I'm so glad you found me. It's like we were meant to be together today."

Becca melted under his touch and sensitive words. A slight moan escaped her mouth as he nibbled and sucked on her lower lip. She felt his hands caress her neck, shoulders, and back. And, not sure exactly what to do, she mirrored his actions. It soon became apparent that though inexperienced, she was still effective, as she could feel Nico's hardness pressing against her leg.

Nico's hands migrated to her breasts. Through the silky fabric of her bathing suit he massaged her nipples until they were hard and stood at attention. He gently nipped them with his teeth before slipping the straps down her arms far enough to expose her breasts to the newborn moonlight.

"Your breasts are beautiful."

"Wait." Becca insisted in a breathless whisper, sitting up. Her list of lovers was a short and undistinguished one, and even though her body was begging to continue, she was hesitant. Shouldn't they spend more time together before they had sex? More than anything, Becca was afraid of Nico's reaction when he learned that her come-hither walk and talk was more an act than a lifestyle.

"What, gorgeous? Tell me what's wrong?"

"I haven't . . . well . . . it's just that I haven't done this much and, well . . . what if someone sees us?"

"Don't worry. Nobody is going to see us way out here. And on the very off chance that somebody does, they'll just think that I'm one lucky dude," he told her while massaging her breasts.

"I'm not sure we should do this," she said, trying to maintain her focus.

"Don't you like me?"

"Yes."

"Good, because I like you. Let me show you how much," he lobbied before replacing his hands with his mouth. He sucked and licked her nipples individually before pushing them together and devouring both in one mouthful. It was an action designed to shake any residual apprehensions, and judging from the aroused moans and close-eyed, dreamy look on Becca's face, it had done its job. She no longer had the power or the desire to resist him.

Craving skin-on-skin contact, Nico once again pulled away, this time to quickly unbutton and remove his shirt and pants. Stripped down to his bathing trunks, he lay on top of her, his mouth and hands moving wildly over the length of Becca's body. And after awakening every nerve ending between her head and toes, Nico slipped his hand under her skirt, pushed her swimsuit to the side, and let his fingers explore her inner woman. He fingered her gently, judging the scope of her desire by her body movements and vocalizations.

Becca, feeling wet and ready, remembered the condom Cris had given her. What should she do? Her body was on fire and, looking at Nico's face contorted with such intense pleasure, she wondered if she really wanted to ruin their first time together with talk of safe sex? She'd just finished her period so she was sure pregnancy was not an issue, but what about all the other stuff? Was there really any harm in doing it unprotected just this one time?

Always trust your gut. Safe is sexy, so be smart. Pia's advice raced through Becca's head.

"Nico, I have a condom," she cooed in his ear.

"You came prepared. You've been waiting for me, haven't you?" Nico said, taking the condom from her and quickly putting it on. Within seconds he was back to grinding his pelvis slowly into hers. Nico continued to tease her with his tongue, hands, and penis, his words acting as an additional aphrodisiac for both of them.

Unable to hold out any longer, Nico slowly penetrated Becca, letting the tip of his engorged penis slip and slide in the juices of her desire. With each thrust he went deeper, enjoying the rub of every crease and crevice of her vagina.

Nico covered Becca's mouth with his and he reached down between her legs and wet a fingertip with her juices. While he pumped her, Nico massaged Becca's clitoris into orgasmic frenzy.

She swallowed her screams of pleasure while her body erupted into wave after wave of her first orgasm. Nico continued to ride her, his pace becoming more frantic as he approached his own orgasm.

Becca looked at him and saw that his eyes were closed and his face was contorted and tense as he rode his way to ejaculation before collapsing on top of her.

"Oh my God, that was amazing," he declared, and kissed her on her forehead.

Becca smiled, thrilled that she had pleased Nico. Snuggled up to his body, she listened to the sounds of the waves and tried to dissect what had just taken place. She didn't feel as she'd expected she would. She had successfully seduced the hottest guy in Chicago, had lusty, adventurous sex, and despite her inexperience had managed to satisfy him to the point of being called amazing, and yet Becca didn't feel like a winner. She didn't understand. Nico had made all the right moves, said all the right things, and brought her to her first rip-roarin' orgasm, but something was still missing.

It wasn't until Becca was at home curled up in her own bed that she realized what that something was. Not once this evening had Nico called her by name.

Chapter Twenty-eight

Pia climbed into the cool conditioned air of Flo's Navigator, happy to be out of the grueling July heat. She'd flown to Dallas from Houston, where she'd been all week, overseeing production on a cable special featuring Beyoncé Knowles. Florence had generously offered to meet her at the airport so they could spend the afternoon together.

"Flo, you really didn't have to pick me up. I could have easily booked a car and met you at the hotel."

"That's not how we do things here in Texas. We take care of family," Flo said with a wink. "Besides, if you think I'm gonna be hoppin' on anybody's subway when I get to New York this fall, you've got another thing comin', missy. Becca and I are expectin' the royal treatment."

"Done. And speaking of Becca, have you talked to her?" Pia asked.

"Not in a while. What's that girl gotten her pretty panties in a twist about this time?"

"She called me to ask for advice. She's fallen in total lust with some bartender."

"Well, that didn't take long." Pia filled her in on the romantic adventures of their young friend, and to Pia's surprise, Flo listened but spoke very little.

"Looks like whatever she picked up at the workshop is paying off, though in some ways she seems more confused than ever," Pia concluded.

"You know, that WMS workshop went a lot deeper than just

teachin' us how to bat our eyelashes. Seems the more we tap into the sensual side of ourselves, the more confused we get. On one hand we're feelin' all confident and lusty, but on the other hand those feelin's are makin' our lives hella complicated."

"I know mine is, but how so with yours?"

"When you live in the moment, you start really noticin' how much life has to offer. Makes you start lookin' at your own," Flo explained as she eased onto the highway. "I'm tryin' to figure out how I got so comfortable livin' such a small life. I mean, to some folks it might look pretty big—big house, big car, big social life—but really I'm just livin' large in a really tiny world."

"It's the whole big fish, small pond syndrome."

"Yeah, but it's when you start wantin' to swim the ocean that things get crazy," Flo said wistfully. "Suddenly the fishbowl, even if it is an aquarium, just isn't enough anymore. But enough of this sad-sack crap. How you and that baby doin'? You have to look for it, but I saw that little bump."

"I know. It's hard to believe that I'm almost five and a half months along."

"Is he movin' yet?"

"I think I felt a little flutter or two, but I'm not really sure. It's kind of creepy and mind-blowing all at the same time. And I don't know the sex, so my secretary refers to the baby as Pomegranate or Pom for short."

"Sounds like one of those Hollywood baby names."

"Her thought exactly."

"It also sounds like a nickname a daddy should be comin' up with."

"You sound just like my mother. When she saw the picture of me and Valen in the *New York Post* after the Reston Walker event, she almost flipped. It took me two weeks to convince her that he is not the father.

"She doesn't talk about the baby other than to ask how I'm feeling, but she'll ask me about any guy she thinks I might have even said hello to. She's ready to hook me up with anyone, just so long as I'm married before the baby is born."

"She'll come around." Flo predicted. "Have you told the senator?"

"No."

"So you don't plan to?"

"I haven't decided," Pia answered, concentrating on the Dallas landscape whizzing by her.

"Well, darlin', wait much longer and he'll figure it out for himself. You can't keep this a secret forever. I'm surprised he hasn't noticed the bump yet."

"He's never seen me naked."

Flo's eyes left the road long enough for her to frown at Pia in disbelief.

"Why are you surprised? Remember me? I'm the one who's only had sex once in five years," Pia cracked. "I told him I was celibate. Look, he's never around and I'm still traveling too. Since our date on the Empire State Building I've seen him twice—once at the Walker event and then again for our private book club meeting. It's been a month since then."

"What kind of relationship is that?"

"A lovely friendship that suits both our purposes at the moment. We talk on the phone at least once every day and e-mail even more. But actually seeing each other is complicated. Valen doesn't need to be distracted by any press scrutiny over his private life, and frankly, even though I can't stop thinking about sex now, I'm content to avoid the physical aspect of our relationship. We're both perfectly happy being pals."

"Maybe you can convince your mama of that load of crap, but sugar, this is me you're talkin' to. You've been blubberin' for weeks about this man. Even Stevie Wonder could see how far gone you are, and now you're tryin' to convince me of this horse manure? Girls in love aren't satisfied with just phone calls and occasional visits—at least not for long. 'Specially when they aren't even conjugal visits," Flo said as she pulled into the parking lot of the Fairmont Hotel in downtown Dallas and turned off the engine.

"First off, nobody on this side of the car used the L-word. I am just enjoying the feeling of dating and having an interesting man in my life again. Valen and I have the perfect romantic friendship. More than just buds, but none of that messy love stuff."

"And that's enough?"

"I know it sounds silly, but I love being wooed again. I love that Valen sends me flowers and cards and silly little e-mails to let me know he's thinking about me. I love watching him on television and allowing myself the tiniest moment of pride, even though sometimes I'm in total opposition to his politics." Pia smiled through her tears. "And I love that he cares about the country and the world. He has passion for lots of things, especially his work and me. I've missed that so much, so even if I can only have it for a couple months, it's worth it. I'll store the memories and the feelings, and when I'm up at three A.M. nursing, I'll let my heart feed off those recollections."

Flo listened to her friend and wondered if Pia could hear herself talking out of both sides of her mouth. She could deny her feelings for Valen—hell, maybe she really didn't even realize their intensity, but it was clear as the beans in chili that the girl was in love.

"Sorry about the waterfall. Hormones," Pia explained, wiping away her tears. "I cry at dog food commercials these days."

"Pia, I know all about bittersweet," Flo admitted, dropping her comedy mask long enough for Pia to see her pain.

"Like you were wishin' for a baby, I was wishin' that Dan would come home and want me again and our marriage would go on just like it had. Well, I got my wish and now I don't know if it's what I want."

"Did he change that much while he was gone?"

"He didn't, but I did. Hell, at fifty-three years old and after twenty-six years of marriage, all of a sudden I'm horny as a toad. Me, with the grandma bras! Who had seen that comin'?"

"I saw it in San Francisco when you were flirting with that dentist," Pia teased.

"I have to tell you somethin' I can't even tell Miriam. Sometimes at night, when Dan's snorin' away, I lay there thinkin', What would my life look like if I hadn't asked him to come back? And then like you said, I let my heart feed off the memories of what it felt like when Dr. Clay Bickford was lookin' in my eyes and makin' me feel like he just wanted to gobble me up."

"Call him."

"I've thought about it, but no. I mean, what would be the point? I am married and I'm tryin' to make that work. I owe it to myself and to Dan. But sometimes I can't help but wonder."

"Sounds like we really are in the same boat," Pia remarked.

"Yeah, so let's stop rowin' for a minute and go have lunch before you have to get back to the airport," Flo said as she checked her face in the mirror before opening the car door. "We can get you a glass of milk and me a martini and I'll tell you how I was flirtin' my big behind off a couple weeks ago."

"You?"

"Don't sound so surprised, sugar. I bagged me *two* prize steer and won five dollars to boot."

"Girl, you're dangerous," Pia said, both stunned and amused.

"As Joey would say, downright nuclear!"

⁂

Pia touched down at LaGuardia airport at 9:36 P.M., and by 10:25 was home lying back in her bathtub, covered in rose-scented bubbles. She was exhausted. Traveling and baby-making was hard work. Pia planned to finish her warm, leisurely bath, read her nightly section of *What to Expect When You're Expecting*, then kick back and relax until sleep demanded her body's full attention.

She sunk farther into the sudsy water and, as it was prone to do these days, her mind drifted to Valen. She knew from his earlier e-mail that after a grueling day of campaigning he still had a long night of glad-handing and speech-making ahead of him. She didn't anticipate hearing from him until tomorrow morning. In the six weeks they'd been "buddying around" together, it had become an endearing routine for her to wake up each morning to an e-mail or phone call or both.

For the zillionth time, her imagination drifted back to the exact moment their lips first touched. There was something magically delicious about Valen's kiss, and no matter how many times she thought about it, it still had the same impact and produced the same chain reaction—a lip-biting smile, a belly-warming sensation, and the immediate craving for another and another and another.

Pia lifted her hand from the soapy water to caress her mouth, reactivating the electric residue of Valen's lips. Of the thousands of kisses Pia had received in her lifetime, never had a man kissed her with such a soul-connecting quality. And never had a kiss made her so curious to know a man from his core.

The time was quickly approaching for Pia to make a decision about

Valen. She was either going to have to break it off or let him know about the baby. Pia rubbed her slightly protruding tummy, noting that either way, she had only a few weeks left before her secret was revealed to the world.

The phone rang, bringing Pia back into the moment. She shook the water from her right hand and reached over to pick up the receiver.

"Hey," Valen said. His voice sounded strained.

"Hey. I was just sitting here thinking about you."

"Okay."

Pia's concern level immediately shot way up. Usually, no matter how tired, Valen would respond with some kind of remark that was equally endearing and suggestive. But tonight, despite the usual fatigue that lay beneath every conversation, she could hear a weariness that went beyond exhaustion.

"You okay? You sound . . . funny."

"It's been one tough night. Look, I know it's late, but may I come over? I just really need to be with you right now."

"Of course. Valen, you don't sound like yourself. Did something happen?"

"We'll talk when I get there. Thirty minutes?"

"That's fine. Is there anything you need?"

"Just a hug. See you in a few."

Pia hastily climbed out of the tub, dried off, and lotioned up. She was confused about what to wear. It was nearly midnight and she was tired as hell, but pajamas didn't seem appropriate. Regular clothes felt out of sync as well, so she chose a loose-fitting caftan in her favorite shade of purple. It was the perfect blend of chic, casual, and camouflage.

A few quick swipes of mascara, a sweep of bronzer, and natural lip gloss, and Pia was done dressing with ten minutes to spare. She was going to need every single second. Whatever was troubling her friend—and something definitely was—he needed a place that felt safe and serene. A place where he could feel vulnerable and unburden his troubles.

Pia took the next eight minutes to breeze through her front room, turning on the water fountain, lighting the candlescape in the fireplace, and frantically searching for her favorite relaxation CD. With less than a minute to spare, she dimmed the lights, finishing the transformation of her living room into a tranquil oasis where Valen could find peace.

Ready, Pia plopped back on the sofa to wait. She'd kill for a caffeine-packed Tab energy drink right now. She was exhausted and wanted to sleep, but she would power through. Valen needed her, and Pia wanted him to know she could be depended on. Ten minutes later than expected, the intercom buzzed and the doorman let her know that Mr. Bellamy was on his way up.

Pia opened the door and stood in the threshold, waiting. The ding of the elevator bell announced his arrival to her floor, and she watched as he approached. Tonight, the virile and energetic man she was familiar with was lost behind a fatigued, battle-weary warrior. Valen stepped inside and without saying a word drew Pia into his arms for a long, tight, and desperate hug. The pair stood in the foyer, frozen like a sculpture, holding each other for comfort and in concern. Not one word was exchanged, but none were needed. The look on Valen's face said it all. Whatever had occurred tonight had shaken him to his soul.

Pia broke their embrace and helped Valen remove his suit jacket and tie and led him by the hand to the couch. She poured him a glass of white wine before sitting and snuggling up against him. The pair sat there for minutes that seemed to go on forever, but there was no awkwardness in the hush, just a comfort level so great both knew that filling the air with words wasn't necessary.

Valen sipped his wine and absorbed the serenity around him, letting the soft serenade of the music unwind his frazzled nerves. What bliss to walk into such a calming environment and into the arms of such a beautiful and understanding woman. How did Pia once again know just what he needed to soothe his battered ego and disillusioned psyche? She just seemed to have the uncanny knack of anticipating his mood—whether it be playful, serious, or passionate.

"They threw Oreos," he said, finally breaking the quiet.

"I don't understand."

"I was in Buffalo at a rally, standing at the podium and outlining my 'Respect Yourself' campaign, and there was a contingent of loud black Democrats in the room, which is normal. There are hecklers in every crowd. Usually I can deal with them, but five minutes into my talk they started pelting Oreo cookies at me and chanting, 'Uncle Tom.'

"I don't get it, Pia. I was talking about the importance of respecting yourself and acting in a dignified manner with the expectation and the demand, even, that others do the same . . . that's why I don't get it. How is that being a sellout?"

"I'm so sorry."

The pain in Valen's voice caused Pia to cringe. It was unbelievable how protective she felt toward him and angry at her own political brethren for hurting him so. Political opinions aside, why did folks have to be so cruel? She rested her head on his chest and let him talk, instinctively knowing that he needed the opportunity to purge his anger more than discuss the events of this evening.

"The Democratic machine has been trying to paint me with that brush since I announced my candidacy . . . pulling out that 'he's not really black' bullshit."

"This sounds just like media-hungry ignorance at work," Pia offered, fighting to stay awake. It was near midnight, and her pregnant body, encouraged by the relaxing atmosphere, was demanding sleep.

"It *is* showboating and ignorance from the opposition. *And* bigotry *and* playing the race card. It's all that bullshit wrapped up in a goddamn cookie. If you want to go toe-to-toe with me on my stance on the issues, bring it on, but don't step to me with insulting acts of cowardice."

Hearing no response, Valen looked down to find that Pia had drifted off to sleep. His anger and disappointment reduced, he took a deep breath and leisurely finished his glass of wine, enjoying the feel of this woman he adored sleeping next to him. She was like a warm and cozy security blanket, and he was so grateful to have found this incredibly soft place to land. Pia Jamison was everything he wanted in a woman. She was beautiful, funny, and sexy. She also had her own life and interests, and a sharp mind that was as intelligent as it was independent.

Valen wanted this woman for his own, and just as soon as this grueling election came and went, he was going to do everything in his power to make her want him too.

"I love you," Valen revealed, his voice just above a whisper, his mouth stretching into a wide, wondrous smile at the realization. Slowly, so not to disturb her, he cautiously eased off the couch and gently scooped Pia up into his arms.

Valen made his way back to the bedroom, making one wrong turn along the way. Apparently, Pia had been getting ready to retire when he'd called, as the linens were already turned down. He gently placed her on the bed and lovingly tucked in his sleeping beauty. Valen stood and watched her snooze for a moment, forever etching her lovely face into his memory. A powerful yawn broke the spell, reminding him just how tired he was. He'd love nothing more than to slide right into bed beside Pia, but he was being picked up early to begin another tedious day of morning meetings and afternoon campaigning in Long Island. Valen had to get back to his apartment and prepare.

He turned and was reaching for the light on the bed stand, but the book caught his eye. Why would Pia have a book on what to expect during pregnancy? He picked it up and began flipping through the pages until he reached a marker holding the chapter on traveling during pregnancy. Valen pulled the bookmark in order to peruse the page and realized it was a photograph—a sonogram, to be exact. He took a closer look at the grainy image, not understanding most of what he was seeing.

The only thing that was one hundred percent clear based on the name and date stamp, was that this was Pia's baby and the sonogram was taken two weeks ago. There were other letters and numbers on the image, but Valen had no clue how old the fetus was. A confused frown lined his brow as crazy thoughts began running through his mind.

Pia claimed to be celibate, yet she was pregnant. Why had she lied to him?

Valen returned the image and the book to their proper place and took one last look at Pia before turning out the light. He turned and exited the bedroom, his steps as heavy and plodding as when he arrived. He was stunned and felt like he'd been sucker punched. Suddenly, like an image in a kaleidoscope shaken and turned, the lovely scene between them had shifted and changed into something totally unrecognizable.

Out in the hall, he felt the vibration of his Treo and cursed. He was so tired of always being so damn reachable. He opened the file to his mail and clicked on Ed's latest, marked urgent. Apparently the *New York Post* was endorsing his rival. Reading the words, his face stung as if he'd been physically slapped.

A perfect fucking ending to a perfectly fucked-up day.

Chapter Twenty-nine

Pia checked her BlackBerry once again on her walk in to work. Still no morning message from Valen. She knew he had an early start on another demanding day, but she was still surprised and slightly worried. Last night she'd seen the fragile side of this man she adored, and while the hurt to his pride ran deep, the pain inflicted on his spirit by such an insensitive display of disrespect went even deeper. She hoped she'd managed to cheer him up last night before Mr. Sandman delivered his knockout punch, but Pia had no indication of his mood after he'd tucked her in and left.

She slipped the device back into her purse and continued her stroll. Pia stopped when something blue in a store window caught her eye. A sly smile broke out across her face as she turned around and hurried inside.

While the clerk at the toy store wrapped her purchase, Pia filled out the gift card: *Next time you'll be ready. Hugs, Pia.* If this didn't cheer Valen up and score her big-time brownie points for being clever and sweet, nothing would.

❧

"Morning Dee. Can you please messenger this over to Valen Bellamy's apartment?" Pia asked, dropping the shopping bag on her desk as she breezed by.

"Sure. And Benita had to move your yoga session to this afternoon. You were free, so I confirmed it."

"Fine, and when you get a minute I need you to pull the Sony contract and the storyboards for the Blue Diamonds shoot."

"I see you and little Pom have gotten your second trimester boost of energy."

"That's right, and we'll be cracking the whip around here." Pia laughed as she settled into her desk chair to begin her workday.

For the rest of the morning, Pia answered her outstanding e-mails, returned at least a dozen phone calls, and settled a dispute between the art director and stylist. Every so often Valen would slide through her thoughts, evoking a happy grin. She was eager to hear from him and get his reaction to her surprise gag.

Pia left for a lunchtime appointment with Dr. Montrae, and after receiving a healthy report at her checkup, returned to the office. Pre- and post-appointment checks of her BlackBerry left her disappointed, but she was sure that Valen was simply too busy with his crazy schedule to contact her.

"Did that contract go out?" Pia asked Darlene.

"Yep, and the rough cut from the Houston shoot came in."

"Okay, I'll look at it later. Any calls?" she asked, working her way around to what she really wanted to know.

"He hasn't called, *chica*."

"He who?"

"He, Tiger Woods. Who do you think? *Pleeeeease.* You're about as transparent as Nicole Kidman's forehead."

"But you sent the package?" Pia asked, giving up the charade.

"Yes, and I called and it's been received—at least by the doorman. They didn't say if it's in his hands yet. What is it?"

"A Cookie Monster puppet."

"Okay, that sounds a little freaky . . . I don't even want to know."

"Good, because I'm not telling."

❧

Pia lay in her bed, staring at the ceiling. It was nearly two A.M. Something was not right. She'd had no word from Valen despite the many messages she'd left on his Treo and office and home phones. In their six weeks together, patterns had been established and personality traits had emerged. Today he had broken all of them, and Pia was worried.

She reached over for the remote and turned on CNN. After ten minutes of watching and hearing nothing about the U.S. senatorial candidate from New York, she decided he hadn't been shot, hurt, or arrested and shut off the television.

Pia plopped back down on the pillow and closed her eyes, willing sleep to return, but it fast became apparent that the sandman had moved on. She attempted the counting thing, but instead of sheep her last encounter with Valen kept leaping through her mind. From his phone call to his arrival to his finding comfort in her arms on the sofa, she examined every detail of their evening together and could determine nothing that would cause this breach of communication.

Maybe he's mad because I fell asleep on him, Pia considered. Though she doubted it, as he had carried her into her bedroom and tucked her into bed. Pia remembered waking up the next morning wishing he had stayed.

Tucked me into bed. Oh my God, she thought, abruptly sitting up. Pia reached over and turned on the bedside light. There it was, sitting right where it had sat for the last five months: her pregnancy book. If Valen was at all curious, which she knew he was, he'd probably picked it up and found the sonogram. And even if he hadn't gotten that far, he at least had cause to wonder.

"Fuck!" she shouted into the early-morning air. No wonder he hadn't stayed the night or contacted her. Valen was too busy wondering what the hell was going on. Damn it! She should have been honest with him from the very start. Now things were going to be so much more painful and messy.

Pia sat there lambasting herself for every wrong decision she'd made lately, not telling Valen the whole truth about her pregnancy being the worst. After thirty-five minutes of mentally flogging herself, she decided to call him. Yes, it was very early in the morning, but at least she knew he'd be home, and if he was avoiding her, the element of surprise might force him to talk. Or at least, Pia hoped he would.

She picked up the phone and dialed his number, trying to keep back the tears and the terrible thoughts that were swirling around her head, ready to swoop down like vultures on roadkill. Maybe if she was terribly lucky this would all work out, but she wasn't feeling particularly optimistic. After three rings an obviously tired voice said hello.

"Valen, it's Pia."

There was a long pause before Pia heard a click on the line, causing her to burst into tears. He'd hung up on her. He was so hurt and angry that he couldn't even speak to her. Pia didn't know what to do. She ruled out calling back; Valen had been pretty clear about not wanting to talk to her. *Perhaps an e-mail,* Pia thought, going to retrieve her BlackBerry. There was no point in trying to save a relationship that was doomed from the get go, but hopefully she could explain. And apologize. And make him believe that though she'd been less than forthcoming, she had only his best interests at heart. It took forty-five minutes to compose and edit the reasons for her actions and the excuses for her deception. But sitting before her in black and white, the words seemed too cold and unfeeling to send. Pia sat and deleted her thoughts letter by letter until they were back into cyberspace and then collapsed on her bed and cried herself into a fitful sleep.

At 6:45 A.M. the continuous buzz of her intercom woke her. It was Paolo informing her that Mr. Bellamy was downstairs. The news was like a jolt of caffeine, immediately awakening Pia to face her future. Pia told the doorman to send Valen upstairs before jumping out of bed and into the bathroom to fix the damage a tearful, sleepless night had produced. Her eyes were puffy and swollen, as were her nose and lips. Pia pulled on a robe and brushed her hair back off her face. She sighed into the mirror, resigned to her appearance. She felt a mess; she might as well look like it.

Valen's knock was light and tentative. Pia stood on the other side of the door, willing him to listen with an open mind before turning the knob.

"Hi," she said.

"I know it's very early, but I want to put this behind me before my day begins in earnest," Valen said, forgoing any pleasantries.

"It's okay. I've been up most of the night anyway. Let's go sit down."

"No. I won't be staying long. I'd rather talk to you here."

Valen's words hit her with an icy chill. This was definitely not a good sign. She looked into his face and saw a distance in his eyes. Where she used to see affection and desire, she now saw coldness and pain. Pia could feel the crack in her heart widen.

"Why did you hang up on me last night?" she asked timidly.

"I'm sorry—I didn't mean to be rude, but I wasn't ready to speak with you. Frankly, I am livid with you and with myself for being such a sucker. I'm only here because I need some answers before we nail the coffin shut on this relationship.

"Why, Pia? Why didn't you tell me you were pregnant? We know it's not my baby, so what were you trying to do? What was your motivation? Personal? Political? Why the hell didn't you tell me you were carrying another man's child while you were seducing me into loving you on the top of the Empire State Building? I'm assuming that you were pregnant then."

Valen's angry barrage of questions hit her like shrapnel. Even his admission of love, tucked within his angry accusations, was shot down, falling dead at her feet.

"Well, were you?"

"Yes."

"How pregnant are you now?"

"Nearly six months."

"You said you were celibate, and as much as I wanted . . . as difficult as it was, I respected that."

"I am . . . I was . . . I am . . ."

"Make up your mind. Get your lies straight," Valen replied angrily.

"I'm sorry. I should have told you."

"You're damn right you should have. Forget the fact that you lied to keep from having to make love to me. Do you know what potential fire you were playing with? How you could have derailed my entire candidacy? This isn't a game, Pia. I've got political enemies scrutinizing every word I say and dissecting every part of my life, trying to dig things up that might contradict what's on the record. For God's sake, they threw fucking cookies at me in an attempt to embarrass me in public.

"I can't be a candidate running on family values and self-respect and have a girlfriend pregnant by another man. The press would have a field day ripping me apart. I thought you understood that."

Girlfriend?

"I did. I do."

"Thank God I found out before the press or the Democrats did."

"I would nev—"

"So now I get it," Valen continued. For the first time in their relationship he was listening but not hearing what Pia was saying.

"When we first met you wanted nothing to do with me. I pursued you and you pushed me away time after time. Was that before you found out you were pregnant and needed a father for your child?"

In hurt and anger, Valen's mouth had taken on a life of its own, spewing out words and accusations he neither believed nor meant to say. He reached for the doorknob, but Pia caught his arm by the wrist.

"Just give me five minutes to explain," Pia begged, breaking into tears. Valen refused to look at her, but he stayed, standing stiffly in the middle of the foyer with his arms folded across his chest like protective body armor.

"It's not necessary, because right now I'd find anything you say difficult to believe."

"Well, believe that I was always planning to break it off with you as soon as I started showing. I knew the political ramifications were too great and I was determined to protect you, but I just wanted to be with you for as long as possible, even if there was no future for us."

"That's even worse. You let me fall in love with you, all the while knowing that you were planning to dump me? Are you that selfish that my feelings meant nothing to you? Did I know you at all?"

He said it again—he's in love with me, Pia's heart, noticing all the things her brain did not want to hear, informed her.

"All I can say is, I am so very sorry. Valen, it *was* selfish of me. But we always said that we were just friends," Pia said, noticing him wince at the word.

"You don't believe that any more than I do." Valen looked deeply into her eyes and then abruptly turned and opened the door, trying to block the sound of Pia's weeping. "Last night, while you were asleep, I told you I loved you—" he began.

"Thank you," she whimpered, not letting him finish. She was shocked by her words. This wonderful man just said he loved her, and "thank you" was all she could come up with?

" 'Thank you'? How polite," he said, hiding his pain behind sarcasm.

"I don't know what love is, Valen. And that's why I'm so afraid of it," Pia said with a truth that was as new and surprising to her as it was to him.

He paused and said nothing before continuing through the door. Once in the hallway, his body collapsed on its frame. "I could have shown you, if you'd only given me the chance," he muttered to himself before trudging down the hall and out of Pia Jamison's life.

Inside her apartment, Pia slid down the wall to the floor and began to sob. She'd always known this day was unavoidable and thought she was prepared for the inevitable, but Pia hadn't anticipated how thick the hurt and anger that now clung to her would be.

As she sat on the floor feeling sorry for herself and Valen, Pia felt a flutter in her abdomen. She forced herself to calm down and sit perfectly still. There it was again—the baby was moving. Pia covered her belly with a protective self-hug and leaned her head back against the door.

The irony of this situation was nearly intolerable. She had stopped looking for love, made a plan, and gone on with her life. Then Valen had stepped into her world, wrapped her up in his warm and comforting embrace, and lifted her toward the heavens. And now, as if part of a heart-stopping aerial act in Cirque du Soleil, she'd taken a furious drop to earth and its harsh reality—she had gotten the baby she'd always wished for but lost the man she'd always dreamed of.

❧

"She said she didn't know what love was and that she was afraid of it, but she never said she didn't love me," Valen revealed to his campaign chief. He was grateful for the trustworthy ear, as keeping this ache inside him was too excruciating.

Ed poured his boss another cup of coffee and allowed him to expel his pain. It wasn't quite noon yet, but he had canceled all of Valen's appointments, sensing his need for a mental health day. This situation with Pia Jamison had rocked his boss off kilter, and Ed needed him to get back on track—fast.

"Val, it was the only thing you could do. We've gone over the scenario a hundred times. You could try to keep the relationship under wraps as long as possible, but in the end, in this political climate, someone would find out, and then what?

"The 'Respect Yourself' campaign is finally getting the attention it deserves. It was genius to extend it past individual family values into global family values."

"That was Pia's vision, not mine. I took that from her."

"Okay, she's a smart woman, but let's face facts—you don't know all that much about her. For all we know she was working for the Dems to set you up. Or she might just be some power-hungry gold digger who gets her kicks screwing power players instead of ball players. Either way, it's not pretty."

"No. I won't believe she was out to hurt me or my campaign," Valen insisted.

"Okay, we'll give her the benefit of that doubt. She might love you, who knows, but the bottom line is, she lied. And not just a little lie— a potentially life-altering, career-ending lie. If you stay with her and the Democrats or the liberal press get wind of the situation, your entire family values platform will go down the toilet, along with your credibility and political career. This is a no-win situation for everyone. You did the only thing you could do."

Valen simply sipped his coffee, trying to swallow the unfairness of it all.

"Val, when you're sitting in that Senate chamber, you two can try again, if that's what you want. But right now we have to concentrate on what you *need* to do, which is cut all ties with Pia Jamison and win this election."

Success

is

found

not

in

what

you

have

achieved,

but

rather

in

who

you

have

become.

Chapter Thirty

As *The Today Show*'s Meredith Vieira finished up her interview with the modern screen legend Meryl Streep, Pia puttered around the kitchen, preparing her latest breakfast craving—cinnamon toast and deviled eggs. It was already 8:50 A.M. and she should be out in the fresh September air making her way to the office by now, but she proceeded with no sense of urgency. Now seven months along, she was feeling larger and more cumbersome since the baby's recent growth spurt, and *hurry* was no longer an active word in her vocabulary.

With tea, toast, and eggs before her, Pia sat down to eat and catch the local news segment. Following stories on a three-alarm fire in Staten Island and a paralyzed Long Island man who fathered triplets was an update on the midterm elections, which were now heating up. As expected, Valen Bellamy had breezed through last week's primary election, securing his spot on the November ballot for the U.S. Senate seat. But the general election was a different story. The contest between him and the Democratic incumbent was predicted to be one of the tightest races in modern history. The latest polls showed Valen trailing by a mere three points, making it a statistical tie.

Pia stopped chewing when Valen's handsome but obviously tired face appeared on screen. He looked good. Still impressive and charming, still sounding committed and caring. Unable to stop herself, she reached up and caressed his face, still wishing today, like every day since they'd last spoken two months ago, that things could be different between them.

" 'Respect Yourself, Be Respected' has grown into a national movement with a mission to reclaim our individual and national dignity to become the greatest America we can be. But without action and financial commitment behind this movement, it will fade into distant memory like other ineffective, slogan-only campaigns. I will fight to find the money and build the momentum to take back our airways, support our families, and provide for our citizens. We will take back our pride as a people and a country and be respected by the world as the superpower we are, not because we demand it by force, but because we earned it through valor," Valen said, looking straight into the camera lens.

"Oh, he's a pro, Pom. In thirty seconds he managed to tout bipartisanship, family values, and foreign policy, and look and sound damn good doing it," she told her unborn child. "And he also stole my 'Just Say No' argument," she added, feeling both proud and flattered that in some small way she had had a positive impact on his campaign.

"As Valen Bellamy continues to crisscross the state, bringing his message of hope and opportunity directly to New Yorkers, he has become the Democrats' worst nightmare," the local NBC reporter voiced. "If he continues to draw support from black Democrats willing to cross party lines, the party's dominance in New York may end, making Mr. Bellamy the first black Republican elected from New York to the U.S. Senate."

The piece ended and Valen vanished from the television but not from Pia's thoughts. It was almost as if she were mourning the death of a loved one. Not a day went by that she didn't wake up with Valen Bellamy on her mind or go to sleep without wishing him good night. Though she didn't like to watch him on television—the image was too immediate and alive—she followed his campaign in the print media with an almost sick obsession, praying each night that, despite his Republican leanings, success would find him and his dreams would came true. Valen was a good man. He deserved to be happy.

"Hey, what are you doing, somersaults in there?" she asked, rubbing her belly. After a quiet start, little Pom had become quite active these past few weeks. Kicking, punching, hiccupping, all hours of the day and night, letting Pia know that her baby was alive and well.

Her question was answered by another kick, which set off a waterfall of teardrops. The combination of seeing Valen on the television and the baby's activity was too much of a reminder of the profound loneliness that had usurped her life. In her head, giving birth and raising a child alone seemed like a simple proposition, but in actuality, especially after her romantic friendship with Valen, she realized that her mother had been correct all along. She deserved to raise a family with a man she loved.

Love. Pia rolled the word around on her tongue. It had an odd, unfamiliar taste. In Pia's experience, love was a strange, exotic dish—a mix of familiar and foreign ingredients that always seemed to taste good going down but inevitably left her with heartburn. Over the years, just as she avoided curry, she'd learned to avoid the condition and the men who caused it.

Pia quickly ran through the list of people in her life that she'd truly loved. Her mother and father, of course; her sweet PopPop, whom she adored but who died when she was just five; her lovely grannies, Mimi and Bertha; Jeffrey, her first true love; Rodney and Lamar; hell, she even loved Dee's crazy ass; and Florence Chase was fast moving up the list of the soul-sisters she loved and who she knew loved her back.

But when she dissected the register, it was the women who were still there in her corner, loving her unconditionally. Every man on her list who had loved her had left her—including her father.

Why couldn't she and Valen have remained just pals? Why had he complicated everything by claiming to love her? His feelings came with the natural hope and expectation that she would love him back. And frankly, despite her proven ability to turn a man on in bed, Pia had to admit that she was a less skilled lover outside the bedroom.

Did she love Valen? She knew she adored him and had come to think of him as her best friend. She thought about him incessantly, and every thought was smile-producing. She worried about him, and lusted after him, and she had shared everything—from the mundane to the sublime—with him. But was that love? Aside from the lusting part, didn't she behave the same way with Dee and Flo?

Pia finally rolled into the office at ten-thirty in a cloud of general malaise. She would have taken the day off but she had a meeting at eleven-thirty that she couldn't miss, and besides, staying at home would only mean a day of feeling sorry for herself.

"Dee, could you please call Benita and cancel my session this afternoon?" Pia requested as she dragged herself past Darlene's desk and into her office.

"Sure. Your mom is . . ." Dee managed to get out before Pia disappeared into her office, ". . . waiting for you."

Pia walked into her office and was at her desk before she realized Maizelle was sitting on the sofa, a large shopping bag at her feet, reading the *New York Times*.

"You're running late this morning," her mother commented to a surprised Pia. "Are you feeling okay? You look tired."

"I am fine. Just a lot of things going on. This is a surprise," she said, coming over to deliver a quick peck to her mother's cheek. Though the tension between the two had eased considerably, Maizelle's reluctance to discuss the baby left Pia feeling anxious and judged.

"It says here that Valen Bellamy is pledging to build a bridge between Democrats and Republicans. Does this mean you two are still in touch?"

"No, we're not. He's moved his campaign forward without any further input from our company," she fudged before scrambling to change the subject. Valen Bellamy was one topic Pia did not want to delve into with her mother. "Why didn't you tell me you were coming in? We could have had breakfast or lunch."

Maizelle gave her daughter a look that made it clear that she was well aware something had transpired between her daughter and the candidate beyond work. But she let the issue go, out of respect but also because the look in Pia's eyes demanded it. "I'm meeting Madeline in a bit, but I wanted to come by and drop something off to you."

"What's that?"

"Now, I know you don't like yellow," she said, reaching into the bag and pulling out an infant's pima cotton drawstring gown on a tiny satin hanger, "so I picked up mint green."

"Mom, it's so sweet," Pia said tenderly, fingering the cloud-soft material. "And this is really sweet of you."

"And I got a few other things," Maizelle said, picking up the shopping bag and handing it to Pia. She pulled out item after green, yellow, and white layette item. She felt deeply touched that her mother was finally coming around to accepting the baby.

"Thank you," Pia said, swallowing her tears. "You're going to spoil this baby rotten. There's nothing left to get for the shower Dee has planned but thinks I don't know about."

"That's what grandmas do. We spoil our grandbabies . . . and their mamas." Maizelle opened her arms to pull Pia into a warm, accepting embrace. "Pia, I've prayed a lot on your reasons for having this baby. And I asked God to help me put aside my feelings and concentrate on yours. And while I'm not happy about the way you went about it, this is your life and you're a grown woman."

"Thank you for understanding," Pia said as the tears fell.

"I think I do understand, sweetheart. When I try to picture my life without you, it is impossible to even imagine. And I wouldn't want you to miss out on the kind of joy you've brought to my life. So, if this is the way it has to be, I will accept it."

"Mom, you don't know how much that means to me and how much I needed to hear you say that today."

"I was saving this for the birth day, but that's two months away, so I decided to give it to you now as kind of a peace offering." This time Maizelle pulled from her pocketbook a small jewelry box. "And the beat goes on," she said, handing it to her daughter.

Pia opened it to find an eighteen-karat-gold heart filled with three small gemstones—amethyst, peridot, and citrine—floating inside. "It's beautiful," she said, picking it out of the box to inspect it closer.

"It's a mother's heart with yours, mine, and the baby's birthstones in it. As long as he or she is born any day in November, we're okay."

"Mom, if you don't mind, I'd like to think the heart is Daddy's and he's holding us all inside."

"That's perfect," Maizelle said, touched to the core by her daughter's sentiment. "He'd love that. He loves you, Pia, and he's proud of you. And so am I."

Pia sat clutching the necklace and clinging to her mother in love and gratitude. It felt good to know the total spectrum of her mother's love again. Pia had missed their close relationship. And for that moment, she felt just a little less lonely.

As soon as her mother departed, Pia picked up the newspaper and, without looking at Valen's picture, threw it in the garbage. She then called Darlene into the office.

"Grandma Dearest is starting the no wire hangers' thing a little early," Dee said, picking up the satin hanger while inspecting the baby bounty Maizelle had delivered.

"Leave my mother alone. She's finally come around. And I can't tell you what a relief it is. I really missed her."

"Something else to celebrate," Dee said, rubbing Pia's belly. "We should have a party."

"Don't think I don't know you've been planning one for weeks. When is this embarrassing shindig taking place?"

"The date has been set and invitations sent. It's the second Sunday in October. We didn't tell you because we all know you can't keep a secret, so don't you tell Pom. It's a surprise."

Chapter Thirty-one

Cris and Becca walked into the Uptown Bar as if their names were on the lease. Becca felt nervous energy fuel each step as she navigated her way through the lounge and into the bar. And though she may have looked assertive and bold to the inquiring eyes watching her assets stroll by, inside she was feeling anything but.

Since Becca and Nico's lusty romp on Oak Street Beach in June, they'd talked twice on the phone and hooked up for sex once in the span of seven weeks. Though she visited him each week at the bar, summer was over and they hadn't gone out again, and neither had she heard from him. Sidelined first by work and then a cold, she'd been calling him at the bar for the past two weeks to no avail. She'd left a message each time, but he hadn't returned any of her calls. She didn't know where he lived, and his home phone was unlisted, so Becca had no other choice but to come to the bar and find out what was going on.

It was only nine P.M., but the Uptown was more crowded than usual on this Thursday night. The throng around the bar was three deep, emitting a contagious energy and a damn near deafening din that managed to drown out even the house music. Becca and Chris pushed their way into the crowd to find the reason for all the hubbub.

"Shots! Shots! Shots!" The masculine chant rose from the center.

Sliding by several guys wearing Chicago Bulls paraphernalia, Becca found Nico pouring shots for a horde of guests there for a bachelor party. Quietly standing out of the fray, at the far end of the bar, was an impeccably groomed black man who appeared to be in his early fifties. Of medium height, well built, and strikingly handsome, he stood there, occasionally stoking his well-groomed salt-and-pepper goatee while keeping his eyes glued to Nico Jones.

"Why don't you wait over there?" Becca suggested, pointing to Mr. Goatee.

"With pleasure." Cris smiled as he slid through the drunken humanity and over to the corner to do what he did best—flirt, eavesdrop, and speculate.

"Excuse me," she repeated, while making her way to the bar. "Hi," Becca said loudly over the crowd, giving Nico a big happy-to-see-you smile.

Nico returned her grin with a friendly head nod and sauntered over to her.

"Hey, gorgeous," he said. "What's your pleasure?"

"It's Becca," she informed him, totally recognizing his classic line.

"I know that. Where you been, gorgeous Becca?" Nico said.

"At work, mostly. Hey, did you get my messages? I've been calling for a couple of weeks."

"No. It's rough around here when it comes to getting messages."

"Oh. Okay. So . . . what's up?" she asked, trying to talk over the noise.

"Not much. Just chillin'."

"I mean, what's up with *us?* I thought maybe we could go out again this weekend. It's been a while," Becca said, loud enough for the woman rudely jostling her for position to hear.

"Can't this weekend. Gotta work."

"Maybe Monday or Tuesday then?" Becca continued, wondering if she sounded as desperate as she felt.

"I don't know. I might be busy."

"So that's it?" Becca was confused. Where was the sweet, flirtatious man she'd watched the sunset with? And had sex with twice?

"Look, gorgeous—"

"Becca."

"Hold on," he said, stepping to the corner of the bar to refresh Mr. Goatee's drink. Delivering a cognac and a broad smile, Nico chatted for an amicable minute before moving on with a fresh twenty-dollar tip in hand.

"Hey, gorgeous, what's your pleasure?" Nico flashed his toothy grin at the tall redhead resting her bountiful bosom on the bar. "Long time no see—where you been?"

Becca listened, repulsed by Nico's newly revealed "playa, play on" persona. Apparently everyone was gorgeous, and satisfying them—whether through libation or libido—was Nico's self-appointed mission. It was apparent now that Pia had been right. Nico had taken advantage of her inexperience and crush. He'd talked the talk, fucked the fuck, but when it came down to walking the walk, he stumbled over Becca's feelings like a drunk on moving stairs.

"Shots! Shots! Shots!" the chant went up again. Nico delivered the redhead's apple martini and slid down to the other end of the bar to pour tequila for his rowdy patrons. It was clear that Becca was forgotten in the mayhem, though it was just as clear that she'd been forgotten long before she'd arrived.

Becca felt the sting of salty tears mixing with mascara. The last thing she wanted to do was break down sobbing in front of Nico and his adoring audience. Through a veil of tears, she spotted Cris conversing with Mr. Goatee and signaled it was time to leave. Cris finished chatting up his bar mate and joined Becca. He waited until they had cleared the crowd and were outside to speak.

"So what did he say?" he asked gently, sensing her mood.

"You were right—he's just not into me. How did you do?" she asked, making it clear that she was done discussing Nico. "He was cute."

"Too old. I couldn't get into him. But you'll never guess who he is."

❧

"Flo, you comin' up?" Dan bellowed from the bedroom. "It's eight-fifty-seven."

"Yes, I'm on my way," Flo called back. Since they discovered them three weeks before, the shows *Mafioso* and *On Call* had become must-see TV for the Chases. Every Thursday at nine they settled in to watch Dan's favorite, a cable program detailing the personal and professional life of a New York crime boss. *Mafioso* was followed by a network hospital soap/drama set on the left coast. It followed the loves and lives of the staff of Mercy Hospital and was Florence's absolute favorite program.

Flo climbed the stairs with a tray laden with their favorite snacks—tortilla chips and guacamole for him and, in keeping with her new diet, almonds with fresh sliced mango and strawberries.

"You brought the beer?"

"Yep," she assured him as she waited for him to clear the space on the bed of the newspaper. Task completed, Dan took the tray from his wife so she could settle in beside him.

At nine on the dot, the credits came up and *Mafioso* began with an execution-style murder of a member of a competing family. As is common with cable shows, the scene was graphic and brutal, complete with blood and brains spraying the windshield. It made Flo squirm and look away. She didn't much like the program—it was way too violent and crass for her tastes—but to be fair Dan didn't really care for hers either, which was way too chick-friendly for his. But their watching each other's favorite programs together was important to Flo. In her mind, Thursdays at nine had become a solid show of commitment and compromise and an encouraging sign for the survival of their union.

Forty-five minutes and three Heinekens later, after a barrage of murder, mayhem, and wanton sex, the credits rolled, shutting *Mafioso* down for another week. Florence happily commandeered the remote, flipping the channel to ABC. She'd been looking forward to this episode all week, waiting to see if the chief of surgery would learn that he was operating on his father's love child.

Flo snuggled up on Dan's shoulder, ignoring his beer and guacamole breath, and watched the drama unfold. Just as the paternity of Dr. Carvin's patient was to be revealed, they went to commercial break, leaving Florence on the edge of her seat and giving Dan the opportunity to run downstairs for more chips and dip.

"Will you please bring me up a diet peach Snapple?" Flo requested.

"Sure. Be right back," Dan assured her as he headed toward the door.

Commercial break over, Florence's attention once again turned to the saga of Dr. Carvin and his sordid secrets and relationships. She sat engrossed in the stories of her beloved Mercy Hospital staff, not realizing until forty-seven minutes into the show that Dan had not returned with her drink. He had missed nearly the entire episode.

Ten minutes later, Florence read the credits in an effort to block her frustrated tears. She had tried redecorating. She'd tried sex and seduction. Tried surprise and shared interests. Nothing was working. How much longer was she to keep trying to reengage a man who seemed uninterested in reengaging with her?

She clicked off the television. Dr. Cavin's saga was over for another seven days, but hers threatened to drag on. What was Dan thinking? She had to know.

Florence marched downstairs, prepared for confrontation but wanting clarification. Was he still bored and unhappy with their life together? Was he contemplating leaving her again? She knew they had three months to go before their agreed upon six-month reevaluation, but she needed some kind of interim report.

"Dan?" she called out, not finding him in the kitchen or the family room. "Dan?" she called again.

"In here," he said from the library. There he was, sprawled out on the couch, Snapple on the table, watching championship boxing on HBO.

In another uncharacteristic move, Florence walked right into the library and headed straight for the remote. A surprised Dan watched as she clicked off the television and sat on the coffee table, facing him.

"Why didn't you come back upstairs?" she demanded to know. "I thought we were watchin' my show together just like we watched yours. Plus, I asked you to bring me a drink, which—after all the damn beers I've delivered to you—seems like somethin' you could have managed to bring me."

"I'm sorry, Floey. I had the Snapple and came in here to check out the fight, just for a second, just to see who was winnin'."

"And?"

"And Bambino was beatin' the crap out of the champ and I thought it would be over in that round and I didn't want to miss it. Next thing I know, it's round eight and you're down here lookin' for me. I'm really sorry."

Flo was taken aback by his seemingly sincere apology. It deflated the hurt and anger, clearing the way for her questions.

"Dan, are you any happier now than when you left? I mean, what are you thinkin'? Do you still want out?"

"Woman, what gave you that idea?"

"I don't know. You don't seem like you're really into us . . . into me," she said, bracing herself for whatever was to come.

"Florence, first, let me apologize now for bailin' on you like I did. I'm not sure what got into me, but I just needed some time. Seems like with the boys gone and it just bein' the two of us, everythin' was feelin' different. But now I'm back and I'm here wantin' to stay. Like I said, the bachelor life just isn't meant for me."

"Then you're happy with me? With our life together?"

"I can't lie. You aren't the same gal I left and that's takin' some time to get used to, but far as I'm concerned, we'll just chalk me leavin' up to a midlife crisis and extended vacation. That okay with you?"

"Yes, darlin', it certainly is," Flo said, joining him on the couch for a big hug and kiss.

Florençe left Dan downstairs to finish watching the fight and went upstairs to dress for bed. She sat at her vanity, going through the rote motions of removing her makeup while sorting out her thoughts, a jumble of divergent ideas. On one hand, she was relieved to find out that her fears about Dan were unfounded. Dan was simply trying to adjust to the new, sensually improved Florence. She would simply have to be patient and keep taking those baby steps.

On the other hand, if she was so pleased by her husband's emotional state, why didn't *she* feel satisfied? While Dan was adjusting to her being a different woman, she was trying to make peace with the realization that he was the same man. The new Flo seemed to want something more. Perhaps that was the reason she found herself constantly thinking about Dr. Clay Bickford.

Chapter Thirty-two

"No, absolutely not. Tell them my schedule is committed," Valen replied while going over his schedule for the upcoming week with his staff.

"Done. One other thing. Let's not worry, but this is definitely something to put on our radar," Ed told his boss, handing him an article titled, "Whites Take Flight on Election Day."

"Can you bottom-line it for me?" Valen asked, trying to concentrate on the speech he was preparing for his upcoming appearance at New York University.

"Analysis by a Yale economist shows nationally that white Republicans as well as independents are twenty-five percentage points more likely to vote for a Democrat when the GOP candidate is black. The bottom line is, this could mean an additional one or two percent of the vote going to the other side."

"That's sobering," Valen said, shaking his head at the absurdity of it all. "So much for party loyalty."

"But the Dems are just as fickle. White Democrats are thirty-eight percent less likely to vote along party lines if their candidate is black."

"Okay, so what do we do about this?"

"Well, we've spent a lot of time reaching out to the African American and Hispanic voters who are disappointed with the Democrats, and to moderate Republicans tired of the inefficiency of partisan politics. It's October fifth. We've got one month until the election; maybe we need to concentrate more on the GOP's base and let our final push be to the conservatives," Ed suggested. "Talk more about some of the basics such as abortion, gay marriage, and faith-based initiatives. Let them know we haven't forgotten their needs."

"But those have never been my issues. I mean, that's out-and-out pandering."

I find it difficult to see you as anything more than an opportunist. Again Pia's words, this time from their initial meeting at the Marriott Marquis, came back to him. In their short time together, with her sincerity and penchant for telling it like it is, she'd become a major sounding board and source of comfort and inspiration. Valen still didn't understand how they'd gotten to this empty place. She'd been so honest about everything else. Why had she chosen to lie about her pregnancy?

"Valen, we're talking twenty-five percent GOP flight," Ed said, bringing him back to the present.

"We're also talking about my integrity and character. I have campaigned this far on what I believe, not what I thought people wanted to hear. I'm not about to start now. I've got to get this speech finished," Valen said, dismissing his staff.

Once they'd departed, Valen put his head in his hands and tried to exhale the feeling of being alone and overwhelmed. It seemed no matter how much progress he made in trying to open closed minds and alter negative opinions, it remained a one step forward, two steps back proposition. Feeling the gurgling in his stomach, he opened his desk drawer to retrieve his antacids and instead grabbed a handful of blue fuzz.

Valen pulled the Cookie Monster puppet from the drawer and ran his hand across the soft fur. As always, his face betrayed him with a childish smile. The day it arrived, its juvenile quality had hit way too close to home, mocking him about Pia and her pregnancy. But with the passing time, the toy had become a sentimental reminder of a woman he still loved and desired.

So often these past four months, when the craziness of his day had finally quieted and he was alone, the ache for Pia's touch or the sound of her voice became overwhelming. Many times he wanted to call and ask her opinion about something that had popped up on the campaign trail, or just slip into her calming embrace and put the day behind him.

Having the benefit of hindsight, Valen realized now what a treasure he'd lost. Pia was not only insightful and intelligent but amusing and entertaining as well. She had a charmed quality about her that had rejuvenated his zest for living life in all its fullness and had brought a sanity to his hurry-up-and-work existence. Pia Jamison was the only woman he'd been involved with—including his ex-wife—who made experiencing joy as important as pursuing his ambitions. She had made him stop and smell the roses, but now he was standing in the garden all alone.

But she lied. Told you she was celibate when her pregnancy proved otherwise, his mind argued.

She had been wrong for not telling him about the baby, but he so regretted not giving her the opportunity to explain herself. He should have been more accommodating and fair. Instead, he'd let his sense of betrayal consume him. Looking back, he was sure she was neither part of some dastardly plot to ruin him nor some unwed mother out to trap a husband and father for her child. Pia was an intelligent, sensible woman of a certain age. It was not uncommon these days to run across successful professional women who had opted for single motherhood. She must have had a good reason, but, after so decisively and unkindly cutting her out of his life, he would never know the truth behind her decision.

But what about the baby?

Good question. Even if she had the best possible reason for not telling the truth, Pia still came with baggage—living, breathing baggage that would in many ways dictate his life for the foreseeable future. He was fifty-two years old. Valen was not interested in raising any more children, his or otherwise. That stage of his life was over.

So the truth that he loved Pia remained, but so did the question: Was having the woman he adored and who made him feel alive again worth eighteen more years of child rearing?

☞☜

Pia woke up early on the morning of her shower and, as she did every new day, spent a few minutes talking in bed to her unborn child. She was due in less than a month, and her body had now taken on a highly uncomfortable beached-whale quality.

"So, Pom, Valen is going to be a grandfather soon," she said, discussing with the baby things she refused to utter to anyone else. "And the election is coming up. It's going to be close, but I hope he pulls it off. Between you and me, for the first time in my life I'm voting Republican. It's the least I can do to make up for everything.

"I miss my pal, Pom, but he and I just weren't meant to be. I was meant to have you instead."

Though Pia had given up a lot in order to have this baby, she'd come to terms with the enormous reality of maternal commitment and sacrifice. No matter what regrets or disappointment she might have in her own life, the comfort and happiness of her baby were now paramount. Still, it seemed cruel that her timing had been so off. If she'd waited a few more months to be with Grand, she would have met Valen first and maybe things would have been very different.

"Pom, you've been awfully quiet these past few days. Getting kind of tight in there, huh?" she said, pushing away her guilty thoughts and stroking her tummy. "Well, not much longer, sweet pea. In just a few weeks from now we'll be spending our mornings face-to-face."

She rolled her cumbersome body out of bed, took her first of the day's many bathroom breaks, and headed into the kitchen to fix her now standard pregnancy breakfast of toast and deviled eggs.

Pia ate her breakfast and climbed back into bed to watch her favorite weekend program, *Sunday Morning*. She was enjoying a story on the creative designers behind functional art when the phone rang.

"Good morning, sweetie. How are you feeling?" Maizelle's voice rang through the receiver.

"Big, bloated, and exhausted, but okay. I think the baby is worn out from all the work I've been doing trying to get things tied up at the office. Pom's been very quiet."

"How quiet?" her mother asked.

"I don't know, I haven't felt a kick or anything for the past day or two."

"I'm sure everything's fine, but pay attention to it."

"I will," Pia responded, feeling the flush of concern. "It's normal though, right? I mean, the baby is getting bigger and there's not that much room to move around."

"I'm sure that's all it is, Pia. Now, what time are you and the car picking me up to go to the shower?" Maizelle asked, changing the subject and hoping she hadn't needlessly alarmed her daughter.

"It starts at two, so I figured the car could pick us up at two-thirty. No need for the guest of honor to arrive before everyone else."

"Okay, I'll see you then. And Pia, don't worry. The baby is fine."

Bothered by the suggestion, Pia hung up and immediately went to her computer and Googled the words "fetal movement." The first entry she looked at did nothing to put her mind at ease: "A fetus that is not well will move less. Mothers should pay attention to their baby's activity, particularly in the third trimester." The article also suggested that the expectant mother lie down and if five pokes, kicks, or wiggles were not felt within two hours she should call the doctor.

Pia promptly went back to bed, taking the burn of fear and helplessness with her. She stayed there all morning, watching television and catching up on her magazine reading, but it was difficult to focus, and Pia found herself begging both the baby and God to let her know things were okay.

"Please, Pom, give Mommy a kick or a hiccup. Anything to let me know you're well," she pleaded. Pia tried not to panic, but intuitively she knew that something was terribly wrong and she felt powerless to fix it.

Ninety minutes later, with still no movement, a quietly hysterical Pia first called Dr. Montrae, who insisted she get down to her office immediately, and then her mother, who promised to rush right over and meet her.

Pia got dressed and went outside to hail a cab. She felt as if she were inside a bubble, totally oblivious and removed from the activities occurring on the street around her. She purposely tried to stay in this state in order to keep the frightful thoughts circling her head from swooping down and overtaking her.

She and Dr. Montrae arrived within minutes of each other. Pia undressed and waited on the treatment table while her obstetrician quickly prepared for this unexpected examination.

Please, God, let the baby be all right, she prayed frantically as Dr. Montrae spread the cold gel on her skin and moved the transducer over her belly. The concerned look on her face while she studied the screen was obvious, and Pia immediately started crying. She reluctantly looked over at the monitor and saw for herself flat lines where the baby's vital signs should be.

"I'm sorry, Pia. The baby died," Dr. Montrae said, holding her patient's hand while delivering the devastating news.

"But how? Why? What did I do wrong?" Pia sobbed.

"You did nothing wrong. But we won't know for sure what happened until you deliver," the doctor said, crossing the room to retrieve a box of tissues.

"Deliver?" Pia screeched. The idea of going through labor and delivery to produce a dead child seemed unjustly cruel. "How does one deliver death into the world?"

"I know, I know," the doctor said, giving Pia a supportive hug. "But at this point we don't have much choice. We can either induce labor or you can wait for it to occur naturally, which typically will happen within two weeks. I would not advise surgery."

"I can't carry around my dead baby for two weeks. I just can't. I can't," Pia said, sobbing on Dr. Montrae's shoulder.

"That's perfectly understandable. We'll schedule the procedure as soon as possible. In the meantime, I'm giving you a prescription for something to help you relax. I'm so, so sorry, Pia. I know how much you wanted this child. Lie here for a few moments. I'll be right back."

Dr. Montrae left the room, trying not to cry herself. This part of her job never got any easier. She walked into the waiting room, where Pia's mother sat anxiously awaiting some report. She could tell by the doctor's face that the news was not good.

"She needs you right now. Take all the time you want."

Maizelle followed the doctor back to the examination room and found Pia curled up on the table, rocking gently and crying. She lifted herself into a sitting position as soon as her mother walked into the room and immediately collapsed into her arms. Maizelle said nothing but prayed to her God, asking for an explanation for this spirit-crushing event and for the strength and wisdom to guide her broken child through it.

An hour later, Pia was back in her bed, resting, thanks to the prescribed sedative. Maizelle was there watching over her daughter when she called Valen Bellamy's name. Pia had convinced her that he was not the baby's father, but she had not been so convincing about the true nature of their relationship. Mai had suspected all along that there had been more between them than work, but whatever it was or wasn't, it was apparently over.

It wasn't until nearly two o'clock that Mai remembered the baby shower. She called Dee's cell phone and broke the sad news, asking her to discreetly inform the guests that the shower was canceled.

"No details, Darlene," Maizelle insisted. "Let's protect Pia's privacy. We'll let her decide how to handle things when she's ready."

"Okay, Mrs. Jamison. Please tell her I'll call and check on her tomorrow. I'm so sorry," Dee said, shedding sad tears for her friend. "If there is anything I can do, please let me know."

"Maybe there is one thing," Maizelle said. "Do you know how to reach Valen Bellamy?" A tear for her daughter rolled down Maizelle's face. To be heartbroken twice in such a short period of time seemed so unfair.

Chapter Thirty-three

One week after delivering and cremating her stillborn son, Pia stood gently twisting the birthstone necklace her mother had given her. She, Maizelle, and Darlene, all dressed in white, stood barefoot in the surf, waiting for the late October sun to set over the Atlantic Ocean. In deference to Grand Nelson, Pia had chosen the Sag Harbor beach for their baby's memorial service because eventually these waters would connect to Aruba's—the place they'd met. As per their agreement, Pia never told him that she was pregnant, so there was no point in telling him that their child had died due to an undetected knot in his umbilical cord. But in this small way, Pia felt she was paying her respects to the man who had graciously and unselfishly tried to make her dream come true.

With the cold ocean water rushing between her toes, Pia felt tinges of guilt and resignation interlaced with her grief. She had unfairly pinned so many high hopes on her child that she had to wonder had it all been too much for his little spirit to uphold. Pia had taken her lifelong desire for a child into her own hands and become a mother by any means necessary. But apparently God had other ideas. Motherhood was evidently not meant to be a destination on Pia's road map.

"The sun is setting. Are you ready?" her mother asked, giving her daughter a hip-to-hip hug. Maizelle was trying to stay strong for Pia, but the death of her grandchild had hit her much harder than she'd expected. Standing here in this grief-stricken moment, she felt a sense of shame for months of denying Pia and her child the unconditional love they deserved. She'd spent far too much time being caught up in her own shame and concern over what people would think of her because of Pia's decisions. Because of her selfishness, Mai hadn't properly celebrated and enjoyed what should have been one of the happiest times of Pia's life.

"To those of us who knew and loved my baby, he will always be known as Pomegranate or Pom, as we affectionately referred to him," Pia said with a small smile to begin the memorial. "Dee named him that as a joke. At the time she said it was because he was like a little seed growing inside me, and since Gwyneth Paltrow already had dibs on the name Apple, we had to come up with another fruit. We laughed, and from then on referred to the baby by this sweet nickname.

"But after . . . well, recently I decided to look up the word, and what I learned amazed and comforted me. The ancient Greeks associated the pomegranate with death and rebirth, while to modern Greeks it represents *agatha,* or the good things in life. It is also a Christian symbol of the Resurrection.

"So I know we named him appropriately," Pia said, squeezing the hands of her mother and friend. "And I have to believe that Pom's death will eventually cause some kind of positive rebirth in all of us.

"Officially, my son's name is Charles Nelson Jamison, named after my father and his. And I am trusting you, Daddy," Pia said, looking up into the heavens, "to look after my . . . angel." The words caught in her throat, causing her to pause, and Maizelle's weeping, mixing with the gentle lapping of the ocean waves, filled the space.

Pia motioned to Darlene and then watched stoically as the two women lit eight floating candles. Pia then followed by launching eight gardenias into the water—one for each month her baby had lived inside her. As the sun dipped into the horizon, she and the others watched the flowers and flickering flames head out to sea.

"It is said that we all come into this world with a specific purpose. Some people arrive knowing exactly what their mission is and live their lives fulfilling that purpose. Most of us, though, arrive with some vague notion that may take us the better part of our lifetimes to understand. But even with this uncertainty, we still manage to touch others and change lives, usually unaware of just how much until something unexpected happens.

"Pom's life was short, his mission still unclear," Pia continued.

"He came and went in an instant, taking with him a lifetime of hopes and dreams. But his presence was felt, and without ever taking a breath he touched us and left a tiny, eternal imprint on our hearts. I love you, son."

Pia concluded her remarks, remaining eerily calm while the others wept openly. Pia held Darlene's hand, handing her a fresh tissue to dab her eyes and blow her nose, and then rested her head on her mother's shoulder, watching the lights float farther away from the shore.

"That was beautiful, Pia," her mother said, finally breaking the hush. Pia remained quiet as Maizelle shot Darlene a questioning glance.

They were worried. When Pia had first learned of the baby's demise she had broken down and for days was inconsolable. But following the induced labor and delivery, she'd settled into this unnaturally contained and unemotional state in which little seemed to touch her.

The drive back into New York City was quiet and uneventful. Both Dee and Maizelle came upstairs to help Pia get settled in. Inside they found several new bouquets of flowers—including a Texas-size arrangement of white peonies and calla lilies from Florence and Becca. Tired from the long day, Pia decided to retire early. Dee volunteered to cook a light dinner while Mai kept her company.

"It was a beautiful memorial," Maizelle said, sitting at the breakfast counter and peeling an orange. "I was pushing her to have the service at the church, but I'm glad she didn't. This was better and more meaningful for Pia than sitting in a church full of folks she didn't know."

"It was touching and powerful. And it was important for Pia to say good-bye her way. I know she appreciated you understanding that," Dee said as she gently seasoned the eggs to make omelets. "This has to be so sad for you too."

"There is nothing worse as a parent than knowing your child is hurting and you can't kiss away the pain like you could when they were little."

"It also makes it hard to help when she's so closed down," Dee said. "I know it's only been a couple of weeks, but it's like she's in this unreachable zone where nobody can touch her."

"I'm very concerned. Best I can tell, Pia hasn't shed a tear or expressed any kind of real emotion since the procedure. I've talked to her about getting grief counseling from Pastor Saxton, but she's not interested. I wish she'd just open up and at least tell us what she's feeling."

"I guess grief affects people in all kinds of ways."

"Pia has always been pretty private. She was five when her grandfather died and eighteen when her father passed, and she was the same way. She kept everything bottled up inside her, just like now."

"So how can we help her?" Dee asked as she served Maizelle's omelet and toast with a supportive smile.

"I'm not sure there is anything *you* or *I* can do."

"I agree with you. We're not the one she craves comfort from."

"So what should we do?" Mai asked.

"I know that you were planning to spend the night here with Pia, but you look exhausted. Why don't you go home? I'll stay with her. Maybe we'll have a chance to chat," Darlene replied with a wink in her voice.

After Maizelle left, Dee looked in on Pia and found her asleep. She tidied up the kitchen and proceeded to make herself comfortable on the sofa in front of the television. But instead of paying attention to the program, she continued to worry about her friend. Ever since things had ended with Valen, Darlene had seen sutble signs of despair, which now had catapulted into full-fledged depression since the death of her baby. Pia barely ate, refused to speak to anyone other than Dee and her mother, and spent her days either sitting in her bedroom, staring out the window or sitting on the sofa mindlessly watching cable news. Sleep came only with the help of sedatives. Dee couldn't be sure, but she guessed that Pia's thoughts were typical of those who experience this kind of tragedy—alternating between wondering what she did wrong and why she was being punished.

"You don't have to stay and babysit me," Pia said, emerging from her bedroom.

"No problem, *chica*. Besides, your cable reception is better than mine," Dee said, trying to keep things light. "Are you hungry? I can make you an omelet or something."

"I'm good," Pia said, joining her on the couch with the coverlet Flo had made in memory of Pom. She'd asked Dee to send all of the baby clothes from the shower and had pieced together a beautiful one-of-a-kind quilt. It was heartbreakingly thoughtful, and it had become Pia's security blanket of sorts. The blanket and ceramic baby shoes from the hospital, engraved "Charles Nelson," were the only baby items that Pia kept as an open reminder that she'd once had a child.

She and Darlene sat in comfortable silence, watching reruns of *Sex and the City* on TBS. Neither was paying much attention to the episode, as each was lost in her own thoughts—Pia going over the sad and touching events of the day and Dee wondering how to bring up the very delicate subject of Valen Bellamy.

"That Carrie really loves her some Mr. Big," Darlene said, easing her toes into the troubled waters.

"I know. The sorry thing is that he really loves her too but is just too scared to admit it."

"There's a lot of that going on," Dee commented, wading farther out into the potential riptide.

"Meaning?"

"Meaning that you should call Valen. There's too much unfinished business between you, and . . ."

"And you think by calling Valen somehow I'll feel better about losing the baby? Or, worse, he may come back to me because I did," Pia replied, her voice still flatlined.

Pia couldn't explain that because of the nagging guilt she felt, getting back with Valen would never be an option. It was her fault she'd engaged in the emotional tug-of-war of wanting her child and wanting Valen. Pia could only believe that her internalizing the disappointment of not being able to have both had somehow broken the spirit of her baby, causing her to lose him forever.

"I really wasn't thinking about it like that," Dee said, totally lying. "I was thinking that you seem to be the only one around who can't see how much you love him. And I was thinking that just because you lost one love doesn't mean you have to lose both."

"You think too much."

"That's it?"

"I don't want to talk about this. It's over. I've accepted it and I'm moving on. But there is one thing you can do for Valen."

"Name it."

Pia left the couch and went into her study, returning moments later holding a business envelope. "You can mail this for me tomorrow."

Darlene looked at the sealed envelope. It was addressed to the Board of Elections.

"It's my absentee ballot. The race is too close, and he needs every vote he can get."

Dee tried to contain her smile. The fact that Miss Liberal Lucy was crossing party lines for the first time in her voting life was all the convincing she needed. Pia had always counted on her to keep her life straight, so the way Dee saw it, getting her boss and Valen Bellamy reconnected was just one more thing to add to her to-do list.

"Will you get that?" Pia asked, referring to the ringing phone. "Please take a message. I don't really feel like talking to anyone."

Darlene picked up the phone. It was Florence Chase checking up on her friend.

"Hi, Flo. Well, it was a tough day and she's resting. But I'll tell her you called . . ."

"Wait, I'll talk to her," Pia said, taking the receiver from her surprised secretary. "Hey. Thank you so much for the beautiful flowers and the coverlet. It's very special."

"You're welcome. How you holdin' up, sugar?"

"I've had better days."

"Well, I'm not gonna keep you. I just wanted to let you know that Becca and I are thinkin' of you and sendin' you lots of love. We're lookin' forward to seein' you soon, but don't you worry about pushin' our reunion off until you're feelin' up to company."

"No, I've already postponed it once. And even though I look and feel like anything but a weapon of mass seduction, I don't want to cancel. It'll give me something to look forward to, because right now there's not much going on in that department."

"I know, darlin', and as much as you think you'll never get over this hurt, while it won't ever go away, it will fade to a dull ache over time."

"Maybe" was all the agreement Pia could commit to. "You'll call Becca and let her know?"

"I will. Now you go rest, and darlin', you call me anytime, night or day. If you need to cry or bitch or moan, I'm here for you."

"Thanks. See you in December."

Chapter Thirty-four

Pia was awakened by the smell of bacon wafting under her nose. Bacon could mean only one thing. Her mother was up cooking her yet another breakfast she wouldn't eat. Filling her stomach had seemed so important when she was pregnant—first to ward off the morning sickness and then to fuel and sustain the growing life inside her. But her baby was gone and so was her appetite—not only for food but for life as she'd known it.

Pia was as confused by her reaction to Pom's death as everyone else around her. When she'd first learned that he had died, the pain swept over her like a tsunami, destroying her life and then quickly receding, leaving an eerie calm behind. Inside she was hurt and heartbroken, but just like when her father had died, or after the horrific tragedy of September 11, or even when Valen had told her he loved her, there was an impermeable numbness about her. It was as if her heart was layered in bubble wrap, protecting her from any feeling—good, bad or otherwise.

She sat up in the bed, letting the sunshine hit her face, and for the first time in weeks, a small smile decorated her face as she woke. Election day in New York would be a pleasant sunny November day. Bad weather could be crossed off the list of potential reasons voters might stay at home.

Pia had been secretly looking forward to this day and was happy it had finally arrived. Today gave her something else to concentrate on besides her grief. She would stay in and watch the news and follow the election returns. All the main pollsters—*New York Times*/CBS News, *New York Post*/Fox 5 News, and the Marist Poll—predicted a virtual deadlock between Valen and his rival, Democrat Betsy Franklin. Only one, the Quinnipiac Poll, had Franklin leading by as much as eight points. Valen had picked up a late-minute endorsement by the top elected officials of color in the New York State Legislature, and Pia was hoping that this would help kick him to the top.

Despite what she'd told Dee, Pia had not fully accepted Valen's walking out on her, and she hadn't moved on. She missed their romantic friendship, with its camaraderie, compassion, and sexual tension. And though she knew a future for them was not possible, in many ways Pia was happy she still felt so strongly for him. It proved that despite her crumpled heart and years of shutting down and closing off her emotional and sexual sides, she was feeling again.

But feeling what?

That question left a niggling sensation under her skin, causing Pia to get up and stretch. She tried to pinpoint just what was bothering her as she glided through a modified yoga sun salutation. She had completed the series of poses and was sitting down to rest on the settee when a huge aha moment descended on her and the answer to her question emerged from within.

Feeling everything.

She hadn't known at his conception, when learning of his death, or while standing on the beach releasing his spirit to the sea. The reason had remained unclear until this exact minute. And the fact that this moment of revelation included thoughts of Valen made it all the more poignant. Suddenly everything was making so much sense.

Her lost baby's mission had been to open her heart and teach her how to *feel* again. Since losing her father so many years ago, she'd been running on neutral, with a smooth, even emotional range—never high, never low—moving through life without any true emotional commitment. *Not* feeling had become her normal state of existence.

Even the mysterious cool charisma that defined her sensual self was a mask she hid behind. When it came to her personal life, she'd become an observer, because to participate meant to put her feelings on the line and risk being vulnerable. After years of feeling hurt and abandoned by men, beginning with her grandfather and continuing with her dad and Rodney Timble, Pia'd closed down her emotional side and tried to find personal passion through sex while allowing lust to replace love.

And when that didn't work, she'd shut down her sexual self and constructed a false serenity around her. At home, Pia had let the Zen-like atmosphere she'd created, with the soothing new age music, calming candlelight, and affirmation cards, become a cocoon insulating her from the highs and lows of her life. In addition to her yoga practice, she had been posing all of her adult life.

Pom had changed that. Her pregnancy and his death had forced Pia to tap into the emotional reserves she'd been storing up since shutting down production on her sentiments. The pain of losing her child was too powerful to self-medicate away with champagne and mood music. But with the grief and anguish came the realization that she could be whole, though only if she had the courage to chose to be.

Another bolt of enlightenment hit her. This was why she didn't know how to translate her strong feelings for Valen into the actions and words necessary to keep him. He had told her he loved her and she had ignored him in the most polite way she could think of. But why? Yes, she'd avoided a physical relationship with him because of her pregnancy, but Pia now saw that being his buddy was also a way for her to remain emotionally unavailable. Instead of giving herself to him in totality, she'd held back, keeping the depth of her feelings in reserve.

Remembering the pain on Valen's face when he'd repeated his declaration caused the storm clouds to gather over her heart and threaten a deluge. She blinked back the early sprinkles as she picked up her BlackBerry from the nightstand and typed in Valen's e-mail address. She left the subject line blank and typed the words she hadn't uttered to a man since Rodney broke her heart, and even then she wasn't sure if she fully understood the concept.

I love you too. Pia stared at the words and took inventory of her bodily reactions. A warm sensation crept through her body, culminating in a small smile that ignited her tears. It was true.

Are you going to send it? her heart inquired.

No, it's too late, her head quickly responded.

Why?

Because you lied to him and hurt him and put his candidacy at risk. He doesn't trust you.

Her heart had no reply, and Pia tossed the device on the bed as the tears rained down, and she sat alternating between sobs and laughter, purging her years of pent-up hurt and grief and allowing them to be softened—not replaced—by the resurgence of love in her life and the sorrow of its loss.

Pom and Valen were lost to her, but in the rubble that was currently her existence she would rise and she would feel and she would love and she would live.

"I owe that to you, Pom. Thank you," she sobbed into the morning.

Maizelle had just put the biscuits in the oven when she heard a hodgepodge of noises coming from the bedroom, and she rushed in, spatula in hand, to find her daughter in some sort of controlled hysteria. She was concerned but pleased that finally Pia was releasing her grief.

Sure that Pia was still grieving the baby, Maizelle dropped the spatula, got in the bed with her daughter, and gathered her into her arms. She held and soothed her, just as she'd done throughout the years. Pia continued to cry and before long her sobs became whimpers and the whimpers became sniffles.

"Why don't you go shower and I'll finish your breakfast," her mother suggested.

Pia gave her mother one last squeeze, disengaged her body, and headed off to the bathroom. Mai was about to get up when she rolled over onto Pia's BlackBerry. She picked it up to put it on the nightstand and couldn't help noticing the message.

I love you too.

Maizelle became even more interested when she noticed the message was addressed to Valen Bellamy. Her maternal side kicked in, suggesting to Mai that here was her chance to help make Pia's pain more bearable. Hearing the shower, she decided to call Dee and get her to weigh in on what Pia was sure to find a *mom*umental act of meddling.

"Do it," Dee said without hesitation. "It's not like you wrote it. You're just making sure it gets delivered."

"She said 'too' so that means Valen said it first," Maizelle rationalized.

"All the more reason."

Mai agreed, then looked toward the bathroom, closed her eyes, and hit Send. She dropped the device back on the bed where she'd found it and padded back into the kitchen, smiling all the way. If Valen loved Pia and Pia loved him back, it seemed crazy for them to be apart, especially now. In Mai's eyes, if Pia was willing and ready to love, Valen was the perfect candidate.

Pia emerged from her shower feeling both mentally and physically refreshed. She quickly got dressed and made her bed, refusing to spend another day holed up in her bedroom grieving. She picked up her BlackBerry to place it on its charger and noticed with great dismay that her message had been sent.

I know I didn't send it, she told herself. *She wouldn't. Oh, God, she did.*

"Why, Mother?" Pia asked, marching into the kitchen.

"Because you finally figured out what all of us knew for months. And we decided it was in both your best interests to send it," Mai told her, not the least bit apologetic.

"We? We who?"

"Dee and I talked while you were in the shower. It was apparent to both of us that you and Valen were at some sort of impasse and needed a little push."

"First the workshop and now this? She really crossed the line this time."

"Don't blame Darlene. I was the one who made the final decision. What workshop?"

"It doesn't matter," Pia said, unwilling to even try to explain that concept to her mother. "Dee knows better, and for that matter, so do you."

"I know *you,* Pia Clarice Jamison. And all your life you have needed a push toward things you were interested in but afraid of. Remember in high school when I wanted you to apply for the Links Debutante program? You absolutely refused, and what happened?"

"I won the scholarship," she muttered.

"And you had a great time. And you didn't want to do that summer abroad thing your senior year at college, but I pushed you into going, and what happened?"

"I met Larry Holland . . ."

"Who?"

"Who worked for WJLA-TV and hired me as a production assistant when I graduated."

"So maybe this push will be just as fruitful," Maizelle suggested. "Pia, Darlene and I both love you. We're only trying to help."

"It's a lot more complicated than you understand, Mother."

"Pia, I don't know exactly what went on between you two, but maybe if you'd told him how you really felt, it wouldn't have gotten so complicated. And now the ball is in his court. If you two are meant to be, you'll know soon enough."

❧

By the eleven o'clock news, it was clear. Despite a valiant effort and inspired campaigning, Valen Bellamy had failed to win the election for U.S. senator from New York. The entire state was stunned, as the winning margin for Senator-Elect Betsy Franklin had left most pollsters way off the mark. What had been billed as a virtual deadlock had proven to be a 23 percent margin of victory for Franklin. Whatever the reasons for the miscalculations, Valen was not to be the champion tonight.

Forty minutes later Pia sat with her mother, once again in tears, heartbroken for the man she now realized she loved as he delivered his concession speech.

"I am disappointed," Valen stated after congratulating his opponent and thanking and commending his hardworking campaign staff and volunteers. "But tonight marks only the end of this particular campaign. I will not retire from politics because I will not abandon the great citizens of New York State, neither will I abandon the causes we have fought so hard to bring to the forefront." Valen delivered his concession speech with the same graciousness and dignity with which he'd run his campaign, and Pia was mightily proud.

The ball is in his court. Her mother's words ran through Pia's head. She was certain things were probably much too hectic and disappointing for him today for Valen to even look at e-mail, let alone tackle such an unexpected and thought-provoking message. Still, Pia wondered what response her mother's boldness would bring.

It occurred to Pia that despite a lot of praying and campaigning on both their parts—she for a baby, he for office—neither of them had achieved their professed dreams. She wondered why. Why did the feel-good gurus of the world build you up to believe that everything was possible, that dreams did work out as long as you believed, and as soon as you started believing—*BAM!*—the jesters of the universe found a way to let you know that the joke was on you.

⇢

At 2:17 A.M., Valen sat in his dimly lit study, quietly getting drunk. He'd run a gentleman's campaign, one he was proud of, and yet the voters had turned him away. The second-guessers and armchair quarterbacks were already chiding him for being too soft in this crazy world of million-dollar, mudslinging neo-politics, upset that instead of confronting the negative ads and cookie-throwing audiences he'd taken the high road and pressed forward with ideas instead of insults. In the weeks ahead, further analysis would determine if the white flight Ed had feared had actually played a part in his defeat, but Valen had remained true to himself, and with that he was satisfied.

He poured himself another drink. The hardest part of losing was coming home to an empty apartment. He'd left the Hilton Hotel, where hundreds of volunteers were gathered together to commiserate; had sent his staff and son home to be with their families; and here he was, alone in his study, entertaining his regrets. His intoxicated mind wandered back to the last time he'd felt this down and how he'd immediately retreated to the place where he'd felt comforted and understood. He'd sought refuge in Pia's arms, and somehow she'd managed to make everything right. He'd fallen in love with her that night. And then it had all come crashing down at his feet.

Damn, he wished he could step back in time before the lies, the secrets, and the good-byes. He took another swig of scotch and tried to erase the hurt, anger, and disappointment that had crested this evening with his political defeat. With every sip, his head became cloudier while the truth became clearer—it wasn't drink he needed. It was Pia.

Valen saw the message light blinking on his Treo. He sat watching it, hoping that between the alcohol and the light he could hypnotize away this horrid feeling. He had no intention of checking it. He was not ready to sift through the many condolences and next-step messages waiting for him. Valen drained his glass, shut the damn thing off, and took his exhausted, defeated butt to bed.

Chapter Thirty-five

"Happy birthday, dear Florence, happy birthday to you," the waiters finished the traditional song with a flourish and Flo blew out the candles.

"Sorry about the dancin'," Dan apologized when they departed. "I had no idea they'd be all booked up. But we can just finish up here and go on home."

Florence simply continued to sip her coffee and eye her birthday slice. She'd requested just one thing for her birthday: to go dancing. But after one swing and a miss, Dan had given up, and instead of out shaking her groove thing, here she was, sitting in front of a slice of carrot cake. She hated carrot cake. Apparently he'd forgotten that about her too. Flo tried to push aside thoughts of the time and effort she'd put into planning his red hot birthday surprise, but the resentment welling up inside her wouldn't allow it. She hadn't expected the same level of treatment, but certainly something different from what they'd done to celebrate her birthday every year since the boys had left home—dinner, gifts, home to bed.

"Time for birthday presents," he said on cue as he pulled a red foil gift bag from under the table. "Happy birthday, Floey."

Florence looked for a card and, finding none, pulled the first item from the bag—the complete DVD set of season one of her favorite show, *On Call*. She was pleasantly surprised. Perhaps she was being too hard on her husband. It was a thoughtful gift. "Thank you, honey."

"Now you can catch up on last season," Dan said, pleased with himself for getting it right. "There's more."

She reached back into the bag and pulled out a large size bottle of Jean Natè, and this time her expression wasn't so delighted.

"What? You like Jean Natè."

"No, I simply wore it because *you* like it. But I changed my scent months ago."

"Really?" His pleasure deflated.

"Yes, really. I don't wear this anymore. I wear Chanel Nineteen. And I've never liked carrot cake."

"It's like I don't know you anymore."

"No, you don't, and I'm not sure you ever did. Why don't we go?" Flo suggested, decisively ending the celebration.

Dan paid the check and escorted his wife out of the Strip Steak House. With the cool November air kissing her cheeks, she stood in the parking lot, waiting for Dan to unlock the door. The clouds drifted in the sky, revealing a bright yellow full moon. It was absolutely beautiful. She loved when the moon was full. It made her feel as if she really did live on a planet that was floating in space.

"Oh my God, Dan, look. Isn't it amazin'?"

"It's the moon, Flo. Ya miss it tonight, it will be back tomorrow. Now let's get in the car and get home."

Flo stood looking into the sky and realized that living in the moment alone wasn't nearly as gratifying or delicious as sharing any moment with someone as interested in life as you were, who loved you and you loved in return. And right now, bathed in the light of her birthday moon, Florence could not say definitively if Dan Jeb Chase was that someone.

❧

It was eleven-thirty when Florence left Dan snoring in the bed and hauled the large wicker basket from upstairs down to the basement. She was in a reflective mood, not surprising, considering her earlier thoughts. She normally did the laundry during daylight hours, but spending the last minutes of her birthday alone, washing clothes, was Flo's attempt to abate her frustration.

Walking across the laundry room, Flo placed the basket on the folding table with an exasperated sigh. She robotically sorted the clothes, poured the detergent into the water, and began placing Dan's whites into the suds. Instead of immediately closing the top and moving on to the next task as she would usually do, Florence stood mesmerized by the agitation cycle rotating back and forth, pulling the dry clothes under water, drowning them in a sea of foam.

With no provocation, she slammed the top shut, her stomach churning up her own buried agitations. Something besides disappointing birthday plans was gnawing away at her sense of contentment. Perhaps it was that her fifty-fourth birthday celebration coincided with the end date of the agreement they'd made six months ago to sit down and reevaluate their relationship and future together.

Leaving the rhythmic swish of the machine in the background, Florence trudged back upstairs to make a cup of tea. Sitting at the table, stirring honey into her cup of chamomile, Flo realized that despite Dan's declarations of domestic happiness, she was no longer sure of her own.

Dan had left her for six months because he was bored and had returned because he'd discovered he was too old to be a bachelor. Apparently in his time away he'd determined that comfort trumped monotony and had come home, happily settling back into his same routine. His meals were cooked, his underwear washed, and his minimal sexual needs met. Sometimes she thought it would have been better if he had left her for another woman. At least that would be proof that Dan still felt alive and energetic.

Florence had her husband back, and now she was the discontented spouse, but her dissatisfaction went so much deeper than simple monotony. When had she ceased being comfortable in her own life? The need to explore the world and her place in it left Florence feeling as if she were about to burst through her skin.

Florence felt out of place everywhere she stood. From the outside looking in, things looked pretty damn perfect, but inside she felt as if she'd been running on automatic pilot, doing what she'd always done for years out of habit, not happiness. Despite their recent troubles, Dan had given her a good life, and lately she'd felt guilty for wanting more, but she was dying a slow death. The suffocation of her passion and zest for love and living was proving fatal to her marriage and her soul.

When Dan had left, Flo had been panicked and afraid. Marriage to Dan had been her way of life for twenty-six years, and the thought of existing without him had unnerved her. In desperation she'd allowed Miriam to pack her off to the Weapons workshop in search of ways to put a spark back into Dan's eye and make him want to come home and stay married.

But something had happened in San Francisco. Florence had become more interesting to herself. She now wanted more of something different. She wanted joy and wonder and love in her life. Now, months after the WMS workshop, Flo could no longer ignore the growing realization that she had outgrown her husband, her marriage, and her life as it had been.

As Florence refilled her teacup, she decided exactly what she wanted for her birthday. Leaving the cup on the counter, she went to the kitchen desk and turned on the computer. In the time it took to boot up, Florence allowed herself to imagine the taste of freedom dipped in curiosity and rolled in adventure. Once online, a hungry Flo went to the AOL travel page. Ten minutes later she'd performed the most spontaneous act she had in years and booked a seven-day, six-night vacation in Barcelona, Spain, deciding her destination based on Clay Bickford's enthusiastic recommendation. She would leave the day after Thanksgiving and would fly through New York on her way home to keep her reunion with Pia and Becca.

Forget dinner and dancing in Dallas. Flo wanted to take her celebration outside the confines of Texas. She wanted to take in the Catalan architecture, strut down La Rambla, dance all night, and then take a sunrise dip in the Mediterranean Sea.

But this was so much bigger than simply taking the party abroad. Florence was experiencing an amazing bout of wanderlust. She needed to bust out of this suburban way of life and expand her world beyond this all American cowboy existence. Not just see the world, but be a part of it. And she wanted to do it alone.

Florence had no idea how Dan would react to her desire to spend time by herself in Barcelona. Frankly, she didn't care. He had taken his sabbatical from their marriage, and now it was her turn. The decision to return or not would be pondered while sipping Spanish red wine and eating spicy tapas and getting better acquainted with the exciting new woman within.

Chapter Thirty-six

Valen rocked back and forth in the hospital glider with his sleeping granddaughter, Isobella, in his arms. The pain of this month's earlier defeat seemed far away as he stared down at this tiny new branch of their family tree. She was a perfect reason to celebrate Thanksgiving. Ten fingers, ten toes, the sweetest pouty mouth, and though he had yet to see for himself, he'd been told that Isobella had inherited his light gray eyes.

For the second time this year, Valen Bellamy fell in love.

"You look like a natural, Dad," Robbie said reentering the hospital room after escorting his wife, Stacey, on a prescribed walk around the floor.

"It's been a long time," Valen said, trying but failing to remember his own son being this new.

If Valen was to be honest, he'd sleepwalked through his son's upbringing. Always too busy becoming and then being a success, he had let slip by so many important moments of Robbie's life, which he either did not attend or barely noticed. Truth be told, he'd fathered a child but had never truly been a hands-on dad.

"It will all come back to you. I've already got you down on the babysitting rotation."

"Robbie, you know Dad's too busy for that," Stacey said.

"No, Stacey. If it's okay with you two, I plan on being a regular visitor in this lovely lady's life. As fate has dictated, I'm going to have a little bit more time on my hands."

And nobody to fill it with, he thought as Isobella began to whimper and squirm.

"Sounds like somebody's hungry," Stacey declared, which was Robbie's cue to deliver his daughter to her mother's breast.

Valen stood and beamed proudly as his son lovingly placed Isobella in Stacey's hands and huddled around his girls. He was proud of his son and grateful to his ex-wife. She deserved the majority of the credit for raising such a strong, compassionate, and loving black man. But the sight of Robbie with his family also underlined the pain and loneliness he'd been experiencing since the night he'd lost the election.

With kisses all around, he bid his good-byes, promising to visit again soon, and headed down the hall. Passing the nursery window, Valen stopped a moment to gaze upon the new souls that had recently graced the world. His mind immediately went to Pia. She should have given birth to her own little bundle by now. He scanned the tiny faces lined up in their bassinets, looking for one that somehow resembled Pia. He knew it was a silly act of desperation, but in an odd way it made him feel closer to her.

Why are you torturing yourself like this?

Pia and her baby's father were probably at this very moment making plans for a future together. Or maybe the guy had dishonorably ditched her and his paternal responsibilities. Valen had no idea, because he had been too quick and too pigheaded to allow Pia to explain the details of her situation. He'd made a huge mistake by simply letting her go with no further discussion. He'd been so worried about his public image, he'd given up on the one woman who had given him a taste of true love. So perhaps it would be best for all if he just gave up and moved on with the remnants of his life.

Valen pushed the confusion to the back of his mind and left the hospital, headed back to his apartment. It was time to regroup, get back to business, and face the fact that his professional life may very well be all he had left.

With the *Monday Night Football* game playing in the background, he sat on the couch, sifting through hundreds of unread postelection e-mails still taking up memory in his Treo. Some could be answered by his staff, but others—like those from the governor and head of the RNC—needed his attention. Valen worked diligently answering and/or eliminating at least eighty e-mails before reaching the one that caused a sharp intake of breath.

I love you too.

The roar of the crowd filled the room as the New York Giants scored their second touchdown of the game. The timing was exquisite, and Valen burst out laughing. Pia Jamison loved him. That was definitely something to cheer about.

Ed had been damn near clairvoyant. If he wanted Pia, now was the time to move on it. The election was over and he could clearly see opportunity in his loss. His life was his own again. There was no constituency to kowtow to, no press following his every move. He had four years to get his private life in order before he ran again. Four years to love Pia back. Four years before the public scrutiny started up again. But by then, they'd be a solid family.

A family of three. Do you really want to dive headfirst back into fatherhood?

Truthfully? No. But a few more years of child rearing was a small price to pay for a lifetime of contentment. And maybe through Pia and her child, he'd actually learn to enjoy his life, not just work his way through it. Valen once again tossed aside his Treo. Work could wait until after the holidays. Right now he had other, more pressing and definitely more lovely things to concentrate on.

Twenty minutes into their walk, the snow began to fall. Pia felt the icy flakes hit her face, a chilly reminder that winter as well as the holiday season had officially arrived.

"I'm coming back to work next week," she informed Darlene.

"I thought you were waiting until after the New Year."

"I was, but it's time to get myself together and start being productive again. I'm going crazy just lying around mourning my baby."

"Losing a child is not something you get over easily, *chica*. You can't brush it aside and pretend it didn't happen. You have to take all the time you need to heal."

"I know. I'm not brushing it aside, but I need other things to think about. Plus, working will help keep my mind off the holidays. I'm not really feeling the Christmas spirit."

"I'm feeling right Grinchy myself," Dee said. "I miss Hector. He called from Iraq this morning and sounded so lonely. It's always so much tougher to be apart during the holidays. That's why I didn't want to go home for Thanksgiving."

"Mom and I are glad you're spending it with us, even though we're kind of pathetic—like a lonely chicks club or something."

"I know there are probably a hundred things I should be grateful, for, but somehow being around all my family just makes me feel worse. You know, like I have to be strong and happy even though I feel like shit."

"I hear you. I know that I have plenty to be thankful for, but right now all I feel is that it's been a year full of pain and drama with nothing to show for it."

"I can't believe Valen never answered the e-mail." Dee blurted out the words she'd been wanting to say for weeks. "*Chica,* I'm sorry I interfered. I was just trying to help. I really thought it would turn out differently."

"Yeah, well, somewhere deep inside I thought so too, but I guess Valen had other ideas. We'd better get back and finish dinner. Besides, I'm freezing."

"Me too. I wish Hector were here to warm me up," Dee said, putting her arm through Pia's as they walked through the accumulating snow.

"I know. But maybe hot chocolate will suffice."

"Maybe hot chocolate with a little Frangelico tossed in," Dee insisted.

"Now you're talking."

By four o'clock the lonely chicks club was sitting around Pia's dining room table, feasting on Maizelle's traditional meal of turkey, cornbread stuffing, corn pudding, string beans, and homemade rolls. Following dinner were all of Pia's favorite desserts, homemade apple pie a la mode, red velvet cake, and fresh fruit. With no thought to diet or dress size, the women dug in and thoroughly indulged. Between bites, the discussion consisted of every possible topic except the two taboos—men and babies.

"I'd like to propose a toast," Pia announced, raising her glass. After several glasses of wine, Pia found she was actually enjoying herself. "It occurs to me that I do have something to be thankful for—the two of you. Thank you for your love and support and for helping me get through this really hard time. Dee, for holding down the fort and being my friend. And Mom, for accepting me as I am and loving me in spite of myself. And I am very grateful for your slammin' red velvet cake. Thank you," she said, blowing kisses across the table.

"And I want to thank God that Hector is alive and halfway through his tour. And for you, *chica,* for being such a great boss and friend and for having such an amazing *mami* who can cook like this."

"I guess it's my turn," Mai said. "I want to thank Dee for all the love and kindness you have shown my daughter. She's never had a sister, and you are the closest thing she has. And Pia, I am so grateful to have such a strong and wonderful daughter. You are my light. I love you. God has blessed all of us."

The women touched glasses in a grateful toast, genuinely happy to be sharing this moment together. Through good food, good drink, and good friends, the irritations and disappointments that lately had clouded their daily existences were momentarily forgotten.

The ringing phone cut short their merriment. Strangely, when Pia picked up, there was nobody on the other line. "Must have been a wrong number," she said, returning to the table.

"Pia, Pastor Saxton has been asking after you. I thought maybe we should invite him over for dinner during the holidays," Maizelle said as they all cleared the table.

"So much for never meddling in my life again," Pia said. Amused by Maizelle's never-say-die attitude, she burst into laughter, followed first by Darlene and then her mother as they finished cleaning the kitchen. Their laughter was interrupted by the buzz from downstairs.

"Mom, you didn't ask Pastor Saxton over here, did you?" Pia asked on her way to answer the intercom.

"No, dear, not yet."

"Who?" Pia asked into the receiver. "Okay, tell him to wait five minutes and then send him up. Thanks, Paolo."

Pia took a moment to listen to and enjoy the song her heart was singing. And just as quickly, the music stopped. Valen had come to her, but was it by his own volition?

"Okay, which one of you is responsible for this? 'Fess up now, you traitors."

"*Chica,* what are you talking about?"

"Valen Bellamy is down in the lobby. Now which one of you invited him here?"

"Not me," Dee said, looking at Maizelle.

"Not me," Maizelle said, looking at Pia.

"Well, don't look at me. What does he want?"

"I don't know, but you might want to brush your teeth and spruce up that coif before you find out," Dee suggested.

"And put on something decent," her mother added.

Pia shook her finger at both of them and mouthed "Beeyotch" to Dee behind her mother's back before scurrying into the back to freshen up. As soon as she left the room, Dee and Maizelle, both with huge smiles on their faces, grabbed their coats and handbags and quickly departed.

"Did you?" Dee asked again in the hallway.

"Really, I didn't," Mai replied before the two exchanged high fives and stepped onto the elevator.

Pia walked back into the living room with freshly brushed teeth and hair, looking casually chic in a cream-colored velour hoodie and pants. She was nervous and quickly found another thing to be grateful for this Thanksgiving day—wine. She poured half a glass and gulped it down. Only then did she realize that the house was quiet.

"Mom? Dee?" Receiving no reply, Pia added one more item to her gratitude list.

Valen's knock was soft and tentative. Knowing that he was on the other side of the door caused Pia to freeze with temporary paralysis. Why was he here? To give her his heart or break what was left of hers into a gazillion minuscule bits?

"Only one way to find out," she said to the face in the mirror as she checked her makeup and steeled herself for whatever was coming.

He knocked again, this time louder and with more determination. Pia opened the door and took in a greedy eyeful. Valen looked good but tired, and his shy smile let her know that he was feeling as tentative as she was. She wanted to give him a big hug and tell him how sorry she was about the election results, but she simply stood leaning on the door, contemplating Valen and the small gift bag and a burgundy bunch of mini calla lilies in his hands.

Valen scanned Pia as well. She was more voluptuous than when he'd seen her last, and it was clear from her body shape that she'd given birth. Her face also bore the revealing signs of sleep deprivation.

Still, Pia looked lovely, and it took every ounce of restraint he had not to leap across the threshold and kiss those soft, full lips he'd spent the past months missing so much.

"Happy Thanksgiving," he said, swallowing his desire. "Uh, these are for you," he said, handing her the calla lilies, their stems tied with a burgundy satin ribbon.

"Thank you." Pia accepted the bouquet, and with her ivory clothing, Valen couldn't help thinking she looked like a bride. The look became her.

"Happy Thanksgiving to you too. Come in," Pia said, finally moving aside so he could enter. Valen placed the gift bag on the table as she helped him off with his *GQ*-worthy shearling coat and hung it in the closet.

"Can I get you a glass of wine?" Pia asked, further delaying the reason for his appearance.

Valen refused her offer. He wanted to stay clear-headed for the conversation to come. There was too much at stake tonight to blow it with alcohol-induced misunderstanding. Pia invited him to make himself comfortable while she put the flowers in water. The apartment smelled like holiday love—a mishmash of favorite foods layering the air with aromatic scents. It was also very quiet. The baby must be asleep, he concluded. Valen sat on the couch and quickly scanned the room. Isobella had only been home a few days and Robbie and Stacey's entire apartment looked like a ransacked Babies R Us store. Surprisingly, other than a blanket and tiny ceramic shoe, he saw no signs of an infant. Valen concluded that Pia, chic mother that she was, kept all the baby gear in the back.

"Sorry for arriving unannounced, but I thought the element of surprise might work better to my advantage," he explained.

"And surprise was necessary because . . . ?"

"Because it's been a long time and I didn't want to risk your refusing to see me. But with the baby I figured you'd probably be staying put."

Valen noticed the change in her eyes and chalked it up to residual anger over their last conversation, more pointedly his disapproval over her pregnancy.

"Was that you who called earlier and then hung up?" Pia asked, adding things up.

"Uh, yes. I was just checking that you were home."

Pia turned her head slightly and smiled. She was secretly pleased she'd driven him to such high school antics.

"Valen," she said, returning and putting the vase on the coffee table, "I'm really sorry about the election. I know how hard you campaigned, and you deserved to win. I even voted for you."

"Thank you. That means a lot, more than I can tell you."

"I hope you were sincere about what you said in your concession speech about running again. This country needs you—even if you are a damn Republican," she added with a teasing smile.

"I was and I will. But first I need to take these next few years to get some personal things in order," he said, getting closer to what he came to discuss.

"So you were just in the neighborhood?" she asked, waiting for him to mention her mother-sent e-mail. She'd already decided to take ownership for sending it if he did.

Though he'd gone over this conversation a hundred times in his mind, sitting here with Pia in kissing distance, Valen didn't have a clue where to begin. So he just said the first thing on his mind.

"I'd love to meet your baby."

Valen watched as Pia's body crumpled before releasing a tidal wave of tears. Instinctively, he reached out and drew his sobbing woman to his chest. "Shh," he said in a soothing voice as he stroked her hair. "Whatever it is we'll make it better, I promise." He was totally perplexed by Pia's reaction, but at this very moment comforting the woman he loved was more important than understanding the reason for her tears.

Pia fell willingly into his arms, not realizing until now how much she needed him to help her heal. She allowed herself to release the storm of pent-up emotion she'd been holding in since delivering her stillborn son. In the safety of Valen's embrace she purged the sorrow and guilt over the losses of Pom, Valen, and her father, and for all the years she'd spent repressing her emotions. Eventually her sobs became whimpers before dissolving into the hiccups.

"There is no baby, Valen. I had a little boy, but he died."

No words seemed adequate, so Valen simply hugged Pia tight, shielding her body with his, wanting desperately to protect her from any further hurt.

She told him everything that had been on her heavy heart since the morning he'd walked out on her. Pia started at the very beginning from her years of no sex then moved on to her gynecological issues to taking the WMS class to breaking her celibacy with Grand Nelson and their agreement.

"He doesn't know about his son?" Valen interrupted to ask.

"No. It was part of the agreement. There was to be no contact until the baby's first birthday."

Pia disentangled herself and went into the bedroom to get a Kleenex. When she returned she held two boxes—one full of tissues, the other full of heartbreaking memories.

"I've never shown this to anyone. Not even my mother," she said. Pia took a deep breath and opened the handcrafted, wooden treasure box, actually a humidor that once belonged to her father. One by one, Pia pulled from it the proof that her baby had existed—a lock of Pom's hair, his footprints, and her hospital bracelet.

Valen listened with a chest full of compassion as Pia told him of the tragic turn her life had taken in the months since they'd been apart. He cursed himself for not being around to help her through this misery.

"It was very quiet in the delivery room. Eerily quiet. No cry of life. No excited announcements. They cleaned him up—thankfully he hadn't begun to . . . well, you know—and wrapped him in a receiving blanket. He was wearing a tiny blue hat, just like all the other babies. If you didn't know he was stillborn you might have thought he was just sleeping," Pia told him, recounting the moment they placed her tiny angel in her arms so she could say good-bye. "Except for that one brief moment in time, I never got to hold him again."

The muted sounds of their pain commingled and drifted skyward. Pia had not spoken of this to anyone, and it seemed fitting to express her deepest hurts to the man she loved and thought of as her best friend. She was so grateful that he'd finally come.

Valen wept, remembering how just days ago he was rocking his precious, hungry granddaughter to sleep. He could not imagine the horror of holding her still and lifeless little body. The mere thought made him shudder.

He allowed Pia to cry for as long as she needed, vowing that pain like this would never touch this beautiful woman again. He was moved that she'd shared all of this with him as it brought them closer and made Valen only love her more.

"Pia, you asked me why I came today," he said once her sobs had subsided. Valen gently lifted her face by the chin so he could look into her tearful eyes. "I just got your e-mail."

"But I sent it weeks ago."

"It came the day of the election, and truthfully, I was so worn out and depressed that I shut off my Treo and didn't pick it up again until a couple of days ago. But when I saw your message it made everything, including losing the election, bearable. I realized that as long as you loved me, nothing was that bad and anything was possible. I hope you'll realize the same thing."

Valen brought his lips down to meet Pia's in a life-changing, love-affirming kiss.

Pia settled into his kiss, relishing the words she'd always thought she wanted to hear but had been running from nearly all her adult life.

"I love you too," Pia told him, running no longer.

"When did you know?" Valen asked, his smile as wide as the sky.

"I think it happened when we were dancing at the Empire State Building," she said between sniffles.

"I think it was sooner than that," he teased.

"Oh, really? And just when do you think I fell for you?"

"When I told you that I was no longer interested and yet you continued to pursue me. Showering me with gifts and then wearing that incredible dress to the Met just to tempt me. Those moves had 'I love you' written all over them," Valen joked.

"Uh, you do realize that I was just trying to save my job at that point?"

"Yeah, any excuse. Say it again."

"I love you."

"One more time."

"I love you, Valen Bellamy," Pia repeated, enjoying the way the sweet words warmed her like hot fudge on a warm brownie.

"Then marry me," he said. "With you, my life makes sense. *I* make sense, and now there's nothing to stop us from being together," Valen said. He hadn't come over intending to propose tonight. He'd planned on waiting until Christmas, but now just seemed like the right moment.

Pia sat and stared into Valen's eyes before standing and walking over to the window. She ignored his question and instead watched the snow continue to fall, noticing how bright the night appeared with the glow from streetlights reflecting off the snow. Usually she loved the hushed quality of snowfall, but this evening she could find no peace in the stillness.

There is nothing to stop us from being together. Valen's words pierced her joy, causing it to evaporate into the night.

Why was nothing easy? She'd finally allowed herself to fall in love and to revel in her feelings, and yet even through the euphoria of love she still had to contend with crushing disappointment.

Valen crossed the room and wrapped his arms around Pia, enjoying the warmth of her body pressed against his. Her silence seemed appropriate. She'd been through a lot, and he was sure his sudden proposal had created the need for reflection.

"I do love you, Pia."

She totally believed that Valen loved her. Just as she was positive that she loved him in return. Love was not the issue. The problem was that Valen wanted to marry her only now that there was no child. And that was unacceptable. If he didn't want her with the baby, he didn't deserve her now.

"I can't," she whispered.

"Can't or won't?" he asked, turning her around to face him.

"Does it matter? The bottom line is I'm saying no," Pia said, her hurt slowly morphing into an armor of indifference.

"You don't want to think about it?"

"There is nothing to think about," Pia said, avoiding his probing eyes. She was back to protecting herself from this disastrous thing called love. "What I need is for you to go."

Valen's thoughts sped through his head like a bullet. He didn't understand. Just moments ago they'd both professed their love for each other, and now she was throwing him out? At what point had things gone so terribly wrong? Did she not believe in marriage? Was there something else she was keeping from him?

She just lost her baby. Of course it's too soon to think about marriage. That

was the rationale that made the most sense to him. After years of
wanting to have a child and the physical and social hurdles Pia had to
get over to conceive, only to lose her child so close to delivery, she was
in no frame of mind to decide on the rest of her life. What was he
thinking? It was thoughtless and selfish for him to have put his desire
to be with her above the emotional crisis she was currently dealing
with. He should have been more compassionate. He should have followed his original plan and waited.

"Pia, talk to me," he pleaded.

After such an emotional, gut-wrenching outburst, she had nothing
left. She didn't want to talk. She just wanted to be left alone so she
could begin to get over this latest ironic chapter of her pathetic love
story.

"There's nothing left to say . . . except good-bye," she said, turning
back to watch the snow.

Valen paused for another few moments before giving up. He
kissed the back of her head, noticed the tense rise in her shoulders,
and strutted across the room to retrieve his coat. He was down but
not defeated. Valen refused to repeat his earlier mistake and give up
without explanation, but enough had been shared today.

"Pia . . ."

Her silence drove him to open the door and make his exit. It
wasn't until he'd reached the lobby that he remembered the gift he'd
brought. He wasn't sure if he should leave it and risk upsetting her all
over again, or go back and retrieve it, guaranteeing he'd upset her
again.

Leave it, he decided. There'd been enough drama for one day.

Chapter Thirty-seven

Pia turned around as soon as she heard the door close behind him. She was almost grateful for the earlier waterworks, because there wasn't a tear left in her body. She could not believe this was happening to her. Who was the cosmic jokester who kept dangling happiness in her face and then pulling it away like with Charlie Brown and that goddamn football?

Pia wandered back to the couch, poured herself another glass of wine, and blew her nose for the millionth time. She reached out and gently stroked the flowers Valen had given her. They were beautiful, just the type she would have chosen for her walk up the aisle. Oh, well.

The phone rang but Pia refused to answer it. It was probably Valen, her mother, or Dee, and she wasn't in the mood to talk to any of them. Instead, she curled up on the sofa and turned on the television, flipping through the channels, looking for some mind-numbing program to take her thoughts off recent events. She stopped on a TBS showing of *The Wizard of Oz*, allowing herself momentarily to get caught up in the residents of Munchkin Land before her mind drifted off again.

Maybe she wouldn't go back to work next week. Maybe before the WMS reunion she'd take a trip somewhere warm and beautiful. Somewhere where it would be easy to forget all the crazy twists and turns her life had taken recently. Somewhere where Pia could wipe her personal slate clean and come back in the new year and start all over again. Was that possible? Did such a place exist?

Just where the hell do I find my Emerald City and great Oz? Pia thought, yawning as her eyelids got heavy. *I'm just like that damn Dorothy—cute shoes, a motley crew of romance-impaired friends, and not a clue which way to turn.*

It was 9:46 P.M. when Pia opened her eyes. She yawned and stretched, waking herself just enough to lock up the apartment and drag herself to bed. Too much and she'd be up all night rehashing her pathetic life.

Pia got up and walked to the front door to check the locks. She flipped off the entry light and was headed back into the living area when she noticed the gift bag Valen had put down and apparently forgotten about. "Tomorrow," she instructed herself while one by one she turned out all the lights leading to her bedroom.

She undressed and went through her nightly beauty regimen. Keeping the curtains open so she could see the falling snow illuminated by the streetlights, Pia slipped into bed, pulled the comforter under her chin, and closed her eyes. She remained like that for all of thirty seconds before curiosity grabbed her by the hand and forced her to turn on the lamp, jump out of bed, and retrieve Valen's bag.

Crawling back under the covers, Pia took a deep breath. No matter what the contents, she was sure it would somehow turn the drama up a notch.

She timidly reached inside, the sound of crinkling paper broadcasting her progress until her hand touched something soft and fuzzy. Pia pulled out the Cookie Monster puppet holding a note taped between its hands. Immediately her face burst into a tearful smile, which widened into open-mouthed surprise when she read the words on the envelope: *To Baby Jamison.* Following another huge, bracing exhalation, Pia opened the note.

Dear Baby,

We haven't met yet. I'm afraid I don't even know your name, but I will soon. I wanted my first gift to you to be special, and this certainly is. Your mommy gave me this puppet at a time when I was feeling very down and unsure of myself. It made me laugh and reminded me that life is only as bad as you think it is. It is one of my most treasured possessions, and I want you to have it. I plan to play with you and Cookie Monster regularly, because it is my hope that one day soon, you, your beautiful mommy, and I will be a family. It's taken me a long time to get to this place, but I know I'm going to love you because I dearly love your mom and you are such an important and special part of her.

Love, Valen

"Oh my God. He did want the baby," Pia said, giving Cookie a fur-squashing hug. "Cookie, did you hear that? He wanted to marry both me and Pom.

"When am I going to learn to let the man speak?" she asked the little blue monster as she hopped up and down on the bed with joy. She could have avoided all this angst if she'd only let Valen explain. Pia fell out flat on the bed as she tried to think. She had to see him. And she had to see him now, and in the perfect place. It was nearly ten-thirty, which left little time, but she didn't care. It had to be there.

With Cookie Monster cheering her on, Pia picked up her BlackBerry and sent Valen a message requesting his presence. After sending it, the thought occurred to her that he may not look at his e-mail, and she decided to call.

Instead of a live voice, Pia got Valen's voice mail. She paused for a moment to swallow her disappointment, then left a message.

"Hi. It's me. It's after ten and I just sent you an e-mail. Please, please, read it and then meet me before midnight. I have so much to say to you."

Pia jumped off the bed and raced into her closet. Just what did one wear to propose? Considering the weather, she decided that it had to be the warm, outdoor equivalent of the sexy little black dress. Something with a maximum seduction quotient. In her mind that could mean only one thing—après ski wear. Pia hurried through her makeup application, added a spritz of her favorite cologne, and quickly pulled on a winter white cashmere turtleneck and matching wool stretch pants tucked into snuggly fur-lined boots. She added a silver fox-trimmed down parka, fur hat, and gloves. Pia was ready to hit the door when inspiration struck. She checked the clock. It was already eleven. She was cutting it close, but the additional details would be perfect.

Pia stripped off her gloves and scooted into the kitchen to make a thermos of hot chocolate. While she waited for the milk to warm, it dawned on her that if she was going to do this properly, particularly in such a world-famous romantic and now personally sentimental location, she should have a ring.

Think. Think. You're creative—come up with something, she commanded herself.

"Reynolds Wrap," she exclaimed, clapping her hands.

Pia ripped away a small five-inch-wide strip of foil and folded it lengthwise several times to eliminate any sharp edges. She then twisted the material into metallic rope and looped it around her thumb to create a shiny silver band. Perfect. Pia slipped the makeshift engagement ring into her pants pocket, poured the cocoa into a thermos, and sped out the door to meet the rest of her life.

⊗∽

Pia arrived at the Empire State Building twenty minutes before closing. She stepped into the empty elevator, visualizing the moment to come as the car began its ascent to the eighty-sixth-floor observation deck. Somewhere around the fiftieth floor, Pia realized she was humming. And not just any song, but her happy song. She was humming a classic tune she'd learned in nursery school, "If You're Happy and You Know It." Over the years it was the one melody that reflexively burst into her head whenever she was feeling particularly gleeful.

". . . then your face will surely show it," Pia sang before clapping her hands and walking out into a cloud's-eye view of the winter wonderland below. Snow flurries whipped around her head as she immediately turned right and circled the deck, looking for Valen. Just as she nearly completed the lap and was beginning to worry, she noticed a familiar shearling coat and the man inside it, his hands in his pockets, looking out into the snowy night.

Pia walked toward him, her steps hushed by the fallen flakes, and reached out and wrapped her arms around Valen's body. She laid her head against his back and allowed herself to soak in the silence and revel in the moment. Everything that wasn't her and Valen was cleared away by the winter wind. There was no cold, no pain, no fear or misunderstandings. Just the two of them standing on the top of their world, finally together.

Valen stepped forward and spun around, bringing his lips down on hers and devouring any words about to be spoken with his ardent kiss. Their mouths and open eyes spoke a silent language of love, clearing up all the confusion and miscommunication that had gone on between them for months. At its end, their mutual tongue-tangling proclamation was clear: Love will not be denied, no matter how messy it starts or how complicated it becomes.

"Pia—"

"Me first," she commanded, holding her gloved finger to his lips. "I have something to say and I need you to listen.

"I said no to your proposal tonight because I thought you wanted to marry me only now that there was no baby. I didn't know until I found Cookie Monster and your note that I was terribly wrong."

"It's true," Valen said, breaking Pia's rule. "It took my losing the election to finally figure out what was important to me. And that was you—baby, liberal politics, and all.

"If I had won, I'd be a senator, but it would have been such an empty victory. I've wasted so much time without you because I let my staff and the voters dictate whom I could and couldn't love. I am so sorry."

"It's so crazy that it took both of us losing the thing we wanted most to bring us together. Going through my baby's death forced me to look at aspects of myself that I was keeping in the shadows and refusing to deal with. Losing Pom hurt so much, I couldn't avoid feeling anymore. Through the pain I realized why I'd spent so much of my life avoiding love—because I was afraid that any man who loved me would leave me. I know my baby came and stayed long enough to teach me how to feel love again.

"Valen, I never believed that marriage was for me. In fact, though I was hell-bent on becoming a mother, I never thought I'd ever be a wife. Well, motherhood is no longer an option, but here I am, standing in front of the only man I've ever truly loved and wanted to spend the rest of my life with."

"Well, you already know how I feel about that," Valen said, his eyes and voice dewy with gratitude.

"So you still want to marry me?"

"More than ever."

Pia turned to squarely face the man she loved, removed his gloves, and took his hands into hers. With tears that for the first time in weeks were cried out of pure, unadulterated joy, she proceeded.

"Then I, Pia Clarice Jamison, take you, wonderful, patient, smart, funny, sweet, sexy as hell Valen Bellamy, to be my husband. To have and to hold, to love and cherish, until death us do part," she vowed.

Happiness broke out on Valen's face as Pia reached into her pocket and pulled out her handcrafted ring. With his amused eyes looking on, she squished the foil back into shape and held it between her thumb and forefinger. Pia slid the foil band onto Valen's ring finger, laughing the entire time. Valen held his hand up into the light and admired her handiwork. He loved it and everything it represented.

"And I, Valen Kermit Bellamy—"

"Kermit?" she interrupted with a laugh. "Who am I marrying?"

"Shush. I, Valen Kermit Bellamy, take you, brave, beautiful, thoughtful, sensuous, sexy, and very wise Pia Clarice Jamison, to be my wife. I will love you and protect you and drop at your feet all in the world that is good and sweet until death us do part," he said. To Pia's great surprise, Valen stripped away her glove and reached into his pocket and pulled out a small box. He flipped the lid, revealing a three-carat Asscher-cut diamond set in platinum.

Pia held the box while Valen took the ring and slipped it on her finger. It was half a size too big and wobbled slightly, but Pia's deep intake of breath let him know how beautiful she thought it to be.

"But your ring is better," Pia said through her wide smile.

"Ah, but yours, my darling, is priceless. I love it and you. Now, do I finally get to kiss my bride?"

Their lips found each other and sealed a marriage that while not legal was as real in their hearts as any officiated church ceremony. They stood happily holding each other, exhausted by the struggle to get to this place but elated knowing that the hard times were behind them. Now, with hearts united, there was nothing life could possibly throw at them that would ever be this difficult again.

"Time for a wedding toast," Pia said, pulling away and retrieving the thermos from her purse.

"You've thought of everything," Valen said as she poured him a cup of steaming hot cocoa.

"The last time I invited you up here, I promised you an evening to remember. Now I'm promising you a *lifetime* of memories. To us," Pia said, raising her cup.

"To love." They touched cups and drank the hot chocolate, warmed by both the drink and the moment.

"I promise you, Pia, that from the time the sun comes up on our real wedding day until the time we are separated by the inevitable, I will make our life together an affair to remember."

"*Real* wedding? Darling, tonight was so real that I am expecting a honeymoon," she said, giving him the tried-and-true WMS eye smile and lip bite combo.

Valen's only answer was to crush her lips with his and, after delivering a toe-curling smooch, grab her hand and practically run to the elevator.

"Where are we going?" Pia asked through her laughter.

"To the first hotel we come across," Valen said. "I can't afford to have you change your mind. It would absolutely break my heart."

"Why would I change my mind?"

"Who knows when that celibacy thing might kick back in," he joked.

It dawned on Pia that abstinence was a thing in her past. She'd finally found what she'd been holding out for all these years—sex that was driven by love, not simply lust. Pia smiled broadly, realizing that in Valen she had landed a magnificent "twofer." She loved him *and* lusted for him, and right now she wanted very much to make love and solidify the bond that had begun between them tonight.

Two hours later, Valen and Pia were curled up in each others arms, totally satiated. The first time, their lovemaking had been urgent, hungry, and enjoyable. Valen was a skilled and generous lover and knew all the right moves to make her cry out with passionate release. And any apprehensions about making love following her recent gynecological trauma were erased by Valen's tender, considerate lovemaking and their mutual and overwhelming need to quell the fire that had been burning brightly between them. The second time was less physically urgent and instead sought to satisfy the soul as well as the libido.

"I have never made love to anyone who gazed in my eyes the entire time," Pia told him, still amazed by the deep and spiritual bonding it had produced. "It was like making love from the inside out. It was so powerful."

"I couldn't help myself," Valen admitted. "You have the most incredible eyes. They pull you in and make you feel as if there is not a more important or pleasurable place to be. I couldn't look away even if I'd wanted to, and I definitely didn't want to."

"Hmm. I love you," Pia said, curling up beside him, enjoying the warmth of his body mingling with hers. They snuggled together, luxuriating in the silent companionship of their newfound joy. "But . . ."

"But what?"

"*Kermit?* I should have bought you the frog instead of Cookie Monster," she teased. The comment brought an onslaught of tickles, and after Pia promised never to make fun of his name again, the torture subsided.

"It was my mother's brother's name," he informed her.

"Speaking of mothers, I have a confession to make."

"What? Yours didn't vote for me?"

"Quite the contrary. You know that e-mail you got from me that said something like 'I love you too'?"

"It said exactly that. I know this because those four words changed my life. What about it?"

"The truth is, well, I wrote it, but my mother sent it. I wanted you to know that now because when she finds out about us she's going to take all the credit for hooking us up."

"Were you planning to send it?"

"We'll never know now, will we?" she teased, thoroughly enjoying their first pillow talk session. "Hey, you have your first official husband/fiancé appearance coming up."

"Oh, really. Where to, and have you cleared this with my staff?"

"First of all, when it comes to home, you are now *my* staff. And second, the event is the WMS reunion. Flo has turned what was going to be basically a sleepover at my apartment into a whirlwind girls' getaway weekend—hotel, dinner, spa, shopping, the works. I think she's trying to cheer me up after everything that's happened."

"Isn't the whole concept behind that workshop picking up men? I mean, isn't bringing me like bringing sand to the beach?"

"Oh, it was so much more than that, and one day I'll fill you in. Anyway, men are invited only for Friday night cocktails at the hotel. You know, so we can show off how much we learned in San Francisco. The rest of the weekend we'll spend picking up sexy *new* men."

Pia's comment once again got his tickle fingers going, inducing a second promise that she would not so much as look at another man as long as she was Mrs. Valen Bellamy.

"Pia?" Valen said as soon as the laughter died down.

"Hmm," she uttered, detecting his mood turning serious.

"I will try my damnedest to be enough."

"Baby, I was just teasing about the other men. You are more than enough man for me. And if I didn't know that before, you certainly proved it tonight."

"Thank you, but I wasn't talking about that. I'm talking about the fact that the two of us are all the family we're going to be. I know how much you wanted to be a mother and how hurt you are that it didn't work out, and I want you to know that I will try my hardest to be enough family for you."

Pia's response was simply to hug Valen close.

"We're going to have a great life. I promise," he said, crushing her in his arms.

"You know where I want to go on our real honeymoon?"

"Where's that, baby?"

"Reethi Rah. It's in the Indian Ocean."

Valen burst out laughing. "Oh, you *are* the wife for me. Now come here and open wide. I want to get lost in those eyes again."

Chapter Thirty-eight

"Yes, exactly like the foil replica," Pia told Dee. "Well, not *exactly*. The jeweler is going to straighten it up a bit," she said, recalling with a smile how she'd had to squish the original version back into shape.

"He's going to love that, *chica*. I'm so happy for you. But you do realize that you're going to owe me for the rest of your life? And I'm going to take great pleasure in saying 'I told you so' *every* day."

"Between you and Maizelle, my sanity is doomed."

"Don't kid yourself. You were *muy loca* to begin with. So how's the wedding coming?"

"Great, but there's really not much to do." She and Valen had decided on a small "official" ceremony, with fewer than a dozen close friends and family, to take place exactly at midnight on January 1. From there they would leave for Maldives to start the new year and their new life together. "I'll fill you in later, but I have to run and meet the girls." Pia said her good-byes and hung up.

From the other side of the room, she heard Brian Williams signing on to deliver the nightly news, which meant it was six-thirty. Where was Valen? They were going to be late for cocktails. Brian had just introduced the second news story when the phone rang.

"Valen, where are you? Becca and Flo are at the hotel, waiting for us."

"I know I'm running late, but I was picking up one of your wedding gifts."

"Sweetie, the wedding is still three weeks away. Plus, gifts are supposed to be a surprise so it's no fair taunting me."

"This is one I want you to have now. I'll be there in five minutes."

Pia hung up the phone, smiling. She gazed down at her stunning engagement ring. It had been on her finger a week now, but she still was not used to seeing it there. How lucky was she to have such a fantastic man? Looking back, Pia was almost glad she'd avoided love prior to meeting Valen. She could not imagine spending her life with anyone else.

A minute later than expected, Valen knocked on the door. Coat and overnight bag in hand, Pia flung the door open, expecting to join him in the hall and continue to the WMS reunion. Instead, Valen had company.

"Oh my God," she said, gesturing them inside.

Sleeping in Valen's protective arms was Isobella. She was bundled up against the cold, with only the center of her face peeking out of her snowsuit, but Pia could see she was a beauty.

"Who's this little sweetie?" she said, gazing first at the baby and then at her man.

"She's an early wedding gift. What's mine is yours, and this beauty is my granddaughter, Isobella Bellamy," he said, taking off her snowsuit.

"She's beautiful, Valen. And so tiny. How old is she?"

"Five weeks tomorrow. You know the saying 'It takes a village'— well, you're now part of my village, and we need you to help raise Isobella. She may not be our child, Pia, but she can be the child in our life. And I know it won't be the same and I certainly don't mean to imply that she is a replacement for your son, but I hope you'll love her and think of her as a part of you," Valen said, handing the baby over to Pia.

She held Isobella to her breast, breathing in her baby smells and experiencing the wonder of her tiny chest rising and falling against her in a way Pom's never had. She remained speechless as a multitude of emotions ran through her—gratitude, awe, wonder, and a great surge of love and regret.

Stop it, she commanded herself. *This isn't Pom and it isn't his replacement.* But her loving husband-to-be had given her back something that with her baby's death she'd resigned herself to losing forever—a child to love and watch grow up.

"Thank you. I am so honored that you would trust me like this.

This is without a doubt the most touching and thoughtful gift I have ever received."

"So you know what this makes you, don't you?" Valen asked, leaning over to kiss his girls.

"No. What?"

"Only the sexiest grandma on earth."

"Hmm. Grandma. Do you think she could call me Mimi? That's what I call my grandmother."

"I like it. Very sexy. Hell, *I* might even call you Mimi."

"Let's go. I can't wait to show off my new family."

Pia grabbed her overnight bag and the gifts she'd gotten for Flo and Becca and followed Valen out the door. She felt like skipping. Never had her life felt so full and so very complete. It may not be exactly the way she'd painted it, but it was a damn masterpiece nonetheless.

Pia, with Valen and Isobella in tow, walked into the bar of the St. Regis Hotel and glanced around for her friends. Before she saw them she heard Flo's loud and excited voice.

"*Buenos noches,* darlin'," she said, the Texas Spanish she'd been using all week slipping out. The shrieks and hugs that followed belonged to both Pia and Becca as the three women hugged and kissed and greeted one another like the long-lost sisters they were. Valen, the baby, and Cris Yang were momentarily forgotten in the excitement.

"Let me look at both of you," Pia insisted, stepping back to admire the view.

They both looked great. Florence, who'd arrived last evening from Barcelona, looked as if she'd lost at least fifteen pounds, but more than that she seemed relaxed and extraordinarily happy. She was decked out in a black St. John's suit and heels thinner and higher than Pia had ever seen her wear. The woman looked ten years younger, and sizzling hot.

"How do you like my haircut, sugar?" she asked, pushing her sexy red fringed bangs to the side. Gone was the sprayed and teased Texas bob. In its place was a soft wanna-run-my-fingers-through-it do. "I got it cut and colored while I was in Barcelona. I figured I'd come back to the States with a whole new look."

"And you did. Your eyes look amazing. I never realized they were that green before. Both of you look great. Becca, you look 'hot,' " Pia said, making them all laugh.

In the months since she'd last seen Becca, the girl had finally gotten her hair and wardrobe straight. She was wearing fitted pinstriped pants paired with a lacy white shirt and tiny cropped vest. A tangle of chains encircled her neck. It was subtle, trendy, and still sexy as hell.

"Love the ring," Pia added.

"How are you?" Becca asked in a gentle, caring tone.

"I'm doing okay. It's been rough, but I'm getting better. And he's the reason why," Pia said, gesturing to Valen to join them.

"Florence Chase, Becca Vossel, meet my fiancé, Valen Bellamy, and my soon-to-be granddaughter, Isobella." As expected, Florence and Becca fawned over the baby until Becca realized who Valen was.

"Whoa. I've seen you on television. You're famous," Becca said, reverting to her starstruck ways.

"Nice to meet you, ladies. Pia has told me all about you."

"Don't worry, I haven't told him *all* about you," Pia said, making them laugh.

"And I want you all to meet my best friend, Cris Yang," Becca said. "He's the one who helped me get out to San Francisco."

"Ladies and gents, there's a martini with my name on it waitin' at the bar. Let's go sit down and get this party started," Flo said.

Valen excused himself to take the baby home, and Flo and Pia lagged behind a bit while Cris and Becca moved into the bar. "Darlin', that man is a total hunk. You didn't tell me he was such a looker," Flo said, locking arms with Pia.

"There's a lot I haven't told you yet," Pia said, holding up her hand to show off her new engagement ring.

"Wow! Now that's a rock!"

"And he's definitely rocked my world. Flo, I love him so much."

"Duh. Like I couldn't see that written on both y'all's faces."

"Yeah, well, your face is telling quite a story as well. I can't wait to hear all about Spain. I hoped you behaved yourself."

"I did not. And just to be clear, I was a misbehavin' fool. In fact, guess who joined me over there."

"No."

"*Sí.*"

"What, you had a dental emergency?"

"I've learned that there are all kinds of emergencies a good dentist can fix."

"What about Dan?"

"*After* the martini, darlin'. Hell, better make that two."

Cris joined the ladies for about twenty minutes before saying his good-byes and letting them get on with their weekend. Over dinner, Pia, Flo, and Becca caught up on all that had been going on in their lives since leaving the Weapons workshop and forging out on their own into the big, bad world of men and romance. After their meal, they took their drinks and moved the party upstairs so they could speak freely and enjoy themselves without feeling inhibited by nosy strangers.

They changed into pajamas, got cozy, and continued their reunion. After poring over the scrapbook Flo had put together chronicling their stay in San Francisco, the conversation turned decidedly personal.

The older women listened with love and concern as Becca admitted to her disastrous hookup with Nico Jones and the distressing things she and Cris later learned about him.

"Turns out that he was playing on both teams, as Cris put it. I'm just glad I was safe. Cris made me get tested for HIV, and thank God it turned out negative," she revealed to a chorus of relieved sighs.

"Like I said, safe is sexy," Pia reiterated.

"I thought that being a hot girl and hanging out with a hot guy, I'd feel different. But I didn't—at least not in a good way," Becca admitted.

"Maybe because you weren't really *bein'* a hot girl—you were only *actin'* like one. I tell ya, since I've been home, so many of Joey Clements's lessons have started to make sense. Like the only way to feel good about yourself is to *be* yourself. But the problem with that is sometimes other folks don't like it or can't handle it. But you can't let that stop you from bein' you."

"I guess I still have some more things to figure out."

"Honey, you're still a baby. You don't get that kind of wisdom until your butt is flappin' behind your knees like mine. Beauty or wisdom. That's the trade-off."

"I did learn something else," Becca said in a sly tone.

"What's that?" Pia asked.

"I *like* sex."

"You know what, darlin'? I think I've learned that same lesson," Flo said as the three exchanged spirited high fives.

"Just no more jumping into bed with somebody just to make yourself feel good," Pia added.

"Unless you've got a toothache," Flo said with a saucy grin.

"Flo, you're married," Becca scolded.

"Yeah, well, about that. Technically, I still am, but I made a decision while I was in Barcelona. Hell, I think in the back of my mind I made it soon after I got home from the workshop. Some people lose their hearts in San Francisco, but I found my sensual self, and damn it, I like the old gal. So I'm not settlin' anymore. I'm gonna live my life and live it well."

"Without Dan?" Becca asked.

"I tried really hard when I got back to Texas, but Dan just isn't the man for me anymore. I know that now."

"Is Clay?" Pia inquired.

"Darlin', I don't know that for sure either. And frankly, it doesn't really matter. On a whim, I called him from the airport while I was waitin' for my flight to Spain. He said he couldn't stop thinkin' about me and I told him the same thing, and three days later we're dancin' the night away at some little club with a view of the Mediterranean Sea, and then the next day nibblin' our way through the Museu de la Xocolata. Ladies, you gotta love any city that has a museum dedicated to the aphrodisiac qualities of chocolate."

"Girl, you are now an *international* weapon of mass seduction. You go, Miss Flo," Pia said.

"And you're practically a married woman and a grandma! Seems like the world is spinnin' in reverse." Flo said, laughing.

"But what about Clay?" Becca wanted to know.

"Right now, Clay is just the steppin'-stone I need to move forward into the new Flo. We'll see what happens down the line. But if Barcelona is any indication of my life to come, I'm gonna need a new panty patrol trip while I'm here in New York. I'm thinkin' pink. *Hot* pink."

The ladies burst out laughing as they raised their drinks to the middle of the table and toasted themselves and their obvious progress.

"Well, speaking of the panty patrol, I have something for all of us," Pia declared, jumping up and retrieving the three gift boxes from her luggage. "One night I was sitting around watching *The Wizard of Oz* and it dawned on me that the three of us are very much like the characters in that movie," she said, passing each one of her friends a beautifully wrapped box. "We went to the Emerald City, a.k.a. San Francisco, to find the great Wizard of Oz—"

"A.k.a. Joey Clements," Flo chimed in.

"Exactly. Each of us had issues about men that brought us to her workshop, where we thought we were just going to learn how to flirt and attract the men we wanted. Instead, we were forced to look at ourselves as *real* women and not just the roles we play while wearing a skirt."

"It was like going to girl school," Becca said.

"Exactly, but even though we learned a lot there, we needed to come home to really master the lessons."

"I'll buy that," Flo concurred.

"So open your gifts. Becca first."

Oohs and aahs mixed with throaty giggles rose to the ceiling as Becca opened her box to find a pair of hot red boy shorts embroidered with the saying "Smart Is Sexy."

"So, I'm the scarecrow?" Becca asked, not sure if she should feel complimented.

"Only in that you needed to find the wisdom to go with your sexy new persona. And you did," Pia said, giving her a gentle squeeze on the arm. "There's no sexier combo than brains and a body, and now you've got both."

"Thanks. Okay, you go, Flo. I'm guessing lion all the way," Becca said.

"It was the big Texas hair," Flo quipped, ripping open a box containing a pair of electric blue satin panties with "Bold Is Sexy" on them.

"They aren't hot pink, but—" Pia apologized.

"They're perfect. And you are absolutely right. I might be as loud as a lion, but I was a real scaredy-cat when it came to gettin' what I wanted out of my life. I had to find the courage to step away from a marriage that wasn't fulfillin'."

"This is fun," Becca said, laughing. "And what about you, Pia?"

Pia unwrapped her box to reveal "Love Is Sexy" sewn across the front of a fuchsia-colored thong. "I'm like the tin man. I needed a heart."

"And that you definitely got," Flo remarked.

"It's crazy. I was so mad that Dee tricked me into attending the Weapons of Mass Seduction workshop. And I had such an attitude. I knew I was rusty, but I really thought I already had and knew it all when it came down to the whole sensuality, flirting, sex thing. But I was so wrong.

"Before the celibacy, I wore the underwear and a signature scent, I lit the candles and sprinkled the rose petals, and once setting my sights on a guy, I knew how to work it until he was in my bed. But what I realized after the workshop was that I was basically just setting the stage and playacting.

"I came to WMS a know-it-all. But when I came home, life sent me on a journey to learn it all, and now hopefully I'll spend the rest of my days living it all."

"Here, here," Flo said, raising her glass.

"Flo, maybe you can trade with Pia for the thong. It's pink," Becca suggested.

"Darlin', I may have dropped a ton or two, but my butt still is not thong-ready. First we're gonna have to address the twin canyons I got gracin' not one but both cheeks."

"Well, ladies, it looks like we are fully evolved weapons of mass seduction," Pia proclaimed.

"That's right. Look out, world! We got heart, we got brains, we got courage, and sexy drawers to boot!"

"And we are definitely not in Iowa anymore!" Becca chimed in as they each stood up and twirled their panties in lacy salute.

Take

the

Weapons

of

Mass

Seduction

tests

and

find

out

just

how

potent

you

are.

The Sensual You Self-Test

1. Shopping, you fall in love with a fur vest. You're not sure if it's real or faux, so you:

a)   Bury your nose in it and smell.

b)   Run your fingers through it.

c)   Check the label.

2. Given a free hour, you would:

a)   Get a massage.

b)   Listen to music.

c)   Clean the house.

3. You're staying at a swanky resort with forty minutes until checkout. You decide to enjoy the balcony and catch a few rays. Do you:

a)   Strip down au naturale?

b)   Lie out in your clothes and let your face get sunkissed?

c)   Find some shade and recheck your itinerary?

4. You're in the elevator on your way up to an important meeting. A sexy, suggestive song is playing. How does the music affect your mood?

a) You'd get into the music and exit feeling energetic and aroused.

b) You'd briefly enjoy the music and the mood and memories it evokes and then put your game face back on.

c) You're totally focused. Your mood wouldn't be affected at all.

5. The first thing you notice about a new acquaintance is:

a) The tone and timbre of his voice.

b) His physical appearance, body, and wardrobe.

c) What he adds to the conversation.

6. Which of the following have you done in the past month? (Circle all that apply.)

a) Put on perfume, even though it wasn't a special occasion.

a) Taken a long, candlelight bath.

b) Tried a new food.

b) Listened to music other than when driving in a car or doing chores.

c) Sorted your sock drawer.

c) None of the above.

7. How do you feel about public displays of affection?

a) Love them. Any place, any time.

b) I enjoy them where appropriate.

c) Please. Get a room.

8. What qualities are you most looking for in a lover?

a) Passion and adventure.

b) Looks and humor.

c) Stability and wealth.

SENSUALITY SCALE

SUPERSENSUAL (Mostly A's): You are a pleasure-driven individual. You enjoy living life through your senses. Because your senses are usually linked to your emotions, you are inclined to be emotionally passionate. Your lifestyle allows you to experience a life of maximum pleasure, but it's important to keep yourself in check, because the search for pleasure can be addictive. So to find happiness, seek balance. Too much of a good thing isn't always so good. But when properly directed, you have the innate ability to use your senses to thoroughly enjoy everything this life has to offer.

SOLIDLY SENSUAL (Mostly B's): You have found a balance between absolute self-denial and complete indulgence. You are able to enjoy and even lose yourself in the sensual aspects of life, but you aren't totally pleasure-driven and know how to keep your emotions balanced. You are able to stay focused and to persevere, even while acknowledging the sensory pleasures around you. Continue to live in the moment and you will intensify your sensual side.

TOO SENSIBLE TO BE SENSUAL (Mostly C's): You are not a very sensual person and probably enjoy more intellectual or practical pastimes. You appear to be tenacious, persistent, and goal-oriented. Like the supersensual, you need balance. You can expand your pleasure quotient by getting out of your head and exploring your world through your senses and by acknowledging how your body feels at any given time. You have only one life, so just make sure that you are not missing out on some sensual pleasures of the moment by always trying to understand.

1. What's your most important flirting tool?

a) Your body.

b) Your personality.

c) Your smile.

d) Not sure if you have one.

2. The last touch you add before leaving for a party is:

a) Glossy lipstick that draws attention to your mouth.

b) A funky, quirky handbag.

c) A charm bracelet that sparkles and jingles when you gesture.

d) A breath mint.

3. You see a man you'd like to meet. You:

a) Sit where he can see and enjoy your come-hither eye contact.

b) Pass him a joke sans the punch line, with the suggestion he come over to hear the rest.

c)   Have a friend go tell him you'd like to meet him.

d)   Wait until he leaves and ask a friend later who the person was.

4. You and your lover are sitting across from each other at dinner. He is seductively maintaining eye contact. What do you do?

a)   Immediately ask for the check and get to a private place ASAP.

b)   Hold his gaze and seduce him right back before playfully sticking out your tongue.

c)   Stare back for a while, smile seductively to let him know you're feeling him, and then look away.

d)   Start talking so he'll stop staring. All that gawking is uncomfortable.

5. A man offers to buy you a drink. You ask for:

a)   Sex on the Beach.

b)   The same beer he's having.

c)   Champagne—it's flirty and sophisticated.

d)   Tell him no thanks, and buy your own drink.

YOUR FLIRTING STYLE

SEXY FLIRT (Mostly A's): You're a woman who sees what she wants and takes it. You've got all the right tools in your bag of tricks, and you know the signs and signals to attract what you want when you want it. In the right dose, you are pure power. Be careful about taking your sexy flirtation too far. Being too sexually overt can cause a multitude of things to occur: you can embarrass yourself, make other women dislike you, and make promises to men you don't intend to keep.

AMUSING FLIRT (Mostly B's): Your allure is your quick wit and wicked sense of humor. You can feel at home in a sports bar or at a poker game. You entice a man by making him feel comfortable around you. And though your "buddy" approach is less direct than those of other femme fantastiks, it can be just as disarming. By not playing the games other girls play, you lower his guard, and before he knows it, he's hooked. But watch that you don't become one of the guys. Find ways to let him know there is a lusty woman sitting beneath that Jets jersey.

ADORABLE FLIRT (Mostly C's): You've got a sparkle about you that attracts attention as soon as you enter a room, but you prefer not to be too aggressive when you meet a man who interests you. Instead, you tend to be subtler in your seduction, sweetly letting him know you're interested but letting him initiate the pursuit. By allowing this man to feel like a man, you're respecting his feelings and protecting your own reputation. With this light approach, know exactly what you want so your feelings are clear to him. Otherwise, you may be left smiling by yourself while some devastating diva walks away with your man.

FLIRTING FLOP (Mostly D's): Ouch! You're flirtability quotient is dangerously low. And lack of confidence may be the enemy lurking within. Remember the golden rule of flirting: People find you attractive when you make them feel attractive. So concentrate on making your object of desire feel special and watch your confidence soar as he returns the favor. Now get out there and practice. You'll be successfully flirting in no time.

The Red Hot Night Sensuality Questionnaire

Knowing what turns your senses on is the key to planning a sexually sensual evening. Take a minute to answer the following questions for both yourself and your partner and use this information to plan and ignite a red hot night.

1) **My/his favorite color is:**

2) **The fabric I/he like(s) touching my/his body is:**

3) **I/he love(s) the smell of:**

4) **My/his favorite musical instrument is:**

5) **My/his favorite food is:**

6) **My/his favorite vacation spot is:**

7) **My/his favorite body part of his/mine is:**

8) **Given a free hour I/he would rather:**
   a) Watch TV.
   b) Listen to music.
   c) Try a new recipe.
   d) Get a massage.

About the Author

LORI BRYANT-WOOLRIDGE is a fifteen-year veteran of the television broadcast business and the recipient of an Emmy Award for Individual Achievement in Writing. She is the author of the bestselling novels *Hitts & Mrs.* and *Read Between the Lies* and is a contributor to several top anthologies, including *Gumbo: An Anthology of African American Writing*. She is also a founding member of the Femme Fantastik Tour. She lives in South Orange, New Jersey, with her family. Visit her Web site at www.loribryantwoolridge.com and the WMS blog at www.weapons-of-mass-seduction.blogspot.com.